SYNC

K.P. KYLE

 ALLIUM PRESS OF CHICAGO

Allium Press of Chicago
Forest Park, IL
www.alliumpress.com

This is a work of fiction. Descriptions and portrayals of real people, events, organizations, or establishments are intended to provide background for the story and are used fictitiously. Other characters and situations are drawn from the author's imagination and are not intended to be real.

Book and cover design by E. C. Victorson
Front cover image: "Scenic night landscape with Milky Way
and highway in Finland" by Jani Riekkinen/Shutterstock

ISBN: 978-0-9996982-3-5

Library of Congress Cataloging-in-Publication Data

Names: Kyle, K. P., author.
Title: Sync / K. P. Kyle.
Description: Forest Park, IL : Allium Press of Chicago, 2019.
Identifiers: LCCN 2019007154 (print) | LCCN 2019011371 (ebook) |
ISBN 9780999698242 (Epub) | ISBN 9780999698235 (pbk.)
Subjects: LCSH: Space and time--Fiction. | GSAFD: Science fiction
Classification: LCC PS3611.Y58 (ebook) | LCC PS3611.Y58 S96 2019
(print) |
DDC 813/.6--dc23
LC record available at https://lccn.loc.gov/2019007154

Praise for *Sync*

"Kyle's adventure moves fast, ably handling both the science of multiverse theories and the thrilling dangers represented by the lab's goons. Some questions remain open at the end…but they don't diminish the book's fun and excitement…an engrossing multiverse adventure."
—Michelle Anne Schingler, *Foreword Reviews*

"A mind-bending, thrilling story of parallel universes with real-world consequences, *Sync* twists and turns until it delivers a final explosive punch."
—Jamie Freveletti, bestselling author of *Blood Run*

"The stakes and the villains throughout remain realistic and believable, and Brigid's aggressive normalcy lends her great charm as a protagonist. There's a solid supporting cast as well; even relatively minor characters like Jason's family get strong, poignant moments to shine and to help save the day. A well-executed debut whose compellingly human cast enriches the standard 'parallel universe' science-fiction trope."
—*Kirkus*

"If you're tired of preposterous protagonists who never misstep, pick up *Sync*. Featuring flesh-and-blood characters facing impossible odds and uncertain futures, Kyle tackles the mind-boggling concept of parallel universes to deliver this twisty, fast-paced adventure."
—Julie Hyzy, bestselling author of *Virtual Sabotage*

For Alice, the best big sister, and for The Brothers, Nick and Alec

ONE

One different choice, one tiny change, would have changed everything.

   If she hadn't chosen to visit her mother in Vermont that day. If she hadn't been driving home at that exact time of night. If she hadn't been distracted, wallowing in the realization that she was destined to a life of mediocrity and obscurity. If she hadn't been terrified of following her mother's path toward the fog of dementia, confusion, helplessness. If she hadn't drifted to the side of the road at that precise moment, and if she hadn't seen the lanky, hooded figure in the headlights, standing there in the freezing rain, holding out his thumb.

A million alternate realities, but she was only following the one.

She'd been driving for an hour or so at that point. The wipers smeared flecks of sleet and ice across her windshield, obscuring vision already obscured by the tears that obnoxiously would not stop welling up and spilling out of her eyes. She kept thinking she had it under control, kept taking a couple of those vaunted deep cleansing breaths and trying to focus on happy thoughts, happy memories. Wipe eyes, sniff back the drips of cry-snot, force a smile. Picture a sun-filled kitchen, lemonade in a dewy pitcher dampening the blue tablecloth, her bare legs swinging off a chair too tall for her to touch the ground, thighs slowly becoming imprinted with the woven mesh of the seat. Her mother holding a report card, beaming at her, pride spilling over into her voice. "Straight A's. I knew it. Smartest girl in the—"

The image morphed, distorted, evaporated, and suddenly she saw her mother's aged face, twisted with fear and fury, and a small pot of shamrocks flying toward her head and smashing on the wall behind her.

A sob burbled up from inside somewhere, unexpected, unwanted. Her chest shook with the effort of suppressing it, but her eyes flooded again.

"Don't worry about it," the nurse had told her. "She's just sundowning. It happens. Don't take it personally." Sundowning? What a fucking misleading term. It sounded like someone going to sleep or something, settling down for the night. Instead, it seemed, it meant losing what little lucidity might have clung onto the vestiges of her mother's tattered, ruined mind.

She'd been forced to flee, then, scrambling out of her mother's bedroom amid shrieks and howls, leaving the staff to clean up the shattered pottery on the floor.

She blinked, tried to clear her eyes, tried to focus on the road. The headlights lit up the specks of ice in the air but didn't do much to illuminate the highway. Which is probably why she didn't notice the person standing there, standing where no one should've been standing, where she had no reason to expect someone to be standing, way too close to her car, so that gasping she had to swerve blindly away before stomping on the brake and screeching dramatically to a stop.

卐

How in the holy fuck had he ended up in Vermont? How? Forty-nine other states and all of them must be warmer, friendlier, kinder. Vermont, it seemed, was an endless stretch of back roads, all of them icy and muddy, with occasional off-brand gas stations that never had any real food for sale, or for scavenging for that matter. Sullen attendants and empty trash cans. The rain had seeped under his jacket, soaked his knit hat and his jeans and shoes. Where were Ben and Jerry anyway? He hadn't eaten for three days.

He was hitching, or trying to, though he hated the idea of it. He hated being indebted to a stranger, he hated being in their car and seeing their noses twitch in revulsion because he knew he smelled—he couldn't recall the last time he'd bathed—and he hated the simmering fear that they might have an ulterior motive for picking him up. He wasn't good at hitching. He didn't trust his fellow man, not these days. But tonight he was starving, cold, and tired, so he stuck out his thumb in the dim hope that someone would stop and let him sit in a warm car, and maybe he would move a little faster toward wherever he was going.

And, wonder of wonders, the brake lights of a car that had swerved to pass him suddenly lit up like a carnival. Like a miracle. Like a beacon of freedom—well, that might have been the hunger talking. But a car did indeed brake, and even stop, and wait for him to jog up to the passenger window and peek in.

It was a small car, a hatchback, two passenger. A middle-aged woman with graying hair in a tangled ponytail was driving. She peered at him with puffy, red-rimmed eyes, clearly anxious. "Uh…hey. You need a ride?"

"Yeah, yeah, yeah…thanks, thanks so much." Then he was in the passenger seat and pulling the door shut, and hoping things would turn out all right, hoping it wasn't a mistake, hoping he wouldn't regret it by the morning.

⌘

Good lord, he stinks.

He'd curled his small frame into the passenger seat with his duffle on his lap, leaning into the door, eyes cast downwards. The little car filled with the smell of unwashed hair, body odor, and a faint sweetness that was more difficult to place. Still, it was hard not to feel bad for him—he was visibly shivering, uncomfortable, tense. She cracked a window despite the cold. *Hell, I have to breathe.*

The opened window appeared to awaken Lithium, and a small black nose appeared over the guy's shoulder.

"So. Where you going?" Forced amiability. Pretend to be happy and friendly and maybe it'll happen. She had read that in an article somewhere, on the Internet, and surely the Internet wouldn't lie to her.

He paused for a few seconds longer than normal. "South. Nowhere specific. Maybe New York."

"You're just out here wandering with nowhere to go?"

"Yeah…uh…well, sort of." He paused. "No, I…uh…I was living with my aunt, and she…uh…I had to leave, and I thought maybe you know…'cause I've never been to New York…and so, yeah."

The small black nose poked the back of the guy's ear, sniffing inquisitively.

She glanced at him sideways. He was no more relaxed than when he'd gotten in, but he finally raised his head and gazed out the windshield into the darkness. His eyebrows furrowed slightly. *Shit, is he making up this story? Why make up a story? Is he running from someone? Is he a criminal? Fuck. Why did I pick him up?* There was that faint, sweet odor again. It tickled her brain, she couldn't quite place it. She took another peek at him. He had several days' worth of sparse facial hair. Underneath, his cheeks were gaunt, his eyes hollow. He wore a knit hat over longish hair that appeared partially matted. She took a deep breath, stifled a gag, smiled politely. At the very least, the sudden concern that she was sharing a car with a homeless madman or criminal sort of helped displace the aching, heavy sadness that always followed a visit to her mother.

The little black nose was now roving around the guy's left cheek, behind his eye, under the base of the knit hat. He squirmed away, twisting around to try to see behind him.

"Right. Okay, well, I'm heading to Boston, so I can get you that far. Do you have somewhere to stay?"

He turned forward again, stared out the window. "No, I think I'll just get on a train…like if you drop me at a train station, that would be great, or somewhere close by…or, you know…I mean, thanks."

Goddamn. What is that fucking smell? It was driving her crazy. "Yeah, that's no problem."

Silence. Awkward silence. She wondered how people were supposed to interact with potentially crazy hitchhikers. Was there a guide for this sort of thing? Should she turn on the radio? Would that be considered rude? How long should they sit in silence before it wouldn't be considered rude?

The nose had now realized there was something more interesting under the knit hat and was snuffling underneath it.

She peeked at the guy again. Honestly, he didn't seem like a crazy person, or even a criminal. He just seemed like a scared young man. He stopped shivering, relaxed slightly, looked like he was fighting a grin even, wiggling away from Lithium's inquisitive snout. Lithium's nose managed to displace the hat a little, sniffed deeply a few times, paused, snorted and withdrew. The guy lost it finally, giggling and curling around to see what had been so interested in his head, and Lithium very solemnly sniffed and licked the tip of his nose.

This was just too much. "Lithium," she protested. "Stop, please..." *That fucking dog.* But she felt herself grinning, too. She couldn't help it. *Oh! Right. Names. People are supposed to introduce themselves. That's a thing normal people do.*

"What's your name?"

He jerked, startled. "J-John."

"Okay, hi. I'm Brigid."

"Hi."

And recognition came swooping in. *Ketones! That's the smell. Ketones. Well, shit. That's not good.*

"Look, I'm sorry, I don't mean to pry, but are you a diabetic?"

That got a reaction. He turned, obviously bewildered, pushing Lithium's still investigating muzzle out of the way. "What? No. Why would...why?"

"Are you sure? It's just, you—" She looked at him again, took in the sunken eyes, the hollow cheeks. "Are you absolutely sure? Have you checked your blood sugar? When did you last eat?"

⌘

Reservations he'd held since getting in the car dissipated rapidly once the dog in the backseat appeared. He'd always liked dogs, and the appearance of a small brown canine face behind him instantly reassured him. *Bad guys don't keep dogs, do they? Or if they do, they're scary and intimidating. Big, threatening, ripped.* This one was smallish, maybe forty pounds, leggy and lean with short chestnut brown fur, a long narrow snout, half-cocked ears, curious brown eyes. And a damp black nose, which had slowly and carefully hoovered every accessible square inch of his face and neck. And once the dog sneezed under his hat, he lost it. He turned, giggled, cupped his hands behind the dog's ears, scratched, and the woman asked him if he was diabetic.

Fuck. What? Why? What? Shit, she knows something. She isn't a random person after all, she's a plant, or something, this is a trick...Diabetic? Why would I be diabetic? Who would ask me that? Wait, does she know something? Am I a diabetic? What if I am? Did they make me diabetic? Is that even possible? Fuck. Fuck. Fuck!

"When did you last eat?"

He tried to calm himself. He was on the verge of panicking. He looked up, back into the face of the dog behind him. Clutched the car seat. Wasn't quite sure when he'd stopped petting the dog. *Okay, relax. Maybe it was an innocent question.* He focused on slowing his breathing and realized she was waiting for a response.

"It's been a few days, I guess. Why do you think I'm diabetic?"

"You smell ketotic."

What the hell does that even mean? "What...what is that, what does that mean?"

"Ketones. You have ketones on your breath. I can smell it. Diabetics get it when they don't get their insulin. But also people on...like...the Atkins diet. Or starving people."

He was silent for a few moments, listening to his racing heart. Ketones. He'd never heard of ketones. "Three days. I mean, that's when I ate last. Three days ago."

She gazed out the front windshield, neutral. Blinked a few times and finally her eyes flicked in his direction again. "We'll stop at the next gas station. Convenience store. Whatever."

He turned to stare fixedly out the window. His stomach had condensed into a pit of anxiety at this point. He hoped they were just stopping to get a snack. Maybe? *Maybe she's kicking me out. No, she could kick me out anywhere. So, probably to get a snack. But I don't have any money. But she has to know that, right? I mean, obviously I have no money. So, we're stopping to get a snack and she's going to pay for it. And then she'll expect something as payment. Will she? What do I have to offer? Sexual favors?* He gazed out the window. Maybe she'd spot him a dollar and not ask for anything back and, just maybe, drop him off somewhere with a nice candy bar under the assumption that he was not in fact diabetic and...

Oh shit, she's licking my ear right now. She definitely wants sexual favors. She definitely wants sex—

Oh wait, it's the dog again.

She pulled the car into a gas station.

⊞

"You want to come in or wait in the car? Either's fine. I'm just gonna grab some stuff."

He looked paralyzed. She thought for sure he was going to stay frozen in his seat, but no. His eyes were fixed on the door to the mini-mart like it was the entrance to Eden. He followed her into the store almost involuntarily, skulking, head turtled into his damp and grimy sweatshirt, hands balled in his pockets. Like he would prefer being anywhere else in the world but was unable to resist the allure of the fluorescent bulbs. She tried to walk casually, but it turned out to be hard to walk casually, because the more she thought about walking casually the more she walked like she didn't know how to walk and was trying to fake it based on a magazine article she'd read once, and the whole thing just made her feel super awkward. *Well, fine.*

She wandered through the aisles looking for food that approached "not junk." Nothing. Literally nothing was not junk. *Why do they even sell this shit? Pork rinds?* She crouched down by the "nuts" to scrutinize the "hot chili peanuts" and "honey glazed cashews" and realized the guy was standing in the corner wolfing down a Snickers. She stood. He froze, gagged, coughed chocolate and nougat out of his nose, wiped his suddenly watering eyes.

"Let's just be clear. You are absolutely sure that you're not diabetic? Because that's not going to help, if you are."

He shook his head.

"Right. Okay. Fine."

She returned to the nuts, selected the cashews because they seemed the least noxious, grabbed a couple of bottles of water, set it all on the counter. "And also a candy bar. My friend ate it already. Thanks. Oh, and a thing of jerky."

The guy—John?—the guy had vanished from the store. She wondered briefly if he'd just taken off, but he did have a duffle, so she supposed he was waiting in the car. Yes, in fact, he was crouched down in the front seat again, evidently trying to avoid Lithium, who'd wiggled half into the front seat with him. Most of what was visible was canine rump and wagging tail. She got back into the car, and Lithium paused in his attempts to lick any leftover chocolate out of the kid's beard to give her a perfunctory tongue swipe. The car now smelled largely of body odor, ketones, and chocolate. She was not convinced this was an improvement.

"Get back, Lithium." She wrestled him back to his place in the backseat, then had to adjust her belt buckle as it was pinching the roll of fat over her belly. She handed John the bag of snacks and he rummaged through it, pulling out the jerky and a bottle of water.

He drank half the bottle in one go. "Thanks. Sorry, thanks. I was just really..."

"You wanna make a friend? Give the dog a piece of the jerky."

He twisted around and offered a piece of jerky to Lithium, who snatched it, dropped to his haunches, gnawed happily. John turned around, jerky in his own mouth, smiling a little shyly. "What's his name? Or...uh...her?"

"He's a boy. Lithium."

"That's...huh. That's kind of a...kind of an unusual name."

"Yeah. Because he keeps me sane. Get it?"

"...No."

"Because lithium is a medication for depression."

"Oh, okay..."

Definitely more relaxed now. Progress, she supposed.

"That's funny. Is he a...um...a service dog?"

"No, not a service dog. Not even technically a therapy dog, or emotional support dog, or whatever they call them. Though maybe I should get him one of those orange vests, start taking him on planes and stuff."

Unfortunately, now the car also smelled of jerky, so she cracked a window again. John pulled his coat tighter around him, leaned against the door methodically chewing and drank the rest of the water. Lithium's head popped up again between the front seats. Evidently, he'd finished his snack and was looking for more. John reached over and stroked his head, scratched his ear. Lithium shook his head and whined softly.

"Can I give him another?"

"Nah, sorry pup. That shit is terrible for him. Also terrible for you, but whatever. He'll eat when we get home."

They drove on in silence, conversation having been exhausted presumably, or John exhausted more likely. Sixty miles from Boston. She should be home by ten, if she was lucky. And then a nice dinner, and a nice glass of wine, and a nice evening curled up on her sofa with her dog, and...ugh...this guy. He was presumably planning on...what? Spending the night on a train station bench? Getting kicked out for being obviously homeless? Buying a train ticket with money that he clearly didn't have? *Ugh.* That charitable glow she was hoping for, picking up this hitchhiker, was starting to morph into guilt. *Why? Why?*

⌗

"Hey, so, what are your plans exactly when we get to Boston? I mean, I don't want to pry or anything, but you want to go to the train station?"

He'd started to doze off but wrenched himself awake. "Yeah. Yeah, that'll be fine. Thanks."

"No, I mean, there's not going to be a train this late, I don't think. Do you have a ticket?"

"No. I'll just get whatever when I get there."

"Yeah...yeah. Okay. Do you have money?"

Long pause. "I'll be okay."

"Do you have any friends in the city? Or family? Anyone you can stay with?"

He shook his head. He was getting kind of nervous, all of these questions. Also, his scalp was starting to itch again, under the damp hat, now that he was warmer. He kind of wanted to take it off, but he was afraid of what his hair might smell like. Or look like. Or both.

There was a prolonged silence, while the woman—Bridget, her name was, he was pretty sure—while Bridget stared out at the road looking conflicted, chewing her lower lip. Finally, without changing expression, she said, "Look, I have a guest room. Why don't you stay with me tonight, you can get cleaned up and have something to eat, and I can drop you off in the morning."

He froze. He didn't know how to answer. His initial gut response was to politely but firmly decline, insist on going to the train station. He didn't know this woman. *What does she want? Who's she working for? What's this about?* But under that, deep down, he really, really wanted to say yes.

"No strings. Just, you look like you could use a good night's sleep is all."

God, though, he wanted to say yes. A bright flash of a possible shower. Just the notion of a bed. He wanted that so badly. He wanted this to be real. He wanted this to be a genuine offer out of human decency. He wanted desperately to believe there were good people, that a good person was with him, that he might trust this person. After all, she had a dog. *Dog lovers can be trusted, right? Except Hitler, who was a dog lover. Shit. But still.*

"That is, so long as you're not a psycho killer or anything. Then we might have a problem." She laughed wryly, a half smile, and glanced over.

He stared blankly into the dark. "Yeah...ok, yeah...I mean if it's not a problem, okay, that would be...that would be really great." *And please, please don't be the wrong thing to do, please be the right choice.*

"Cool. Good. There's not going to be anywhere to spend the night at the train station anyway, you know. So good, we'll just head to my place. It's not big, and it's kind of dirty, so please no judgement, though. I mean, there's lots of dog hair." She gave a terse smile, the kind where people sort of purse their lips and grimace.

Quiet again for a while. The dog had curled up and was presumably sleeping in the back, with no further promises of jerky. He was feeling more and more awkward. He should say something. Try to have a conversation, try to seem normal. He suspected she'd rescind the offer if she got the impression he was an escaped mental patient or a creepshow or something. *Right, so, normal. Normal conversation. Ask a polite question.*

"Where do you live?"

"Southie. South Boston. You know, where Whitey's from?"

"Who?"

"Really? Whitey? The gangster? You don't know him? Where'd you grow up?"

Pause. This was a mistake. He'd hoped to steer the conversation to her background, not his. Well… "The Midwest. Indiana."

"Oh. Well, you know that movie with Jack Nicholson, *The Departed?* Jack Nicholson's character was based on Whitey. Yeah, he came from Southie. But he was gone long before I arrived." Silence. "It's becoming a lot more gentrified now, you know. Fewer gangsters, more yuppies. People resent it, some people, like the old school neighborhood, but I think it's just progress, you know? Nothing's gonna stay the same forever."

"They resent you?"

"Me? Nah, not me. I'm not a yuppie. Yuppies are young and upwardly mobile. That's the definition, the acronym, remember from the '80s? I'm not young or upwardly mobile. I'm middle aged and complacent." She grinned at him.

"Ha. That's funny."

"Mmm. You won't feel that way when you hit forty."

He leaned back against the car door again. He had a lingering anxiety in his belly. There was still a chance this could turn into a weird sexual favors sort of situation. And there had been security cameras at the convenience store. He saw one after he was halfway through the candy bar, and he thought he'd vacated the place in time, but really, who knew. In the end, it came down to the fact that he was tired, wet, cold, dirty, and still hungry, and the promise of a bed and a shower were too seductive.

Just please, please, please don't be a mistake.

Please.

꒲

Once they pulled off the interstate, it was only a few minutes to Brigid's place. A couple of stoplights, not much traffic at that hour. They drove down Broadway, past the local police station, the housing projects. The incongruous upscale food market was closed but the sketchy old bars were still open, as per the dusty neon lights in their windows and huddled smokers loitering outside their doors. She'd been in a couple of them with some of her more adventurous friends in the past, the long-ago past. Free pool, and the bartenders dealt coke. Only a 30 percent chance of getting stabbed, and the beer was okay.

She had to circle the block twice to find a parking spot. She grabbed Lithium's leash as he hopped out of the back, led John up the front steps to her door. Her apartment was smallish, for a two bedroom. She actually wasn't sure it qualified as a true two bedroom. The second bedroom—the guest room—was barely more than a closet. She lived on the first floor—kitchen in the front, den and guest room next to the kitchen. Her own bedroom was in the back, adjacent to the back door.

"Sorry about the mess. I wasn't expecting company and, also, I'm a slob." He said nothing. "Okay, well, the guest room's in here. I'll get you some sheets…sorry the bed isn't made, forgive the clutter." There was a pile of gardening tools in the corner, relics from an attempt to start a mini-garden a few years back. The bed had a half-constructed herb bed on it, which she removed and shoved into a hall closet already overfilled with empty moving boxes and abandoned shoes. "I'll get you a towel. You can have a shower and I'll get some food together. Hang on a sec."

"Thanks." He dropped his duffle onto the bed.

In the kitchen, Lithium was waiting expectantly by the food pantry, tail waving. She threw kibble into his bowl and he dug in happily. It took a bit longer for her to locate a towel and sheets. She gave John the towel, ushered him into the bathroom, made the bed once she heard the water running. His duffle, frankly, smelled almost as bad as he did. She frowned at it, went to her own bedroom, ruffled through the bureau until she dug up a pair of oversized track pants and a t-shirt. She left those on the guest bed and went to the kitchen to put a pot of water on. She didn't have much food in the house, but she always kept a box of spaghetti and jar of sauce for dinner emergencies. She rarely ate spaghetti herself, but it was easy to cook and filling. Besides, she was hungry.

⛶

He stood in the bathroom for a few minutes, uncertain, still not sure if he should cut his losses and just run out into the street. But no, that would be weird at this point. And a shower…though the idea of being naked in a stranger's house was kind of terrifying. The door had a lock on the knob. He turned it, slowly, muffling the click of the lock. Looked at his reflection in the mirror over the sink, at the grime on his face, his matted hair, the bags under his red-rimmed eyes. He turned on the shower to let the water warm up, pulled off his clothes. His muddy jeans had dried in the car, and they accordioned stiffly, like new poster board, as he pushed them down.

He stepped into the water. *Oh. Oh god.* It was glorious. The water pressure dug through his hair to pummel his scalp, heat running over his head and shoulders, warming the core of him. For a few minutes he stood motionless, just watching the swirl of gray runoff twist into the drain. It was almost sexual, it was so pleasant. He literally never wanted it to end. And the soap—well, there was rose-scented body wash and, for a second, he thought, *But that'll make me smell like a chick!*— but then he rubbed a handful of it into his hair, working through the mats, scrubbing his face, scrubbing his armpits, vigorously scrubbing his crotch. Rose-scented grayish lather ran off his legs, pooled around his feet. This was the greatest thing he'd ever experienced. This was nirvana. This was glory. This was the rapt—

There was a rapping at the door. "Hey, uh…John?"

He froze. A rush of adrenaline surged to his extremities, blooming into an unpleasant tingle. "Yeah?"

"I left a change of clothes on your bed. Thought you might want to wash your stuff. Okay?"

Oh jeez. "Oh. Okay. Thanks."

"Also, there should be a spare toothbrush in the medicine cabinet."

It took a few seconds to relax again, but he did, relaxed again into the water, closed his eyes, stood there until his fingertips shriveled and the water didn't register as hot anymore, stood there a few moments longer, before he willed himself to shut off the shower. Rubbed himself dry and knotted the towel around his waist, almost left the bathroom before he remembered the toothbrush, which was new and unopened and next to a tube of toothpaste. His hands were shaking as he pulled the toothbrush out of the packaging and spent what seemed like the next hour furiously brushing all the filth and slime and grit off his teeth. He'd almost started to consider a filmy coat the normal state of teeth. By the time he finished, he was spitting bloody flecks into the sink but, once he rinsed the blood out with several cupped handfuls of water, he nearly felt like a real person again.

The clothes she'd left on the bed consisted of a pair of track pants and a green t-shirt featuring a drunken Santa, drunken reindeer, drunken elves, and the line "Merry Christmas, You Bastards!" He felt kind of goofy putting them on, but there was an intoxicating odor of tomato marinara coming from the kitchen. Suddenly, he didn't care much about what he looked like.

In the kitchen, he found Bridget stirring a pot of boiling pasta, a glass of red wine in one hand, her lips stained purplish. She'd re-ponytailed her hair, which was dark auburn and threaded with kinky gray streaks. "Hey. Feel better?"

"Yeah, tons. Thanks."

"No worries. You smell so much better. You want a drink? I have wine, or there are a couple of bottles of beer in the fridge. Oh, sorry. I should've asked. Are you a drinker? Like, if you're in AA or something, I'm gonna feel like an asshole."

He smiled. "No, I'm not in AA. Sure. Beer would be good." The jerky'd been way too salty, he realized. She opened the fridge, handed him a bottle and an opener labeled "Harpoon Oktoberfest 2010." He drank deeply, and the beer hit him hard. He hadn't had a drink in a long time. He felt dizzy and dropped onto a stool, elbows on his knees.

She set her wine glass on the counter. "Keep an eye on the stove. I'm gonna throw your stuff into the wash."

Dimly, he thought he should be embarrassed that a strange lady would be handling his underwear.

Also dimly, he thought the rest of his clothes were as gross as his underwear. He closed his eyes, heard a hiss from the stove and jumped up to stir the pot, which was starting to boil over.

⌗

They took plates of spaghetti and a big bowl of salad into the den and sat on the sofa, eating off their laps. John wolfed the food down in great greedy bites. She worried he was eating too fast and would barf it back up. There was still an undercurrent of desperation from him, the sort of vibe you get from feeding a stray dog. The same sort of hopeful trust in a stranger. She'd seen it before. She was a sucker for it, truth be told. Lithium lay at her feet, head up, ears cocked, eyes bright, waiting for any morsel that might make its way off the plates and onto the carpet. She picked at the food, not terribly hungry. Well, this was an outright lie, but spaghetti has a ton of calories, and she'd already had two meals that day and was already like thirty pounds overweight. And, though she didn't want to admit it to herself, she was kind of self-conscious about eating in front of a sort of stranger. So she nibbled at the pasta and ate mostly salad but had another glass of wine because wine has no calories. She leaned back on the arm of the sofa with a leg curled under her, watching John. His hair was clean now and, with the mats mostly gone, it was black and shiny and scruffy. Hard to establish his age. He had that haunted look and gaunt cheeks that prematurely age a person but, truthfully, underneath the wispy beard he had a young face.

"What were you doing, really, walking along the road out there? Do you actually have an aunt in Vermont?"

He paused shoveling food into his mouth, chewed slowly, kept his eyes down.

"I mean, it's your life, you don't need to tell me. But you look like you're running from something. You're kind of, I don't know, jumpy. And also hungry. Your aunt is a pretty terrible aunt if she didn't feed you for however many days."

He swallowed, inhaled deeply through his nose, set his fork on his plate. Lithium took this as a suggestion that he was done eating and bounced over to sit by him, hoping to snap up any leftovers. John closed his eyes for a moment, straightened his shoulders, met her gaze. His eyes were clear and dark brown, almond shaped, framed by black lashes.

Funny the way boys get the pretty eyelashes sometimes.

"It's a…a long story. I sort of…" He rubbed his hand through his hair. "I got unlucky. Lost my job, didn't have a bank account, didn't have a place to stay. Your basic…you know."

She nodded. "Parents?"

He hesitated. "Yeah. No. They, uh…I don't really want to talk about this, if that's okay."

"Yeah. Sorry."

He reached for his beer, drank the last of it. Picked up his fork again. Lithium appeared visibly disappointed.

"How old are you?" She realized she was being pushy at this point, but the wine had made her bold. Bolder. It made her care less anyway.

"Twenty-seven."

"Oh, huh. That's the age people tend to die."

He started, stared at her with wide eyes, frozen mid-bite with noodles hanging out of his mouth. It would have been comic, but he looked genuinely panicked.

"No! No, that was a weird thing to say. I'm sorry. I just mean, that's the age that a bunch of famous people died. You know? Janis Joplin…uh, Jimi Hendrix…Kurt Cobain. They were all twenty-seven. There's a conspiracy theory about it, I think." She was blushing, she could feel it. *Stupid fucking thing to say. Who says that?*

He nodded slowly, resumed chewing, but thoughtfully. He swallowed and added, "Amy whatshername, with the hair."

"Amy Winehouse! Yeah. So, okay. What were you doing before you…what was the job…that you lost?"

"Nothing special. Uh, bartending. What do you do?"

"Bartending! You should make me a cocktail."

"Yeah…" He scraped the last of the sauce off the plate with his fork. Lithium's eyes tracked the cutlery. A filament of saliva slipped gracefully from the corner of the dog's mouth to the carpet. "It was mostly...like, pouring beers and stuff. Nothing fancy."

"Hmm."

He looked around the room, at the framed photos of old vacations, department store art prints, an Ansel Adams photo of a tree and moon, a wooden stick resembling a baseball bat flattened at the end mounted on the hallway wall. "What's that thing?"

Brigid beamed a bit. "It's a hurling stick. I got it at the Irish festival on the south shore a few years ago. You know hurling? It's an Irish sport. It's insane. It's like soccer, sort of, but they use a hard little ball, and they pick it up and whack it with that stick."

"I've never heard of it."

"Yeah, it's not well known, but I saw a demo match at the festival, it was crazy. I don't know how people don't just get flat out killed during the game."

He set his plate down on the coffee table. "Thanks. For dinner... and everything. I really appreciate it."

Lithium grumbled impatiently.

Brigid reached over, refilled her wineglass. "He wants to lick your plate. You can give it to him. He's my dishwasher. You want another beer?"

"No, that's okay. I'm pretty wiped out, you know. Thanks." He set the plate on the floor and Lithium polished it clean. "I think I might crash, actually."

⌸

He crawled into bed still wearing the gaudy green t-shirt and track pants. Bridget had transferred his clothes to the dryer and he could hear the rumble from the other side of the apartment. A weirdly comforting sound, a running dryer. It sounded like home. His head was still spinning slightly from the beer, or maybe from the meal, or maybe just from having a warm dry place to sleep and clean hair and a full stomach. He wasn't sure how long it had been since he'd

17

last had all three of those luxuries. Months. Since he'd fled the lab. The bed was small, the mattress thin, but it was at least cushioned, and he could pull the blankets around him and feel warm and safe.

He hoped.

There was a camera at that mini-mart.

His eyelids drooped. He let himself fall backwards into the sweet promise of sleep and oblivion swooped in to embrace him.

But still…there was a camera at that mini-mart.

⌗

She considered closing her bedroom door as she got into bed. There wasn't a lock on it so, if this guy ended up having malevolent intentions, closing the door wouldn't really do much good. Honestly, she didn't feel like he was a bad person, though. Maybe that was the wine talking, but he seemed sort of sweet, innocent. *Well, but they all seem innocent until they turn out to be psychos, though, right? Jeffrey Dahmer probably seemed innocent at first.* Still, she left the door open.

Lithium hopped up onto the bed beside her, flopped down. She kissed his head between his ears, curled herself around him. Drifted off to the noise of the thumping dryer.

It was sometime later that she woke again.

The dryer had stopped. The place was silent, but something was off. Lithium was still lying next to her, but not sleeping. His head was up, his ears pricked, his body tense, vibrating. He was staring into the darkness with an almost aggressive intensity. And he was growling. No, not growling. He was snarling.

She went cold, seeing him. She looked around the room, but it appeared to be empty. No sinister figures lurking in the corners or in the doorway. But Lithium was upset, his hackles up, lips pulled back. And, in one smooth motion, he leapt off the bed and slipped down the hall toward the guest room.

⌗

He woke abruptly with the realization that someone was in the room with him. Sat up, saw something in the doorway—something shadowed, menacing, reaching toward him. His chest tightened, he clawed backwards away from the thing in the door, terrified, unable to think even. He heard a set of scratching arrhythmic taps, a throaty rumble, a roar of pure rage. The dog barreled into the room, homed in on the intruder, leapt upon it without hesitation, snapped onto it. The creature howled, cursed, spun—

He closed his eyes, focused, pushed himself out of sync, pushed himself just a little. Opened his eyes. Still sitting upright on a bed, in a room empty and dimly lit, the loudest noise the pounding rush of blood in his ears. Cool air on his exposed skin—the t-shirt and track pants were gone. He took a couple of deep shaking breaths to center himself. Things were peaceful, things were fine, he was safe. All he had to do was get out of the house, run down the street a bit, re-sync back, and he should be fine. That is, he would need to find clothes, but that was…well, he would figure that out later. Maybe just hide out somewhere until things blew over, settled down. Maybe he could find Bridget and get his clothes back. But he was thinking too far ahead. The important thing was that he was safe…for now. He spent a few moments to calm himself down, eyes closed, letting his mind clear, until he felt ready to move.

He tried to stand up but couldn't move his legs properly—there was something holding them down—there were two extra legs. A pair of legs fused into his. One emerged at knee level, one at hip, but he couldn't move himself without dragging them along, and—

Oh, god.

He twisted around. A young woman was lying in the bed. His torso rose out of her pelvis like some nightmarish centaur. His clothes were gone but he appeared to be emerging out of a hole in her nightgown. She was blinking sleepily, confused at being abruptly awoken. She stared at him, stared at the fusion of their abdomens, horror dawning on her face. He could feel her pupils dilate, feel the terror reel through her because it reeled through him too, could predict the screaming that was coming—

He relaxed a bit, re-synced, returned to Bridget's guest room, to where he'd come from. Naked now, cold, shaking, but to his relief alone in the bed, sitting on top of the sheets and the green t-shirt and track pants. And the room, now brightly lit, no longer contained a shadowy menacing figure but instead a woman embracing the limp body of a dog, rocking back and forth, sobbing.

卐

She'd hesitated for half a second after Lithium jumped off the bed, frozen, her heart imploding with an anonymous terror. She hadn't even thought about it clearly—just a brief and hopeful, *Maybe it's fine*, flickering at the back of her mind. But of course it wasn't fine, something was very wrong, so she flung off the sheets and ran after Lithium. Almost without thinking, she'd snatched her hurling stick off the wall as she passed. The guest room door was open—she was sure she'd heard it close last night—but it was open. She glimpsed Lithium as he tore into the room, heard a clamor of snapping and crashing and an angry yelp. An angry human yelp. *Shit, did he attack John?*

She bounded into the room, halted for just a moment. There was a man in the room, not John but a man, hulking and huge, in a leather jacket over a flannel shirt, spinning and twisting to try to evade Lithium's flashing teeth. But Lithium was young and lithe and furious, and his teeth would not be evaded. He clamped down on the man's leg. The man howled, pulled out a gun, pointed it at Lithium, who yipped once and dropped away. Brigid instinctively swung her stick, clocked the shadowy figure on the head with all the strength and fear and rage within her. The stick fractured and splintered. The man stumbled. She recoiled, swung again, hit him in the elbow with the remnants of the stick. Hit him again and again and again. He lurched out of the room, down the hallway and out the front door with her in pursuit. She slammed and locked the door behind him, though it occurred to her that the locked door had not prevented him from coming in. She paused, panting, shaking.

Lithium wasn't with her.

He should be with her. He should be with her. A spike of dread flashed through her as she bolted back to the guest room. She hit the light switch and her heart froze when she saw Lithium's body limp on the floor between splatters of blood.

She dropped to the floor next to her dog, shaking, keening. "No, no, no no no no, Lithium, wake up, wake up, please, please." She couldn't breathe, she felt sick. She pulled his limp body onto her lap, wrapped her arms around his chest. Her hands were trembling. Her entire body was trembling. *This isn't possible, this cannot be possible, I can't lose him, not Lithium, not him.* There were a couple of wires coming out of his neck, between his shoulders, leading to a little pistol-shaped thing on the floor. She yanked them out, buried her face in his fur, refusing to face this horror, this palpable, impossible horror. Not Lithium, anything but this, she could not lose him. "Lithium, please, please wake up, please…please!"

His body jerked a little bit, his leg twitched.

She pulled back, holding her breath. *Did his chest move? Please…let his chest have moved…* She groped around over his ribs, searching for a heartbeat. *Is that a heartbeat?* It was hard to feel anything, she was shaking so badly. She put her ear to his chest, listened, but wasn't sure. *He feels warm, doesn't he? He's okay, right? He has to be okay. Please be okay.* She stroked his head, his ears. He blinked.

He blinked! He definitely blinked.

He had a heartbeat now, she could feel it. He was breathing. He was moving his legs. He was whining. He was alive. She lost it again, just sobbing, wailing with relief, clutching his body to her.

Finally, she remembered that there was someone else in the room, looked over to the bed—

"Why the fuck are you naked?"

卐

He'd forgotten about the nakedness. He jumped, looked down, pulled the sheets over himself, not sure how to react. His head was spinning, and he could feel the promise of a migraine lurking in his temples.

"I…" *Shit. Shit.* He had absolutely no idea what to do. No idea what to tell her. He had to run, to just be somewhere else. He tensed his shoulders, clenched the sheets in his fists, shut his eyes and pushed himself out of sync again. A little further this time, a little harder.

He opened his eyes in darkness and cold, no bed now. The drop to the ground was jarring, the floor rotting wood with broken planks scattered around. He appeared to be in a derelict, or semi-demolished, building. There was a large blue tarp flapping gently to his right, where there should have been an exterior wall. A rat squeaked and scurried through a hole in the wall to his left. The basic layout was the same as Bridget's guest room though, the hallway and front door still there. His head was throbbing now, every heartbeat bringing a flash of light behind his eyes. He had to concentrate, focus on the phase he was in, but he was out of practice, and the effort was more than he was prepared for. He managed to pull himself to his feet, stumbled toward the tarp, pulled it aside and saw to his dismay that there was a six-foot drop to the sidewalk. God, his head. The pain was overwhelming. Dizzy, he lost his balance, stepped backwards to catch himself and stepped on something sharp. He cried out, tripped, lost his focus…

And was back in Bridget's guest room, standing now by a window, swaying. He put a hand on the wall to steady himself, the other on his head, which did precisely nothing to relieve the pain. His knees buckled and he fell to the floor, fingers laced through his hair, nails digging into his palms. He tried to steady his breathing, but nausea came rushing in and then spaghetti came rushing out. He curled up against the wall, eyes squeezed shut, still naked and trembling in a puddle of vomit.

⌗

"John…John."

Lithium seemed to be back to himself, sort of—distressed, panting, eyes manic—but basically himself. He kept slipping out of Brigid's hands, circling her, letting her hug him, wriggling loose again.

Brigid had managed to calm herself down a bit as well, still shaking violently with jerky breaths but at least under control. But confused. *What the fuck. What the actual fuck. Who was that guy? Why was he here? Was he after John? Who is John? Why is he naked?* And, somewhat more troubling, she thought he'd disappeared for a minute. She was staring at him on the bed, then she couldn't see him, then he was standing by the window. She must've imagined it, or her perception was skewed due to trauma, or she'd sustained a blow to the head or something. It confused her, but there were bigger problems. Not just the pool of half-digested pasta that was soaking into the corner of the rug, more the possibility of the intruder returning.

Also, John appeared to be injured or something. He was crouched against the wall, one arm wrapped around his abdomen and the other pulling on his hair, his face contorted, eyes shut, breathing shallow. A thin trickle of blood ran from his left nostril down to his lips, where it mixed with regurgitated marinara sauce. His ribs were visible with every inhalation.

She let go of Lithium, pulled herself onto her knees, looked around. There was blood splashed all over the place. The thing she'd mistaken for a pistol had been kicked to a corner, and she realized now that it was a Taser. Lithium seemed to be uninjured, other than the two puncture marks on his neck where the Taser electrodes had hit him, and those were only minimally bleeding. The rest of the blood seemed to have come from the intruder. *Well, good job, doggy,* she thought. *I hope that bite gets infected.* She crawled over to John, who was still basically unresponsive. *Why is he naked, though?* This bothered her. Because, truthfully, the house was not that warm, and his bedspread was not that thick...something felt wrong. He was grimacing, still not opening his eyes, his breathing short and choppy. She put her hand on his shoulder and he gasped, jerked, gulped air a couple of times before his eyes finally slid open a fraction.

"I'm...sorry. I'm sorry. I'm sorry."

She pulled the top sheet off the bed and wrapped it around him. "It's okay. We're all okay. Just hold on. I need to grab my phone. I'll call 911."

He jerked again. "No! No...please. Please don't do that." He wiped the blood from under his nose, but the trickle reappeared. "Please. Just give me a few minutes. I'll...I'll get out of here, but please...just wait."

"Why? Do…do you know what happened? Do you know who that was? What's going on?"

He shook his head, tensed again. "No. I mean, no…sort of. He was here for me. He was after me. I'm so sorry. I'm so sorry…your dog—"

"He's okay. He got Tasered, I think, but he's okay. I should probably take him to the vet to make sure. But what do you mean, he was after you? Who was he?"

Lithium moved behind John, sniffed him under the sheet, sniffed around the vomit, around his mouth, lingered under his nose, licked the blood before he withdrew. He clicked his jaws a few times, resumed panting, but his canine forehead was wrinkled. He looked at Brigid, clearly distressed.

"Come here, baby. It's okay." She embraced her dog and some of the tension started to ease out of her shoulders. "John. Seriously. Tell me what's happening."

John took a deeper but still shaky breath. "I have to get out of here." He struggled to right himself but failed and slipped back down to the ground. His face was a rictus of pain.

"Is he coming back?"

John nodded. "Yeah…someone's going to come back. They found me, they'll be after me."

"The police?"

"Yes. No. No, but…" He shook his head, wiped the trickle of blood from his nose. Another trickle replaced it.

Brigid rested her head on Lithium, arms still around him. She gazed at the broken figure before her. She was feeling calmer, more in control now. Lithium was okay, so she could face everything else. What were her options? Well, she could call the police and have them come and take John in for whatever he was wanted for, then they could track down that dickwad who had fucking Tasered her dog and hopefully they'd Taser the fuck out of his fucking dipshit nutsack; *or* she could wait for that dickwad to come back and then Taser the fuck out of his fucking dipshit nutsack herself; *or* she could pack Lithium and John into the car and drive away, go on the run until she could figure the whole story out.

That was the issue, really. She didn't know the full story. She didn't want to turn John in without knowing why he was running. She felt kind of responsible for him.

Oh, great. You've bonded already. Good going. This is why you don't feed strays, for fuck's sake.

She knew what she ought to do. Obviously. She ought to call the police. *They'll straighten everything out, right? It's their job. And then I can get back to my normal life.*

But she had a feeling that things would end badly for John in that case.

Also, I hate my normal life. It's boring as fuck.

"Get up, get dressed. We're getting out of here."

⌗

He had to get up. He pressed his hands against the floor, tried to push himself to his feet.

He failed.

He leaned back against the wall, shivering, looked around the room. There were splashes and smears of blood over the floorboards and rug. Broken pieces of wood scattered around. Vomit, of course. He closed his eyes for a moment, wincing at the pulsing pain in his temples. He tentatively scooted himself backwards, away from the puddle of vomit, toward the bed. Where were his clothes? Right, in the dryer. The t-shirt and track pants should still be on the bed though. Where was Bridget? What if she was calling the police? He had to get up.

He took a deep breath, focused on ignoring the pain in his head, used the bed to pull himself upright. Found the track pants and t-shirt, put them on, wiping his mouth on the shirt. *Can I maybe slip out the back door?* There'd been a back door…but he couldn't leave like this, he'd freeze to death, and that guy might be waiting for him to emerge. *Where's my coat?* His head started spinning. He sat down on the bed. *Fuck. Maybe I should just give up.*

Bridget and Lithium reentered the room. "Oh good, you're dressed. Here, I found some Vicodin," she said, handing him a couple of white pills and a glass of water. "We're going to try to make a break out the back door. The car's not far. Do you think he knows my car? Guess it doesn't matter, it's not like I have a spare." She left the room, returned with his duffle messily packed, his coat, and a backpack. She snapped a leash on Lithium. "Are you ready?"

"Yeah."

"OK. Shoes, get your shoes on. Can you run at all?"

"Yeah, I think…"

"Good. I'm gonna need you to carry your bag."

He pulled on his shoes, braced himself, managed to stand and pick up his duffle. She pulled out her phone, led him to a back door through her bedroom. He could see a small wooden deck out the back, with steps leading to an alley. "You see the car there? At the corner?" He nodded. "OK. I'm gonna open the door. You run, I'll be right behind you. Ready?"

He nodded again.

She opened the door.

He ran.

⌘

Brigid let John get about halfway to the car before she hit the *Talk* button on her phone.

The dispatcher answered after a couple of rings. "911, what's your emergency?"

She answered, "Someone broke into my house," dropped the phone, shouldered her backpack, and tugged on Lithium's leash. They ran toward John, who'd made it to the end of the alley, where he was leaning against the corner of an apartment building. She unlocked the car and pushed him into the front. Lithium hopped into the back. She pulled out with as much control as she could manage, wrestling with her seatbelt and resisting the urge to speed. She turned the next four corners at random.

"Can you see anyone behind us?"

Shit. John appeared to have passed out. *Very helpful.*

Well, she didn't see anyone in the rearview mirror. She circled a few other blocks to be sure, darting through the housing projects and down back streets, then finally headed toward the Seaport. When she was confident there was no one behind her, she pulled up next to an ATM and withdrew all the cash she could. Which, owing to daily withdrawal limits on her debit and credit cards, amounted to about $1,200. *Who knew I had so little in accessible liquid assets.*

She continued taking random turns and arbitrary streets for a while before getting onto the interstate and then Route 1 heading north, past strip malls, fast food places, a giant plastic dinosaur. The single most depressing strip of tarmac in the state, in her limited experience. There was a motel there, in Saugus—the Fronds. She'd never been there herself, but she knew someone years ago who'd told her it was a fleabag, and she thought an anonymous fleabag was what they needed.

And a fleabag it was. Everything about this establishment just oozed despair. What was that feeling, when you just gave up and accepted the shit that your life is? That was what it oozed. Letters hanging off the signs by the road read, "NEW ROOM, FREE HBO, WHIR POO, LOW RATES." Even the lobby seemed to be drained of color, as if it had been filmed through a blue filter. Though that might have been the fault of the fluorescent lightbulbs that semi-lit the place.

Brigid approached the front desk, leaving John and Lithium in the car. A bored, middle-aged, overweight man looked up at her as she approached. Purplish bags under his eyes, deep lines around his mouth. *Well,* she mused to herself, *it's three o'clock in the morning. Maybe he shouldn't be shamed for looking like shit at this hour.*

"Hi. I need a room."

"How long?"

"A…a night, I guess. Maybe two. A night."

The man sighed, wiggled the mouse attached to his computer. "You mean until the morning, or until tomorrow morning?"

"Tomorrow morning. How much is that, until tomorrow morning?"

"It's $150 a night, so $300 till tomorrow."

She blinked. "Wait. One night. $150. Right? This night is pretty much done."

"Lady, it's three AM. Check-in time is four in the afternoon. You want to check in now, it's two nights."

She glared at him, exhaled slowly through her nose. "Fine. Two nights. I mean, that's bullshit, but fine."

He shrugged, took her money and gave her a key. Not a keycard, a key. *Wow, this place would be fucking quaint, if it wasn't so clearly a shithole.*

It took some doing to wake John up. In hindsight, maybe the Vicodin had been a bad idea. But she managed to shuffle him into the room and drop him onto the bed, before returning to fetch Lithium. She locked the door, looked around the room—a television from the '90s, a bedspread half-covered by the unconscious John, a stained armchair—*Oh god, why is it stained? What is that stain?*—and a dilapidated bureau. A stereotypical shit motel room. She was kind of floored that it should even exist.

She was exhausted. Wired, but exhausted. Not yet processing the events of the past few hours. She collapsed onto the stained armchair— *Don't think about it, just don't think about it*—and pulled out her tablet. What were the odds the place would have Wi-Fi?

Long, it turned out. Very long odds.

She curled herself around the tablet. The chair had a weird smell to it. *Probably semen. Old, dried, fermented semen. Ugh.*

Lithium hopped up on the bed and nestled down next to John. *Well, the dog still seems to like him anyway. Can't be that bad.*

〇

He woke up to sunlight streaming into a strange room. Lying on top of the covers on a strange bed, a little brown dog next to him. The events of the previous night came trickling back slowly—Vermont, hitching, Bridget's apartment, an intruder, a jump, another jump, a meltdown, then things got fuzzy.

Where was he? How had he gotten here?

The dog noted he was awake, hopped up, wagged his tail, woofed brightly.

"I dunno, puppy. What do you want? I don't have anything." His voice was hoarse, unfamiliar.

He pulled himself up, looked around. A motel room. An ancient TV on an ancient bureau, a stained armchair, worn carpet. At least his head wasn't hurting anymore. He was hungry, though, and thirsty. He stumbled to the bathroom and drank three plastic cups of odd-tasting water, savoring the feeling of the cold washing through his chest and stomach. He pawed through his duffle, pulled out a blessedly clean shirt and jeans, and changed out of the track pants and garish green t-shirt he was still wearing. He sat down on the bed and found a TV remote tethered to the bedside table. Clicked through scrambled porn until he found a morning news show. Perky people talking perkily about stuff that didn't matter, the weather for the next five days, some human-interest story about a sick kid, breaking news about a home invasion and a missing woman—

Whoa, shit.

Oh, shit.

His hands felt numb. *Bridget's face is on the news. Her face, her face! is on the news. What do I do? What do I do? I have to get out of here. Yes, I have to do that.* He looked around the room. His duffle was in the corner. *I can grab that and run, just run down the road. Wait, what road?* He had no idea where he was. Looking out of the window was no help. All he saw were a few cars in a dilapidated, overgrown parking lot. Trees that looked dead, gray skies. A cold, steady drizzle falling. He couldn't even figure out which way was which. He could go out there, start walking in any direction, see how he went, but the idea of heading out into the cold again made his throat tighten. *I'd be exposed out there. I'm exposed in here.*

The little brown dog was sitting next to him by the door, looking expectant. What was the dog's name again? Thorazine or something?

There was a note on the door, hanging off the doorknob, secured with a hair elastic. He hadn't noticed it before. He pulled it off and read:

John
I had to run out for a bit. Don't panic. I'll be back soon. There's food on the bureau.
Brigid

He hesitated a moment, briefly confused by the signature, and turned around. There was a Sonic bag on the bureau. Hunger rushed back, displaced the panic. *Oh right, barfed last night's dinner.* He was still starving. Starving, and also exposed. Inside the bag, he found three breakfast burritos (all cold) and some French toast sticks (also cold), all of which he wolfed down, and it was the greatest experience of his life, or at least the last few days of his life. He sank onto the bed, chewing, looked at the dog who was staring hopefully at the last bit of burrito in his hand. Gave the dog the bit of burrito. Slumped over, tried to think. *She said she'd be back. Of course she'll come back, she left her dog here. She wouldn't leave her dog. And she helped me last night. Really, there's no reason to assume that she'll turn me in at this point, right? Unless last night was a ruse, or unless something happened today to change her mind.* He wanted to call her, find some reassurance about what was happening, but it had been a long time since he'd had a phone…and he didn't know her number…or her last name, for that matter.

The television continued to drone on. An ad for a personal injury lawyer.

Maybe I should wait. If I leave, where would I go? Should I trust her? What if she comes back with police or something? What if this is how I get caught?

The TV switched to some sort of talk show. A bunch of obese people who looked like they just couldn't be bothered to dress in something other than pants with elastic waistbands before appearing on national TV. A white, middle-aged man in a suit with an absurd mustache talking at them, literally shaking his finger. He shut it off. The little dog jumped up on the bed, dug himself a nest in the discolored bedspread, circled, flopped down.

I need to be ready to run again, that's all. I need to prepare myself.

He closed his eyes, cleared his mind, focused on his breathing.

centered divider

Brigid sighed and leaned her forehead onto her fingertips, arm braced on the chair's armrest. She'd honestly thought this entire undertaking would've taken maybe an hour, but now she'd been sitting in the police station for the past three hours, watching the clock advance and fretting about what John might be doing back in the motel room.

After seeing her face on the morning news, she'd decided to return to Southie to file a police report. That's all they'd need, she figured, an APB out on her. Should she get picked up, that would leave John in the lurch. So, having taken Lithium out for his morning constitutional and having grabbed some fast-food breakfast, she joined the morning traffic rush, crept back into the city, walked into the local station, and explained her situation. After some confusion, paper shuffling, inspection of her ID, and more paper shuffling, she was escorted to the back of the station where she sat on an uncomfortable plastic chair staring at yellow cinderblock walls, trying to get her story straight in her head. She was permitted to borrow the front desk phone to call work and tell them she wouldn't be in for a couple of days, what with the break-in and all. They sympathetically explained that all missed time would have to count as sick days. Ultimately, a man in a rumpled suit showed up, belly hanging over his belt, thinning hair gray at the temples, bags under his eyes, with a vague air of exasperation. He sat down, pulled out more paper, peered at her over his glasses. An officer? A detective? She wasn't actually sure who would be in charge of home invasions. When he introduced himself as Detective O'Leary it was with the nasal vowels and displaced terminal "r"s of deep-rooted Bostonians.

She explained—nervously and fearing that her face was giving her away every time she stretched the truth—that she'd been peacefully sleeping in her own home when someone broke in. That she fought him off with a decorative hurling stick—here she also had to explain what hurling was, and why she should have such a stick hanging decoratively in her home. That she called 911 but, in a panic, fled to a safe place and…oops…must have left her phone behind because it was no longer with her. That she saw the news report in the morning and came in to report the incident.

"Why did you leave the scene?"

"Well, I was scared, you know. A man broke into my house…and I didn't know if he was going to come back or not…so of course I ran."

"Why didn't you go directly to the police? Why did you wait so long?"

"I'm sorry. I just…I panicked. I wasn't thinking clearly…and you know I lost my phone…I didn't know how I would…contact…well, I don't have a good excuse, I guess, I just…I just wanted to go and hide, so that's what I did."

"Where'd you go?"

"I went to a safe place. No offense, but I'd rather not say where exactly…you know I'm still scared that the guy might track me down. I don't even know who he is or why he broke in, but it's really freaking me out to be honest…so—"

"He won't. We have him in custody. Where are you staying now?"

"That's great to hear, but I'd still just rather not say. If you need to get in touch with me that's fine, just email me. I'll be checking. Did he say why he broke in? What did he say?"

"We can't discuss that at this time, ma'am, but we have it under control. Were there any other witnesses present at the time of the incident?"

"No, no…just me and my dog. I live alone."

"No one else was present? Because it seemed like both beds had been slept in, as if you'd had a guest."

"No, no. I mean, I did have a guest a few days back and I just never got around to cleaning up…but no, there was just me."

"Who was your guest?"

"No one, just a friend…well, I mean, not exactly a friend, but someone I met who needed somewhere to stay for the night. So I let him crash… but that was like a week ago, give or take. Look, to be honest, I didn't even get his full name…he said his name was Dave. He just stayed for one night and then he caught a bus the next morning."

"You let a stranger spend the night in your house?"

"Yeah, I know. It sounds dodgy, but he seemed fine. He didn't do anything…he's gone now."

"Ma'am, that's very dangerous…not a good idea. Good way to get yourself hurt."

"Yeah, I know but, like I said, it was fine."

The detective showed her a mug shot of a heavyset man with a black eye, stitches on his forehead, and a swollen, deformed nose. "Have you seen this man before?"

"No, is that the guy? I couldn't see him well last night, it was dark. But I definitely hit him, so probably. Who is he?"

"We're going to need to fingerprint you, so we can exclude prints at the scene."

"Really? Do you? But you've arrested the guy already. Why do you need to fingerprint the scene? I mean it just seems like kind of a waste of time."

In the end, she allowed herself to be fingerprinted. Bickering the point seemed like a useless undertaking. That process took another hour, and then she had to look over the report and verify that it was factually correct, and sign various forms, and leave a contact email address, and insist again that she didn't want to disclose where she was currently staying. She asked if she could have her phone back, but they said it was evidence and that they had to keep it.

Finally, the detective shuffled all the papers into a manila folder, sighed and said, "Well, ma'am, guess that's all we need for the time being. We'll email you if there are any developments."

She gathered up her coat and left. Took a deep breath once she was back in her own car and massaged her temples. *Lord, what a pain in the arse.*

She'd need to get some more cash. And John. She'd left him alone in that motel room. *Odds are he's taken off. Well, hopefully he left the door shut. I'll be pissed as hell if I get back and find Lithium missing.* She drove down the street to the nearest ATM, an old grimy thing which was mounted on a wall next to a sketchy bar. Double-parked the car and withdrew another $500 from her diminishing reserves.

She drove back to the motel with some moderate agitation, fretting about her dog. Which was, of course, unnecessary as she found both John and Lithium waiting quietly in the room. John had changed back into his own clothes, jeans and t-shirt and flannel. Lithium jumped off the bed as soon as she opened the door. John was sitting in the armchair, legs crossed and eyes closed. His hair was mussed and there were circles under his eyes, though he looked marginally better than he had when she'd left him on the bed that morning. He opened his eyes, blinked a few times, focused on her.

"Hey. Dude, you're on the TV. On the news, I mean. I saw you on the news this morning. People are going to be looking for you." His voice was hoarse.

"Yeah, I know. It's okay. I took care of it."

"What? How?"

"I went to the police this morning. Filed a report."

John's eyes widened in evident panic.

"It's fine. I didn't tell them about you. Anyway, they picked up the guy. They showed me his mugshot. He's all sorts of beat up, not to brag. I didn't recognize him, though. Do you know who he was? We actually haven't really had the time to go over this, but what was happening there? Who was he? Why was he after you?"

Silence.

"Look…look. I'm not mad or anything. I'm…curious. You know, my home was broken into, I'd like to know why. And I want to know what's going on with you. You're acting like a…did you see that video of the lizard with all the snakes after it? You, you're acting like that lizard. So, yeah, I'm curious. And, if it helps, you can trust me. I'm not going to turn you in or anything." *Maybe I shouldn't be promising these things so blithely. For all I know, he's a serial killer with a trail of dead hookers in his wake. In that case, I should probably go ahead and turn him in.* "John. Come on."

He closed his eyes, sighed.

"Jason."

"What?"

"Not John. Jason."

"You definitely told me John."

"Yeah, I'm sorry. I lied about that. I…I thought it would be safer, you know, if you didn't know who I was…like if you didn't know my name. In case you were, I don't know…in case someone found me."

"Someone clearly found you anyway."

"Yeah. It wasn't a great plan, I guess, in hindsight."

Sigh. "So, okay, tell me, Jason, why did someone break into my home in what appeared to be an attempt to assault or abduct you?"

⊞

Jason leaned back in the armchair, rubbed his eyes. "It's a long story. Like, really long. Are you hungry? I'm hungry."

Brigid eyed him balefully. She looked irritated. She clearly wasn't an idiot, she could see that he was trying to dodge the question. He probably should have just left, earlier. This was going to end up a shitshow. Well, but he was actually hungry. It was past noon, and fast-food breakfast burritos, it turns out, are not particularly filling.

"Fine. But we'll order in. You can start talking. You want pizza? We'll get pizza." She picked up the phone, then hung it up again and started opening drawers on the night stand. "Shit. Have you seen... like, a takeout menu or something?"

Jason slumped.

"Oh, stop pouting. I'll go ask the front desk. Actually, you know what? Take Lithium out to go do his business while you're waiting. There's probably a plastic bag around here somewhere. His leash is on the bureau."

Jason obediently snapped the leash on the dog and followed him through the drizzle out to the edge of the tree line. He did not bring a plastic bag. It struck him that a pile of dog shit could only improve the aesthetics of this patch of land.

He realized, upon reentering the motel room, what an interesting moist, yeasty odor adorned the place. Now moist, yeasty, and wet-doggy. Still, it was dry. He found a threadbare towel in the bathroom and dried his hair, then tried to dry off the dog, who wiggled, spun, and shook himself off.

Brigid returned. "Right, we have some pizza coming. Hope you like pepperoni. God, it smells in here." She took off her jacket and shoes, jumped onto the bed and sat cross-legged. "Well, get started. Let's go."

⌗

"I signed on for the money. It started out as a research study, you know like the ones they advertise on the bus? Make however much money, expenses covered, commit to eight months, and have some tests run... seemed easy. And I didn't have much money, I had to drop out of college the semester before, and the study promised $10,000. Ten thousand! You know, for that I could've re-enrolled, finished my degree." He paused, sighed, rubbed the bridge of his nose. "It really did seem, like...too good to be true. So I signed up, and then there was this...you know, interview sort of process, and I got selected, me and nine other people. Ten total—five guys, five girls."

"Girls? How old were they?"

"I don't know. My age, give or take."

"Then women."

Jason looked at her blankly.

"Women. Girls are children."

"Okay..."

"Look, I know this is off topic, but I have a thing about the...the... the automatic, like, infantilization of women. It's...it's not necessarily offensive, but it's kind of low-key degrading."

Jason blinked. "Okay, five women. The head of the lab was this lady...woman, Dr. Hernandez. She was really cool, so down to earth. She treated us like we were...part of her team, you know...like we were important. It was really critical to her that we all understood what she was studying, you know...why...how we were supposed to be, like...a part of it. How we were contributing and why we were doing it."

"What was she studying?"

Jason laughed a little. "Right, so...I'm not going to be able to explain it very well. But it's sort of like this...you know the whole multiverse theory? The idea that there are multiple parallel universes?"

"I mean, I've seen the *Twilight Zone*, if that's what you're talking about."

"Yeah, okay, sort of. Okay, so...you know the Schrödinger's cat thing? You put a cat in a box with a poison, but the poison is in a bottle and there's a 50 percent chance of the bottle breaking or whatever, and you shut the box, and then while the box is shut the cat is theoretically both alive and dead."

"She killed a cat? What the fuck?" Brigid didn't consider herself a cat person, particularly, but this sounded pretty sociopathic. *A messed-up sort of scientist, this Hernandez character.*

"No. No one actually killed a cat. This was a...uh, like a thought experiment, you know? Theoretically, you killed a cat, maybe, but then maybe the cat didn't die. So, it's both alive and dead until you open the box and see."

Brigid relaxed a bit. "Seems to me a cat in a box would let you know if it were *not* dead."

"Well, this is a soundproof box, I guess. That's not the point. Anyway…so one of the…so there are the two possibilities, alive or dead, and when you open the box you see…let's say you see a dead cat. So, the theory is that there's another parallel universe where the cat is alive."

"Right…okay, sure, I guess?"

"So, apparently, there's a lot of debate about whether this alternate universe is a real thing or not. Like, a lot of scientists study it. I think Stephen Hawking wrote about it, in that book about time."

"Yeah, I don't think I read that one."

"So, but Dr. Hernandez, right? She figured it out. That's what the whole thing was about. She said the alternate universes are there… like physically really there, but they're on a different like wavelength or frequency or something, so they're there but we can't see them. Different phase. Like harmonics. And what we were doing was, we were learning how to shift to those other wavelengths. We were learning how to jump to other universes."

卐

Brigid stared at Jason. Her eyebrows were mushed together, and her lips were pressed into a thin line.

"Yeah, I know, it sounds like bullshit."

"Mmm-hmm."

Jason took a deep breath, walked to the center of the room, away from the furniture. He balled his fists and closed his eyes, focused on clearing his mind, took several deep breaths…and pushed himself out of sync.

Rhythmic squeaking and panting in a darkened room, the shades drawn against daylight, the smell of fresh cigarette smoke but stale tobacco, with a rancid undertone. He stood motionless for a moment or two until one of the two figures on the bed noticed him, gasped, hissed, "Shit, what the fuck?" Then there was a comic flurry of arms, legs, exposed buttocks, and pants entwined around ankles before he shifted back into sync and stood, naked, before a clearly mind-boggled Brigid.

Lithium barked.

Brigid said nothing, just stared, mouth hanging open slightly. Jason gathered up his clothes from the floor and pulled his pants back on, returned to the chair, leaned against the back of it, massaged his temples. His head spun, he felt nauseous. He smiled, a bit wanly, at Brigid. Lithium sniffed his pants, his ankles, stepped back and barked again.

"I think he smells it. There was cigarette smoke there...and I think someone had like hired the room for an hour. You know?" Another wave of nausea hit him. He sank down into the chair, tried to focus on breathing again. *Do I smell like smoke, actually? I'm not sure. Stupid thing to get hung up on.*

Brigid remained silent.

Jason slumped over. *What was I expecting? No one's going to take this sort of thing in stride. Honestly, if she isn't freaked out it probably means she's a plant, working for someone, somehow, or something. Though she could still be acting. Who knows.*

"Maybe you should start at the beginning."

Jason looked up. Brigid was on the bed, leaning back against the wall, arms crossed over her chest, gazing at him, face tense but calm.

Jason nodded. "Yeah. Okay. Like I said, I signed up for the money."

TWO

But he hadn't stayed for the money. He'd stayed for a girl. A woman. He remembered that sunny Monday in May when he'd walked into the lab to meet the other experiment participants. Ten of them total. Himself and four other guys—Pedro, Moe, Chris, Tyrone. Five women—Ji, Angela, Kechia, Diana. And Molly. Molly with the frizzy hair and wide smile, clever brown eyes, snarky wit. She maybe wasn't the prettiest of all time, but she was cute. And funny. And smart.

Dr. Hernandez explained the basics of the experiment. After several weeks of training, she'd implant a small device—which she called a quantum distractor—into the back of each of their necks, at the base of their skull. The device would sense changes in certain neurotransmitters and this would, theoretically, trigger a phase shift. The phase shift would allow them to jump to an alternate universe, where they would collect data. They would shift back after a designated period of time programmed into the distractor. So they signed contracts and non-disclosure agreements and giggled among themselves about being lab rats.

∴

"Wait. I don't understand. These...jumps, they're caused by what exactly?"

"Well, so it's located by the brainstem, and it reacts to certain...uh, hormones I guess that your brain releases? Nerve impulses. That sort of thing. I'm a little fuzzy on it, to be honest."

∴

The first few weeks at the lab were actually pretty fun. Mostly exercises, like learning how to control their physiologic state. They had to learn to control neurotransmitter expression, and the first step was to induce a sort of mental blank page, a state of Zen. So, lots of meditation. Some yoga. All very holistic and new agey. Jason started to doubt the seriousness of Dr. Hernandez's research, truth be told, after a series of grueling days of aromatherapy and acupuncture. But whatever, it was easy. Come in, spend six or eight hours on various meditative activities, give a few blood samples, maybe have an EEG or EKG or blood pressure check, then go home in the evening. A few times, he had an MRI of his head and neck, which was less fun, since it made him claustrophobic. But they were given a stipend, to pay for food and rent and essentials. It felt like getting paid to do nothing. Life was good.

The ten subjects started spending more time together than apart—going out for drinks in the evenings, getting to know one another. Some of them started hooking up a bit—Diana and Pedro, Tyrone and Chris. Jason found himself gravitating to Molly, sitting next to her, making inside jokes with her, partnering with her during exercises at the lab, walking to the bars with her. Thinking about her when they were apart. Thinking about her pretty much all the time.

They had a bunch of classes together, as a group. Concentration-type things. They tried mindfulness centered meditation, where they all sat in a circle and focused on breathing. The idea was that they would allow their minds to wander, become distracted, make a mental note of the distraction, release it and refocus on breathing. After some time, they were supposed to reach a state in which feelings and thoughts and other distractions were separated from the mind. Once they became adept at this, they started training on the stimulation of physiologic responses, to control the expression of specific neurotransmitter releases from the brainstem. It felt like a sort of mental "push." It was hard to describe.

Jason did a good job with his meditation when he practiced on his own, or when he was in a class without Molly. But, whenever she was in the room, she was the only thing on his mind. He would dutifully sit cross-legged, close his eyes, focus on deep breathing, and her face would drift up behind his eyelids. He would breathe and wonder if they would be getting dinner together that night. Let it go, breathe, and remember that she'd suggested they go catch a show at Metro. Let it go, breathe, and see her laughing uproariously at his attempts to sing Raffi songs when six of them played a drinking game a few nights before. And, eventually, the corners of his mouth would involuntarily turn upwards and he would open his eyes and peek at her, and inevitably she would snicker back at him.

He looked forward to seeing her every morning, the room brightening as soon as she walked in the door, feeling an actual physical flush of warmth behind his ribs when she looked at him and smiled. That dizzying rush when she laughed at something he said, the way he broke down helplessly at every joke she cracked. God, watching her lips widen into a grin over her perfect imperfect teeth, watching the dimples appear magiclike on her cheeks, even just seeing her blink, everything in slow motion, everything played back again in his head when he wasn't with her. And one night, finally, he walked her home from the bar, and at her doorstep she leaned against his shoulder and slipped her hand into his, and suggested he come in for a cup of coffee. He asked her, "Coffee, really?" and she giggled and answered, "No, not really," and he followed her into her apartment, and it felt so natural, so normal, like his whole life he'd just been waiting for this piece to fall into place. This…this was not a hookup. This was forever. This was real.

∴

"Was this maybe your first girlfriend?"

"No. She wasn't. And she wasn't just a girlfriend. She was…it sounds kind of…I don't know, melodramatic, but for real. She was my soulmate. She was everything to me. So don't take this the wrong way, but don't…don't belittle this. Don't mock me."

"Okay. Sorry. Go on."

∴

Maybe three or four weeks in, they had the devices implanted. Little metallic cylinders, about an inch and a half long. He was given a mild sedative and a local anesthetic, and lay face down on a surgical table. A small incision was made at the back of his neck, then there was some unsettling prodding around back there while they asked him to move his hands or wiggle his toes. He felt lightheaded and weak for a while afterwards, kept stumbling and losing his balance, but after a few days everything seemed to return to normal.

There was a two-week period of in-house recovery after the procedure, for monitoring purposes, they were told. During that time, they stayed in the lab complex, in an area set up like a dorm. Jason was assigned a room between Moe and Tyrone but he barely spent any time there. By that point, he and Molly had become basically inseparable, and he stayed with her most nights. After two weeks, when the sutures were removed from their incisions, they were allowed to return to their off-campus homes at night, and Molly moved in with Jason.

∴

"Where was she living before?"

"She had a couple of roommates in an apartment by the lakefront. She gave them like two weeks' notice before we had the implants put in. I guess she kind of knew where she was going. I had a studio place, kind of a shithole, but I liked living alone. It was a couple of blocks from 57th Street, so pretty convenient, and I didn't have much stuff. Still, it was kind of crowded with two people. But good. I mean, we were happy."

"Where was this?"

"Chicago. South Side."

∴

Those weeks, right after she moved in, were glorious. Every morning, Jason would wake up, see the mass of puffy hair—her hair was wild, had a life of its own, and she never tried to tame it—on the pillow next to him, sometimes flatten it a bit just to see it bounce back up, laugh to himself, sometimes laugh out loud. They would lie in bed for hours, she'd watch TV or read, he'd rest his head on her ribcage, his hand on her hip. She was both soft and firm, lean muscle under a reassuring cushion, no bones uncomfortably jutting out. He just loved everything about her—the dimpling on the back of her thighs, the perfect smooth brown expanse of her back, her slightly crooked teeth. She liked to watch romantic movies and mock them, liked to pick apart pseudo-science in action or sci-fi movies, or medical dramas—"Goddammit, why does every episode of *House* involve a brain biopsy? Who biopsies that many brains?" She was smart and ambitious, planning on applying to med school after the project was done. She was a college graduate, had a bachelor's in chemistry. Sometimes, she'd come home late because she'd spent half the afternoon or evening talking with Dr. Hernandez or her staff. Even from the beginning, she'd ask to see Dr. Hernandez's research, her notes and theories, trying to understand how the distractors worked, the origins of alternate worlds. She could understand so much so easily, whereas Jason would get confused and let his mind wander off and then come back and try to fake his way into their conversations. It made him self-conscious, the difference between them—she was so far out of his league, so much better than him. What was he anyway? Chubby, not quite ugly maybe, but a far cry from hot, kind of dim, mediocre. He wondered sometimes why she was with him at all.

But she liked him. She really did. He remembered the way she looked at him, the way she talked to him. He remembered one summer afternoon, the two of them lying in front of an oscillating fan, the sticky heat inducing a sort of drowsy, heavy torpor.

She sat up, fanned her t-shirt in a halfhearted attempt to cool off, and announced, "You ever been to a blues club? We should go. We're going. Tonight."

Jason tore his eyes away from the TV screen, glanced over. "What? Do you even like blues?"

"Of course I like blues. Everyone likes blues. It's obligatory. Around here, it's obligatory."

"It's Thursday."

"Thursday is a fine day for the blues. Any day is a fine day for the blues." Singing, grinning. She didn't look like she felt particularly bluesy.

Jason shrugged, looked back at the television, suddenly bored with the movie he'd been watching. Doubly bored by the commercials that had replaced it. He dug around for the remote in the cushions. "I dunno. I'm not really that into blues stuff. It all kinda sounds the same to me."

"Heresy! Heretic. You're just uneducated. All the more reason."

"I'll be the only Asian there. It'll be weird."

She snort-laughed. "You will not, you asshole. Besides, there's nothing wrong with expanding your horizons. Venture out of your comfort zone and all that."

He gave up on the remote, looked back to her. Her face was lit up, eager. He felt his apathy weaken under the onslaught of her enthusiasm. "Eh…"

"Yes. Yes. We're going. I'll buy you dinner. It'll be fun."

It took them nearly an hour to get there, since it was some place way up north of the river. When they arrived and found the blue neon sign flickering in the twilight, Jason suddenly thought he must not be dressed right. There was a line of swanky-looking people forming outside already. He'd be turned away at the door. Molly looked great, as she always did—even without effort, she always did—but he was wearing a somewhat oversized and faded t-shirt that did little to hide his gut, and there were stains on his jeans that he hadn't noticed till they were already on Metra. He hesitated, dragged his feet—literally—but Molly pulled him into line, oblivious to his discomfort.

"You're gonna love this place. It's supposed to be one of the best." She tugged her shirt down—it was riding up a little, exposing a bit of her midriff—and dug her fingers into the pockets of her jeans. "Argh. Why are these pockets so shallow? Tell me. What is the purpose of these useless pockets?" She pulled her fingers out again. "I need a blues song on the lack of decent pockets in women's clothes. Think they'll do that?" She started singing, shaking her head and snapping her fingers. "My lady-pants, they ain't got no place to put my hands…they ain't got no place to put my phone…they ain't got no place for shit—"

He laughed. "Stop. Please."

"No place for nothin'…I got some pointless, stupid, pocketless lady-pants."

"That doesn't even sound like blues."

"What? Yes it does. I sound amazing." She beamed at the bouncer, who was laughing, clearly entertained. They handed over their IDs, entered the dim crimson haze within, her arm around his waist, hugging him to her. She leaned up a bit, whispered into his ear, "Thank you for doing this, for coming out tonight." She hugged him a little tighter. "You're my favorite person in the whole world."

In that moment, the stains on his jeans, the pooch of his stomach, they just didn't matter anymore. Every insecurity, every self-doubt, every uncertainty he felt about himself, all of it vanished when she said that. Her perfection, projected, reflected onto him.

Glorious. A glorious time.

Δ

Activities at the lab changed after the two-week recovery period. On the first day Jason was back he was isolated, put in a sterile white room—white floor, white walls, white table, and white chairs—fitted with electrodes over his scalp and an EKG monitor and a blood pressure cuff. The beeping of the EKG and hissing of the cuff were more ominous than reassuring. He was particularly anxious because he felt alone. Molly was at home, and he hadn't seen any of the other lab rats in the hallways or heard anything from them that morning. Dr. Hernandez sat across from him, looking anxious but eager, flanked by her postdoc Erin, who was taking notes on a tablet. Vijay, the research assistant, was on the far side of a one-way mirror on the wall to Jason's left, presumably running a camera.

"Right, Jason, are you ready? What's going to happen is, I'm going to switch on the quantum distractor. What I want you to do is take a moment, try to focus and relax, and then start your breathing exercises. Okay? If we are successful, when you are ready you should be able to move to an adjacent universe. Take a look around, try to make a mental note of everything that you see, and hear, and otherwise sense, yes? The distractor will switch off after sixty seconds, which should allow you to re-synchronize, and that will bring you back here and we'll see what we have. But don't worry if we are not successful. Remember, this is only our first trial. No pressure, eh?"

He nodded, inhaled through his nose, focused on his breathing, focused on relaxing, but he felt like his heart was pounding so hard it must have been audible. He tried to remember his meditation techniques, released his death grip on the chair arms, visualized his happy place...thought about Molly.

He heard a quiet "click" when Dr. Hernandez switched on the device, sensed a sort of humming in the back of his neck. He took a few more breaths, closed his eyes, and began the breathing exercises. Tried to push himself.

Nothing happened.

He opened his eyes, stared plaintively at Dr. Hernandez. "Shit...I screwed up, I'm sorry. Let me try again. I can do this."

"It's fine, Jason. Just relax. No pressure, remember? Again, this is our first trial. We'll just take a few minutes, try again. Go back to your focused meditation. I think you are a bit nervous, no?"

Meditation again. Inhale, focus on the sensation of filling his lungs, expanding his chest. Exhale...slow, controlled. Let his mind empty. *Molly said she'd cook dinner for me tonight.* Inhale. Exhale. Empty mind again. Inhale. *Maybe we'll rent a movie.* Exhale. *Like* Transformers. Inhale. Exhale. *No, she definitely won't go for that.* Inhale. *She'll want to watch an indie movie, one of those movies that has a big star who's put on forty pounds, so you can tell he's authentic, and a banjo-heavy soundtrack, and a weird solemn kid with giant eyes...*

"Jason, how are you doing?"

Oh, shit. Right. Focused meditation. "Sorry, wait. I got it. Hang on."

Ten more minutes of mindful breathing and emptying his mind before he reached a sense of peace, transcendence, whatever. His mind floated around in his skull, pleasantly void, and off in the distance he heard Dr. Hernandez say, "When you're ready, Jason," and he gave his brain a little nudge...

It was hard to describe the sensation of that first phase shift. A buzzing that wasn't a buzzing. A tremor that came from within but also without. Not exactly painful, not exactly pressure, but not exactly not. It just felt...alien. Unnatural. Forced, even. Every part of him suddenly felt very slightly...off.

He opened his eyes, panting. He was sitting, naked, in an identical chair by an identical table next to an identical one-way mirror. No blood pressure cuff, no electrodes. Dr. Hernandez and Erin were missing. He looked around. Things seemed altered, somehow. Sure, the nakedness was part of it—no one had warned him about that, so he felt exposed and cold and confused, and his head hurt, behind his eyes. But more than that. In front of him, the table looked the same, but something about it was subtly wrong.

∴

"What do you mean, 'wrong'?"

"Have you ever had a dream where you're in, like, your own house, for example, but then you start to notice that things aren't where they're supposed to be? Like there's a door that isn't where there really is a door?"

"Um. Okay. The door was in the wrong place?"

"No. But it's wrong…the dream-door is wrong. But, in your dream, it's also where it's supposed to be, because it's a dream. So your brain tries to make both things true and you get confused, and you start trying to convince yourself that the door either was always there or isn't really there. And then you wake up and go, 'Well, that was a weird dream.'"

"So…the table was in the wrong place?"

"I'm not doing a great job of explaining this."

∵

He stared at the table, and the mirror, and the blank walls for some time trying to get his brain to come to terms with what he was seeing. It was a strange sensation. He had the impression that as soon as he looked away from the table in front of him, it would disappear, or maybe he would just forget that it existed. Like it would slip out of his mind, leaving no echo, no trace in his memory. He wondered if his recollections of his own home, his own origins, were similarly tenuous. He wondered if he'd forget about his own universe entirely if he were to stay here too long. If that happened, would he remember to return home? Or would he be stranded here? His heart started pounding. He couldn't stop staring at the table, the somehow not-right table, and his head was spinning, his palms sweating.

The door opened, and a strange man looked in, started, jumped back out and slammed the door, then an alarm started wailing. Jason's heart leapt up into his throat. He sprang out of the chair, pulled it in front of him, looked around in a panic. Should he try to open the door? Break the mirror-window? How long till the distractor re-synced? He was dizzy, lightheaded, breathing hard. He felt another weird buzz, the alarm stopped, the room shimmered, and then the room wasn't there at all. He found himself in an empty lot, the sun hot on his bare shoulders, reedy grasses up to his waist and scratching his legs. The bones of long-collapsed buildings lay around him, the lake mirroring the sun in the distance. He froze, panting, turned slowly around, staring at the endless wasteland. *Fuck. Fuck. What's happening? Shouldn't I be back in the lab? What I am supposed to do?* His head was killing him. He felt nauseous.

The abandoned lot shimmered and vanished. There was a weird sucking sensation in the back of his mind, and he literally stumbled backwards and steadied himself on a wall. He was in a familiar room.

He was back in the white room.

He was standing behind the chair, his clothes piled on the seat and floor, the electrodes and monitoring equipment scattered around. He was weak, his head pounding. He dropped onto his knees, shaking. Dr. Hernandez stood behind the table with an anxious face, while Erin typed madly into her tablet.

"Oh, sweet Jesus. Thank God. Thank God." Dr. Hernandez covered her mouth with her hands, dropped them, beaming. "I was worried for a minute. We lost track of you. I was worried you weren't going to return, but ah, here you are, wonderful! Wonderful."

Jason nodded and vomited.

Each of the subjects, in turn, underwent these experiments. After Jason, Dr. Hernandez made sure to have robes available at arm's length. Not all of them succeeded right off, though. Most of them didn't, in fact. Jason was the only one who managed it the first go-round.

After every trial, they were debriefed. If they were successful, they were asked to describe what they saw, and what they heard, and how they felt. Regardless of the outcome, they were subjected to a barrage of tests—blood and urine and physiologic parameters. After all the questions and the medical tests, they were given juice boxes and cookies, as if they were recovering from a blood donation, which Molly found hilarious. Sometimes, they also got painkillers or nausea medications.

∴

"So, yeah, it turned out I was the first one, and they hadn't expected the clothes and monitoring stuff not to, like, jump with me, even though, when you think about it, it makes sense. Like, in hindsight."

"It does? Why?"

"Well, so, the device affects the organism that it's implanted into, right? But like clothes and things aren't part of you, as an organism. So they stay behind. I used to have an earring, too, but that fell out. I lost it."

"Oh. Well, I'm so sorry to hear about the earring. But why does the device not fall out? It's not a part of you, right?"

"Yeah, I'm not sure. I think it has something to do with, like, it initiates the shift, like it controls the waveform that dictates what universe you're in. So I think it has to travel with you. Or maybe it's an organic thing. I'm not sure, like, it looked metallic, but honestly I never actually asked."

∵

"What did you see, Jason? Let's start there. Just an overview."

This was after the fifth or sixth successful visit he'd made to one of the alternative universes. He winced at the needle prick as Erin drew a little vial of blood, then a second vial, before she finally withdrew the needle. Closed his eyes and tried to picture the scene he'd just left. "There were...uh, I was in a building. High ceiling. A big wooden desk...had a whatsitcalled...blotter on it, some papers and books and stuff. Big glass windows." The room had been brightly lit, sun reflecting on a gleaming floor. Red, though, part of the reflection was red, red light through the window. "Oh. Stained glass. There was a design, like...a bird...a stork, maybe? Or a crane? On the window." He concentrated. The window in front of him...what was to the left of it? "There was a photo on the wall, it was framed, it looked like those pictures of the president that hang in the post office? Like a government guy."

Vijay typed on his tablet, murmuring. "Possible government building. Crane or stork."

Dr. Hernandez peered over Vijay's shoulder at his notes. "The man in the photograph, can you describe him?"

"Black hair. In a ponytail, I think. His clothes were kind of…weird. He was wearing a blue suit with those like military shoulder things and beaded stuff, patterned beads I think, underneath." Jason pictured his face. Stern expression, angular features. "I think he may have been…Indian?"

Vijay looked up. "Indian?"

Jason glanced over. "Oh. Not India-Indian. Like, American Indian."

Vijay returned to his tablet. "So, not Indian."

"Native American, you think? Or First Nations?" Dr. Hernandez sounded intrigued. "Did you see anyone else? Did everyone look ethnically similar, or would you call it more of a heterogenous population? Could you identify any specific national or tribal identification?"

Jason shook his head. "No. I was only there a minute, no one came in or anything. I think that's all I can tell you." He rubbed his arm, over the bandage Erin had stuck on it, hesitated before he ventured, "Um, Dr. Hernandez, can I ask you something?"

"Of course, Jason. What is it?"

"I don't, like…I don't really get why you want to know these things. I mean, I don't really get why it matters. I thought you just wanted to find out if, like, if these parallel worlds existed, right? And you did…so, like, who cares what's in them? I mean, what does it matter, a picture on a wall?"

Dr. Hernandez was quiet for a moment, regarding him, as if she was unsure how to answer. "Well, Jason, in a sense you are correct. My training is in quantum physics, not sociology or demographics or even economics. And yes, the core question that I set out to investigate has been answered.

"But that does not mean that the investigation has concluded, does it? There is so much more to learn. Right now, we are just gathering data points. Everything is so new. We are still in the very early stages of exploration. When we have enough data, enough little puzzle pieces, we will put them together to see what sort of picture emerges, and from there we will be able to develop specific avenues of research. So many different fields need investigation, you understand? What are the variables that dictate to which parallel reality you are able to travel? Can you control it? Can we control it? And if so, to what end?

"You asked why I care about the picture on the wall. I confess, I have a tendency to wonder, to leap to possible conclusions. On this trip, for example, maybe you were in a government office, and the picture on the wall was of a Native American. What could that mean? Is that particular Chicago populated by predominantly indigenous peoples? In that universe, was there a European invasion of the Americas? If so, did it fail? What makes that reality different from ours? Where in our history did the timelines diverge, and what was the butterfly flutter that triggered it? What sort of social and economic developments after that divergence led to the disparity between realities we see now? What tragedies were avoided, what opportunities were missed, and vice versa? And, once we understand some of these patterns, perhaps we can use that understanding to help direct our own futures. To avoid tragedies, to reach for greatness. To elevate humanity. You understand? We have found proof of parallel realities, and this opens up an infinite number of new possibilities.

"But we have a long way to go. We are just beginning. So, please continue. Did you see anything out the window? Buildings, or a city, or wilderness, or the lake? Try to remember."

⌸

Generally, there was one trial per day, and afterwards the lab rats were allowed free time while Dr. Hernandez, Erin, and Vijay presumably recorded and analyzed their findings. Sometimes, they'd run a trial elsewhere, like a library or museum or whatever, try to research that alternate universe by reading newspapers or whatnot. Unfortunately, there were almost always other people around during the day. Those trials were awkward. They weren't particularly fruitful, either, as it was hard to gather data while people freaked out around them. What Jason found funny, though, was that people didn't tend to freak out about him appearing out of nowhere. They freaked out because he was standing naked in the middle of a museum or library foyer or whatever. He guessed they just assumed they hadn't seen him before, hadn't seen him walk in and strip. Anyway, Dr. Hernandez started holding trials periodically at night, to lessen the chances that they'd run into other people.

As he became more experienced, Jason found that he had some degree of natural skill. After the first month of trials, he started to figure out the nuances of jumping. A light push led to a jump to a world not so different from his own. A harder push led to a more noticeably different world. Dr. Hernandez theorized that the more similar worlds were branches from relatively recent sets of potential outcomes. By the cat-in-a-box allegory, the box was only recently opened and the consequences of finding the cat alive instead of dead had not become significant. The further in the past that the hypothetical box had been opened, the more differences there would be between the two worlds.

∴

"Why does this keep coming back to the cat and the box?"

"Well, okay. So, look at it this way. Say like a week ago I, like, maybe went to the supermarket and was trying to decide what cereal I wanted, and I bought Lucky Charms instead of Cheerios. Right? So, in this world, this is a world in which I have been eating Lucky Charms for a week. But there is another world where I've been eating Cheerios for a week, and I could jump to that world, and because it is based on a difference that was a week ago, it's a little bit of a bigger jump, so everything is a little bit more different, right? Because of the butterfly effect and all. But maybe say yesterday, I had the option of having like an egg for breakfast instead of Lucky Charms. I didn't, I had Lucky Charms, but there is then like another world where I had an egg, but that happened just yesterday, so it's a little jump. And things are not so different."

"The variation in universes must be mind blowing."

"Well, I mean, replace my breakfast choices with like the president deciding whether or not to nuke North Korea."

"Ah."

∴

Sometimes, the alternate worlds were pretty similar. At Jason's first trial, he shifted to a nearly identical room—if not for the 'other-ness' and the headaches he might not have realized it was an alternate at all. When the trials took place in the white room with the one-way mirror, occasionally he would find other people in the room. Another scientist in a lab coat, or some random dude with a notebook. Usually they were shocked to see him, sometimes just surprised. Like they'd known he was in the other room but hadn't expected him to walk in the door. One other-scientist told him that she'd been working on the same project but hadn't found any success. She wanted him to stick around, answer a bunch of questions, and he did for about five minutes before the distractor shut off and he returned home.

∴

"So, you would sometimes like go to another world, and there would be another you, or another group of people, in the same project, doing the same thing?"

"Sometimes. Sometimes not. Like once the other-lab was an office building, and I ended up standing in front of some guy in a suit, with, you know, all those sort of knickknacks on his desk? Like the hanging balls that you click back and—"

"Yeah. Okay, but so does that mean that there are a bunch of other, like, alternate worlds where people are doing the same...what is it, phase-jumping experiments?"

"Yeah. There are some. But usually the participants are different, like it wasn't ever any of the ten of us that I saw."

"Yeah, I get that. But, so here's my question. Why don't we see people from other realities jump into this one? Shouldn't that be happening kind of all the time?"

"Oh, yeah, that's a good point. Molly asked Dr. Hernandez that, too. I think they decided it was because the odds of someone jumping into ours, it's possible, but it's unlikely, because there are an infinity of other universes out there and, I'm not sure how many, but a finite number of universes that have people who theoretically can phase shift, and in those universes there's only about ten people who can do it, give or take, so the odds of someone from another universe finding their way here is pretty infinitesimally small. There's also the issue of, like, even in very similar universes where Dr. Hernandez is working on the same thing, I couldn't find any one where they had succeeded. Like, this might be the only one."

∴

There was always the possibility of materializing into space that was already occupied by something else, like a piece of furniture or wall or whatever. If it was inanimate, it would shift itself around him, as if the matter itself, on an atomic level, just moved aside to make room for him. But if it was a living thing, another person or animal or something, they would actually merge together. These experiences left him shaking and nauseous. He would end up with his entire body fused into the other person, sometimes with an arm sticking out or an extra face out of the side of his head, sometimes joined by a single appendage. It tended not to last very long, as he would become unable to control his involuntary responses. Usually a few seconds of escalating panic and then a second jump to a second alternate world. He didn't know what happened to them after he jumped out. He hoped they were okay. He didn't want to think about it too hard.

About two months after the distractor had been implanted, during a nighttime trial, Jason stood on an alternate Lake Michigan beach watching a distant storm sprinkle lightning onto the lake. Gusts of sand scoured his skin, the wind unpredictable and violent, whipping his hair into his eyes. The storm looked to be approaching. He hugged his arms around his chest, nervous, threatened. He wanted to go home. And just like that—like he'd nudged himself back to his natural phase—he returned, fifteen seconds early and without the deactivation of his distractor implant.

Dr. Hernandez was delighted at this development. "This is tremendous…tremendous, Jason, such a leap forward! Though I am unclear as to how this happened. We will need to investigate this further. Erin, have you noted this? Make a note of this. Yes, we will look into this further…" Jason was pretty happy about it as well, as it released him from his reliance on the distractor. Frankly, spending too long in any one alternate universe was unnerving and, after a few minutes, it also gave him a headache and a stomachache. Much longer than that and it gave him a migraine. Jump too far, or for too long, and he could end up nearly incapacitated.

These physical effects did not go unnoticed. Jason returned from one trial with a nosebleed that refused to stop, leaving drops of blood all over the floor and drips down the front of his t-shirt. Another time, he looked in the mirror and was shocked to see that the white of his left eye had turned diffusely red—a broken blood vessel, it turned out. Dr. Hernandez and her crew put him through a new barrage of testing after the nosebleed incident. He never heard about the test results but, after that, Dr. Hernandez cut back on his participation.

Despite that setback, Dr. Hernandez was giddy with the overall progress the ten of them were making. Most of the subjects had managed to make at least brief, short jumps, though Tyrone was still struggling. As far as Jason knew, though, he was the only one not dependent on the distractor—he was the only one who could re-sync himself. He tried to initiate jumps on his own, without the distractor being activated, though this was trickier and met with failure.

It was around this time that Wilders appeared.

Wilders. There was something off about him from the start. Jason disliked Wilders, disliked his slicked back blond hair and the expanse of upper gums that were exposed whenever he twisted his face into an oily, leering smile, disliked that he wore business suits under a lab coat, because that was, well, stupid. No one who wore a business suit under a lab coat could be trusted, and who slicks back their hair anymore? He looked like a reject from an '80s finance movie.

He had initially been just a background presence—first behind the one-way mirror and invisible, then standing behind Dr. Hernandez as she set up her equipment, then sitting at the table during post-jump briefings. He had an unnerving habit of helping himself to juice boxes, which Jason felt was presumptuous of him, given that he hadn't actually performed any quantum maneuvers. Honestly, Jason had a bad feeling about him from the start. He suspected Dr. Hernandez did as well, as her normally ebullient personality became muted and guarded when he was around, and a few times Jason caught her flicking irritated glances at him. Erin and Vijay were also visibly on edge.

Gradually, Jason realized that all of his interactions with Dr. Hernandez were being monitored by Wilders. In fact, every time he saw Dr. Hernandez it seemed Wilders was hanging around, lurking. Making suggestions before trials. Questioning the value of whatever data had been collected. Once, he leaned over Dr. Hernandez's shoulder and tapped something out on her laptop. Jason couldn't see what, but Dr. Hernandez slapped his hand away, her eyes burning with rage. She slammed the laptop closed and politely but firmly asked Jason to excuse himself. He lingered in the hallway listening to her rapid-fire, staccato outbursts from within, but wasn't able to discern much of what she was saying.

Then, one chilly day in early October, all of the lab subjects were summoned to a meeting and were given the news—Dr. Hernandez was gone, and Erin and Vijay were gone, and there was just Wilders with his absurd business suit and lab coat and a set of unknown, anonymous lackeys in jumpsuits. Something about Dr. Hernandez's funding being pulled, and the experiment being taken over by this new team because they had the backing of the people paying for the project. They were assured the project would continue as planned and that everyone would be paid as promised at its conclusion, but some minor changes would be implemented. For one, no more living off campus. Everyone was to move back into their dorm rooms. Their stipends were being cut back as well. The justification was that they no longer needed to pay for their own rent, and food would be provided by the project. Also, the experiment was now subject to greater security—cameras were installed in the halls and in the dorm common areas, cell phones were confiscated, and the Wi-Fi in the lab disappeared. In order to prevent leakage of sensitive information, all communications with the outside world were forbidden. Going forward, any off-campus trips would be chaperoned by a member of the jumpsuited research team.

This did not go over well with the lab rats. There was much shouting, much anger, much demanding to know what had happened to Dr. Hernandez and her team, and some threats to walk out. All of this was met with the cool reminder that exiting the experiment at this time would nullify the contract regarding payment, and that discussing the details of the experiment with any person or organization would be considered breach of contract as per the NDA they'd signed, and that any such breach would be met with prosecution. So, while they were free to leave, they would be leaving with no money and no rights to talk about what had been going on. Oh, and they would need to have their implants removed before they could leave.

Jason and Molly had some differences of opinion about how to respond to these changes. Jason was distressed that Dr. Hernandez was gone, but he was still excited about the experiment, excited about his ability to cross into parallel universes. "This is a superpower, sort of...right?" he argued to Molly. "Just because the researchers have changed, the science itself is still the same, right? I don't like Wilders much either, but the ends will be justified...nothing's really changed... we just have a different boss. Right?"

Molly didn't agree. "No. There's something dodgy in the way he's taken over the lab. You don't see that? It doesn't bother you? What happened to Dr. Hernandez? I can't work with him. Dr. Hernandez was always happy to share her findings with me. But him? He won't even talk to me. He won't talk to any of us. He doesn't even treat us like people...he's the sort of slimy creep who hunts endangered animals for sport." She dropped her voice. "And he's not a scientist. He...he has some other agenda. He's taking us down a dangerous road, Jason, you can't see that?"

"That's ridiculous," Jason responded, maybe trying to convince her, maybe trying to convince himself. She just glared at him and shook her head.

It was the cameras, though, that really got under their skin. The sense of constant surveillance, the lack of privacy. They were assured that the cameras were only in the common areas and hallways, but Tyrone came out of his room one day shouting that he'd found a camera installed in the air duct which was spying on him. He ripped it out of the wall and was standing in the common room shaking the broken thing at the camera in the corner, cursing enthusiastically and creatively, when a couple of anonymous lackeys showed up with platitudes and apologies and escorted him out of the dorm. He never returned. The story was that he elected to leave the project of his own volition. But, still, all his personal belongings were left in his dorm room for about a week afterwards, as if forgotten or abandoned. Weird. Suspicious.

Lying on Molly's bed, Jason found himself staring at the air ducts, wondering. They started hanging sheets or papers over the ducts when they wanted to be sure they were alone, though they were never certain that actually accomplished anything.

It was during one of those times when they'd hung a sheet over the air duct that Jason first managed to make a phase shift without the extrinsic activation of his distractor implant.

∴

"You what now?"

"I jumped to another universe on my own. Without them having to turn on the implant."

"Huh…and this was possible…how?"

"I'm not completely sure. I don't know if they turned it on at some point and just forgot to turn it off, or if there was like a malfunction, or what. But it was a…like, a turning point for me because then I could jump around outside of the lab. I don't know that anyone else was able to do it. Molly was trying but she never managed, and she never managed to come back without the distractor's help either. I did spend a lot of time rubbing my neck. You know, maybe that was it."

"Yeah. Okay. That makes total sense."

∴

Molly was asleep, curled up in her bed. Jason was suffering one of his occasional bouts of insomnia and was staring at the luminous alarm clock display, bored and kind of restless. So, with nothing else to do, he tried to push himself into a jump. Tried with no success for half the night, but finally he felt a shimmer, saw the clock blur briefly. He looked at Molly's slumbering form, feeling a rush of excitement, closed his eyes, pushed himself gently but insistently, as if he was trying to focus his vision. He felt a familiar unnatural tremor. The bed vanished from under him and he fell onto a concrete floor. He opened his eyes to a cold, empty room, broken glass under a window, graffiti on the walls and empty beer cans scattered in the corners. Gunshots sounded off in the distance, he heard the thin wail of a siren. Out the window he could see an overgrown empty lot bordered by a chain-link fence. A shadowed figure trotted along the fence, stopped, saw him, paused for a moment and bolted away. *Christ, this is worse than Detroit,* he thought. *I've gone to Chi-Detroit.* He grinned, triumphant, and allowed himself to re-sync back to his own room.

After that first jump, he practiced whenever he felt he could get away with blocking the air vents. It was always a little bit dodgy—the dorm rooms were on the second floor and, once, he jumped too far into a universe in which the building did not exist, and he sprained his ankle in the fall to the ground. It could've been a lot worse, but there happened to be a convenient thick layer of vegetation there instead. He still barely managed to control how far he jumped—only a general idea of how far from his own reality, never precise enough for him to predict what he would find when he arrived. But it was getting easier. He practiced as much as he could—days when he had nothing scheduled with Wilders, late at night after Molly had gone to sleep—always being careful to hide his activities from Wilders and his crew.

Meanwhile, the experiments were getting more intense. The jumps Jason made with Wilders were still mostly random, undirected. Jason never knew where exactly he was going to end up, though he tried to control it. He thought maybe if he could standardize how hard he pushed himself for every jump he would reliably return to the same alternate timeline and maybe, if he could manage that, he could train himself to predict where he was going. Wilders didn't seem to have any interest in that aspect of the experiments, so Jason largely kept his repeated failures and frustrations to himself. Wilders seemed to be particularly interested in finding ways for him to carry objects back and forth between universes and, to this end, he performed a variety of increasingly uncomfortable trials. He had Jason swallow some sort of tracking capsule, but that didn't work, just left a bile-stained capsule sitting inside his shirt on the chair when he jumped. He tried similar trackers placed under Jason's skin, or inserted rectally, which were met with similar, but more painful, failures. Anything Jason tried to carry back with him from an alternate universe would disappear when he re-synced.

But one day, not too long after Wilders took over, Jason opened his eyes after a jump and felt a shock of recognition. Sun shining through a floor to ceiling window with a red stained-glass crane. A portrait of a man, looking stern and important and familiar, staring at him from the wall.

Jason scrambled up from the floor where he'd fallen, heart racing with excitement. He ran over to the desk, pawed through the documents lying on the blotter. He couldn't read them, the letters seemed all scrambled up, but the letters were familiar—the English alphabet, at least. He tried opening the drawers, but they were locked. A computer monitor came to life when he wiggled a cordless mouse. An open text box and the word "Ensaluti" appeared on the screen. A login screen, he supposed, so he typed "password" hopefully, but the password was evidently not "password." He abandoned the desk, scanned the rest of the room—a digital clock was set up high on the wall opposite the portrait, over what looked like a diploma or fancy award. On it, he recognized one word— "Miami"—which struck him as odd. Miami, he'd have to remember that. He could hear noises, a commotion, developing beyond the closed door. He dashed over to the glass wall with the red crane, looked outside to a courtyard, brick walkways along flowering bushes, a fountain set in the center featuring a stone turtle. Men and women walking back and forth, ignoring him or maybe not seeing him. Maybe it was one-way glass? What had Dr. Hernandez asked him, the last time he was there? Do they look alike? He studied faces. Some of them looked alike. Black hair, dark skin, looked kind of Hispanic, maybe. But not everyone.

The door behind him opened and several people ran in, yelling at him, yelling at each other, words he couldn't make out. Two men in uniforms twisted his arms behind him, bracing him in place. A few more moments of shouting back and forth while Jason stood frozen and silent, and then a blonde woman approached him, quieted the room, and asked "*Kui vi estas?*" When he didn't answer, she tried again. "*Qui êtes-vous? ¿Quién eres tú?*" Shook her head in frustration. "Who are you?"

Jason barely had time to register some sort of foreign accent before, panicking, he re-synced back to Wilders's lab.

In his excitement, he started babbling even as he put on a robe, sat in a chair, and was fitted with a blood pressure cuff. "I've been there!

I've been there before! It was…" He tried to order his thoughts, clarify his recollections. "I was there with Dr. Hernandez, it was the place with the Indians, I mean the Native Americans, she thought, but there were other people, they tried to talk to me…one of them spoke English, but the rest I didn't understand—"

Wilders cut him off. "You did not manage to transport our tracker." His aide finished with the blood pressure reading, extended Jason's arm and prepared to take a blood sample.

Jason started. He'd forgotten about the tracker. They'd had him try swallowing it again this time, and he hadn't thought about it afterwards, but now he could see it sitting on Wilders's desk on a sheet of white paper, damp and discolored. "Oh. No, I guess. But…I saw, on the wall, the word Miami, it was written on a…like framed document-type thing."

Wilders regarded him blankly for a moment or two, finally asked, "What exactly do you expect me to do with that information? If we can't manage to manipulate those other universes, or at least gather information that will help us control our own future, then why do I even bother sending you across? You need to learn how to be more useful to me, Jason."

Jason fell silent. He didn't know how to respond. Dr. Hernandez would've been thrilled with the details he'd brought back. She would've drilled him with questions, taken copious notes, and done something constructive with the information. He felt himself sag, physically and emotionally. His head was starting to hurt, and he felt suddenly drained, like a teenager who'd disappointed his abusive father.

The aide withdrew the needle from Jason's arm, stuck a bandage over the little bleeding spot, took him back to his room.

∴

"Did you ever find out what that universe was all about?"

"No. I never got back there. I don't think any of the others went there, either. After a while, I just didn't think too much about things I'd seen in other universes any more. Didn't seem to be any point, I guess. I don't know."

∴

All of his fellow lab rats were showing signs of stress at this point. Ji chewed her fingernails to the point that her fingertips had specks of blood on them pretty much all the time. Angela took to spending every waking moment curled up on the common room sofa, mindlessly eating whatever she could scrounge from the communal kitchen. Moe could no longer reliably succeed at his trials and became withdrawn, distant and moody. He spent a lot of time playing his guitar, singing softly in his room. Jason was able to listen once, hidden out of eyesight.

Where did I come from,
and what am I supposed to be doing?
I have no idea.
My soul is from elsewhere,
I'm sure of that,
and I intend to end up there.

Jason approached him tentatively, curious, to ask, "Did you write that? It's…that's pretty profound."

Mo shook his head, wrapped his arms around the guitar. "No. Rumi. He was a poet. My dad used to read his stuff to us, me and my sister, when we were kids. It makes me feel better."

Jason found solace with Molly. She was bitter and angry at losing Dr. Hernandez, but she was emotionally stronger than any of the other subjects. Whenever he came out of the lab feeling confused and distressed and hurt, she was there to wrap her legs around him and pull his head to her chest and stroke his hair. Molly never came out of the lab confused or distressed or hurting. She only came out pissed.

More and more frequently, Jason was getting headaches, blinding migraines that would linger for hours or days, no matter what meds he took to control them. Sometimes, he would make a jump and come back with a bloody nose, or with another broken blood vessel in his eye, making him look demonic. Once, he started coughing up blood. He spent the next week having blood tests, X-rays, and MRIs of his chest, but no one ever told him what was wrong. He asked Moe about it, about whether he'd also had similar problems, but Moe only averted his eyes and suggested that Jason take it easy. But Kechia spent a whole week bedridden, Pedro was missing for a day and returned alarmingly pale under his normal bronze, and Diana stopped eating nearly entirely, declaring there was no point since everything eventually just came back up.

Several of them started hanging around outside of the labs where the experiments were taking place. They weren't allowed inside, not while one of them was in a session, but they would stand in the hallway by the door, listening and waiting for whoever was inside to come out, waiting to ask them what had happened. A lot of the time, it was a good way to predict what their own future sessions would involve. One November day, Jason, Angela, Molly, and Chris were lurking by the door to the lab where Pedro was having a session, trying surreptitiously to listen in. There was a clamor, a ruckus in the lab, they heard shouting, things falling, more shouting, then an alarm, and a few minutes later some lackeys came rushing down the hall with a gurney. When the door opened, they could see Pedro on the floor thrashing, eyes rolling, bloody foam oozing from his mouth. Wilders was standing in the corner, barking into a cell phone, while his assistants tried to hold down Pedro's flailing limbs. They got him onto the gurney and rushed him down the hallway. Molly and Chris tried to follow, but the gurney was pushed past a set of swinging doors that locked shut as soon as they closed. Molly banged on the doors, shouting, demanding to know what was happening, but no one responded. When they returned to the lab, Wilders was still there. He pushed past without acknowledging them, left them alone in the hallway, freaked.

Pedro did not return to the dorm. Not that night, not ever. They were told that he'd also elected to voluntarily leave the project, for unrelated health reasons. Again, it felt weird. Suspicious.

Jason's skill at initiating his own jumps was improving steadily, though. He tried to explain the process to Molly, but he didn't understand it well himself. He wasn't quite sure if his ability was because of a defect in the implant or some sort of inherent skill of his own. He would've preferred the latter. It made him feel important, special. Molly had tried a few times, but the only time she managed to jump outside of the lab setting was once, when she and Jason were in the middle of an especially passionate bout of lovemaking. The sheets around them vanished and, startled by the cold, they looked around and realized they were in a strange room, on a strange bed. Molly gasped, wrapped her legs around Jason, pulling him deeper into her. He thrust a few last times before finishing and, in that triumphant moment, they returned to their own bed.

She laughed, panting, delighted. "Ha! That was fucking incredible, that was amazing..."

He felt a swell of pride that he'd been able to do that for her, wrapped his arms around her and pulled them under the comforter again. "Merry Christmas, Moll. I love you."

∴

"Whoa. Seriously? But I thought you said that you couldn't...co-transport... you couldn't transport things with you."

"Yeah, but this was different. Maybe because she was another living thing, and we were...um...I guess...joined? Or maybe it had to do with...like, that she had an implant also? I don't know."

∴

Jason amped up his secret universe-hopping activities for a while after that, hoping maybe he could figure out how to teach the trick to Molly, or find a way to replicate it. He realized the recklessness of what he was doing one night in January when he was alone in his dorm room and he made a jump into an other-apartment that was crashing down around him. He heard explosions nearby, saw dust puffing out from under the door, froze for a moment in panic before diving under a doorjamb as a chunk of wall took out the floor he'd been standing on. *Shit,* he thought, clinging to the doorjamb and staring at the void that had nearly swallowed him, gasping the frigid, dusty air. With a massive effort, he gathered his thoughts and re-synced home, clinging to the bathroom door, panting, shaking, coughing, wondering what would happen if he were killed in another universe.

It was at breakfast the next morning that Angela finally declared that she was done with the project—her actual words being, "Fuck this fucking noise." She demanded that Wilders release her from the program, and he appeared happy enough to comply. All she had to do was sign a bunch more non-disclosure papers, legally rescind her right to payment, and have the implant removed. She signed the papers without hesitation and asked how soon she could get it taken out. Jason had a bad feeling about the whole thing. Molly had a worse feeling. But Wilders gave his consent, and Angela was scheduled to have the procedure for distractor removal the following day.

The distractors had been implanted in a surgical suite on the first floor of the lab. There was a viewing area on a mezzanine above it. During the original implantation procedure, there had been a smattering of strangers in the viewing area. Jason hadn't given that much thought at the time, but when Angela had the distractor removed, he and Molly chose to watch the procedure. Jason was a bit reluctant—not being a particular fan of scalpels or bleeding, the whole idea made him more than a little nauseous—but Molly convinced him to come. She perched on the edge of her seat, face pressed to the glass, staring intently at the activity below. Angela saw her, grinned, gave her a thumbs-up before settling face down onto the surgical table.

"Should be easy," Jason mused, anxious. "Same as putting it in, right?"

Molly grunted noncommittally.

There were three unknown people in surgical gowns and masks present, doctors or surgeons or something, rearranging a set of gleaming surgical instruments on a table. One injected a local anesthetic into the back of Angela's neck, scrubbed the area, placed a drape over it. The doctors gathered around Angela's prone figure, one of them holding a scalpel. Wilders stood in the corner, appearing visibly annoyed under his mask, arms crossed. The surgeon leaned in, nicked Angela's neck, started poking around with his shiny instruments while another daubed away the trickling blood with gauze squares.

Things seemed fine for about ten minutes, before it all went to hell.

Angela twitched once, abruptly disappeared. All the surgeons jumped back, stared at the empty surgical drapes lying on the table, looked at each other. A second later, Angela blinked back onto the floor, pushing the table over so it crashed to the ground. She fuzzed a bit, vanished again, reappeared, and now she was agitated, reaching back at her neck which was producing a rhythmically pulsing geyser of blood. She screamed, screeching, clamping her hands over the wound in her neck. The doctors tried to hold her down, tried to pull her hands away, but she flickered out again and reappeared on the floor, scrambling, trying to stand up but still spurting blood between her fingers. The doctors grabbed her, pulled her back onto the table, held gauze over the wound.

Wilders shouted, "Sedate her!" But the IV that had been so carefully placed earlier was lying useless on the floor. She wasn't struggling anymore, though. There was so much blood, everywhere. Sprays across the floor, across the walls, across the glass in front of Molly's anguished face. Even through the horror, Jason wondered how it was possible...so much blood from such a small wound? She was soaked in it, swimming in it...but the bleeding gradually lessened, no longer a river, just a stream, a trickle. Angela's arms fell down over the edge of the table, her hands limp, her eyes unfocused. One of the doctors pushed her onto her back, knelt over her, started doing chest compressions. Another, cursing, tried to place a fresh IV into her arm. Someone was rifling through a set of drawers and yelling things like, "Atropine" and "Epi," while Wilders snapped, "Blood, we need blood!"

But it was useless, Jason could see it. She was gone. They were pounding on a corpse. They got an EKG going, looked at the flatline, pulled out the shock paddles.

"What the fuck do they think that's going to do?" Molly snarled, tears on her face, her fists on the glass.

Three minutes later, everyone just stood motionless, staring in horror at the pale, bloody, naked body.

∴

"Jesus fucking Christ."
"Yeah. Things got really bad. None of us could really figure out what happened. And it was...everyone had nightmares afterwards...or couldn't sleep at all."

∴

No one was eager to volunteer to have their implants removed after that and, since that step was obligatory before leaving the program, none of them asked to leave. Molly dug out her old NDA forms, read and reread them, looking for a loophole. What she found, instead, was an addendum that all implants must be recovered at the end of the project.

"Do you think that's legally binding? I mean, if we can argue that it's dangerous to remove them?"

Jason didn't know.

"I mean, it makes it sound like we're all going to have the implants removed at the end of this anyway," Molly pressed. "Will they do that? I mean, given what happened to Ang—" She stopped, choked a little bit, took a few breaths before starting again. "Given what happened. And honestly, we don't know about Tyrone or Pedro. I'm not into conspiracy theories or anything, but we have absolutely no idea what happened to them."

Still, Jason would've stuck it out. He was basically a trusting person and, much as he didn't like Wilders, he didn't actually think the man would intentionally endanger anyone. *Monsters like that only exist in movies, right?* He was willing to believe that either they would've figured out how to safely extricate the implants or not required their removal after all. So long as they weren't activated they were useless, so what harm could it do to leave them in?

∴

"Except for yours."

"Yeah."

∵

But then Molly told him that she was pregnant.

Evidently, she'd been suspicious for several weeks. They were always careful, always used protection, but then her period was late, or rather it was absent, and then absent again, so she took a chaperoned trip to a drugstore—she and Diana and Jason, who wanted candy—where she apparently managed to shoplift a pack of pregnancy tests.

They were both positive.

∴

"How did that happen?"

"I think it was that time we, like, jumped together. We..." Jason blushed. *"We lost the condom."*

"Oh."

∴

She waited for a week before she told him. It came as a shock—not just the news of the pregnancy, but the fact that she kept it hidden from him for a solid week. Why hadn't she told him? Didn't she trust him? He lashed out, confused and hurt, and she retaliated. That was the only time he could remember that they'd gotten into an actual angry, shouting fight. He couldn't even recall exactly what he'd said or what she'd replied, just the hurt, the sense of betrayal that wounded him. Finally, she stormed off, left him sitting on his bed cradling his head in his hands, the anger draining out of him and leaving only dread that he might've lost her, that she might leave him. The very thought chilled his blood. He lasted maybe half an hour before he ran after her, found her sitting in her own dorm room with tears on her face. He literally fell to his knees apologizing, begging her forgiveness, wrapped his arms around her waist and buried his face in her lap. He held on until he felt her body relax and she began to stroke his hair.

When his emotions calmed a bit, he was able to start to process the news. It was hard to understand how he felt. Excited? Scared? Both? He was not ready to be a parent, to raise a child—he felt like he was barely managing adulthood as it was. And they'd been careful! They always specifically took measures to avoid this, to avoid being caught off guard like this. It was unfair! Or was it a sign? Maybe this was a message from...he wasn't sure, a higher power, from the ethos or from the universe—from his universe—that it was his destiny, to raise a family together with Molly. Maybe?

Molly, though...she was scared. Terrified. "Pregnancy changes your body, physically and physiologically changes your body," she told Jason. "I don't know how this will affect phase shifting. I don't know whether the baby will come with me or not. I don't know if it will spontaneously abort, or whether it'll be damaged, you know? What if this shifting... what if it's teratogenic?"

Jason shook his head, puzzled.

"Teratogenic—causes birth defects, permanent congenital injuries? We don't know. Honestly, we don't even really know exactly how shifting...all this phase shifting...is affecting us. This is all uncharted. There are so many things that could go wrong. I don't know if I should even keep this baby." She shrugged, bitterly, then. "And I'm not sure I'm gonna have a say in the matter."

He wanted to get her—both of them—out of the project. If they asked to go, they would have no money. Though, suddenly, that seemed so trivial. He could dismiss those concerns with, "We'll figure it out," but there was the issue of how to get the devices un-implanted. The idea of going through what Angela had gone through...well, that was out of the question.

They didn't tell Wilders or his lackeys about the pregnancy. Molly was afraid of what Wilders would want to do when he found out, and so was Jason. This wasn't a long-term solution, though. Already, she must've been about two, three months along. Eventually, she would start to show, Wilders would figure out something was up. She could get away with the baggy sweatshirt look for a while, but the weather was warming up. March slipped into April, the snow melted, shoots of grass started to appear in the mud of the grounds outside.

And then she vanished.

The official explanation was that she'd chosen to terminate her participation in the study. This was a lie, of course. She never would've left without telling Jason. They'd talked about it, at length, had discussed all of their options and some non-options as well. On the last night they spent together, she suggested that maybe they were getting ahead of themselves, that she needed to come clean to Wilders, see a doctor, get a prenatal checkup or whatever, make sure they knew what was going on before making any decisions. He went to bed in his own room when she said she was going to read for a while and, when he woke up, she was gone. Her room was emptied. Nothing left, no clothes, no pictures, none of her books or notes. Her laptop was gone. Her room as gutted as Jason felt.

Jason was frantic without her. He refused to participate in the experiments, refused to eat, refused to bathe, refused to speak to the lab staff—except to demand to see her. Stopped talking to the other lab rats. Moe especially tried to reach out to him, tried to remind him that he wasn't alone and that he still had friends, but he could only snarl back at them until no one wanted to make an effort anymore. He spent the nights wandering the halls, banging on staff doors and shouting at the jumpsuited guards behind them. He was blind with grief, mad with loss and confusion.

He started sneaking around the lab after hours. He had some limited control over accessing the locked rooms. He would make a jump outside of a locked door, walk to a spot he thought was on the other side of the door, sync home. It was so simple in theory as to be absurd. He explored the first floor of the lab this way, found no Molly, no dorm rooms, nothing that would indicate she might have ever been there. Nothing on the first floor but the cafeteria and experiment rooms, the MRI, a lounge, but no hidden rooms that might be housing a pregnant woman.

The upper floors were more of a challenge, since at the spot where he sometimes landed the entire building would turn out to be missing. At this point, he could sort of control how far he jumped, but the process wasn't entirely reliable. It was kind of like playing that Canadian broom-and-ice game, curling. If he didn't push hard enough, not enough had changed and doors were still locked. If he pushed too hard, suddenly he'd be standing in a barn or a hospital or some random person's kitchen. Once, standing on the second floor, he'd jumped to the end zone in an empty stadium and fallen fifteen feet to the artificial grass below. Had it been concrete, he probably would've broken an ankle. Anyway, he didn't jump from the upper floors after that.

"Weren't there, you know, other people around? In these alternate universes that you were jumping into?"

"Yeah. But I only went at night, so they were mostly sleeping, or gone home or whatever, I guess. I'd go from a corner of the room because people weren't likely to be there. A few times, I'd jump and there'd be someone there, and they'd freak out a bit. But, most of the time, I managed to sneak around unnoticed. I'd usually even manage to find some clothes, but most of the time I didn't really care, because I'd lose them as soon as I jumped back."

"So, night is night in other universes?"

"Time seems to be basically constant. Relatively speaking."

∵

About four months after Molly's disappearance, he managed to break into the research library, where all the records from the experiments were kept. Much of it was password protected, all of it was kept in locked file cabinets. A security camera watched silently from the corner. Jason ignored the camera, broke open a file cabinet drawer, then a second, a third. He finally found a folder labelled *Lincoln, Molly* and, on the last page, a report. An autopsy report.

Multiple localized cerebral infarcts...Evidence of extensive hemorrhaging in pulmonary and uterine tissues...Evidence of altered renal and hepatic function...Death attributed to DIC with multi-organ failure likely secondary to preeclampsia complicated by premature induction of parturition.

His hands shaking, eyes blurring, he managed to read most of it before he was caught and dragged, fighting and screaming uselessly, to the white room by a pair of jumpsuited thugs.

Wilders joined his crew in the white room to interrogate him. They pushed him into a chair, cuffed his hands behind him. The cuffs bit into his wrists and the vinyl seat of the chair was sticky against his bare skin. He refused to talk. They were suspicious, obviously. They figured he must have managed to jump, given that he showed up out of nowhere and naked in a locked room. They couldn't figure out how he'd done it, though. They asked him nicely, they asked him less than nicely, they threatened, they cajoled, but Jason just stared off into the middle distance, his throat tight, nauseous. Nothing they did really registered. Later on, he couldn't even recall the specifics. "Premature induction of parturition" kept ringing in his head, back and forth, like a nightmarish auditory pendulum. Parturition? Childbirth? What had they done? What did they do? Eventually, they issued a last set of threats and brought him back to his dorm room.

It was days before he was able to function again. A few. Several. Many. At first, he just lay on his bed, his bed that felt so strange and unfamiliar and empty, curled up, sometimes shaking with repressed sobs, sometimes limp. He didn't eat for a week, though Moe and Chris would bring him food a few times every day, shake him by the shoulder, mutter encouraging or sympathetic words. But, eventually, shock and despair gave way to anger and that gave way to fear, and he started to believe that none of them would survive this project, that the plan from the beginning was that every subject would be ultimately terminated. And that was when he decided he had to run, he had to leave, so he made a plan.

It was a simple enough idea. Much like sneaking around the lab. Jump to another world, run outside, jump back, run away. By this time, the dorms were being locked every night. Every stairwell had an alarmed door. The entrance to the building involved a locked door, a vestibule, then a second locked door. Most of the locks required a keycard to access. Jason's room had a camera on him at all times. The lab structure was a stand-alone building, currently surrounded by a chain-link fence with razor wire on top—a recent addition. It was located not far from Jackson Park and the 63rd Street Metra stop. The surrounding neighborhood was heavily populated, so Jason's original plan to just jump back and take off down the street had to be modified. He would need to find some clothes. He would need some money. But there was a Walgreens down the street a bit—that was where Molly had shoplifted the pregnancy test. He would just need to remember how to get there, hope it would be closed.

It went off without a hitch, in the end. Well, without many hitches. His first jump was to a nearly identical lab, a familiar room, with a stranger sleeping in his bed and unlocked doors. He went down to the ground floor, but the exterior doors were locked. He jumped again, as far as he could, found himself standing in a crumbling building in a derelict neighborhood, sirens in the distance, boarded up apartment buildings lining the street. He tried to get his bearings as the familiar pain-dagger stabbed through his temples. His nose started to bleed again, his ears started ringing. He ran naked down the street, sliced up his feet on shards of broken glass scattered on the sidewalks.

Fortunately, it was a warm August night, and the whole place seemed abandoned. But, unfortunately, he couldn't figure which way led to the location of the drugstore. He re-synced back home, staggered down the street, hiding as best he could, but by the time he managed to make it to the Walgreens he was barely able to stand and retched up whatever bile happened to be sitting around in his stomach. He broke the glass door with a brick, pulled a t-shirt off the rack, then a pair of sweatpants and some flip-flops. He checked the register for money but found it empty, so he took off running with the store alarm blaring behind him. He ran as far as he could, maybe six blocks, found an alley, crawled behind some trash barrels and curled up. By some miracle, the police didn't pick him up and by some other miracle Wilders and his goons—who must have been looking for him—didn't find him. After a day or two, he was strong enough to start walking.

He didn't stop until the night Brigid found him by the side of the road.

THREE

Brigid was quiet for a few moments, waiting, but evidently Jason had finished his story. "But what about the others in the lab? Moe and Chris…and whoever else?"

He shrugged, looked away. "Diana. Ji. Kechia. They're still there, as far as I know."

"Why didn't you go to the police? I mean, it sounds like all sorts of illegal shit was going on in there."

"I couldn't. I mean, I was going to, at first. But I was scared, so I didn't right away, and then I started thinking, if they were after me, you know, the first place they'd check would be with the police, right? And they had the authority, it was their lab, we'd signed all of these forms, we'd sort of signed away our rights."

Brigid shook her head. "I don't think it works like that."

"But, no, listen…I saw myself on TV…there was a report on the news, it had my picture and they were saying I was wanted for larceny and assault. But I didn't assault anyone, I swear. I did steal some stuff, but nothing big, and I didn't…it was a lie, and I know it was Wilders, I know it was him. The police, they were in on it, somehow." He dropped his eyes. "I was scared. They killed—" His shoulders twitched, spasming involuntarily. "They killed Molly. And they would've killed me. They're still after me. If they catch me…" He shook his head, still staring at his feet.

Brigid glanced at the clock. Most of the day was gone. The pizza was eaten, the crusts given to Lithium. This story Jason had been spinning was really too much. She still wasn't quite sure what had happened earlier, that disappearing act—some sort of trick, misdirection or something. But it was diverting anyway, better than her usual boring life. Sort of exciting, in a weird sleeping-in-a-semen-stained-armchair way. Something to tell her hypothetical grandchildren about.

"Right, well." She stretched, cracking her back. "We've got the room for one more night, and your nefarious hunter has been arrested and is in jail, so I think we can relax for now. Okay? And tomorrow we can figure out the next step. Tonight, I don't know, let's just watch some of that free HBO or sit in the 'whir poo' and get some proper rest."

Jason smiled a little. "Yeah, that was the plan last night too, right?"

"Well, it was. Yes. But you know, we have a lot more information now. So, if someone should break into this fortified stronghold of a motel room, we'll be ready."

"Yeah? You have another baseball bat?"

"Hurling stick. Jeez...though that one did seem to fall apart kind of easily. Makes me wonder if it was legit."

"Okay. But can we order another pizza? I'm, like, starving."

Instead, Brigid piled them all into the car, drove to a steakhouse down the road a bit, ordered a ton of takeout, got a six-pack of beer, took it all back to the motel. It was getting dark at this point and there were some very questionable individuals skulking around the parking lot, but they all seemed like straightforward sexual perverts. No worries there. Brigid switched on the free HBO, but the free HBO was showing some shit movie neither of them wanted to see, so they flipped through the channels between bites of steak and fries and swigs of beer.

Brigid had the remote and switched stations restlessly but hesitated finally on one show. Jason looked up. Brigid brightened. "Let's watch this. I like this show. You know it?"

"Um, maybe. What is it?"

"It's about two sexy brothers who sexily fight monsters and demons."

"Oh..."

~

He was back in his Chicago studio, lying on his lumpy futon, Molly curled up against his belly, flicking through channels until she stopped on a scene in which a young, sweaty, shirtless man was doing pull-ups in a motel room with an incongruously grumpy expression.

"What is this? You're watching this?"

"Yeah, I love this show. This is a great show. Why, you don't like it?"

"Is it a great show, really? Or are you just watching it for that guy with the abs?"

"Well, that doesn't hurt."

"Hmm…is that what you're into, though? Waxed chests and, I don't know, steroids?" Jason glanced down, sheepishly, at Molly's head on his stomach. His well-padded, kind of prominent, ab-less stomach. He doubted he'd be able to manage a single pull-up, grumpy expression or no.

"You're being a bit uncharitable there. I'm sure he worked hard for that waxed chest. But no, sweetie, you can relax. That's not what I'm into."

"Oh, okay then." Stupid as it sounded, he did relax.

"I'm really much more into his frumpy angel sidekick."

~

Jason dropped his piece of steak back into the Styrofoam clamshell, almost smiling, throat closed, face flushed hot. Tears started to leak out. *Molly. Goddammit, Molly.*

Brigid looked over, said, "Oh, shit, dude. I'm sorry. What is it? We don't have to watch this. Are you okay? What happened? We can watch something else. I'm sorry. You okay?"

"Yeah. No, I'm fine. I was just…Molly liked this show, too. It just sort of reminded me, that's all. I think, you know, it's been a long time since I talked about her as much as today, I think I'm just sort of…sort of on edge, I guess." He wiped his eyes, poked at his food.

The little dog whined softly, apparently upset. Brigid changed the channel, left it on some god-awful comedy with a laugh track. She was quiet for a moment, then ventured tentatively, "Do you want to talk about it?"

"No. Not really." He wiped his eyes again, sniffed, avoided her gaze. "It's fine. Sorry. We can maybe talk about something else."

Brigid kept staring at him. "Oh. Okay...what do you want to talk about?"

"I don't know." Uncomfortable silence again. "Uh. Hey, um...how come you misspell your name?"

Brigid grinned wryly. "I don't misspell it. It's the Irish spelling. B-R-I-G-I-D. It's the other way that's misspelled."

"Oh."

"My mother, she's always been really proud of being Irish. I mean, in Boston it's not really that unusual, but I grew up in Connecticut... not that it's that important, I guess. And I mean, technically, she's I think only half Irish, but still. Irish-American pride."

"Oh."

"I'd just been to visit her ...before I picked you up. I brought her a little pot of shamrocks for St. Paddy's."

"She lives in Vermont?"

"Yeah. She lives in a care center up there." Brigid's face became clouded, distant. "I try to visit her...as often as I can, I guess. Though, if I'm being honest, I don't go as often as I really could. It's...well, so, now she's got Alzheimer's. So it's kind of emotionally...difficult, going to visit her. And, you know, she doesn't always recognize me anymore, so I'm not sure if she gets anything out of it either." She sounded uncertain.

Jason wondered how much she was trying to convince herself.

"I think I'm sort of a stranger that comes to see her, and is that beneficial? Maybe. Yeah, it must be. I mean...the staff up there, they do a good job, I'm happy with them, but they can only spend so much time with one patient. So at least she gets some attention when I'm there." She shrugged. "I suppose."

"I'm sorry. That must be hard."

"Yeah. It is hard. It is...really...hard." She sighed, stared off into the distance for a while. Shook her head. "Alzheimer's is a bitch of a disease. There's a family history of it, my great-aunt had it as well, and I think a great-grandparent, so you know she was always a bit worried about it. And then when she first developed signs...well, that was the worst, actually. When she realized what was happening, you know, knew what was in store for her. Because it's not all at once. You don't just wake up one morning and not know who your children are. At first, she'd forget words, for example, do that thing where you're like, 'What's the word for this, it's on the tip of my tongue.' And that's not that unusual, right? I do that all the time."

Jason nodded.

"And yeah, every time, it scares me. Every time I forget a word, or a name, or what I was just reading or whatever. But yeah, so that, and then she started having trouble doing things like reading the newspaper, she had trouble like understanding what she was reading, and she'd get frustrated. And react to things differently. She started getting agitated, upset, at the littlest things. I couldn't really predict when she'd have a meltdown. Which was another whole thing, because my mother had always been so...even. Even keeled. I can't remember a single time during my childhood when she lost her temper, lost her cool. And that changed, like, her whole personality started to change. And it became really hard, taking care of her, especially because...you never think you're going to need to take care of your own mother. Or I didn't anyway. Even though we both knew it was a possibility, I just hadn't prepared for it, really at all."

"She was living with you?"

"I moved in with her, yeah, after the symptoms first started. I thought I could handle it. But turns out I couldn't. I just...it was too much. Between that...and also my marriage was falling apart, which was maybe related to it. That was why I had to put her in the nursing home. Which she was not on board with. There was a lot of shouting, she was really bitter about it. But I mean, in the end, I don't think I really had a choice. Neither of us did."

"Yeah, I mean that's what it sounds like." Jason tried to sound sympathetic. It came out just sounding uncomfortable, though Brigid didn't seem to notice.

"But, you know, it's funny, when I think of my mother, when I picture her, I picture her as she was when I was a kid. Young, like mid-thirties, just a little bit of gray in her hair, which I only even noticed when she talked about it, how gray she was going. I mean, she was amazing. Beautiful, so beautiful...I wonder sometimes, does everyone see their mother as beautiful? Because, to me, she was the embodiment of it. The walking definition of beauty. But I don't know if that was the reality, or if it was, I don't know, imprinting or something. And she was so...involved. My father wasn't in the picture, so she had to work to make a living, and that was hard, you know, we didn't have a lot of money, we were on food stamps sometimes, always had like powdered milk, that sort of thing." She sighed, blinking. "But, still, every night she was there to help with my homework, she read books to me, she cooked me dinner, she was...well, I don't know, in my mind, she was perfect." She shrugged, eyes downcast, and wrapped her arms around her knees. "So that is how I picture her. And then I go to visit her, and it's...she's just...not there. She's just gone. She's sitting there, but she's gone, and it feels like someone stole her away and left me just this... shell." The corners of her mouth quivered, and she rubbed her hand over her face, her voice trembling. "It's almost harder than if she'd just died. Sometimes I wish—"

Brigid stopped talking. She was sitting on the bed with her legs pulled up in front of her, chin balanced on her knees, eyes unfocused and wet, breathing ragged.

Jason wasn't sure what to do. *Should I hug her? Reassure her? What do I say? 'Don't worry, your mom will die someday. Cheer up!'* He settled for saying nothing, just staring sympathetically in her direction. A fairly useless choice, all things considered.

"Anyway...so I'd been to visit her." Brigid laughed, a barking, bitter sound. "I went to visit her, and then I had a good cry in the car with ol' Lith here, and then I was driving home trying to think happy thoughts, and I saw you. I thought, you know, 'This'll be an interesting diversion. If he tries to murder me at least it'll take my mind off other things.'"

Jason attempted a polite chuckle. It felt forced. "Well, um...thanks, though...you know, for picking me up and all. I'm sorry that you were having such a shitty day." He considered. "Also, that it got shittier. It might've been a bad call, picking me up, you know...seeing what happened after."

Brigid sniffed, wiped her eyes with the heels of her palms, grinned ironically. "Pfft, naw. Everyone needs a little excitement in their lives, right? We got out of it all right. And now we get to have a nice cryfest in a motel room, so that's a good time, too." She got up off the bed and stretched, gave Lithium the rest of her steak. "I'm gonna hop in the shower and hit the sack, I think. It's been a long day. Also, I'm going to sleep on the bed tonight. That chair is not what I'd call 'comfortable' in the classic or literal sense. I don't mind if you share the bed, though. I think we can agree no one is going to get the wrong idea."

Jason nodded. "Okay. I'm just going to stay up for a while, though. Watch some TV, if that's okay."

⊞

Brigid woke up to thin sunlight filtering through the curtains. Jason was still sleeping, on top of the covers, wearing the same clothes from yesterday. He was snoring softly. She crept off the bed, dressed, took Lithium to the tree line for his morning business and then drove along Route 1 till she saw a Starbucks. She bought some breakfast food and coffee, sat down with her tablet to check her email. Fifty-eight new emails. Fifty-six of them were junk.

One was from work.

> Tried to call but had to leave a voicemail. Any idea when you will be joining us again?

Oh, for fuck's sake. It's been one day. She chose to ignore it. The other was from the Boston PD—Detective O'Leary asking her to return to the police station to try to ID a suspect and answer some questions. She replied to that, told him she'd be there in a few hours. She checked Facebook. Nothing of import—pictures of babies, pictures of food, people whining about headaches, links to articles she didn't read. She didn't update her status.

On an impulse, she looked up "multiverse" on Wikipedia. Read the first half of the article, clicked through about fifty links, ended up just as confused. There was apparently some debate as to the existence of parallel universes, some debate as to whether the absence of such could be definitively proven. Various proposed forms of multiverses, a myriad of terms she'd never before encountered. Bubble universes. Hubble volumes. String theory. M-theory. Black hole cosmology. Eventually, she realized she was no longer reading, just skimming for words she recognized. So she gave up, bought a newspaper, returned to the car, and gave Lithium the other half of her cinnamon scone.

They were going to have to check out of the motel today. What should they do? Go back home? Go to another motel? Maybe she should just put Jason on a train with some cash. But not yet. She felt like she only knew half the story. If he were to leave now…there were still so many unanswered questions.

She returned to the motel with breakfast pastries and a coffee for Jason. He was still asleep.

"Hey, psst, wake up."

He stirred, blinked at her.

"Checkout's at eleven. We need to figure out what we're doing today."

"Right…right."

"I got you some breakfast. You can have a shower. I'm going to need to run back to the police station at some point, too."

"Right…right."

Jason showered. Brigid sat in the stained chair, turned on the TV, watched it absently, thought about their options. Jason came out of the bathroom wearing his jeans but no shirt, drying his hair.

God, he's thin. She found herself wishing she had another scone to offer him.

There was a scar on his abdomen, about four inches long, on the right side, peeking over his jeans.

"What happened there? You get stabbed or something?"

"Appendectomy. From when I was fifteen."

"Oh, okay. Well, these are my thoughts—we can, one, stay here for another night. If you're a fan of this place. Two, go back to my place, which theoretically is safe now because that guy's been arrested. Three, go to a new motel for another night or two."

"Or you could drop me off at the train station."

"Yeah, I mean, that's an option. I don't think it's ideal, personally. I mean, what's your plan? Long term, I mean. You can't just keep running around homeless and starving. You have to have some sort of goal."

"I hadn't really thought that far ahead."

"Yeah, no kidding. Well, look, it's time to start thinking. You're an adult, believe it or not. You told me a bonkers fucking story and, if you want me to buy it, you're going to need to give me an ending. Though I haven't completely ruled out the possibility that you're just schizophrenic."

Jason sat down on the bed. "I'm not schizophrenic."

"Well, I mean, that is what a schizophrenic would say. But, setting that aside, say I do completely, 100 percent, buy into everything you told me last night. Right? Then, just…so many loose ends. Molly, for example. Didn't she have family? Would they know what happened to her?"

"Yeah, she was really close with her sister, actually."

"So, do they know what happened? If not, wouldn't they deserve to? And then, also, don't you still have friends back at the lab? The other, uh, lab subjects?"

"Yeah. There were five left, besides me."

"So, it seems to me that you, as the one person who escaped the lab, have a responsibility to them. Right? They're still in danger, prisoners of this Wilders person. And, on that subject, since he seems to be this… what, mad scientist or whatever, what is he planning on doing with this wondrous ability to hop around between alternate realities?"

"I'm not really sure. Dr. Hernandez said something about being able to share, like, knowledge and stuff, with people in other universes…she said it was kind of like discovering a planet with advanced life forms, like in the movies, and then you can collaborate and stuff. But she also talked about how it was to understand the, like, fabric of reality."

"Um, okay." Brigid was on a roll now, almost enjoying herself. "I get that, it's basically knowledge for the sake of knowledge, right? Very noble. But it doesn't sound like that's Wilders's goal, is it? We're assuming he's doing something evil, or, I don't know, abusing or like corrupting these discoveries." She frowned, briefly frustrated. She wasn't able to find the right words, or maybe she was confused, or confusing herself. "In any event, it seems to me, it's probably dangerous to let him dick around with alternate realities. Once again, you have some degree of responsibility here."

"I didn't ask for—"

"Oh, shut up. Nobody asks for responsibilities. I didn't ask to have to work a shit job in order to pay for my sick mother's care. But here we are. And also, you need your own resolution here. You can't live as a vagrant your whole life. For one thing, you are not good at it. And you don't seem to be enjoying it. And if there's one thing that everyone agrees on, it's that you should at least try to enjoy some tiny aspect of your life. Right?"

"...uh huh." Jason looked sullen.

"Right. So. We have the following things to figure out—one, what to do about your friends still at the lab; two, how to deal with Wilders the sociopath and his pursuit of unlimited power—" Jason snorted— "and three, how to get people to stop chasing you so you can settle down and have a nice boring life like the rest of us. What's the word? Exoneration. Seems simple enough."

"And...also. One more thing."

"What?"

"Molly. Some form of justice. She deserves that."

"Yes, okay. Justice for Molly. Yeah, we can do this. We can do all of this. Easy peasy." Brigid reflected that maybe she hadn't absolutely needed quite so much coffee that morning. This whole conversation was absurd. This whole situation was absurd. She bounced up, faintly giddy. "So, first off, I'm going to go back to the police station today. I can tell them about the lab, see if they will look into it—wait, it's in Chicago, right?"

"Yeah."

"Okay, so, well the Boston police probably don't have a lot of jurisdiction in Chicago, but maybe they can, I don't know, call over or something. I don't know how all that works. Anyway, I'll tell them about it. And we'll check into a new motel for now, just to be safe. A nicer one. And…what's the deal with Dr. Hernandez now? Do you trust her? If we were to track her down, do you think she'd help us?"

"Yeah, I do. She never liked Wilders. And he stole her lab, she has to be mad about that."

"Okay. Step two, we'll find Dr. Hernandez. What's her first name?"

"…I don't know."

Sigh. Minimally suppressed eye roll.

"Well, one step at a time. Let's go find a new motel. One with two beds, maybe."

⌗

Jason was quiet during the car ride. He was uncomfortable with this new development. Not at all sure he was interested in taking on a partner in proverbial crime, not sure if Brigid wanted to be a partner or just push him around, not sure if she even believed his story. Which, to be honest, did kind of sound like a load of bullshit. He himself wondered sometimes if maybe he actually was crazy, had made the whole thing up. Would he know, honestly? Maybe there was no shadow conspiracy after him at all. Maybe he just suffered from debilitating delusions and hallucinations. Maybe none of this even existed and he was actually locked in a padded cell wearing a straitjacket. Was he capable of hallucinating an entire person, like someone to interact with? He looked over at Brigid, studied her features. Auburn hair streaked with gray. Fine wrinkles around her eyes, a little dewlap under her chin, a smattering of freckles. Frown lines at the corners of her frowning mouth. Could he imagine someone like that, out of his own head?

She noticed him staring, glanced over. "What?"

"Nothing."

Brigid drove south, heading back toward the city. She pulled over at an unremarkable motel tucked behind a little parking lot, nondescript sign out front reading "Camelot." Ran into the front office and came back a few minutes later with a room key. "That guy was so much nicer than the one at the last place. You didn't see him, I guess, you weren't really conscious at the time, but he was a dick. Anyway, we got an early check-in, so you can hang out in the room. Should be a TV, you can read the paper. I'll be a couple of hours, at least."

"Yeah, okay."

"Um, if you need anything...I guess call 911 because I still don't have my phone. Kidding. About the 911. I'll be back shortly. You okay to keep an eye on the dog?"

The new room was a massive improvement over the last one. It was actually a cabin, a small stand-alone structure, which was kind of fun. No mysterious stains, no baseline moist smell. Two beds, white duvets stretched over them. Nothing fancy, but clean. Jason sat on one of the beds and watched Lithium make a thorough olfactory examination of the carpet. He glanced at the paper but couldn't muster up much interest in reading it. Turned on the TV, kicked off his shoes, and leaned back on the bed. No free HBO here, unfortunately.

His eyes slid away from the television, unfocused.

～

Summer, some time back.

He and Molly had gone for a walk on the 57th Street Beach. The sand was so hot it burned their feet, the sun off the lake so bright it blinded them. A bunch of kids were splashing around, trying to keep cool, their teenage chaperones in matching t-shirts—a summer camp, he guessed, summer daycare. On the breezes wafted the odors of coconut-scented sunscreen, charcoal grilling, industrial waste. Molly walked barefoot in the water, lamented the sand stuck on her feet when she came out, hopped to a concrete ledge to brush them off. Leaned back on her hands, face toward the sun with her eyes closed, smiling. "Man, you can really smell Gary today. Hey, let's go to the museum, huh? I've never been, I've lived here for how long now? Come on. Let's go get edified. Also, it'll be air-conditioned."

He'd never really been one to go to museums for fun. That was a school thing, right? Wasn't it? Still, she was into it. So they went to the Museum of Science and Industry. They wandered lazily around the exhibits. She was right, it was actually really cool. There was a German submarine from WWII, an interactive demonstration of violent weather, a collection of model ships. Hours they spent in there, till his back and feet hurt from all the standing and walking and leaning slightly over. It was getting dark when they finally left, and they walked back to their studio apartment with the sun setting before them. He remembered feeling so grown up. He had a girlfriend. They'd gone on a museum date, walked home in the twilight, opened a bottle of wine and had dinner at a table. Someday they'd marry and have children, he'd have a good job, and they'd live in a house in the suburbs. Everything falling into place.

Until everything fell apart.

~

Jason's eyes abandoned the television screen and whatever bullshit it was pushing, rested unfocused on the wall. His head leaned against the headrest, his arms folded across his abdomen. Lithium jumped up on the bed, spun a couple of times, curled up against Jason's hip. Jason absently stroked the dog's head.

His whole self was empty. He felt like a void, a black hole, a shell. How was it even possible to miss someone this much? He reflected wryly that when he'd been alone on the side of the road, cold and starving, at least it kept him from thinking about Molly. Maybe he was better off that way.

Maybe he should go back to the lab. Maybe Brigid was right.

Molly was gone. She wouldn't be coming back. But maybe he could find some closure, some resolution.

卐

Brigid was escorted to an interview room as soon as she entered the police station, without any of the confusion or shuffling of papers that had attended her last visit. Which gave her hope that she might be back on the road sooner than she'd expected, though she was a little nervous when the room's door closed. Was this an interrogation room? She was entertaining herself with notions of what sort of nefarious criminals might have sat in her chair before her when a stranger in a suit entered and sat across the table from her.

"Ms. Sullivan."

"Um. Yes?"

"Ms. Sullivan, my name is Agent Smith, I'm with the FBI and I'm here to talk to you about a person of interest we believe you may have been in contact with." He pulled out a badge, opened it, shut it, put it away.

"Oh, right, the guy who broke into my apartment, right? Where's Detective O'Leary?"

"No, ma'am, this is about another individual." He opened a manila folder, slid an 8 x 10 photo over to her. Not a mug shot, maybe a driver's license photo. The face was familiar, but she didn't recognize it.

"No, sorry, I don't know him. Can I see your badge again, please? I didn't really get a chance to look at it."

He took out his badge, handed it to her. She opened it up and made something of a show of examining it. Having never seen an FBI badge, other than on TV, the only conclusion she could reach was that it did sort of look like the ones on *The X-Files*.

"John Smith. Seriously? Is that your actual name? Also, what happened to O'Leary? He's the one who emailed me."

Smith took his badge back. "Yes, ma'am, that is my actual name. Would you look at the photograph again, please? Take your time."

Brigid glanced at it. "I mean, he looks kind of familiar, but I don't—" Recognition hit like a slap in the face. Her hands went cold. It was Jason. Short hair, clean shaven, kind of pudgy, smirking a bit, but absolutely and definitely Jason. *Holy shit. They're after Jason. The FBI's after Jason.* She took a couple of beats, staring at the photo. *What does this mean? Is he right to be paranoid? Well, clearly. Is he a criminal? Is he a psycho killer after all? Shit. Shit.*

"Ma'am?"

The door opened and O'Leary entered. He didn't sit, just stood at the end of the table. His face was neutral. "Ms. Sullivan."

"Hey." She turned back to Smith. "Why do you think I know him?"

O'Leary answered. "We found his prints in your apartment, as part of our investigation into the break-in."

Brigid nodded slowly. "Yeah, okay. Wow, that's quick, isn't it? I'd have thought it'd take longer to get fingerprint results."

Smith opened up a small notebook. "Can you tell me the nature of your relationship with this individual?"

"I don't have a relationship with that individual." Frankly, she was getting a dodgy vibe from this Agent Smith. She wondered if it was an alias. *You'd think he'd have picked a more creative fake name, though.* "It looks like a guy who crashed in my guest room for a night like a week ago. I mean, it sort of looks like him...maybe. I'm not great with faces, though. Who is it?"

"What was his name, this person who stayed in your guest room?"

"John. No, um...sorry."

O'Leary glanced at her but said nothing.

"Sorry." *God, what name did I call him?* "Hang on. John, that's you, right?" She forced a laugh. *Shit. Shit.*

O'Leary chimed in finally. "Yesterday you called him Dave."

"Yes, yes, sorry, I just blanked. Dave...that was it."

"Last name?"

"I didn't get one. He only stayed a night. I took him down to South Station. Far as I know, he got on a train. He told me he was going to New York. Who is he? What did he do? Why are you looking for him?"

"I'm sorry, ma'am, I'm not at liberty to say."

"Well, I'd just kind of like to know if I had a psycho staying in my home. Is he connected to the break-in? Why would you not be at liberty to say?"

"It's part of an ongoing investigation."

She could be wrong, but O'Leary seemed to sneer, just for an instant, at Smith's justifications. There was a definite tension between them. "Okay, yeah, but is it connected to the guy who broke in? What's going on with him anyway? Can I go back home? Is it safe? Is someone else going to show up? I think I deserve some answers. A little information anyway. Don't you?"

O'Leary stepped up. "Our investigation does seem to indicate a connection, Ms. Sullivan." Smith glared at O'Leary. "We found a similar photograph to this one in the suspect's car. That means there's cause to believe that the two knew each other, or that the suspect was, in fact, in pursuit of this individual."

"Well, what has the suspect said?"

"Nothing. He lawyered up."

"Oh, well, bully for him. So you're saying someone may show up at my home again, looking for, uh, Dave here? That's what we're getting at."

"I would say that is a possibility, yes. However, we are prepared to offer you protection, a police escort to monitor for any suspicious activity."

"Thanks." She shook her head. "I mean it, Detective, I appreciate the offer. But, honestly, what is he wanted for? What did he do, that the FBI is after him? Is he a terrorist? Or a murderer? Or a rapist?" *Ha ha*, she thought, *like the FBI would prioritize chasing rapists. Well, serial rapists maybe. Would they?* Actually, she wasn't sure. She realized that was a pretty cynical line of thought.

Smith shook his head. "That's classified, ma'am. Please give me the details of your interaction. Where and under what circumstances did you meet him?"

Brigid sat back, eyed Smith distrustfully. Told him that she'd picked up a hitchhiker in Vermont, and that she let him stay in her guest room for a night, and that she took him to the train station at his request. She lied about the dates, backdating things by a week to try to justify why she hadn't brought it up earlier. Wondered if she should just come clean and explain that she had him holed up in a motel in Saugus. She was fairly sure lying to the feds was a crime, something that could get her into major trouble, but she didn't trust this Smith character. O'Leary, yeah, he seemed on the level, but Smith just had this smell of illegitimacy around him. He struck her as someone who was imitating what an FBI agent would look and sound like, with the suit and tie and curt demands for information. Even O'Leary didn't look convinced.

Also, at this point admitting that she had him holed up in a motel in Saugus would just be...well, really difficult to explain.

Smith scribbled notes on a legal pad, as he continued to prod her for details. He questioned her motivations, her justification for picking up a stranger, asked where "Dave" had been going, where he was coming from, why he was in Vermont, what was he wearing, what he'd told her about his past, what train he got on, if she actually saw him board…on and on and on. Just as she thought he might be winding down to the end, he asked, "Did you have sexual relations with him, consensual or nonconsensual?"

Brigid snapped at that. "For fuck's sake. I would've mentioned it if he'd raped me, don't you think? Not the sort of thing I'd forget."

O'Leary murmured, "Not everyone does. Report a rape."

Brigid threw him a look. *Argh. Fine. Fair point.* "Well, he didn't. And it's none of your fucking business if we did or didn't have sex *consensually*. This isn't fucking *Big Broth*—"

Smith interrupted to ask what she'd seen in her guest's luggage. O'Leary sniggered quietly to himself.

Brigid glared at both of them, irritated, annoyed that the whole thing was taking so long. Went back to answering their questions. Monosyllabically.

By the time both Smith and O'Leary were satisfied with her story and allowed her to leave, three hours had passed. She was hungry and grumpy and annoyed with the entire system, though predominantly with Smith, who refused to explain why he was looking for Jason or suggest any reason that her attacker should be doing the same.

She stopped to use the bathroom on the way out. *Way too much coffee this morning and way too much sitting around in a fucking interrogation room with some creepshow G-man.* She hadn't even realized how badly she needed to go till they told her she was free to leave. There weren't any paper towels in the bathroom. Also, she noticed, the feminine hygiene dispenser was broken. *Fuck's sake. What are taxes supposed to pay for anyway?* She wiped her hands on her jeans, left the bathroom and ran into O'Leary, who was apparently loitering in the hallway.

"Ms. Sullivan. Before you go. This is my card. Just know, if you need help for any reason, call me. Okay? We're here to help."

"Thank you." She slipped the card into her back pocket.

"Once again, it would be very helpful if you could tell us where you're staying."

"Thanks. I'm fine. I'm staying at a motel, everything's fine. I'll check my email again tomorrow. Any idea when I can get my phone back?"

"Well, that's part of an active investigation, so not any time soon, I'd say. You might want to go ahead and get a new phone. Keep in touch. Take care, now."

She returned to her car, stopped at a convenience store to pick up some food and kibble and toys for Lithium, and returned to the motel. Circuitously, and staring at her rearview mirror probably more than she should have. No one seemed to be following her, though. *Getting pretty good at this noir-life business, I guess.*

When she got to their cabin, she found Jason sleeping on the bed, Lithium curled around his legs. The little dog jumped up, tap-danced around her, wagging his tail. She dropped some kibble in a pile on the bathroom floor and he set to eating it. She collapsed into the armchair, leaned her head back and regarded the somnolent body of the psycho or terrorist or serial killer with whom she'd chosen to share a room.

Jason awoke to find Brigid curled up in the armchair with her tablet. Her eyebrows were furrowed, her expression tense. Whatever she was reading evidently held her in rapt attention. The dog was lying on the floor chewing on a plastic bone. He raised his head and thumped his tail when Jason sat up.

Brigid looked over. "Oh, you're up. Sleepyhead."

Jason sucked in air, stretched his back. "How was the police thing?"

"Well, the FBI showed up with a picture of you."

Jason froze. His throat closed and his heart started pounding. "What?"

"Yeah, they lifted your prints from my place, I guess. Seems you're wanted for something. Not sure what, they wouldn't tell me. Perhaps you might have some idea."

Jason sat motionless, eyes wide. Didn't want to ask but didn't know how to avoid it. "What did you tell them?"

K. P. Kyle

"Well, I told them I dropped you off at the train station and you took a train to New York. So now I've lied to the FBI. So that's fine. And that also leaves open the somewhat glaring question of why they're looking for you." She raised her eyebrows pointedly.

Jason was silent.

"Because it does sort of imply that maybe you are a dangerous individual with criminal intent."

"I'm not."

"Ah, all right. So happy to hear that. Certainly I'll sleep better at night."

This frustrated him. *Shit, she slept just fine for the last two nights, right? Well, one. For the last one night? And I haven't done anything to her, right? And she still doesn't trust me?* "I'm not. I told you the truth."

"Jason, I'm serious. Tell me why the FBI is looking for you." She set the tablet down. "Look, I'm on your side. I am. But this is getting into seriously muddy waters here, like this is potentially arrest-level duplicity on my part, and I want to know what the deal is. Okay? Just be straight with me."

"I *am* being straight with you. I told you everything. I told you, I got out of the lab, I knew they'd be looking for me. Maybe it's not the FBI. Maybe it's a trick, maybe it's one of Wilders's people. But I haven't done anything wrong. I haven't broken any laws." Actually, that was a lie. He had done a fair amount of shoplifting and petty larceny in the past seven or eight months. Still, that shouldn't trigger an FBI manhunt. "I haven't broken any serious laws."

She sighed. "Okay. But bear with me here, Jason. In the event that I need some form of support, some substantiation for your story. How exactly do you propose I find it? Can you give me any sort of concrete proof that what you told me is factual? If you can't, can anyone?"

He slumped back against the wall. "I mean, I don't know. Maybe... maybe? There's Dr. Hernandez. And her assistants, Erin and Vijay. But I don't know their last names. They were grad students, maybe? But Dr. Hernandez, I mean, she was the head of the lab. She knew everything, at least until Wilders kicked her out."

"So we need to find Dr. Hernandez."

"Yeah, but she probably lives in Chicago. Unless she moved. Or unless something happened to her, like after Wilders came. I don't know. She disappeared, we never saw her again."

"Didn't you have email? Social media? Some form of communication?"

"No, they confiscated our phones and stuff. We weren't allowed online after Wilders came. Something about compromising the project. I did have her email before, though."

"You did."

"Yeah, I mean—"

"So you have an email address?"

"Yeah."

"Jason, you realize I'm sitting here with a tablet. There's Wi-Fi here. You can sign on. Any time."

"I know. I mean, yeah, I know. The thing is, can't they track you, when you sign onto your email, or whatever? Isn't that a way they can find you? I haven't checked my email since...since forever, really. I've been afraid it would lead them to me."

"I seriously don't think that's the way it works. I mean I think you probably need to *send* an email or something. Okay, how about this. How about you dig up Dr. Hernandez's email address, then I can send her an email, we can start a correspondence that way, and we can sort of move forward. Seems legit, right?"

Jason hesitated but nodded.

She handed him her tablet, left him to it while she rummaged around in a bunch of plastic bags. "I got some snacks. Peanuts and whatnot. Dried fruit, which is not as tasty as wet fruit, but you know, limited selection at the CVS, so you take what you can."

Jason looked up. "Did you get any Spam?"

"Spam? Email spam? I guess—"

Jason shook his head. "No, Spam. Like the lunchmeat. Kind of craving a Spam sandwich."

Brigid stared at him. "Are you joking? Is this a joke?"

"No...I mean, it's not that big a deal, but..."

"Spam? Jeez. That stuff is disgusting."

"No, it isn't. I love it. My mom used to make the best fried Spam sandwiches."

Brigid grimaced. "Did your mom hate you or something? Yuck."

Jason shook his head, grinning. "Shut up. It's good."

"Is it, though? Maybe that's the reason you didn't, you know, go home."

Jason's grin faded. "I wanted to go home. I did. But I thought, you know, that my parents' house would probably be the first place Wilders and his crew would check." He shrugged. "So I stayed away. I thought...I hoped it would keep them safe maybe...if I wasn't there." But, mostly, he'd been afraid they'd catch him. Take him back to the lab. Imprison him. Experiment on him. Torture him. He didn't even know what... but the idea filled him with a cold dread.

"Sorry. Sorry, that was out of line." She looked faintly contrite. "Any luck with the emails?"

"Um, there's just...there's, like, too many messages. It's gonna take me a while."

"Good lord, Jason. Just use the search function. I thought you kids were supposed to be good at this."

Oh, right. He found Dr. Hernandez's last message to him, which was dated over a year ago, December 14.

> Jason: I am worried about the lab, I haven't heard from any of you. I tried to visit but was not permitted on the premises. Please contact me and tell me what is happening. –A. H.

He copied the address onto the notepad function. Looked back through his inbox. There were several messages from his mother dated around the same time.

> Jason: Please call, we're worried about you. Please come home. Tell us what's going on. Love, Mom.

Others from his sister.

> Mom's worried sick. I don't know what's going on with you, but you need to come home.

All of them were dated over a year ago. Other than junk mail, there was nothing more recent. No one had written anything since last January.

He was tempted to respond to both of them, but his finger hesitated over the *Reply* button.

"You good?"

"Yeah." He withdrew his finger, handed the tablet back.

"Right." She tapped away at it, absorbed in her task.

Jason mulled over the emails. His parents *had* been looking for him. He felt bad about that. Guilty. He should have contacted them, somehow, let them know he was okay. Weird that they'd stopped writing, though. Maybe they were mad at him? He hoped they weren't mad at him.

"It seems that email account was closed," Brigid announced.

"Huh?"

"Dr. Hernandez's email. The account was closed." She sighed. "That's a bit of a setback."

Jason chewed thoughtfully on his lip. "But it proves I didn't make it up, right? Did you see the email she sent?"

"Mmph. Ana, by the way. Ana Hernandez. Who does in fact appear to be a published theoretical physicist. I can find a couple of profiles of her, but they're dated a few years back, there's nothing recent. I can't find an address, or a contact number, or anything like that. She was in Chicago, though, at some point."

Jason felt a welcome, though unfamiliar, flush of vindication. "You believe me, then. I told you. Everything I told you, that was all the truth."

"Yeah. I'm on board. Why not."

⊞

Lithium trotted over to the door, pawed at it, whining softly. "You want to go out, pup? Okay." Brigid snapped on his leash, handed the tablet to Jason. "I'm gonna take him for a little walk. You can check the rest of your emails if you want. Maybe just don't send any, but you should be okay to read them."

Outside, the sky was still a drab New England gray. She loved this area, this city, but lord the sun took its sweet time coming back after the winter. Down the street in one direction was one of the thousands (it seemed) of car dealerships, in the other direction was a little shopping center and a mini-golf course watched over by an orange plastic dinosaur. She took Lithium to an overgrown area behind a Dunkin' Donuts to take care of his business and, afterwards, they wandered down a side street which led into some woods. *Probably private property*, she mused, *but whatever. Kind of a nice little stroll.* She thought about letting Lithium off his leash but had a vision of him running into the road behind her and getting killed by a car.

Why am I doing this, this business with Jason? She wasn't sure in her own mind. Maybe it was a distraction, from the pain of watching her mother slowly deteriorate, being unable to stop it. Or from the boredom, the dissatisfaction she got from her job as a telemarketer. After all, what was the point of being a telemarketer? What sort of impact did that make on the world? She was just a shill for corporate America, just going through motions, providing no benefit to anyone, contributing nothing, in a dying industry being slowly taken over by robocallers and spam email.

She thought about her mother, about back when she was first diagnosed, about all the horror and fear that her mother had felt, and how she hadn't been able to help. At the time, she and her then-husband were starting to think about starting a family. But her mother's diagnosis changed that. To be clear, back then, she wanted kids. She wanted so badly to have someone to nurture and raise, to love unconditionally, someone to love her back. She still wanted that. But Alzheimer's is genetic, which meant that she might have it, and it meant that she might pass it on, and she just couldn't take that risk, couldn't face putting another generation through what she and her mom were going through.

Her husband, Will, hadn't been able to understand. He wanted a family. He felt it was part of the contract she'd entered into when she married him. She suggested adoption, but he wanted his own children, not someone else's. *God*, she thought now, *what a jerk*. In hindsight. How could he not have understood how hard it was for her to make that choice, that decision *not* to have children? How could he not have seen how much it hurt her, how much it broke her heart, how much she had agonized over it? As if it was a casual, careless thing. As if she hadn't spent days staring off into the middle distance, aching, feeling irrationally like she had actually lost a child, lost a potential child. She'd spent her entire life assuming she had a family in her future, and now she didn't. So, between the stress with her mom and the constant arguing with her husband, it was no surprise that their marriage failed.

What she should have done, she knew, was cultivate and strengthen her social support network. This was the advice given in every online self-help article, every "personal improvement" book she surreptitiously flipped through in the back of bookstores. She could see her world imploding. She should've spent more time with her friends, should've found herself a hobby, should've worked to keep her life vital.

She hadn't.

It wasn't a thing she could justify, a thing she could explain to someone who hadn't experienced it, but the effort of staying...not alive, exactly, but full of life...it was just too much. Too much effort. She was exhausted, she was sad. The weight of her apathy dragged her down, like a leaden thing in her stomach. She wanted people to reach out to her but didn't have the will or energy to respond. Her friends did reach out, at first, but they were met with halfhearted replies or silence, and one by one they flickered out, floated away to their own lives. Moved to the suburbs, had babies, did what normal people do.

So now she was slipping through her life and, when it was over, there'd be no evidence that she'd ever even been here. She would leave no children, no family, not even any close friends. Only an ex-husband she no longer had any contact with, a mother who didn't recognize her, colleagues at work with whom she never spoke once she left the office. She went days, sometimes, without even interacting with another person. A life of appalling mediocrity. She was just waiting to die.

Lithium spotted a squirrel, leapt forward, jerked on the leash. She let him run after it, tailing him on his lead. He stopped at the base of a tree, staring up, paws on the trunk, wagging his tail. "Think it got away. Sad to say."

Lithium gave up hope that the squirrel would fall out of the tree and returned to the path. The thing was, Brigid reflected, over the past couple of days she hadn't noticed any of that familiar heaviness around her chest, that torpor of the spirit. *Yeah, so someone broke into my home, which could be called less than ideal. Yeah, so Jason may well be a paranoid schizophrenic, or a deranged criminal or con man or whatever.* There was a part of her that whispered that she should do the logical and reasonable thing and tell the FBI about him and just get out of the whole situation, go back home. *I could end up dead or in prison, if things go sideways here. And, realistically, what am I hoping to accomplish? Do I actually believe his story? It is, after all, absurd. No, of course not.*

Except she wanted to believe it. She really did. It was exciting. And frankly, it gave her a sense of meaning, of purpose. She could help this kid. She could get him back on his feet, get him off the street, reunite him with his family, all of that. She could be a hero. She wanted to be a hero. She wanted to save someone. She hadn't been able to save her mother, or her marriage…but she could save Jason.

She and Lithium spent an hour or so wandering the woods before returning to the motel cabin, where she left her muddy shoes by the door.

Jason was sitting cross-legged now, the tablet on his lap. He'd plugged in the charger and so was tethered to the wall. He looked up. "Do you have any like Advil or Tylenol or something by any chance? My head's killing me."

"Yeah." She rummaged around in her bag, found a bottle. "You find anything? On the Internet there?"

"Not really. I got this email, gave the name of the lab—"

"You didn't know the name?"

"I had…I mean…I knew it at one point. I sort of forgot it. Anyway, I looked that up, but I couldn't find anything more."

Brigid filled a plastic cup with water from the bathroom sink, handed it to Jason. He swallowed the pills. "So it sounds like we need to head in that general direction. Chicago. Try to track down Dr. Hernandez. Maybe see if we can get the police to look into the lab. You remember where the lab is?"

"Uh…I think so…probably."

"Okay. We can hit the road tomorrow. I took out a bunch of cash the other day so we should be able to stay under the radar, for a little while at least. Might be a bit dodgy if the police want to talk to me again. But, well, that's a bridge to cross later, I guess."

Jason paused, eyes downcast. "You're okay with doing this? I mean, like, don't get me wrong. I appreciate it and all. But…like, why? Why… what do you get out of it?"

"That's complicated. Maybe nothing. Maybe I'm just looking for a little excitement. Midlife crisis and all." She grinned. "Midlife crime spree. It's all the rage these days."

⌸

They spent most of the rest of the day spitballing ideas and formulating a game plan. Well, that was what Brigid did. Well, that was what Brigid kept saying she was doing. Jason leaned back on the bed, watched her tapping away and scribbling notes on the back of the drugstore receipt. She eventually ran out of space on the receipt, rummaged around in her bag, pulled out various scraps of paper, threw them down in frustration. Pulled open all the drawers in the bedside tables until she found the monogrammed complimentary pad of paper—*Thank you for staying at the Camelot*—then went back to tapping at the tablet.

"What were the names again of the other people you were with… the other, um, lab subjects?"

"Molly, obviously. Moe. Chris. Angela. Ji. Diana…um…Pedro… Tyrone…wait, there's one I'm forgetting. Shit."

"Close, were you?"

"No, I mean, I can remember her face…shit, hang on."

"Well, anyway, how about last names?"

"I'm not sure I ever knew those. I know Molly's, obviously, that was Lincoln, but the others…I think Ji's was…um, Kim? Maybe?"

Brigid arched an eyebrow and went back to staring at the tablet. "If I pull up a map of Chicago, can you show me where the lab's located?"

Jason closed his eyes. His headache had been unaffected by the medication. He felt like there was a gremlin crouched on his shoulder stabbing the back of his head with a screwdriver. With an electrified screwdriver. Dipped in lye. "Yeah. Probably. There was…there was a park, like, down the street, it was walking distance to the lake, close to a Metra stop. I'd recognize it if I was there."

"Okay." She moved her finger around on the tablet screen, groaned, rubbed her eyes and pushed the tablet away. "Fucking hell. I have no idea what I'm doing here."

Jason opened one eye, regretted it, massaged his temples. "Maybe you need a break. I need a break."

"Yeah. You're right. What, you still have a headache? Sorry, dude." Jason smiled a bit. "It's okay. It happens. It'll go away."

Brigid traded the desk for the vacant bed. Lithium hopped up on the bed next to her and spun a couple of times before settling curled against her hip. She scratched his head, rested her hand on his neck. Lithium sort of grumbled impatiently, and she murmured, "Okay, okay," and resumed scratching. Jason watched, faintly envious of her, that she should have this creature so dedicated to her. Since he lost Molly, he felt alone, adrift, untethered. Emotionally, he wanted someone to love him. He wanted someone he could love. Someone who would burrow a little nest against his belly, someone he could wrap his arms around when he felt lonely.

Maybe I should get a cat. Ha, ha.

"How long have you had him? The dog?"

"Um. Let's see. About…four years, I guess."

"Oh. Was he a rescue?"

Brigid sneered a bit. "Everyone says they have 'a rescue.' They buy a fucking goldendoodle and claim it's a rescue. I mean, it's a fancy mutt, but that doesn't make it a rescue. I didn't get him from a rescue organization or from a shelter, but I also didn't buy him, so, well, come to your own conclusions."

"Oh…um…what's a goldendoodle?"

"It's a golden retriever crossed with a poodle. A fancy mutt. No. He is pretty much a rescue. This was back in the fall, about four years ago, I found him. I wasn't looking for a dog, I didn't want a dog. I've never been a dog person, you know? I always thought it'd be too much of a commitment. Which I didn't want. But, one night, I was coming home late, it was raining, like pouring down rain, and cold, and I heard this crying. Sounded like a baby, really. So I went looking, and found him, he was this tiny little puppy, in the gutter, trying to jump up onto the curb, but he was too little. He was so sad, this soaking wet crying little puppy."

"Oh...poor thing. How old was he?"

"Pfft. I don't know. Pretty young. Probably too young to be away from his mother. I never figured out what happened there. I'd never seen a stray dog around. So, I don't know. For all I know, someone chucked him out a car window."

"What?"

"I made that up. I have no idea where he came from. But I found him in the gutter there, and I mean, what sort of monster would leave a puppy in the gutter in the rain, right? So I took him home and dried him off, gave him some milk—which, incidentally, it turns out was the wrong thing to give him. But I didn't know that at the time. He was awfully cute, you have no idea. And I went to bed, let him sleep in the bed, and I woke up in the morning and he was all cuddled in next to me. So, that was it. I was smitten. End of story."

"Wait, what happened with the milk?"

"Oh, yeah, so it turns out you should use dog milk, not cow milk. Funny thing. Apparently, it gave him diarrhea, I had to take him to the vet's, you know, to get him checked out, and they told me. You know they sell dog milk? Isn't that crazy? You can go to the vet and buy dog milk?"

"What?"

"I know, right? What a time to be alive."

Jason leaned back, smiling to himself, thinking of baby puppies. *Aw, man. Baby puppies. Baby puppies are the best. The world needs more baby puppies. This room needs more baby puppies.*

"You hungry? I think I need more than snack food. We should get some dinner. How's your head?"

"Better. Yeah, I could eat. Um, also...most of the snack food is gone."

"Oh, excellent. What do you want to eat? I'm not getting Spam."

Jason giggled. "Dog milk. Really craving dog milk."

Brigid squealed. "Whoa! Jason you made a funny! This is big, kid! Way to go! Pardon me while I notify the press."

"Ha ha…Kechia! Kechia. That was the other subject in the lab. Kechia." *Thank god. I thought for sure I was losing my mind.*

Brigid went back to the tablet, looked up. "Chinese okay?"

"What?"

"Chinese. I'm ordering in. God, the Internet is a magical place."

卐

"So, I don't get it, though. I mean, not entirely." Brigid leaned back, pulled her hair elastic free, ran her fingers across her scalp. Her stomach rumbled. She ignored it. *Come on, Golden Dragon, what's taking so long?* "Well, no. I get why it's, like, cool and exciting to find these alternate universes. I guess what I don't quite understand is, why? What were they trying to accomplish? You know? Did you just...pop over, say hi, pop back again?"

"You mean when Dr. Hernandez was in charge? Or Wilders?"

"Hernandez. I mean, Wilders, he sounds like a different animal. But Hernandez, did she have a goal in mind? Was she working toward something or just kind of poking around?"

Jason looked thoughtful. "No, not poking around, I don't think. I don't...I know she talked a lot about figuring out points of, um, branching? When I was over…somewhere…she always wanted to know details about what the history there was like, see how much was in common with here. You know, how alike they were."

"How alike were they?"

Jason shrugged. "It depended. A lot of the time, it seemed totally random. Really…just completely different."

"Oh!" Brigid sat up, grinning. "Was there a planet of the apes? Did you see a chimpanzee Lincoln statue? My god, suddenly that movie makes so much sense."

"No, I didn't." Jason smiled, a bit ruefully. Almost chuckled. "Sorry. No lizard people, either, I don't think."

"Aw. Bummer. So then how completely different? Did the Nazis win or something?"

"Probably. Probably in a lot of universes. Um, let me think." He dropped his eyes, pensive. "Okay, so languages tended to be the first, the most obvious thing. I think I could recognize English maybe half the time. Spanish once or twice, though I don't really speak Spanish...I mean I can recognize it. Um...at least a few times the alphabet was different, so I mean, I'd see a newspaper or book or billboard or whatever, something along those lines, and I'd have to try to memorize the shapes, but I probably fucked it up. I don't think I was much help."

"I'm sure you were fine."

"No. I mean, I got better at it, but I sucked at first. I'd get back, and Dr. Hernandez would ask me all these questions, and I didn't have answers for any of them. I think I was..." A cloud seemed to materialize behind his features. "I was a disappointment."

"For fuck's sake, Jason." She was surprised by the knee-jerk irritation she felt. Shouldn't she try to be more empathetic? She should. She would. She tried to be empathetic. "No, I'm sure you weren't. Stop beating yourself up." Still, it would be nice if he could pull himself together, get himself out of this funk of his, which wasn't helping anyone or doing him any favors.

Jason shrugged again.

"Well, that aside, what was the point? Why was she collecting information? Did she tell you?"

"Yeah." Jason looked up. "She explained it. Something about...if she could identify branching points, maybe there would be a way to... to correct things? Things that went wrong in the past. Change things for the better. Like, make it so the Holocaust didn't even happen."

Brigid was silent for a few minutes, processing. This didn't make a whole lot of sense, she felt. "So...like, time travel? When did we go off into time travel?"

"No. I don't think. More like change this reality to a better one."

"Doesn't that reality already exist?"

Jason looked confused. "Yeah..."

"So, what, we just take over? What happens to this reality?"

"I..."

"Or, like what's the point, if every possible reality exists, like, we can't just get rid of one, right? I don't get it. I don't get any of it."

"Uh..."

"I mean, honestly, if every possible reality exists, and there's one with no Hitler, and then there's us, and one with extra Hitler...what's the point? There's always going to be realities with bad things. Do we do nothing for them? Do we just say fuck them, not our problem, and make like they don't exist? Do we just focus on *us*? And I don't... how would that even work?"

Jason just stared at her.

Brigid rubbed her eyes. "This is too much for me, honestly. I think I'm just going to turn on the Internet and focus on real, physical, literal things, in this real literal universe right here for a while." She picked up her tablet, flashed Jason a quick smile. "Sorry. Metaphysics just isn't my thing."

The food arrived eventually. They ate out of the cartons. Brigid used chopsticks. Jason tried but he didn't seem to have the coordination he'd once had. The food kept falling out, so he finally gave up in frustration and used a plastic fork. He still had to fight not to wolf the food down, out of habit. But he wasn't really that hungry, or anyway he wasn't starving, so he tried to slow down and enjoy the MSG. Wondered if it would re-trigger his headache. Molly had said something about that once. She never ate Chinese takeout. But he thought it might be worth it. Egg rolls must be one of the greatest things to have ever come out of Asia.

"Wonder why they're called egg rolls," he murmured, around a mouthful of shrimp and snow peas and rice, poking the last roll with his fork. "There's no egg in them. Is there? Where's the egg?"

Brigid shrugged. "I never taste the spring in spring rolls, either. Such are the mysteries of the Orient."

"Yeah, spring...ha." He looked up. "Hey, back in the car, when you picked me up? The other night? What was it you said you could smell?"

"Huh? Well, you, I guess. I mean, no offense, but you were sort of rank."

Jason shook his head. "No. I mean...I know, I was. Sorry and all. But you said you could smell something. You asked me if I was diabetic."

"Oh right!" Brigid leaned back, dropped her chopsticks in the carton of chicken and cashews. "Ketones. You had ketones on your breath. They smell...kind of sweet. It's pretty distinctive." She took a sip of water. "You get ketones on your breath when you aren't metabolizing blood sugar properly. I recognized it because my ex-husband was a diabetic. And not a very good one. He skipped his insulin, like, all the time... was always getting in trouble. The number of times we ended up in the ER...idiot. He'd skip his insulin, his blood sugar would skyrocket, he'd get ketotic, sometimes he'd pass out. The problem was, he tended to be a drinker. Sometimes, he'd start drinking at noon, would forget to take his insulin that night, would be too hung over the next morning, it would go on like that."

"You were married?"

"Yeah, I wasn't always a cynical old hag. Once upon a time, I was a happily married wife. Almost a happily married wife and mother. You know, that was the plan, back then."

"What happened?"

"Well, you know, it's complicated. Marriage is complicated. One day you're in love, you get married, the whole world is at your feet, and then..." She shrugged. "It's not the end of the world. Well, I thought it was at the time." Her lip curled a bit, eyes downcast. "But it's not. I don't blame him. Well, not entirely. I blame him a little."

Jason gazed at Brigid, contemplating. Brigid married. Brigid in a white dress, tears of joy at an altar. It seemed so alien. "Would you do it again? I mean, are you looking to marry again?"

Brigid stared back. "Would I? I don't know. I don't hate the idea of having a partner. But honestly, I think I would find it hard to trust someone, long term. Why? You know someone you want to set me up with?"

"No—"

"Chill, Jason. I'm kidding. Relax."

⌗

They watched a couple of bad TV shows but turned in early. Brigid was thinking they'd start driving west in the morning, try to get as far as they could in the car, ultimately try to locate the lab in Chicago, see if they could find Ana Hernandez, maybe involve the police. They could talk over their strategy in the car—the drive would take all day, if they didn't stop. She snuggled under the comforter on her bed, choosing not to think about the stories about motel bedding and how it is just awash in filth and all that. Lithium nestled down in his favorite position against her hip. Jason was already nodding off on his own bed before Brigid switched off the television.

Several hours later, she was awakened by Lithium scratching at the door. She squinted at the bedside digital clock. 3:22. Lithium whined softly.

"Hold on, hold on, I'm coming."

She pulled on her jeans and shoes and wrapped her coat around the t-shirt she'd worn to bed. They headed out through the parking lot, toward the back of the Dunkin' Donuts again. An ambulance was pulling into the lot as they were walking out, but the lights and siren were off. Behind the donut place, Lithium vanished into the tall grasses, though Brigid could hear wet squirting noises from his direction. *Probably shouldn't have let him have the Chinese leftovers. That was a bad call.* She sighed, stared up at the plastic dinosaur perched on the bluff above her, lit up by a few floodlights under a sickly yellow sky. *Dinosaurs and mini golf. Whatever.*

Lithium was invisible in the grass for maybe ten minutes before he finally reappeared. Brigid pulled in his leash, muttered, "Sorry, puppy," and they headed back toward their little cabin. The ambulance was leaving, lights and siren still off. Guess whoever it was got better. Or got dead.

She entered the cabin, looked around, and felt her heart drop. Jason's bed was empty. The room was dark, the bathroom door open but the light off. She hit the lights—his bed was rumpled, pillows on the floor, one of the bedside lights toppled over. *Shit. Shit. Fuck.* Her throat tightened, she couldn't breathe. There were specks of blood on the sheets. "Jason! Jason! Jason, please! Answer me!" *Shit. Shit.*

The ambulance.

The ambulance…it had come, with no lights, no siren, no fucking reason, it came and then it took Jason and left. He told her someone was after him. Hell, someone just fucking tried to abduct him two days ago, and she'd left him alone in the room, and they'd taken him. *Fuck. Fuck. Fuck!*

She dropped Lithium's leash, bolted out of the motel cabin, pulling the door shut so Lithium wouldn't chase her out, ran to the entrance of the lot and looked down the street. It was a right turn only, and she couldn't see anything that looked like an ambulance, and nothing past the median barrier on the far side of the road, nothing in either direction. *Fuck.* She laced her fingers in her hair, pulled it back from her temples, lips a rictal grimace, eyes watering. She felt dizzy, short of breath, panicking. She spun, raced back toward the cabin, which was in the back of the parking lot, behind a maintenance shed. As she passed the shed, something stung her in the back and there was an awful pain, like every muscle charley horsed at once, and a crackling noise behind her. She fell face first, wanted to cry out, couldn't. Her forehead hit the asphalt, her back arched, arms spasmed, hands clawed against the ground. The crackling noise stopped, there were footsteps behind her. The muscle spasms relaxed, and she tried to push herself up, but she couldn't seem to properly control her movements and her arms just flopped around like marionette limbs. Her breath was coming in ragged gasps. Someone seized her by the shoulder and flipped her onto her back. A man in a suit. A familiar man.

Fucking hell. Fucking sonuvabitch goddamn motherfucker.

Agent Smith.

"You…fucking…dickhead…"

Smith didn't respond, didn't even meet her eyes. Just snapped a set of cuffs on her wrists, dragged her by the arms toward a black sedan tucked back in the shadows, and dumped her unceremoniously in the trunk.

"You…fucking…dick…head!"

He probably didn't hear that, with the trunk lid closed over her. The muscle spasms wore off, and she found she could pound on and kick the inside of the trunk, so she did this for a few moments, but this didn't appear to achieve much of anything, so she stopped. She panted and craned her neck to try to see around the trunk. There was not much to see. It was the trunk of a car. She stomped at the wall, ineffectively.

"*Dick!*" Her voice was starting to sound hoarse.

She could hear a car door squeak open, then the car settled as someone—Smith—dickhead—got in, closed the door. The car started moving, made a quick left, a right out of the parking lot, roared down the street.

卍

Jason had been caught completely off guard when the cabin door opened and what appeared to be a paramedic entered. For a second, he thought, baffled, that something had happened to Brigid and someone had called an ambulance. And then the paramedic pointed a little handgun thing at him, and a pair of barbs hit him in the chest, and the Taser knocked him to the floor.

God, Tasers again.

He tried to jump, to shift, but he couldn't concentrate, he couldn't gather his focus, and he failed. His back arched, he kicked at the bed, clawed at the sheets but couldn't coordinate his limbs. Could only watch in dread as a second paramedic entered the room and the two of them extended and pinned his left arm, shone a flashlight onto it, slipped a needle into the vein at his elbow. A warm fluid sort of wave washed over him. He relaxed, his eyes rolled up, and he found he still couldn't concentrate, but he'd sort of forgotten why he was trying, what it was that he wanted to do. He slipped backwards into a pleasant sort of apathy.

The paramedics loaded him onto a gurney that had mysteriously appeared by the bed. The barbs were pulled out of his chest. He could feel a wetness on his t-shirt, thought dreamily that he was probably bleeding, wondered if it would leave a mess. He tried to roll onto his side, reached for the far side of the gurney to pull himself over, but his arm wouldn't go where he told it. He looked down, saw one of the paramedics pulling restraints around his wrists. They pushed his shoulder back down, wrapped a strap over his chest, pulled it tight.

A man in a suit walked into the room, blinded him with a flashlight, took him by the jaw and inspected his face. The light switched off. "That's him. Good. Get him loaded up, get moving. I'll radio in."

They loaded him into an ambulance. One of the paramedics climbed into the back and locked the gurney into place, the other closed the bay doors and got into the driver's seat. The whole thing vibrated as the motor started. Once the doors were shut, the interior of the ambulance lit up. Too bright. Jason squinted, tried to say something, couldn't figure out how to make words. Tried to open his eyes, tried to focus, couldn't. Something was missing. Someone was missing. He was missing. On his left, there was a fuzzy figure moving around, setting things in place, moving other things to other places. It hung something off a pole above his head, bent over his right arm. Something damp and cold in the crook of his elbow, a pinch. Jason could sense that it hurt, he could register that there was pain there, but it was as if it was all happening at a distance, like he was watching it on TV or something. A slow chill crept from his elbow to his shoulder. He tried to move but didn't have the energy to try very hard.

His eyes shut, his mind wandered...he couldn't keep his thoughts together, everything kept slipping away, like a dream remembered only briefly right after waking up.

The ambulance rumbled on.

⌘

Brigid eventually gave up shouting obscenities and kicking uselessly. Her head was pounding at the spot where it had hit the pavement, and she appeared to be bleeding from the scalp, based on the sticky fluid she felt when she touched the area. The actual color of the sticky fluid was harder to establish, since the only light in the trunk was red, but she felt fairly confident in her assessment that the dickless fuckhead in the driver's seat had caused her to become injured. *That fuck.* At least she'd shut the cabin door. At least Lithium was safe, for now. She refused to allow herself to think about what would happen when the motel manager found him alone in the cabin.

She also refused to think about what would happen when the car stopped, when it reached its destination. She focused instead on rage, on her sheer unadulterated fury. These people had abducted Jason, these people had assaulted her, had stuck her in the trunk of a fucking car like a fucking piece of baggage. This was not law enforcement. This was not FBI. This was a bunch of thugs. And Jason had warned her, he'd known they were coming. She hadn't taken him seriously. All of this, she hadn't taken seriously.

Jason…what was happening to him? She'd taken responsibility for him, hadn't she? And she'd let him down. She'd promised herself she'd protect him, and she'd failed, and now he was missing. Kidnapped. Stolen away.

A muffled voice trickled in from the front of the car. Not-Agent Smith was talking to someone. A one-sided conversation. *Who doesn't put their phone on speaker in the car? Fucking dick.* She held her breath, strained to hear over the car engine and the wind and the irritating pounding of her own heart.

"…yes…successful, subject is en route…panion, I have her con…to the marsh, think there should…pose of a body. Can circle back after… take care of the car and dog…yes, sir, under…."

Ah. To the marsh. Revere, then, presumably…the marsh reservation, which she knew about but had never gone to explore. But it was certainly the most convenient and proximal site for concealing a corpse.

Right. Okay. So Not-Agent Fuckhead's planning on killing me and dumping my body in a marsh. And then "taking care" of Lithium. And doing who knows what to Jason. Great. Fucking fantastic. Brigid glared at the glowing red light that filtered into the trunk, pulled at the cuffs on her wrists but couldn't wrench them off. She remembered seeing in a movie once, a character cut off his thumb to get out of some cuffs. That was not a helpful memory, however, seeing as how she had no knife to cut off her thumb and also kind of wanted to keep the both of them. *Maybe I can find a bobby pin or something to pick the lock. How hard could that be? People do it all the time on TV, right?* Unfortunately, close exploration of the interior of the trunk revealed that it was clean as a hospital ward. No bobby pins from whatever previous murder victims he'd stuck in there, no other small pokey things that might help release her hands. She double punched the trunk lid in frustration. It did not magically open.

Eventually, the car turned off a paved road and onto what sounded like gravel. It slowed to a crawl, and Brigid was bounced uncomfortably around as the gravel was replaced by a dirt road. They finally stopped, the car door opened, the driver got out, and the car door shut again.

Brigid's heart rate skyrocketed. *This is it, then. This is where Not-Agent Dickwad is gonna kill me. Is gonna fucking try to kill me. Is gonna give it his very best shot.* She narrowed her eyes, bracing her feet against the side of the trunk. *Good fucking luck, you murderous shitfaced asshole.*

The trunk opened. Not-Agent Probably-Not-Smith-Either loomed above her.

He reached in, grabbed her by the shirt, yanked.

Brigid reached up with her cuffed hands, seized his collar, pushed off with her legs and pulled her face up to his, roaring, furious, seeing red. Tasting red as well, as her teeth closed over his right cheek. She bit down and ripped off a satisfying chunk of flesh. Not-Smith screamed, staggered backwards. Brigid spat out the piece of cheek and launched herself at him, her weight causing him to topple over backwards. She bit at his face again, couldn't quite reach it. He'd managed to get an arm up, in her way. From nowhere, his fist collided with the side of her head. Her ears rang, either with pain or blind manic rage. Her head spun. She'd fallen on top of him, still clinging to his lapels. He was trying to push her off. She reared up, released his collar, joined her hands, bent her elbows, dropped herself onto him. Drove all of her weight behind the points of her elbows into his chest. The jolt when they connected caused her head to snap forward, and she was momentarily disoriented. She pulled herself back together, whacked him twice on the ear with her left elbow. The side of his face was a glorious explosion of blood and missing cheek. She switched to whack his opposite ear with her right elbow. Not-Smith got ahold of her shoulders and brought his knee up to her solar plexus. That knocked the wind out of her, left her reeling, gasping. She head-butted his nose and he grunted, relaxed his grip. She shoved herself up again, saw her cuffed hands braced on his chest, had a brilliant flash of inspiration. She slid her hands up and around to the back of his neck, twisted them so that she could hook her fingers together behind him, the chain across his throat. Squeezed until the pain of the bracelets on her wrists was just beyond what she could bear, squeezed harder. Veins popped out on his neck and face. His eyes bugged out. He tried to hit her again, but she was too close for him to get any real power.

She braced her elbows, leaned into her hands. Not-Smith's face was turning very red. He thrashed back and forth, knocking her from side to side so her knees scraped the dirt and rocks. He was weakening. He clawed at her arms and face, pulled at her hair. But her fingers were latched securely, and she focused all of her strength and energy on keeping her hands locked together, ignoring everything else. Her fingernails bit into the flesh of her fingers. Finally, he stopped kicking, his arms fell, his eyes rolled up, and his body went limp.

Brigid released her hold on Not-Smith's neck, gasping, her throat and chest burning. Not-Smith didn't move. *Shit. Is he dead? Did I kill him?* She pushed the thought aside, rooted through his pockets. There was a handgun in a shoulder holster, which she pulled out and tossed aside. The handcuff key was in his left back pocket. She pulled it out after a bit of a struggle, got the cuffs unlocked after more of a struggle. Her hands were shaking, and it was hard to control her fingers. She dropped the cuffs and stared for a moment at Not-Smith, trying to figure out what to do, rocking back and forth, literally wringing her hands. *Do I bury him? Dump the body? Abandon him? Jason's still gone. Lithium's still in the motel room. I don't have time to deal with a corpse. Also, holy shit, did I kill someone?* She was wholly unprepared to process this. But maybe she wouldn't have to. Maybe he wasn't dead. She hadn't actually checked.

He wasn't dead.

Thank fuck. He had a pulse. He was breathing.

Oh shit, he isn't dead. He's gonna wake up pissed.

She looked around. The car was parked on a dirt path barely wider than the car itself, in a wooded area. The place smelled damp and sulfuric, with a faint musky undertone. *Right, right...the marsh.* Her nose was running. She pinched it, wiped it on her arm, sniffed. She'd dropped the cuffs into the mud and now, in the shadows, she couldn't see them.

She groped around for an eternity before she found them. She had to drag Not-Smith a few feet to the nearest upright tree, a sapling maybe fifteen feet tall, with a narrow trunk that she could pull his arms around and cuff his hands on the far side. The adrenaline was starting to wear off, and it took all of her strength to pull him those three or four feet. He convulsed for a few seconds as she was dragging him, nearly jerking himself out of her hands. She had barely gotten the cuffs on before he started blinking, eyes rolling back and forth. Brigid leapt back, out of reach, even though she was pretty sure he'd been neutralized, then leapt forward again and kicked him in the belly. "You're still a dick."

His phone was on the passenger seat of the car. She had an idea, dug into her pocket and pulled out O'Leary's card. She couldn't keep the phone, obviously. Phones can be tracked. But she trusted O'Leary. He'd seemed legit, honest. An honest Boston cop. And she'd gotten the sense that he didn't like Agent Smith, even when he thought he *was* Agent Smith.

She dialed the number. After a few rings, she got a sleepy gruff answer.

"Hi, Detective O'Leary, this is Brigid Sullivan, you gave me your card, you were...uh, you were looking into a break-in at my house? And there was this FBI guy there, too? Smith?"

"Yeah..."

"Okay, so, that guy, he's not really FBI. He just kidnapped me from my motel, he Tasered me and then he brought me out to this, like, marshland, up past Saugus, or sorry Revere, I'm not sure exactly where, he said he was going to kill me, but I got away, now he's handcuffed to a tree here and I'm gonna leave the phone. Okay? But I have to go, I can't stay here, but he's here with the phone, but he's not FBI, I can't stress that enough, he's not FBI, okay?" She stabbed at the *End Call* button, had to try a few times as her finger kept missing.

She threw the phone into the woods and got into the driver's seat. The car could probably be tracked, too, but she wasn't about to walk back to the motel.

Fucking hell. No keys. A briefcase in the passenger seat but no keys. She got back out of the car, crept over to Not-Smith, who was half awake now and looked confused and enraged. The keys were in his coat pocket. She pulled them out—dodging a few times to avoid him lunging at her. *Goddammit, of course he put the keys in his pocket. Lord fucking forbid he'd just leave them in the ignition.* She got back into the car, started it up, looked back at the non-FBI man—jerking on the sapling now, he might actually break it—snarled, "Fuck you, fuckhead," and reversed down the path.

It was maybe a quarter mile before she was able to turn the car around and drive forward. A half hour before she finally made it back to the motel, largely since she turned the wrong way onto Route 1 when she finally found it and then had to pull off to turn around, screaming at the highway and herself in frustration.

The cabin door was still closed. She pulled the door open and Lithium bounded forward. She fell to her knees, wrapping her arms around his wiggling frame. Seeing him, all the pent-up fear and horror and pain that she'd been sublimating since she got Tased in the parking lot came flooding back and she collapsed into sobs. She buried her face in his fur, hugged him harder than she thought she probably should, but was unable to relax her arms, unable to let him go.

She couldn't tell how long exactly she knelt there, clinging to her dog, spasming, whimpering. But, finally, she managed to pull her shit together, wipe her eyes, wipe her nose. Jason was still gone.

"Come on," she said to her dog. "We're going."

FOUR

Brigid sat in the driver's seat of her own car, with its safe familiar doggy smell and floating tufts of fur, gripping the wheel, conflicted. The car was packed with her backpack and Jason's duffel, and Lithium was in the back with ears pricked and tail up. She'd left a note apologizing to the motel for the scratches on the door. Lithium had evidently been unhappy with being left in the room for so long. Now that she was ready to go, she knew she was going to drive to Chicago, but she realized she had no idea what to do when she got there. Chicago was a big city, a strange city. She'd been counting on Jason to direct her, but she had no idea where he might have been taken or how to track him down. Or how to get him back. Or how to do any of it. The uncertainty of it all hit her unexpectedly. She was frozen.

She stared out through the windshield at the door to their cabin. Not-Smith's car was parked diagonally in front, abandoned after she'd jumped out and run to the door. She wished she'd kept his phone, in case he had stuff saved on it. GPS coordinates to a secret lair or something. Identities, names, and addresses for all the key players.

Not-Smith's car.

There was a briefcase in it.

Brigid dashed over to the car, grabbed the case, ran back to her hatchback. Once back behind the wheel, she clicked it open, pulled out a bound pack of papers and flipped through them.

It was a dossier. On top was the old, unrecognizable photo of Jason, clipped to a sheaf of personal information. His full name: Jason Bayani Reyes. His parents were Danilo and Jasmine, who had immigrated from

Manila thirty-five years ago, and who currently lived in Springfield, Illinois. He had an older sister named Laura, who was a graduate student at the University of Illinois at Urbana-Champaign. He'd gone to school at Springfield High School, done three semesters at Olive-Harvey College four years ago. It gave his last known address, and a list of known associates and their addresses. There were details of possible sightings over the previous eight months—at a YMCA in Elkhart, Indiana and a soup kitchen in Woodville, Ohio—and screenshots of security camera footage from a Walmart in Buffalo, New York. Several other similar packets, though she didn't recognize the names or photographs.

Until she found Ana Hernandez.

Her heart leapt into her throat. This was it! Ana Gloria Hernandez, MD, PhD, theoretical physicist, born in Cartagena, Colombia. Degrees from MIT, Stanford, and the University of Chicago. There was a list of publications in various scientific journals, but Brigid couldn't decipher any of the titles. She'd immigrated to the US in 1985, became a naturalized citizen in 2002. Her spouse was a David LaGuerre, a tenured professor at the University of Illinois at Chicago, who researched endocrine physiology. He also had a list of publications that flew over Brigid's head. They had one daughter, age eighteen, who was enrolled at Northwestern University. Dr. Hernandez's current occupation was not listed.

But her address was.

Brigid really needed to get going. If Not-Smith's car did have a tracker, surely the police or the not-FBI would be coming to find it soon. She kept the dossier but flung the briefcase out the window—just in case it, too, had a tracker—pulled on her seatbelt, and started the car. Lithium took up his favorite position, his head between the front seats, gazing out the front, eyes bright. Brigid reached over and gave his ear a quick scratch, murmured, "Okay, you ready?" and pulled onto Route 1, southbound.

卐

Jason had to pee. He was still strapped down on a padded gurney, still in a moving ambulance, still with a plastic tube in his arm, his head still swirling. Objects swam around him dreamlike, hazy. He had a vague sense of trepidation, the sense that there was something lurking in the shadows, but he couldn't pin down what it might be. Something was indeed lurking in the light, though. There was a figure in the space with him, mostly sitting quietly, sometimes adjusting the tubing attached to his arm, which distantly hurt. He wasn't sure if this figure was benevolent or malevolent. Maybe he should be scared. He considered maybe becoming scared.

Maybe...but I have to pee.

"Excuse me, sir, but I have to pee," he said—or, more precisely, "Scusasssrr, m'havvameh." But, for some reason, the fuzzy figure didn't react. Jason sighed, scrunched his eyes, tried again. "Ahmma...pfff."

Nothing.

Well, okay.

He peed.

⊞

Brigid drove until she could barely keep her eyes open—which wasn't that long, truth be told, as she'd only had about three hours of sleep to start with—and then she pulled over to a rest stop and bought the largest available shitty coffee, swallowed a couple of painkillers, and kept driving. She headed west on I-90, figuring it was in the right general direction. As the sky lightened behind her, she stopped to buy a map at a New York State welcome center. Turned out I-90 would take her directly to Chicago via Pennsylvania, Ohio, and Indiana. A fortuitous turn, she thought. But the drive was miserable, monotonous. Long hours sitting in the same position, legs cramping, back aching, staring at the unchanging landscape, pavement and trees, and the backs of cars. She stopped at a rest stop a few hours in. A woman in the restroom gasped and recoiled when Brigid walked in. When she saw herself in the mirror she understood why. She looked like a zombie. There was crusted blood over her mouth and chin—a mixture, she presumed, from Not-Smith's face and a cut on the inside of her own cheek, which lined up with her teeth. Her tongue was bitten, too, she discovered when she tried to rinse the taste of Not-Smith out of her mouth. Her nose was bloodied, swollen, purplish, possibly broken. The left side puffed in and out slightly with her breathing, which was concerning. Her temple had indeed been bleeding at some point, and now there were flakes of reddish black in her hair and an ugly scab at her hairline. She washed her face, carefully but with a lot of stinging and wincing. Afterwards, she looked less like the undead and more like a battered wife. A more thorough examination revealed abrasions on both wrists and knuckles, and a nasty violet bruise on her left ribcage, where Not-Smith had kneed her. There was also blood all over her shirt and mud all over her pants. She changed her shirt once she got back to the car but didn't even try to pull on a bra. The pants she left on. *Because who cares, really.*

She managed to make it till about eleven o'clock before even the terrible coffee wasn't enough to keep her awake, and she pulled into a parking lot and closed her eyes. Just for a minute. Woke up three hours later, mostly because she had to pee like a mother, and she cursed and rubbed her face. She took Lithium out to water the grass and ran into a McDonalds to use the bathroom. She bought a couple of tasteless greasy burgers, gave one to Lithium, ate half of the other, gave up and fed the rest of it to Lithium. She wasn't even really hungry. A couple of teeth were loose, so she couldn't chew properly anyway, just sort of mush the food against the roof of her mouth with her tongue. *Gross.*

It was nearly midnight when she finally made it to the outskirts of Chicago. Or, more specifically, East Chicago, which was oddly enough in Indiana. She stopped at a highway motel. She had about $1,100 in cash left, which was plenty for the night. *Shit, where did it all go? Didn't I start with something like $2,000?* Once it was gone, she'd have to use her bank card, and that would surely be tracked. Given the incident with Not-Smith, she really wanted to stay untrackable. The motel wanted a credit card on file. She claimed she didn't have one and offered to leave a cash security deposit instead. Which depleted her available cash even further. She briefly wondered why she was being so paranoid, wiggled her loose teeth with her tongue, and remembered that there were shadowy men with ambulances and Tasers chasing her. *Well, one less shadowy man, but still.*

She hadn't asked if pets were allowed, and didn't really want to know, so just snuck Lithium in through a side door and hoped no one would notice. Hoped he'd be quiet.

She locked the door, left a pile of filthy clothes on the bathroom floor and stood shaking under the shower spray, gingerly scrubbing her face and body. Took another couple of painkillers and finally collapsed into bed.

⌗

Jason blinked. His vision was unfocused, his eyes crusted over. He tried to wipe them but couldn't move his arms. He was slumped forward in a chair. His back and neck ached and when he straightened up it was with jerky, uncoordinated movements. His mouth was dry, sticky. Everything was kind of fuzzy, he couldn't focus properly, and he felt dizzy and weak. Also, his head was cold. That was weird. He tried rubbing his eyes on his shoulder, which was marginally successful, and looked around.

His wrists were in restraints. His ankles, too, by the feel of it. The strap around his left wrist was too tight. It pinched and scraped when he tried to wiggle it loose. There was an IV in his right arm. A bag of clear fluid hanging off a pole next to him was dripping slowly into the tubing that fed into it. He was wearing light green scrubs, stiff and uncomfortable. He could see a familiar table in front of him, a familiar mirror on the wall, a familiar face on the opposite side of the table.

Moe.

"Moe?"

"Hey...hey, man. Welcome back. We were starting to worry."

Jason's mind was clouded. Trying to put a thought together felt like fighting his way through a forest of cobwebs. *I'm in the lab. I'm back in the lab? Shit. How am I back? Did I never leave? No, I definitely left. I'm back, then. How am I back? Where's Molly?*

"Moe. What's going on." God, it was even hard to talk. His tongue felt thick and alien, as if coated with lichen.

"You were...I guess you were brought in last night. Figure they've been looking for you since you bailed, what, last summer? Where've you been anyway? We all kind of figured once you got out, like, the whole project would be shut down. We thought you'd blow the whistle, bring in the cops or something."

"Why are you here?" He squinted, tried to focus on Moe. He looked thinner than Jason remembered him. The Moe he remembered had been sort of a gym rat, who liked fitted t-shirts that hugged his pecs and biceps. This Moe, his shirt hung loosely off him, the sleeves slack over his arms.

"Shit, dude, we're *all* here. You were the only one who managed to get out. I mean, we're all here except for Ji. Me, Chris, Kechia, Diana."

"No, I mean…" It dawned on Jason that Moe was also wearing green scrubs. Weird. Made it feel like a hospital. "I mean why are you *here*, here…wait, where's Ji?"

Moe sat back, glanced at the mirror, rubbed his mouth. "Ji's dead, man. They killed her." He shook his head. His voice was unsteady. "This place…it's a fucking…dystopia. They told us they could kill any one of us, that they were with the government and outside of the law, and they killed her." Moe hiccupped, blinking rapidly. Paused for a few moments. "They killed her, I think just to show us they could. I'm not sure. I do know that at one point she managed to get into their research library—you know, that room with all the computers—I guess that's where they keep all their stuff, their data, and she managed to get in there and was looking through some of their files, and whatever she found freaked her out. She was talking about how it was evil, how the whole place needed to burn to the ground. They came and got her one night, middle of the night, and they took her into the surgery room, shot her in the head." Moe's voice was shaking now. "He made us watch… Wilders. He told us that it was her own fault, that we had to follow their rules…he actually said we had no rights. 'We own you,' those were his words. His exact words."

Jason stared, uncomprehending, mouth hanging open. He couldn't catch his breath. Couldn't wrap his mind around what he'd just heard. It couldn't be true. It wasn't possible.

Moe dropped his voice. "Goddammit, man, where were you? We were counting on you. We needed you." His face flushed, eyebrows knit.

"Why didn't you tell anyone? Send in the cops? Send in someone… anyone? You left us here—" He looked around, as if checking for someone in the corner, hissed, "You left us!"

Jason blinked, shook his head slightly, tried to speak but could form neither thoughts nor words. *I left them. Ji's dead. It's my fault. I left them. No, it wasn't my fault…but it was, I got out, I didn't help them at all, I just ran. Ji's dead.* "I…I…"

"Look, man. I'm sorry. I shouldn't have said that. Just…" Moe sighed, glanced at the mirror again, the one-way mirror on the wall. "I'm actually here because…Wilders sent me to talk to you."

"I…I tried, I was coming back…"

"Shut up. Here's the deal. Things have changed since you left. The four of us, we don't control the phase shifts anymore, pretty much at all. You know how it's triggered by neurotransmitters or whatever? He's pretty much done away with the whole meditation thing. I don't know if he decided it wasn't reliable enough. Me, personally, I only got it to work maybe half the time. Or he just didn't want to have to depend on our…cooperation. I think he suspected that some of us were refusing. Going on strike, sort of. And, yeah, some of us were. But, for whatever reason, now he triggers those phase shifts for us. He's probably got some other goal in mind, down the road. I think we're all, well, Version 1.0."

What? "What?" None of this was making any sense. *Am I dreaming? Hallucinating? Would I be able to tell? Shit. Maybe I'm dreaming. I hope I'm dreaming.*

"The phase shifts, they're more, ah…more precise now, but we don't have any say, we go when and where he says. None of us could ever do it without someone remotely activating the implant, the…uh, distractor. You could, I guess, but we…none of us could. But now…I mean, now we just show up and he sends us where he wants. That's what's happening with us anyway. You, I don't know. That's up to him, I guess. Meanwhile, you're gonna have to sit here on your little cocktail there."

Jason rolled his eyes over to the tubing, the bag of fluid dripping into his arm. "I—"

"It's chlorpromazine. Thorazine. It keeps you controlled, inactivates the distractor, basically. They tried a bunch of drugs on us before they narrowed it down to this one. Maybe 'inactivates the distractor' is the wrong term. It just prevents you from activating it. But whatever... same effect."

Thorazine. This struck Jason, through the haze, as inexplicably funny. "No...Lithium."

"No, Thorazine. Look, it doesn't matter. If you're good, they'll let you just take pills and then you can walk around and stuff. But you have to behave. You have to be good. If you pull anything, if you try another breakout or something...first off, they'll probably catch you and, second, even if they don't, they'll take it out on us. Are you hearing me, Jason? They will take it out on us. They will hurt us. Maybe they'll kill us, one of us. These people, they're fucking inhuman. They're dangerous."

Jason gazed off into the distance. *Ji's dead. I'm drugged. I'm trapped. Where's Brigid? What happened to her? Is she dead? If she is, no one's coming for me. She wasn't in the room when the ambulance came... Maybe she called them, after all. Maybe she's been working with them from the start. Or maybe she's dead.* He nodded, his chest tight, his stomach a black pit. "Okay."

⌸

No evil Taser men came to abduct Brigid that night, or the next morning, but housekeeping came to clean her room because she forgot to leave the *Do Not Disturb* placard on the door. Once the door opened to a flurry of barking, she instantly lost the security deposit. She also had to immediately vacate the room, under the disapproving glower of the motel manager and the annoyed housekeeping lady. Kind of a shitty way to start a day.

She and Lithium had their standard greasy fast food breakfast, which unsurprisingly led to a stomachache, then a panicked stop at another fast food place so she could bolt into the bathroom. Once things were a bit more settled, she pulled out Hernandez's information packet and looked up her address. After about ten minutes of studying a road map of Chicago she'd picked up at a gas station, she located the approximate location. Well, she found the street...she thought...probably. Then there was a lot of driving around, slowly, through unfamiliar streets with fewer street signs than she would've expected, stopping frequently to examine the map again. *Fucking hell, life without a smartphone is impossible.* She definitely remembered having to navigate by map when she was young, but that had been so long ago, and it was so much harder than just following a pleasant GPS lady's vocal directions. So, it took a few hours before she finally found the house with the right numbers on the right street.

She parked and tried to collect herself. The house was a small brick two-story, set close between similar homes that lined the street. It had a little yard bordered by a black lattice edging. There were trees along the sidewalk. An unassuming place. Her heart was pounding more than she'd expected. She was really nervous, now that she was here. *Fuck. What am I doing? How am I going to explain everything? What sort of reaction am I expecting? Do I actually think this woman will be able to help?* She assessed her face in the sun visor mirror. It wasn't pretty. Her nose was still swollen, there was bruising underneath both eyes, one eyelid was droopy and red, her upper lip was puffy and asymmetric. *I look like a crazy person. I'm going to sound like a crazy person.*

But needs must. She had no other ideas for how to track Jason down, short of going to the police, but she found it hard to imagine that they would take her story seriously, and she also suspected she might be extradited back to Boston. She'd left a pretty severely beaten person handcuffed to a tree. And she'd stolen his car. And he had an FBI badge, technically, though she was pretty sure it was fake. So, no… no police, not at this point. And so, yes, Hernandez.

She took a series of deep breaths, steeled herself, and strode confidently up the front walk. Knocked on the door.

Knocked again.

Rang the bell.

Knocked again.

Nothing.

"Fuck," she muttered to herself. Hernandez wasn't home.

She trudged back to her car, leaned back in the front seat. Lithium whined, wagged his tail, sniffed her face and gave it a tentative lick. "Fuck," she moaned again, "what are we supposed to do now?" Lithium offered no solutions, just pricked ears and bright eyes. *Not helpful. Cute, but not helpful.*

Well, theoretically, Hernandez would come home eventually. So, she could sit here waiting for her to show up. *Then again, someone could be looking for me, and someone could show up to check Hernandez's place, right? Not-Smith can't be the only evil shadow not-FBI agent out there. Maybe I should drive around, look for the lab. Maybe I should check on Jason's family ...what other information is in that dossier?* She pulled it onto her lap, flipped through the contents.

Stuff on Jason (she couldn't get over how different he looked in the photo), stuff on his family and known associates. From the map, it looked like it would be a long drive from Chicago to Springfield. Brigid shuddered at the thought of more time in the car. She couldn't find Molly in the dossier. Or the other names Jason had mentioned as participants in the project.

Should I call O'Leary? Shit. I'm tired, I just want to rest. That fucking motel. I want a drink. I want a nap.

卐

At some point, Moe left Jason, still in his chair, still restrained, still with an IV drip-dripping in. Jason wasn't sure exactly when that happened or why. Things still seemed so vague. He also kind of had to pee again. He tugged at one of the restraints, but it was secure, and he couldn't really tug with any particular strength or focus. He wondered if he could maybe manage a jump, just a little one, just a little bit, to at least get him out of his restraints. He tried to collect himself, closed his eyes, pushed himself...opened his eyes. No change. Wearing green scrubs and strapped to a chair. Dizzy from the effort but with nothing to show for it. He was alone, drugged, and needed to pee.

He felt a deep, constant undercurrent of despair. The reason would sort of fade out, now and then, but he was aware of a heaviness in his chest. And then he'd remember—*It's because Ji was killed, and it's my fault, and everything that's happened since is also my fault, because I didn't come back, because I got out and I didn't come back.* And then he'd stop thinking about that, because it hurt, it cut him deep into his core, and he didn't want to face it, so he tried to forget it, and then there was that sense of despair again. The drugs helped, or didn't help, in that he kept forgetting and remembering and then forgetting again.

He wasn't sure how long he was left alone in the white room. Probably not as long as it felt. It did feel like a long time but, when the door opened and Wilders walked in, it felt like it hadn't been long enough.

Jason's stomach managed to drop another level. Impressive, because it had already dropped to what felt like the sub-basement. He expected his heart to start pounding and was kind of surprised when it didn't. But his fingertips went cold, his mouth dry. Drier. He stared at Wilders, who fuzzed in and out unpredictably, reluctant to stay in focus. He looked as odious as he always had, business suited and hair gelled, an aura of menace surrounding him. Jason tried backing up, tried raising his hands defensively, but he could do neither because, *Oh right, still strapped to a chair. Well...* He re-focused on Wilders, felt another flush of fear and dread, un-focused, braced himself.

Wilders sat down opposite Jason, said nothing. Just sat there silently, like a ghoul, or a ghost. Maybe he wasn't there! Jason had a surge of hope that maybe he was hallucinating but, if so, it was a pretty realistic hallucination. Two anonymous men had materialized behind Wilders as well—two aides, he supposed, two goons, two thugs. A complex hallucination, then, a detailed one. A lucid dream. *Does that make sense?* Jason blinked, tried to focus again, gripped the arms of his chair. His head was spinning.

Wilders spoke, finally. "Well, Jason. You gave us quite the chase, young man."

Jason closed his eyes again. His chest felt tight, heavy. He had to concentrate to breathe.

"Jason, we need to talk about your responsibilities to this lab and to the project leaders. I hate to hold you here against your will, but the truth is you accepted a certain set of commitments when you signed on to this project, and you abandoned these commitments when you...you disappeared last summer. Please excuse our...er...our precautions, but our hands are tied." He hesitated, almost imperceptibly. "As it were."

Jason shook his head, kept his eyes down, didn't answer. He was freezing. *Why is it so cold?* His throat closed again against a wave of hopelessness, chased by another of frustration.

Wilders sighed. "Jason. I know you're confused. I know you must have questions. But what it comes down to is that you have obligations to us which have been unfulfilled. You're here to fulfill them. Once these obligations have been completed, you'll be free to go. Until then, you are considered to be our subject. You'll do what we ask you to do, without question or dissent. Is that clear? Do you understand your position in this project?"

Jason moaned softly. His hands were shaking. *Is that from the drugs? Fear? Cold? Why does everything have to be so miserable? I hate Wilders. I hate myself. I hate that I didn't try to expose everything, to fix things, while I had the chance. I didn't try to do anything. I just ran. And now I'm back, and I've accomplished nothing. Useless.*

"Jason. Are you listening? Right now, you may know, we have you on a Thorazine regimen. If you agree to cooperate, we'll take you off the IV drip that you're on now, put you on an oral course, and then you can move back into the dorm with the remaining test subjects. And then, so long as you continue to perform as required for the progression of the project, you can have some degree of freedom."

Jason's eyes were still closed. He tried to coordinate his thoughts into a coherent statement, but his brain was muddled, muddy, sludgy.

"Fuck you." It came out as barely a whisper, tremulous and insubstantial.

"That's not helpful, Jason. I know you're conflicted. I want you to understand. What we're doing here, the research that we're working on, it's of paramount importance. We're talking about changing the course of humanity itself…a leap forward on the scale of splitting the atom. Think about it. Traveling to alternate worlds! Understanding the very fabric of reality, of time and space! This is a field that the greatest minds in history have explored, and debated, and theorized. And, here, we can unlock the secrets of quantum mechanics!" Wilders's eyes burned into Jason, bright, excited. He leaned forward, tapping his spidered fingers on the table. "Think of all the benefits we could reap. The possibility of harnessing these phase shifts, the energy that we could potentially derive from them. We can glean scientific, or... or technical advancements from alternate worlds, bring them back here. Perhaps we can discover methods of time manipulation. Maybe we can learn how to correct mistakes our own civilization has made in the past...see what lies ahead in our future, prevent disasters, save lives. This is a force for good here, Jason. We have the potential to do so much good. If you help us."

Jason glared at Wilders, wishing his head wasn't so fogged. "It's like...splitting the atom."

"Yes, like splitting the atom. A leap forward on a par with."

It sounded rehearsed. Jason wondered dimly how many times Wilders had given this speech. "We bombed Japan...after we split the atom," Jason murmured. He took a deep breath, focused on Wilders, gripped his armrests. "And nuclear...nuclear arms, nuclear war, that's..." *Goddammit, think, form a fucking thought.* "...that's not a good thing."

Wilders sighed. "Yes, you can make that argument. But we also developed nuclear power, didn't we? And I'm not here to debate the benefits or...hmm...disadvantages of nuclear fusion. I'm discussing the project at hand. Quantum translocation."

"Yeah. Quantum whatever." Jason sucked air in through his nose, slowly, deliberately. He couldn't trust his tongue. It was too sluggish, lagging, heavy. "No. I don't believe you. I don't believe you're doing good. You aren't good...you're evil. You're evil." Jason shook his head a little in frustration, which did nothing to clear it. Evil. He sounded like something out of a bad movie. "Dr. Hernandez, she was good. She was working for...for humanity. Where did she go..." He sighed, closed his eyes briefly. "Why is she gone?"

"Dr. Hernandez and I are...were...working toward a common goal. Why would you differentiate?"

Jason snarled, a flash of clarity breaking through. "Because she never killed anyone."

Wilders sat back, folded his hands. "Well, who knows. Things may have progress—"

"Fuck you. You…you aren't even in the same…the same…the same place as her. This, all of this…this quantum stuff, this was her stuff. Her…research. You, you're just…a…a…you're copying. You're stealing her…her stuff." It seemed like there'd been a time when he was able to articulate more eloquent arguments. Once. He squeezed his eyes shut, tried to rub them, but his wrists remained restrained.

"Jason, I've had enough of this. I don't have the time or inclination right now to justify my work, my breakthroughs, with you. But let me be clear, you are faced with two choices here. You either agree to commit to contribute to this project and its ultimate goals—which I stress are of paramount importance for the progression of the human race—or you decline, and we will be obligated to deal with your refusal with severe repercussions."

Jason half-coughed a laugh. "Repercussions." He lifted his eyes, focused on Wilders and, in a burst of anger and defiance, spat at him. "Fuck your repercussions."

The little bolus of saliva didn't manage to make contact with Wilders's face, sadly. It sat on Jason's knee, a thin, slimy symbol of failure.

Wilders glanced to the side, annoyed. "Fine. I'll be clear. Do not make the assumption that your qualities or abilities are unique. You either submit to drug therapy and participation in this project, or your role in this project will be eliminated."

Jason's eyebrows knit, he shook his head slightly again, trying to clear it, failing. Again.

"Do you understand?"

Jason slumped forward in his chair. His face felt hot, the corners of his mouth pulled back. He tried to talk, but it was a challenge. "Eliminated. Like Ji? Like…like what you did to Ji?"

Wilders's expression didn't change. "What happened to Ms. Kim was unfortunate. But it was a result of choices that she made. I regret the outcome, but it was out of my hands. If you make different choices—"

"The fuck it was out of your hands. You did it." Jason's nose closed. He sniffed, but it was a lost cause.

"I did what was required of me. Everyone answers to someone, Jason."

Jason was weeping now, he couldn't help it, couldn't process everything he'd heard in the past however many hours. He felt like he was falling apart. Snot was running out of his nose. He tried to sniff it back in but to no avail, so he gave up and just let it run onto his scrub shirt. Rubbing his face on his shoulder did little to improve his situation. It was worse, naturally, with Wilders sitting there smirking at him. *Trapped. I'm trapped. There's no way out. I have to agree. Right? I have to.*

"Jason."

Jason took a shuddering breath. "I'll take…I'll take the pills." Anyway, he still had to pee.

⌗

Ultimately, Brigid elected to take Lithium for a walk, to pass the time. He'd been cooped up long enough. They drove a little way off, found what looked like a park and left the car in a parking lot by a sign that read *Dan Ryan Woods-West.* The sun was out, but it was still a bit chilly, so she needed her hoodie.

They wandered through the naked trees of early spring, dead grass and exposed soil like a skinned knee. There was an incongruous bald hill, with flat parallel grooves down the slope leading to an open meadow. They wandered past soccer fields and a bike trail, crossed a street to find a small, crumbling stone monument, partially obscured by dried twigs and reeds, that was marked with a plaque reading *Chicago Council of Gold Star Mothers.* Lithium spent a long time sniffing this area, which gave off a faint odor of ancient urine.

A bus stop, where a large woman in a puffy coat was waiting, stood not far from the Gold Star monument. Brigid kept her back to it, conscious of her face—one eye was swollen half shut, and her nose felt huge and bulbous. She felt like she was trying her best to do a disfigured Teddy Kennedy cosplay. "Well," she murmured to Lithium, "it's not like I was ever a great beauty." But still, she wanted her old face back.

For all that, though, she had to admit that deep down she felt something more. Something good. She was almost ashamed of it. She thought she ought to be focusing on Jason and the tragedy of losing him, overwhelmed with guilt and fear and distress. But the truth was, much as she worried about Jason and feared for him, she felt something else entirely about her own self.

She felt pride. That was it. She was proud. She felt strong. She'd been attacked by some maybe-government agent, this shadowy figure armed with malice and a stun gun, and she'd bested him. She hadn't crumpled in fear, she hadn't recoiled and pled for mercy, she hadn't played the part of a damsel in distress, hadn't waited to be rescued. She wouldn't have thought she had it in her, but there it was. And, even now, with everything else that was going on—the presumed ongoing pursuit by Not-Smith's crew, whatever was happening to Jason, the fact that she had no idea how to find him, and, also, that she'd probably lost her job at this point—at the end of the day, she felt good. She felt strong. She felt proud. She grinned, winced, stopped grinning, but she still felt proud.

Weird that being attacked, abducted, and beaten should make her feel so powerful.

Probably some sort of pathology going on there.

An hour or so later, she and Lithium returned to the car and drove back to Ana Hernandez's house.

卐

Wilders's goon removed Jason's IV, wrapped his arm in sticky purple tape. He unbuckled the arm restraints and handed Jason a couple of pills and a glass of water. Jason obediently swallowed the pills and sucked down the rest of the water. His hand was shaking, and the water splashed around his mouth, some of it trickling onto his shirt. *Classy.* The rest of the restraints were removed, and Jason attempted to stand, which was a mistake. The other goon had to come help pick him up off the floor and half-carry him down the hallway to the dorm.

Moe and Chris were sitting in the common room. The two goons dropped Jason onto a chair and left. There was an audible click of a lock when the door closed.

Jason blinked and gazed dully at Chris and Moe. "Hi." He wiped his nose, rubbed his eyes with the heels of his hands. At least he could move his arms. *Yeah, that's nice.* His head was still swimming. Also, his chest itched. He scratched at it and found a couple of little scabs. He scraped one of them off and a drop of blood welled up. He smeared the blood on his finger, sighed, leaned his head against the back of the chair. But the chair back wasn't that tall and his head lolled back against nothing, so he lolled it forward again, leaned onto his knees, cradling his forehead in his hands.

"Jason, you okay?"

Jason couldn't answer. Couldn't move. He laced his hands behind his head. Unfortunately, this somewhat compromised his breathing. He wondered if he should start crying again, but didn't think he had the energy, so he just sat there, elbows on his knees, trying to breathe.

"Hey. Hey now. Come on. It's okay." Someone was standing next to him, shaking him reassuringly on the shoulder. Jason tried to focus on him—a slight figure, green scrubs, light brown eyes, blond hair clipped short. *Chris. Yeah, he always was...just a nice guy, a great guy, I shouldn't have abandoned him here.*

"Chris. I'm sorry. I'm sorry."

"Yeah, I know, J. It's fine. It's fine. Let's get you to your room, right, maybe you can sleep it off. Come on." Jason allowed himself to be helped up, leaned on Chris's shoulder, shuffled into a bedroom. There was a bed, unmade, a naked mattress with folded sheets at the end. He collapsed onto it, waited for the walls to stop spinning. The walls did not stop spinning.

He closed his eyes, curled up.

⌗

Brigid rang the doorbell first this time, waited a few seconds, got anxious, started knocking. The deadbolt slid back mid-knock. Brigid took a step back, smoothed down her shirt, steeled herself. The door opened.

Dr. Ana Hernandez looked pretty much exactly like her photo in the dossier. A woman at the tail end of middle age. Thick, curly black hair laced with silver. Slacks and a button-down shirt, a small gold crucifix peeking out. Dark brown eyes behind black rimmed glasses. And an expression of suppressed shock.

Right, right, because of the face. The hideously disfigured face and whatnot.
"Hi, um…Dr. Hernandez? Ana Hernandez?"

"Yes? Can I help you with something?"

Brigid swallowed. "Yeah, I hope so. You, um…you used to run a lab, right? You were doing research into, uh…" *Oh please don't sound like a crazy person.* "…parallel universes? Or something like that." *I'm definitely sounding like a crazy person, this is no good.* "With…you had a guy working with you…his name was Jason? Is…is that…" Brigid's tongue flicked over her lips, her eyes darted away, which she thought probably made her seem even crazier. "Is that a…an accurate statement?"

Ana Hernandez took a half step back, pursed her lips and looked searchingly at Brigid. She glanced around at the street behind her. "You'd better come in. We can talk."

Brigid followed Ana to a small sitting room. "Have a seat in here. I'll be right back."

Brigid sat down on a sofa by a varnished coffee table. The sofa was neat and clean, the table tidy. On the table were a couple of oversized books and a set of coasters in a wooden box. There was a fireplace built into the wall with ceramic logs. On the mantle were a decorative clock, a vase of flowers, and framed family photos. Bookcases crammed with books lined the walls. The house was spotless. Like a hotel room.

Do real people even live here?

Hernandez appeared from the kitchen, placed a coaster on the table and a glass of water on the coaster. Brigid murmured thanks, picked it up and sipped gingerly. Hernandez sat down in an armchair facing Brigid and crossed her legs.

"Right, then. What is your name?"

"Brigid Sullivan. I'm a friend of Jason's. Jason…uh…" *Oh shit, I can't remember his last name. Well, this is going well.* "Jason, from your lab. He was a test subject, he said. He was part of a project…he, um, he had this implant, he said…it had to do with alternate universes. Is that…is any of this familiar to you?"

"Jason Reyes?"

"Yes! Yes, Jason Reyes. You know him?"

"Yes…yes, he was indeed a subject in a project I worked on. The project was shut down, however. I haven't seen Jason in over a year. Have you seen him? How is he?" Her accent was musical and oddly soothing.

"I think he's been kidnapped. I think he's been taken back to the lab."

Hernandez blinked. "The lab is closed. Shut down. What are you talking about, kidnapped? Who are you exactly?"

"I'm a friend. Of Jason's. Sort of. I mean…okay, this is kind of a crazy story. I picked him up when he was hitchhiking in Vermont two… three…two or three days ago. He told me about the lab, about the stuff you were studying, said you had figured out a way to, um…said you had proof of parallel universes. Does any of that make sense? I mean, I haven't completely ruled out the possibility that he was making it all up." Brigid's brow furrowed. She didn't really believe that. *I'm not sure what I believe, actually.* Saying this sort of shit out loud, though, she was starting to doubt herself.

Hernandez peered at her, guarded, but not denying anything. "You picked him up hitchhiking?"

"Yeah."

Hernandez nodded. "And you're saying…he's been kidnapped? By whom? What makes you think this?"

"Well, because the people who took him also took me. We had a… an altercation. That's why…" She gestured at herself. "You may have noticed this whole face situation."

"You and Jason had an altercation?"

"No! No." *God, this is getting kind of frustrating.* "No, Jason was taken off in this, like, off-label ambulance. Then I was put into the trunk of a car and this man—who'd called himself FBI—tried to kill me, we had a bit of a fight, I got away. I should stress, I don't think the man actually was FBI." *Not sure now why that should be so important. Even the FBI doesn't have carte blanche to just abduct people. Right? Argh, whatever.* "So I came here. Because, when I looked in his car, I found this dossier thing and you were in it."

Hernandez's eyes widened. "Excuse me?"

"Shit. Hang on. I've still got it. I left it in the car. Let me run and get it. I need to check on the dog anyway."

The dog was fine, curled up in the back. Brigid had parked in the shade, with the windows and sunroof wide open, and his leash looped around the back of the seat. He popped up when she opened the door, looking hopeful. She scratched his ears, kissed him on the head. "Things are not going swimmingly thus far," she confided, grabbing the dossier. She checked her watch. The afternoon was cool, but she didn't want to leave Lithium in the car for too long. Someone might steal him or something. Who knows what could happen.

Hernandez hadn't changed positions. She was still sitting in the armchair, legs crossed, looking confused and anxious.

"Hi, okay, right. This is what was in his car. Here's you." Brigid pulled out the sheaf on Hernandez. "And here's Jason, and there are a bunch of other people I don't know. Friends of his, I guess, or something."

Hernandez examined the papers. Her hands had developed a fine tremor and her face was ashen. "I don't understand. How did you get this? What is this? Where did this come from?"

Brigid sat back down on the edge of the sofa, leaned forward and rubbed her arms. "I'm gonna have to start at the beginning, I think."

⌗

At some point, Jason just couldn't hold it any longer and got up to pee. He steadied himself with a hand on the wall, still swaying slightly, trying to aim the stream into the bowl with maybe 70 percent success. Seemed like ten minutes in he was still peeing. *How is this possible? When was the last time I even had a drink?* He took a deep breath and continued peeing.

Eventually, he finished, drained in more ways than one, shook himself and leaned against the wall waving his hand at the flush lever until he connected with it, then leaned a while longer. The purple tape on his arm itched. He pulled it off, dropped it on the floor. He could hear hushed voices in the common room. *I should go out there, face everyone. Can't put it off forever.*

Maybe just put it off one more minute.

Finally, he straightened himself up, tugged on the hem of his scrub shirt and looked at his reflection in the mirror over the sink. His face was unfamiliar. His beard had been shaven, his head shorn, leaving just a cap of short black hair over his scalp. His eyes were sunken, with puffy bags underneath, framed by deep and unfamiliar lines. His cheekbones were weirdly well-defined. *If heroin chic was still in vogue, I'd almost be hot. If the room was dark enough.*

He didn't have the energy to wash his hands, just headed out to the common room.

Moe and Chris were still there, and Kechia and Diana had joined them, sitting next to each other on the sofa. Everyone was wearing the same shapeless green scrubs.

"Jason! Aw, Jason. Thank god." Diana leapt up, pulled him into a tight embrace. "We were so worried, you have no idea. We thought maybe you hadn't made it." Finally, she let go and backed off.

Kechia was waiting in the wings and wrapped her arms around him as well. "Jeez, you're so thin, kid. I hardly recognized you." She looked different, too. She'd always kept her hair sleek and carefully styled, but now it was pulled into a frumpy ponytail, and she was missing her usual eyeliner and lipstick.

"Thanks. It's, uh…it's good to see you, too." *God, that sounds inadequate.* He looked around for a place to sit, lowered himself gingerly into a free chair. His arm was sore. He rubbed it absently. It was bruised at the elbow. The IV, he supposed. He avoided everyone's eyes. He could feel them staring at him.

Diana broke the silence. "Jason. What happened? We've all been wondering. How did you get out? Where have you been, what have you been doing?"

Kechia nodded, pulling her legs under her on the sofa. "Yeah, seriously. It's been forever. We thought you were dead in a ditch." She grinned wryly. "Or that you'd been, you know, taken care of, wink wink."

Jason started to grin back, realized what she was implying and thought maybe it was inappropriate to laugh, decided it didn't matter and besides he didn't have the energy to care, so he nodded. "Yeah. Um. It's kind of a long story. Um…does anyone have anything to eat? Or drink? I'm sorry, I'm just really hungry."

Chris brought him a cup of water and jar of peanuts from the kitchen. "There's not much. They provide meals, these days, but no trips to the supermarket or anything, anymore. You have to make an official request for whatever special stuff you want. They bring in packages once a week, but half the time they don't bring what you asked for. You know, you can complain but it doesn't—"

"Chris," Moe interrupted. "It's not important. Let him talk. I want to hear his story."

Jason nodded thanks to Chris for the peanuts and water, drank most of the water at one go and struggled to open the jar of peanuts. His mind was clearer than before, but still kind of foggy, and his fingers didn't seem to follow his brain's orders particularly well. Also, he was actually hungry to the point that he was shaky. Or he was just shaky. Chris, glowering at Moe, took the peanut jar and opened it for him. Jason shoved a fistful of peanuts into his mouth, chewed and tried to consider what he would say once he swallowed.

Jesus. They're all staring at me.

He suddenly wished he was doing pretty much anything other than chewing a mouthful of peanuts. In a spotlight. While a bunch of people watched. *Shit.* It felt like if he tried to swallow he'd choke. *Too many peanuts. How does someone screw up eating peanuts? Why are they still all staring at me? What do they expect me to say?* He gulped down the mouthful, coughed, swallowed some water, coughed again.

"Jason." Moe sounded kind of pissed.

Jason coughed again, drank the rest of the water, set the peanuts and the glass down on the end table. "Yeah. Okay. What do you want to know? I got out by climbing out a window. And just ran down the road. Hid in an alley. That's it."

"Uh huh. What've you been doing for…the last…what, like eight months?" Moe demanded.

"Well, mostly hiding. You know. Hitchhiked a bunch, just tried to stay on the move. There was a warrant out on me, I saw a thing on TV, a news report, it said I was wanted for assault, larceny." Jason sighed, rubbed his head. "So I couldn't go to the cops. I wanted to, but I thought they'd just arrest me, send me to prison or just send me back here. And I didn't want anyone else to get involved, so I couldn't go home, couldn't talk to my family or…I just kept moving."

"Whoa." Diana sounded sympathetic. "How did you…you know? Money and stuff, places to sleep?"

"Uh, mostly like petty larceny. I did a lot of shoplifting. I guess I *am* kind of a criminal now. And I'd, like, break into places, steal the petty cash, you know, sometimes it's left in the cash register overnight. But yeah, it wasn't easy, I wasn't very good at it." *Didn't Brigid say something like that? What happened to her? Maybe she's still out there. Maybe she's looking for me.*

Maybe she's dead.

He didn't want to think about that.

Moe piped up again. "Did you maybe write a letter to the papers, email anyone, maybe call the cops…anything?"

"Moe, please. Let it go. He was scared," Kechia protested. "Who would've believed him anyway? Going around talking about parallel universes and stuff? He would've been chucked into the loony bin."

"Shut up, Kechia. He could've tried. He could've done something. Anyway, I don't even think they have loony bins anymore."

"What? Yes, they—Don't be ridiculous. You know what I mean. Just go easy on him, that's all."

Jason looked over at Moe, defiantly. "I was coming back. Me and a friend. We…we had a plan and everything, we were going to find Dr. Hernandez. She went to the cops already. We were coming back."

"Well shit, Jason. What happened? Who was this friend? Are they still coming? Hernandez has been to the cops already? What happened?"

Jason dropped his eyes, shrugged unhappily. "No, my friend went to the cops, I mean. We hadn't found Hernandez yet. I don't know. My friend, she wasn't in the room…when they came, when they got me. Both of them—her and her dog, I mean—were gone. I don't know why. I don't know if they killed them, or what."

"Again, who was this person?"

"Brigid, her name's Brigid. She picked me up when I was hitchhiking, in Vermont. Let me stay with her. Cooked me dinner. She was…really nice to me."

Kechia laughed. "Oh ho, she was nice to you, was she? How nice exactly? What did you do to pay for this dinner, hmm?"

"Hey. No. She was just...nice to me. I don't know why. I asked her, she said something about a midlife crisis. I think she was joking, though. But, yeah, like the first night, someone broke into her apartment and she took me and her dog and put us up in a motel for a couple of nights, and I told her everything about what happened here, and she said I had to come back, to get the rest of you out. So yeah. That's what we were doing, when they came and caught me."

⌗

There was a prolonged silence after Brigid finished talking. Hernandez recrossed her legs, rubbed the top of her thigh, exhaled slowly.

Brigid fidgeted with the now empty water glass. "So...I mean, yeah. That's it. That's the whole story."

Hernandez nodded.

The silence became uncomfortable.

"So...what. What are your thoughts, I guess?"

Hernandez pursed her lips. "Still thinking."

"Okay. Um, do you mind if I just pop out, check on the dog again? He's in the car, I'm sure he's fine, I just—"

"Oh!" Hernandez's eyes widened. "Yes! You had mentioned a dog! I'm so sorry, I was so distracted. I completely forgot. You have a dog? You must bring it in. Ah, he shouldn't be in the car!"

"No, I mean, like I said, I'm sure he's fine—"

"No! Go, get him. Bring him in. We still have much to discuss."

Well, Brigid thought while fetching Lithium, *this is probably a good sign. If Hernandez thought I was completely full of bullshit, she wouldn't have invited the dog in, right? Which is something she may regret if he jumps on the sofa as soon as we get in.*

Brigid reentered the living room. Lithium trotted over to Hernandez, wagging his tail, sniffed her pants carefully, and jumped on the sofa.

Dammit.

"I'm sorry, he's...Lithium, please. Get down, bad doggy..."

Hernandez laughed, waved her hand. "No, no. Don't worry about it. He is welcome here."

"I mean, there is so much fur, though. You have no idea, he sheds—"

"Sweetheart, please. You are familiar with vacuums, I assume."

Brigid smiled gratefully and sat back down. Lithium crawled onto her lap and sighed. "Thanks. Your house is so clean, though. You know, mine is just covered with a layer of fur. All the time."

Hernandez beamed back, exuding warmth. "Well, since my daughter went to college, it has been easier to keep things tidy. But I miss a little bit of chaos, to tell the truth." She rubbed her hands together. "Well, right then. We need to figure out what to do now, yes? According to Jason, the lab is still operational…or was when he left. This is confusing, because I have been assured from multiple sources that it was shut down not long after I was evicted. In fact, I have a lawsuit right now pending, to recover my research documents, which were all confiscated when I lost funding."

"Oh." Brigid thought about this. Maybe the lab had moved? "Have you been back to the lab since then, though? Back to the site?"

"Oh yes, of course. Many times. But it is locked, I have no access. I have attempted, my lawyer has served them with all sorts of legal documents, but to no avail. We are merely sent away with the message that it is a government facility and we do not have clearance to enter."

"Is it?" *Oh, shit. Maybe that guy was FBI after all. That might complicate things.* "Government?"

"Oh, I have no idea. They say one thing, maybe they mean another. It is all very shady, very hush-hush. I have gone to the police as well, but they say the same, they have no…no…permission?"

"Jurisdiction?"

"Yes, that's it. No jurisdiction in that area, they cannot get the warrants they need, so they cannot enter."

"Shit. I mean, shoot." Brigid thought for a minute. "Should we go to your lawyer? Maybe I can make a statement, something official? But the thing is, I don't really have any proof. I just have Jason's word. And he's gone." She rubbed her temple, winced a little, sat up. "Wait.

The FBI guy...or not-FBI guy...the guy who attacked me. He may have been arrested. I did call the cops, before I left."

"Oh! All right. That is a place to start."

"Then again, I may be wanted also...I did kind of beat the shit out of him."

"Well, we'll have to check, I suppose. As to making a statement, is that something to do with the police as well? How does that work exactly?"

"I mean, honestly, I'm not sure." Brigid arched her back, stretched her arms. She'd been sitting for too long. "I mean, at this point I'm tempted to just, you know, storm the castle, break into the lab and pull an old-fashioned prison break."

Hernandez got up, retrieved Brigid's glass, took it back to the kitchen and refilled it. "Well, that's an option," she said, thoughtfully, when she returned. "But I think maybe we'll just table it for the time being."

卐

"What..." Jason scrunched his eyes, trying to formulate a coherent sentence. He was sitting in his dorm room, in a white vinyl chair in the corner, his knees pulled up to his chest. Diana was making his bed for him, on her hands and knees on top of the sheets. She glanced over at him. Her hair had gotten longer since Jason had last seen her, and her blonde ponytail fell over her shoulder.

"What what, Jason?"

"What...the stuff that Wilders is doing. Like, you know, Hernandez, she had us going and gathering data on history in other...in parallel... is that the same?"

Diana finished tucking in the fitted sheet, stood up, arched her back. "Well, no. I wouldn't say that what we're doing now really has much in common with what Hernandez was doing." She unfolded the flat sheet, snapped it out over the bed and let it flutter down. "I would say—and correct me if I'm wrong, in my recollection—but Hernandez spent most of her time trying to collect information on the alternaverses. Right? I think she was trying to figure out the timelines, where things diverged, though I'm not sure exactly what she was hoping to learn from that information. Wilders, he does more…hmm." She set the folded woolen blanket down at the base of the bed, pulled the pillow into the pillowcase. "He's not into going to a bunch of different places, the way Hernandez was. He's very focused. The phase shifts are planned, to a specific alternate timeline. Specific to each of us, I mean. I always go to the same alternaverse, but it's different from the one that Moe or Chris or Kechia goes to."

"Why? What do you do there?"

"Well, me, I've basically formed a…what's the best way to put this…a relationship, I guess, a connection, with the people—the researchers—over there. We have a collaboration, you know, with alternaverse, uh, people."

Jason blinked. "Alterna-people? Alterna-Wilders?"

Diana dropped the newly cased pillow, turned around to face him, sat down on the bed. "No, not exactly. I think there's probably an alterna-Wilders there, but we don't work with him. It's another lab, kind of like this one, but the head of it is this other guy, Johnson. We trade data back and forth, you know, compare technologies, systems of government, that sort of thing. I have to do a lot of studying, memorizing, that sort of thing. They're super interested in what's going on in Russia right now. Apparently, over there, the Soviet Union is still a superpower. Wild, right? And I've had to learn a lot about computer coding, which is, like, super boring, but probably important."

"Diana…" Jason rubbed his eyes, massaged his temples.

"Yeah?"

"You keep saying 'we.' Not 'they.' We."

Diana sighed. "Look, Jason. I know you have a…complicated history here. I think about Molly, too. I'm sad she's gone. And I understand why you would consider Wilders and the rest of the staff here to be, I don't know, sort of ghouls or boogeymen or whatever. But there comes a point, you know, when you're actually here—living this life, in this place, in this situation—when you decide you have to make the best of things. I do think that the work we're doing here is important. I'm not gonna lie about that. I think it's important, I think it's gonna change the world. For the better. We're pioneers, in a sense, if you think about it. And fighting with Wilders, fighting with the lab staff, it's…it's not going to achieve anything, it's only going to make things harder for them, and for you. Besides, if you give them a chance, get to know them, they're not bad people."

Jason dropped his eyes. He wanted to argue, but he was tired, his brain still foggy, and she'd been so nice to him since he'd come back. He didn't want anyone else to be angry with him, like Moe was. Still, though. It was hard to understand how she could justify this…this… complicity.

"Anyway. We've made a lot of progress, you know, with our work. Still a ways to go, though. Because any one alternaverse develops a whole new group of branched other alternaverses, you know, as time passes, so it can be hard to define what counts as 'the same.' Because there's going to be a shared history. You know? So, if you say, 'This is the same place, because I've been here in the past,' but there is another parallel alternaverse that you were also in, in the past, which is not the same…you with me?"

Jason picked at the corner of the white vinyl armchair. "Huh. Yeah. Yeah…no."

"Because we have to return to the alloverse—this universe— eventually, and for things to be reliable then we have to be able to return again to that specific alternaverse. If we don't, if we even find a similar, like almost identical one, but it's not the same, or it doesn't share the exact same history, even if we find the same people, we may have to forge a whole new set of relationships. Which is time consuming. And we don't frankly have that much time to devote to that."

"You don't have time? Why? Why not?"

"Oh, yeah." Diana kicked her slippers off, crossed her legs under her. "Do you remember people getting migraines and stuff, back when you were here?"

"Mmm. Yeah. Yeah, migraines, I got a nosebleed a few times…always figured it was because I'd gone too far. You know…jumped too far."

Diana nodded. "Too far, yeah. Too often. Or too long. Anywhere you go, any alternaverse, the longer you're there, the more you're damaged. Or we think that if you try a phase shift that's a massive shift, a significant alteration in your wave function..."

Shit, I don't understand this either. He just nodded.

"...anything like that. Your body doesn't like being part of the wrong universe." She grinned bleakly. "We'd been coming back with microscopic hemorrhages...just...everywhere. Anywhere there are blood vessels, they would start bleeding. I think that was why Pedro had those seizures. I think there was a bleed in his brain that triggered them. Maybe that was part of what happened with Angela as well. We've never really been able to confirm what happened there."

Chris poked his head through the door, tapped his knuckles on the frame. "Dinner's here. Come on out."

᠎᠎

Brigid sat, somewhat uncomfortably, at Ana Hernandez's dining room table. Lithium sat pertly behind her, ears pricked. Ana had invited her to stay for dinner, invited her to stay the night as well, once she learned of the whole motel situation. Brigid had been a little hesitant at first but, given her diminishing financial reserves, she'd gratefully accepted and fetched her knapsack from the car.

She was starting to think it had been a mistake.

Ana was in the kitchen with her husband. David, his name was. He'd come home a short time earlier, greeted her politely, backed up a bit from Lithium's persistent and inquisitive nose. Seemed like a nice enough guy. But now the normal kitchen noises of sizzling and clinking and shuffling were gradually morphing into hushed murmurings of increasing agitation. Something was wrong in there. They were, she thought, whisper-yelling at each other. Whisper-yelling, then hiss-yelling, then finally Ana abandoned all attempts to muffle herself, so Brigid heard her words clearly.

"No. No. Stop it, David. I have had enough. I have invited her to stay and she stays. What would you have me do, eh? What? Turn her away? David, when someone comes to you, someone who needs help, someone who is clearly in...in danger, David, what kind of a person would I be to turn them away? And she is helping Jason. I was responsible for him once and now he is suffering because of that lab, because of the work I started. I cannot turn my back on them."

"Ana…no, Ana, I'm just trying to say—"

"I know what you are trying to say, David, and I reject it. I reject it! I was raised to believe that we as people, as *human beings*, we have an obligation to help those in need. A moral obligation. That is what I expect from myself. What I expect from my daughter, and what I expect from my husband."

"Just…you don't know, you have to be careful, you can't just trust everyone! Ana! Sometimes people don't—"

"No. We help people in this household. We help people who need us, even those we don't know well, even if we are taking a risk. This, David, *this* is a hill I am prepared to die on."

Silence.

Brigid shifted uncomfortably, glanced at Lithium. Wondered if she could slip out through a window without anyone noticing.

The voices in the kitchen dropped to inaudible levels again. A few agonizingly long minutes later, David appeared at the door holding a bottle of wine and a couple of glasses. He smiled at her, a bit sheepishly it seemed. "So. Will you have a glass of wine?"

Brigid shook her head slowly. "No. Thanks. I'm good."

David busied himself with the corkscrew. Brigid watched, fidgeting, trying to collect some courage. "Uh, look, I…I didn't mean to cause a problem. I can leave. Like, it's fine, I can just go to a motel—" *Or the car, I can sleep in the car.* "I really wasn't looking to…to be—"

David looked up, eyes wide, a rueful grin splitting his features. "Oh god, please no. She'll kill me if I let you leave." He shook his head. "I don't think either of us have a choice at this point."

Brigid tried to laugh politely, unsure of what to say.

"It's fine. I'm sorry you heard all that, it must've been awkward, but honestly, it's fine. I'm a little more cautious than Ana, that's all. I mean no offense…meant no offense. I hope you took no offense." His accent was bland and Midwestern. He poured a couple of glasses of wine and took the bottle back to the kitchen.

Ana entered the dining room carrying a bowl of salad and a bottle of salad dressing. David followed her, carrying a serving platter with two salmon steaks on it and a bowl of peas. Ana beamed at Brigid. "You will have to excuse us. We were expecting just the two of us, but we will just divide it up, no problem at all."

David sat down, smiling pleasantly at Brigid, acting as if the previous ten minutes had not happened. "I understand you and Ana have a friend in common." He took the bowl of peas, placed a spoonful on his plate, passed it to Brigid.

Brigid was not a particular fan of peas, but she felt obligated to take a spoonful as well.

"Uh, yes, sort of. One of her subjects, from last year I think?"

"Two years ago," Ana corrected.

"Ah." David nodded as he took a piece of fish. "From the quantum transpositional project. Alternate wave functions. I've heard a lot about it. But I...we'd been led to believe the project was shut down. You know one of her subjects?"

"Yes. He was participating in a study about...um...alternate realities? But, to be honest, I'm not completely clear on what he was doing. I mean, he tried to explain it to me, but I'm not sure he understood it either." She put a piece of the fish on her plate. A smallish one. At the very least she could try not to gobble up all their dinner.

Ana chuckled. "No, he probably didn't. I loved Jason, god knows, but he...well, he had trouble grasping the details, the nuances of our work. Sometimes, I would be explaining our objectives, the basis for our project, and his eyes would just..." She waved her fingers in the air. "Just glaze over. He'd sort of fall into this, well, smile-and-nod sort of pattern."

"Yeah...I mean, honestly, I didn't really understand his explanations either. He kept talking about cats in boxes. Or, once, he went off on this thing about breakfast cereals..."

Ana looked puzzled, amused, as she tonged salad onto her plate and drizzled it with dressing.

"And everything was a wavelength, and he said he was jumping from one wavelength to another. None of it made any sense to me, but then he did pull this disappearing act to prove it. A couple of times, now that I think of it."

"No one really understands Ana's research," David remarked ruefully. "Though we all try. She has to simplify it pretty drastically for it to make sense."

"That is not true." Ana took a sip of wine. "It is a little complicated, but I think I can explain it for you, maybe without cats or cereal." She took a bite of salmon and peas, set her fork down, dabbed her mouth with her napkin.

"Let us first identify the notion of a quantum experiment. This is any situation or happenstance in our world that might have multiple possible outcomes which are not possible to predict using classical mechanics. For example, the roll of a die, or spinning a roulette wheel, or playing rock-paper-scissors. With me? So, for every individual quantum experiment performed in which there are multiple possible outcomes, all outcomes are obtained in multiple different worlds, though the observer may be aware of only one. There is a world in which the die rolls a one, another in which the die rolls a two, and so on. All are alternate worlds, that exist in parallel with each other, at the same space and time. But we, the observer, we can only see the one outcome."

David interjected, "You can make the argument that the roll of a die is predictable given adequate information, using classical physics. Just set that aside for the time being. It's a stand-in for a true quantum experiment."

"Which would be...what?"

Ana beamed. "Well, the original quantum experiment was the double-slit experiment—"

"Stop, stop. That's going to take another hour to explain to a novice. No offense intended, Brigid. Just go with the die roll."

"So, for a quantum experiment which has the two possible outcomes x or y, and one observer, who we'll label 'A'—observer "Ax" will witness outcome x while "Ay" will witness outcome y, with both worlds existing in parallel but independent of each other. There are now two worlds, in parallel, branching off from one world, inhabited by Ax and Ay respectively. These two worlds share a single origin, which is A's world."

Brigid nodded slowly.

"While the two worlds are in parallel, different events may occur in each one—because there has been a difference of outcomes. So, Ax may now witness a new quantum event with two possible outcomes: 1 and 2. The experiment causes a branching of Ax's world into two further, parallel worlds: Ax1 and Ax2. Meanwhile, Ay continues as a parallel of Ax. The worlds are in effect branching off of themselves, but all are still connected by the original world prior to the first quantum experiment." Ana paused.

After a tick, Brigid realized she was waiting for a response. "Yeah. Okay."

"Now, the wave function is the quantum state of physical objects in our universe. It is what determines how the object or outcome is registered by the observer. It holds true for time and position but in a multi-world situation there are multiple states dependent on the potential outcomes of a given quantum experiment."

Brigid could feel a furrow developing between her eyebrows.

"The distractor device works by altering the wave function of the object that the distractor is in. It causes a shift from the original world to an alternate but parallel world with a common origin. For example, if the distractor device were used by observer Ax to shift to the world with experimental outcome y, observer Ax would essentially become—temporarily—Axy, alongside observer Ay."

Brigid remembered something Jason had mentioned. "And there are an infinite number of parallel worlds."

"Yes! The idea is that there are an infinite number of parallel worlds that all branch off from a single original event, which for our universe would be, theoretically, the Big Bang. All the parallel worlds within our own universe are connected and potentially accessible. However, if there were a universe independent or separate from our own, there would be no quantum connection and no way to access it. That would be an entirely new subject within this field, certainly worth investigating in the future.

"Now, with regard to my own project. There were certain un-answered questions we had about this phase shift. Would the subject be able to interact with the alternate world? Would he essentially jump into the alternate version of himself, merging with that identity? What would happen if they shifted into a location with different surroundings…if they were to materialize in the same location as a wall or tree or some other physical object? All of my lab subjects were extremely brave, to venture into the unknown. I hold them all in high regard. And we were gathering much valuable data, because of the work they put in. Jason in particular. He was the first, you know, to make a successful phase shift. That was a day of triumph for us all. Years of labor, leading to that moment."

"He said he had a natural, what was it, affinity for it? It was like a mental push, right?"

"So to speak. I had some not inconsequential assistance from David here, in the development of the distractor. It takes input from neurotransmission expression…electrical impulses from the brain, in a sense. It was a delicate process, both in designing the trigger mechanisms of the distractor and in training our subjects to learn to modulate their intrinsic triggers. Neither was easy. But it was important to me that the subject have the final control of the distractor, that it not be completely out of their hands. Both for safety and for commitment to the project, on the part of our subjects. We wanted them to be a part of it, not just guinea pigs."

Lithium poked Brigid's butt with his nose. She shooed him away. "Wasn't that kind of complicated?"

"Oh, sweetheart. Yes. It was not easy. It took years of research, years of trials. The ten subjects, Jason and his friends, you do not think they were the first run, eh? No, no! They were the first *human* test subjects. But, obviously, there is no way we would have gotten that far had we not had years of reliable, solid data and trials and experiments en route." She sighed a bit wistfully. "This was my life's work. I am happy to hear that Jason has managed to continue, albeit unconventionally." Ana smiled fondly. "I had high hopes for Jason. Though, truthfully, that was largely because of his relationship with his partner."

Brigid looked up. "Molly?"

Ana brightened. "Yes, Molly! What a wonderful young woman. Such potential. I had hoped she would look me up, after the project ended.

Even back then, had she not been a subject, I would have been inclined to offer her a research position. She had such a natural intelligence, this inherent ability to...to comprehend things very quickly. And to extrapolate, you understand? Not just to memorize, but to infer. She can change the world, that one, if she puts her mind to it. Do you know her as well?"

Brigid froze, her fork poised in the air. She stared at Ana in dismay. *Shit. She doesn't know.*

Ana took another sip of wine, picked up her fork. She hesitated when she saw Brigid's expression. "Are you all right?"

Brigid's face felt hot. Her nose, inconveniently and unexpectedly, started running. *Fuck.* She held a napkin under it, over her mouth. "Molly. She's...she...apparently she died. From what Jason told me. She got pregnant, then she sort of disappeared. He found an autopsy report." She put the napkin back onto her lap, set her fork down and looked at her plate because she didn't want to meet Ana's eyes.

After a few moments, though, she had to look up again.

Ana had covered her mouth with her hand. She dropped her hand to her chest, looked at her husband, placed her hands in her lap and looked down. She took a deep breath, slightly tremulous. Her eyes were wet. "That...that is a terrible shame, if it is true. A terrible shame."

Brigid shifted uncomfortably. "It was, uh, one of the reasons...I think the main reason...that Jason left the lab. Broke out, I mean."

"Bad things were happening, you had said. This was what you meant? Molly?"

I...I should not have glossed over those details. It was true—when she'd explained the situation to Ana earlier—she'd left it as 'things in the lab took a bad turn.' She looked up to face Ana. "Molly. And Angela. And...there were a couple of others, I forget their names. One of them had a seizure, I guess."

Ana paled, her eyes widened. David reached over to take her hand.

"I'm sorry. I'm sorry." Brigid didn't know what else to say. She dropped her eyes again.

When Ana spoke, her voice was dark, shadowed. "My lab. My work. This will not stand. This will...not...stand."

田

Jason stared dully at the plastic tray of food in front of him. *Are they serving airplane food now? Where did they get airplane food? Is there some sort of mass distributer for individual terrible meals? Could this possibly be cheaper than just getting TV dinners from the supermarket?* He poked with his plastic fork at the dried crust of cheese that rimmed a small plastic dish of lasagna. *Is that actually cheese?* The plastic tines bent and slid off. He tried again with a plastic knife. The cheese *(cheese?)* defied all plastic incursions. Fortunately, the tray also held a small wilted salad with an individual cup of off-brand Italian dressing, a cold hard bread roll, a square of margarine, and some sort of brownie-type thing in a yellow wrapper. *No need to go hungry tonight.*

"You. Time for your meds."

Jason glanced up at the goon-monkey before him, a thirtysomething guy with a goatee and thinning hair, who was holding out a small paper cup containing a pair of pills. Jason obediently took the paper cup, tipped his head back and dropped the pills in.

"Mouth open. Tongue up."

The goon patted his shoulder approvingly, satisfied that the pills were gone. Jason shrugged away, angry. *I'm not a fucking dog.* The goon left, and Jason resumed his battle with the lasagna. He eventually lost that battle, so just leaned back in his chair with the stale dinner roll, smearing on a layer of margarine, pulling pieces off and eating them.

"Hey, dude." Chris leaned over encouragingly. "We do still get some stuff, you know, that they bring us. I told you, you just need to put in a request. It's not like we live on this shit."

"No?"

Everyone else seemed to be eating it, though. Well, maybe not. Kechia had abandoned the lasagna and was constructing a sandwich with the roll, salad, and Italian dressing.

Moe scraped the whole hunk of lasagna out of the little plastic tub and chewed on one end. He bit off a chunk, tossed the rest back onto his plastic tray. "Yeah," he muttered, "we get treated like kings here."

Diana sighed, giving him a sort of thin-lipped smile, and shrugged.

"It's not ideal, no. But it is what it is. Make the best of it, that's all." But she was just picking at the wilted lettuce.

Jason was suddenly aware of how thin she was, under her scrubs. *Criminy, her arms are like sticks. How did I miss that?*

Kechia pulled out a remote control. "You guys don't mind if the TV is on, right?" She grinned at Jason. "We like to pretend we still have some connection to the outside world, keep an eye on its degradation. Though none of us have been able to vote, so you know…not our fault. Right?"

Jason made a halfhearted attempt at a sympathetic chuckle.

Kechia pointed the remote at the TV and flipped channels till she found the local news. Jason stared at it, grateful there was something he could focus on, but uninterested in whatever it was going on about. There had been a fire somewhere. There was a shooting somewhere. Someone was dead. Another someone was also dead, somewhere else. Jason's eyes slid away. His concentration was ebbing, his mind getting cloudy again. *Must be the pills.*

Kechia's voice drifted by. "That is some bullshit, right there…"

Jason didn't even register what she was talking about. Something on the TV. He leaned his head forward onto his hand but failed to put his hand where his head was going, so he just sort of toppled forward until Chris caught him by the shoulder and pulled him back upright. He tried again, succeeded this time, braced himself against the arm and back of the chair. His stale, half-margarined dinner roll fell out of his hand.

~

Through the fog, in the distance, in the past, he saw himself walking through the streets with Molly. Back when they'd first gotten together, when everything he learned about her was new and exciting. *She* was new and exciting. A couple of years older, a college graduate. She had a *degree*. She was a fully formed person. He was still trying to figure out how to act, how to pretend like he was a grown up. She had wanted, that afternoon, to show off her college campus. Jason didn't really get why. He'd been to college, for a couple of semesters anyway. He knew what a college campus looked like—brick buildings, classrooms, libraries, whatever. But she was insistent, and he wanted so much for her to like him, so he allowed her to lead him down the streets and onto the grounds of her alma mater. And then he stopped, gaping, and exclaimed, "You went to school in a *castle?*"

She laughed, of course, and they meandered through the gothic buildings and by the gargoyles and towers, under latticed gates and over stone bridges, and stopped to sit on a little stone bench next to a pond full of lily pads and turtles so she could point to the building she used to work in, and the café where she used to buy two-dollar milkshakes, and the gratuitously extravagant concert hall where she'd worked as an usher so she could get free tickets. Later, she told him that she hadn't spent that much time there, she'd mostly studied in the utilitarian and pragmatic science library, but she liked to wander around.

It was such a beautiful place. An absurd, unnecessary beauty.

He couldn't see the point. Why have gargoyles leering out from every corner, spires and turrets and towers under creeping ivy? Why bother? But in the end, he could see the reason for it. When she enfolded his hand in both of hers, leaned against his chest, stared up at the architecture with admiration and affection, glowing, he could understand. It brought her joy, so it brought him joy. So he loved it, too, this strange, alien castle in the middle of an urban battleground.

~

"Jason. Jason. Here. Eat your dinner."

He did not want to be pulled out of his reverie, pulled back into the present. There was nothing in the present for him. Nothing that would bring him joy, not ever again, not without Molly.

He pushed away the hands that were proffering him food, shoved the plastic tray away from him. A cup of water tipped over, spilled. Someone cried out in protest. Jason could see his bedroom door, off in the great distance. He pulled himself out of the chair, stumbled, caught himself, shuffled toward the door, and then fell onto the bed. Curled up, hugged himself. But did not cry.

卐

There are few things as disorienting as waking up in a teenage girl's bedroom.

Brigid spent a few minutes staring bleary-eyed at the photo collage on the wall, bedecked with ribbons and banners with inspirational slogans. Photographs of laughing teenagers, making faces; some shots of a girl's lacrosse team on the field, a group portrait. She pushed down the frilly hem of the bedspread and found Lithium's face peering at her. He didn't seem particularly perturbed. His tail gently thumped the bed and he hesitated for a moment before leaping to the floor, where he wagged and woofed impatiently by the door. There were distant clattering sounds, muffled conversation audible. Ana and David must be up already. She rubbed her eyes, rolled over to look at the digital clock on the bedside table. *6:30. Ugh.*

She managed to make it to the kitchen about half an hour later, after spending ten solid minutes staring at her face in the mirror, poking her nose gently with her finger, wiggling her loose teeth, probing her cheekbones. The latter felt intact, so that was something. If she'd thought to pack some makeup, maybe she could've made herself somewhat presentable. *But I didn't, so I can't. So, fine.*

Ana was predictably cheery. Of course she'd be a morning person. She set a mug down in front of Brigid, filled it with coffee. "Milk? Have some breakfast. We've been talking." She nodded at David. "We think today I should talk to our lawyer. You could talk to the police, maybe. Surely they will be able to search the lab, eh? We have probable cause? Well, not the strongest case, no. But we will see. Lawyer first, eh? I will go later this morning. David has some work to take care of, downtown. We can meet him for lunch in the afternoon, if you like. Maybe in the meantime you can look into talking to the police? You had a contact in Boston?"

"Oh, yeah. I have his phone number, uh I *had* his phone number. Actually, I'm not sure...I may have lost it. But he emailed me once... so I think I can get in touch with him. Do you have Wi-Fi? I have a tablet, I can check."

"Excellent! Yes. We will pool our resources, come up with a plan. Eat, have some cereal, or yogurt. What will your dog have?"

Brigid excused herself to take Lithium for his walk and fetched his kibble from the car. When they returned, Ana gave her a slip of paper with their Wi-Fi password on it before she and David left to meet with their lawyer. Lithium ate kibble out of a plastic Tupperware while Brigid opened her email.

Yuck. So many emails. Mostly junk. One from work again.

> We hope you're feeling better. But if we don't hear from you regarding your expected attendance within the next day or two we'll be forced to take action. Please remember that accumulating more than three consecutive sick days requires a doctor's note. We look forward to hearing from you.

Oh, shut up. I just can't...just can't even, right now.
And one from O'Leary.

> Ms. Sullivan: We need you to come in to the station. We have some questions regarding the situation in Revere. Contact me ASAP to avoid complicating the situation.

Her heart lurched a bit. *Am I in trouble? "Situation"?*

She sat for a while, chewing on her thumbnail, debating whether to respond.

I guess I have to...whatever way I look at it, I have to. If I don't, it'll look worse for me. Besides, maybe he just needs to know the details, so he can arraign and prosecute Not-Smith. Right? Maybe he's on my side. Still, maybe I just don't need to mention exactly where I am.

So she wrote back.

> Detective O'Leary: I'm sorry about calling in the middle of the night. I was abducted and assaulted by the man who identified himself as FBI Agent Smith at your precinct. He indicated that he was planning on killing me.

God, this sounds so melodramatic.

I was forced to defend myself, which is how he ended up handcuffed to a tree.

Jesus.

Then I had to drive his car back to my motel, so please note that I didn't steal it. I left it at the Camelot Motel on Route 1. I had to leave the area for my own protection so I am not able to come to the station. I'm sorry about that. But his accomplices also abducted my friend, he was taken to Chicago I think. I think he's being kept prisoner in a lab located on the South Side. It used to be run by a scientist named Dr. Ana Hernandez, but she was kicked out and now we don't know who's in charge but we have reason to believe people are being hurt or maybe killed so we could really use some help.

Well, shit, now this has just gone off the rails. He's going to full on think I'm crazy.

I know you're going to think I'm crazy but look her up, she's a legit scientist, and my friend who was kidnapped, his name is Jason Reyes, and he used to be a subject in the lab and we think he's probably been taken back there. Also, in case it wasn't clear, this is definitely connected to that guy who broke into my condo. Please help.
Yours sincerely, Brigid Sullivan.

Yeah, that should do it.

曱

Jason lay awake on his bed, not moving, listening to voices and rustling from the next room. He could smell coffee. Periodically, someone would peek into his room, and he'd close his eyes and feign sleep until they tiptoed away again.

His head felt a bit clearer than it had the night before. Maybe the pills were wearing off. He wondered if they'd worn off enough to try a jump. *Maybe?* He was still tired, but... *How far would I be able to get this time, though, realistically? I don't have the energy to last very long, not in a...what was it...alternaverse. But still, if I could just make it out of the building...someone would probably call the authorities over a naked man running through the street, right? I could be taken into custody, could tell people what was happening here. Would that be an improvement? Would they believe me?*

Worst case, though, I'd just end up back here. I mean, I have to try. I've done it before, maybe I can do it again.

He closed his eyes, steadied his breathing, cleared his mind. It didn't take that much effort to reach that state of clarity, transcendence, nirvana, whatever it was called. But, when he tried to push himself out of phase, nothing happened. He just got a little light headed.

Well, I guess not, then.

The suite door unlocked and one of the guards—the goateed one he recognized from the night before—entered, pushing a cart loaded with foil-covered plastic trays. A second guard—older, heavyset and heavy lidded—stood by the door, fingering a baton. Jason closed his eyes but had to open them again, reluctantly, as the younger guard shook him gently by the shoulder.

"Hey. Time to get up. Time for your meds."

Jason pushed himself upright, took the paper cup and tipped the pills into his mouth. Looked around for water. No water. *Fucking hell.* He shuffled into the kitchen. The pills were starting to dissolve, they tasted awful. He filled a cup and washed the pills down.

"Mouth open. Tongue up."

Jason glowered at him, tried to rinse the bitter medicinal flavor out of his mouth.

Diana walked into the kitchen, poured herself a mug of coffee. "Hi, Ramon."

The goon brightened. "Hey, Diana. Sleep well?"

"Yeah, for sure. Hey, uh...we getting any deliveries today?"

"Yeah, I think I can drop by." The goon glanced at Jason briefly. "Around two, probably."

"Great. See you then."

Jason stared at Diana as the goons exited. "Buddies, or something?"

"I told you, they're not all bad."

Jason got his own cup of coffee and curled up on a chair in the common room, eying the plastic trays. They smelled like eggs and salt. Like sulfurous flatulence. Flatulent sulfur? The ghosts of half-digested hot dogs belched up after too much beer.

He blew on the coffee. Chris sat down, bit into his toast. Kechia flopped into another chair with a cup of coffee. Moe was missing. Maybe he was still asleep? Jason rubbed his head, sipped his coffee. It was too bitter and too hot. Still, it was better than whatever was lurking in the plastic trays.

"What, uh…" he ventured, staring at his coffee. "Like what happens, usually, as a sort of routine, here?"

Kechia peered up with her left eyebrow raised and half a smile. "Routine? We wake up, we eat some shit food, we wait to see if we're scheduled for an exciting day of torture and villainy, we eat some more shit food, we try to forget about the bleakness of existence, and then we go to sleep again. How's that for routine? Good?"

Jason didn't answer.

"Moe's gone already, you may have noticed," Chris murmured. "Got tapped early."

"I thought he was asleep."

Chris shook his head ruefully. "Moe doesn't sleep, really. Not as far as I can tell. And I'm his effing roommate."

Jason's heart sagged a little, hearing this. They used to be close, him and Moe, well, him and Moe and Molly. They used to hang out, they used to have fun. Moe used to be fun.

~

Midsummer, after Molly had moved in with him, a sweltering July day. Moe had called them and suggested they go out to this one local bar, hide out in some AC, shoot some pool, shoot the shit.

Jason and Molly found Moe in the back, at one of the picnic table-type tables, under a giant mural of a smiling Obama. He was leaning against the wall, one leg on the bench, studying his phone. They sidled in across from him and he looked up, grinned, shut the phone off. There were a few people at other tables, chatting, snippets of conversations occasionally bobbing up, but it was early still and pretty quiet. Jason glanced at the people sitting at the table behind Moe—two girls, one with long disheveled hair in a ponytail, the other sporting a topknot, both in t-shirts and jeans. A pair of backpacks underneath them. Students, then. The one facing away twisted around briefly, ignored Jason and Molly, stared at Moe until he noticed and nodded a greeting. She giggled and whirled back. Jason rolled his eyes. Undergrads.

Moe stood up. "Hang on, I'll get the drinks. What you want? IPA?" Jason shrugged.

Molly shook her head. "Cider. A good cider, not that trashy stuff. Thanks!"

Moe returned balancing two glasses and a brown bottle. Molly took a long sip from her cider. Jason took a smaller sip from his drink, wincing a little at the bitterness. He actually hated IPAs. He drank them anyway because they were so popular, he assumed he must be missing something, or maybe it would just take time for him to develop a taste for it. Thus far, he had not done so. He eyed Molly's cider with envy.

Moe took a swig from the bottle. "Yeah, that hits the spot! I've been dying. So hot."

Jason sipped again. Still bitter.

Molly drained about a third of her drink, looked over at Moe. "Uh huh, for sure. You should've started without us!"

"Didn't want to be rude."

Molly laughed. "We would have forgiven you. Actually, it's funny, I didn't think you drank. Well, I didn't think you were allowed to."

Jason looked at her quizzically. "Because of the…because he's a health nut?"

"I'm not a health nut. I just care about my physique. Everything in moderation anyway. But I think she's talking about religion. You an expert on my religion, Moll?"

"You know, I took a class. I learn things. I'm a smart person, I'll have you know." She tapped her temple with an index finger.

Jason muttered, "Oh," and turned back to his beer. Hoped neither of them noticed his confusion. They didn't. He took a longer pull off the IPA. Maybe the secret was just to suck it all down as quickly as possible. It probably wouldn't be so bad if he chased it with something, peanuts or chips or whatever. He peered over at the bar, tried to see if they sold snacks.

Moe smirked, idly swung his bottle around by the neck. "Yeah, my parents would probably kill me. They're a lot more traditional. But me, I'm a rebel. A maverick. Drives the ladies crazy." He glanced over at the two students, who were studiously pretending to ignore him. The topknotted girl facing them arched her back in a stretch. Her t-shirt bore a university crest—an eagle sticking its tongue out, underneath a book inscribed with the words "Where Fun Goes To Die" in fancy calligraphy. Molly sniggered to herself, watching. Moe shrugged, unfolded himself off the bench. "You guys down for a game of darts? I'll go get 'em."

Jason looked up hopefully. "Get me some chips or something if they have 'em, would you?"

"Yeah."

Molly knocked back the rest of her cider, rubbed Jason's knee. He automatically leaned into her, closed his eyes for a moment. Inhaled her odor, sweat and deodorant and that oil she used in her hair and a faint fruitiness on her breath.

"I'm not sure it's the maverick thing that drives the ladies crazy."

Jason opened his eyes. Molly was eyeing Moe, over at the bar, chatting with the bartender. "Huh?"

"You know. That boy, he's fine. He could be a complete douchebag and he'd still score. Those eyes? I mean, damn. Like the girl in that *National Geographic* photo, right? Women melt before his dreamy gaze."

Jason looked over at Moe, thinking. His eyes. He did have brilliant dark green eyes. Unusual, given his coloring. They should have been brown. Weird.

Molly's eyes, chestnut brown, the right color, flicked back to the two students who were unabashedly staring at Moe now. "Frankly, he's really missing out on an opportunity to be a douchebag. Wasting his time being all, like, *nice* and stuff." She snickered.

"You think he's hot?" Jason felt a tickle of jealousy. *Him? Moe? With his weird green eyes?*

"Jason. Come on. Everyone thinks he's hot." She nodded at the two undergrads. "Ask them."

"I hadn't noticed…I mean, I don't really…like, I don't notice men being attractive."

Molly groaned. "Really? Your masculinity is that fragile? Just admit it, it's not a big deal. He's hot. If you're into that sort of thing, you know, I'm just saying. Human beauty in any form does well to be appreciated, as my sister likes to say." She squeezed his knee again. "But you're the one who got lucky here. You know, he gets all the princesses, sure. You're the one who scored the queen."

~

Was that really how it went down? Was he misremembering? Was he forgetting bits, snipping out the pieces he didn't like? Did she really say that, or did he want her to have said it?

He wasn't sure. He wasn't sure he trusted his memory anymore.

His mind was starting to cloud over. *How long since I took those pills? How quickly do they kick in? Pretty quick, it seems. Wait…but.* "So…but wait. Where's Moe?"

"They came and fetched him this morning. Earlier. He'll be back later."

"Oh." Jason eyed the door. It seemed ominous, now, somehow.

"Don't worry about it," Kechia said, grinning wryly. "They'll come for you, too."

卐

Brigid spent most of the morning staring at her tablet screen, wondering if sending the email was the right move. *Should I regret it? No. Yes? Is there something else I should be doing? What would that something be?*

I ought to be doing something, right? This is pointless, sitting here, wasting time. Shouldn't I be gathering an army, girding up for a heroic invasion, something along those lines? Isn't that what happens in the movies? Or investigating, gathering evidence for some sort of courtroom showdown?

She imagined herself on a witness stand, eloquently and righteously condemning this evil facility, defying a slimy defense attorney who was trying to paint her as unreliable or shifty, but no, her integrity would shine through, none of the jurors would be fooled, the whole organization would come crashing down in a pile of smoking rubble. Flashbulbs would blind her as she descended the courtroom steps to the shouted questions of reporters and journalists. "How did you find the strength and courage to take on such a terrifying and dangerous organization? You, a simple telemarketer with no training or experience." She would be a fascinating subject, this woman out of nowhere, swooping in to save the day.

Except I'm not doing any swooping, or any saving. I'm sitting around with my metaphorical thumb up my metaphorical ass. Savior fantasies aren't going to get me anywhere. But going out there, all on her own…that was scary. Scary and intimidating. *I don't think I could actually accomplish anything. Here, with Ana, I'm safe. Safe and warm.*

She scratched Lithium's head. He looked at her expectantly, grumbled softly and lay back down when he realized she had nothing to offer him.

She sighed, wasted some time wandering the halls of the Internet, checked the news. *The world's going to hell, what else is new.* Checked out some comedy websites. Took a bunch of BuzzFeed quizzes, learned what her dessert choices suggested about her eye color. Waited for Ana to return.

⌘

They came for Jason. They brought Moe back first, in the late morning. He was led in, stumbling, eyes shut, pale, and deposited without ceremony in one of the lounge chairs. He leaned his head on his hand, wrapped his other arm around his stomach, all without opening his eyes. There were weird yellow discolorations around his upper arms.

Diana glanced at Kechia and switched off the television, which had been on some home renovation show. The room fell jarringly silent. Chris went over to Moe without looking at the two goons who'd brought him in, murmured something in his ear. Moe nodded, took a deep breath and allowed Chris to help him up and into his bedroom. Jason watched the scene with something akin to horror. A sort of vague, fuzzy horror.

The horror sharpened when one of the goons walked over to him and took him by the arm. "You're up. Come on."

Jason's eyes widened. He stared, alarmed, at Diana and Kechia.

Diana came over and rubbed his shoulder reassuringly. "It'll be okay. Just take things easy. You'll be all right." She turned to one of the goons, her friend from the morning, and said, "Just...take care of him, okay?" The other guy rolled his eyes and tugged on Jason's arm.

Jason stood up, shaking a bit, and allowed himself to be escorted out of the room. He tripped on nothing as he went through the door. One of the two men seized his upper arm, evidently mistaking his clumsiness for an attempt to bolt.

Ha.

The door locked automatically behind him.

The walk to the white room seemed to take longer than he remembered. Maybe he was walking slower. It did seem to take an awful lot of effort to coordinate his ambulation. He tripped twice more in the hallway. The third time, neither of his chaperones made any move to catch him.

The white room again. Mirror on the one wall. Not a mirror, though. One-way glass. Someone probably watching on the other side. Laptop computer on a table, sprouting a mess of wires and cords. Next to the laptop was a strange device, about six inches long, a black touchscreen on one side and a sort of wand extending from the end. It looked like a modified smartphone-type thing. Chairs on either side of the table. One of the chairs was bolted to the floor. There were straps dangling off the arms. Restraints. The two guards pushed Jason into that chair and secured his wrists onto the arms. He tried not to dwell on the implications of being tied to a chair, tried not to focus on his pounding heart. One of them unlocked and opened a drawer, removed a package—a white paper bag with a clear plastic window, sealed, something bulky inside. He set it on the desk, put on a pair of purple latex gloves, tore open a small packet containing a wet brown swab which he used to scrub both of Jason's upper arms. The brown fluid dripped off his elbows and onto the floor, leaving small yellow splashes. Jason watched, curious, nervous.

The goon opened the package and removed a thick white plastic ring, a collar-type thing. Hinged. He put it on Jason's left arm, over the scrubbed area, and closed it. It clicked as it locked into place. He did the same thing on the right arm with a second ring. The two armbands were snug but not uncomfortable. There were four little slots on each armband. The goon inserted a little chip into each one, like those little memory cards that go in digital cameras. He took out a skullcap with a bunch of electrodes dangling from it and tugged it onto Jason's head, stuck a set of EKG leads onto Jason's chest, under his shirt. The wires from all these gadgets ran into the laptop on the table.

The two goons retreated to the corners of the room, leaving Jason alone in his chair by the table. One of them pressed a button by the door. Nothing happened for a few minutes. Just silence, other than blood rushing in Jason's ears. *Is that real? Maybe I'm making it up.* He looked over at the two men. *What are they supposed to be anyway? Orderlies?* They were wearing the standard white jumpsuit, so maybe. *Why a white jumpsuit, though? They'd be more suited to…what, tracksuits, maybe. Whatever thugs wear. Maybe they're wearing tracksuits and big gold chains underneath the jumpsuits.* The corner of Jason's mouth twitched. *Ha, that's funny.* He imagined them tearing open their shirts, Superman-like, to reveal giant gold-plated dollar sign pendants and Adidas jackets. For a second, he forgot about the terror. Just for a second, though.

His nose itched. *Dammit.*

Wilders came in and sat down in front of the laptop. He was wearing a lab coat. *Over a fucking suit! Again with the lab coat over a suit. And that hair.* Slicked back from his forehead. Too much gel, so it clumped together in tiny linear cornrows. Pale blue eyes, a weak chin, slack lips that somehow always looked wet. An air of haughty entitlement, all the more maddening for being so undeserved. Jason wanted to punch him in his porous bulbous nose. *He looks fucking absurd.*

"All set, sir."

Wilders nodded at his goon—the fat one—opened his laptop and tapped something out. He glanced briefly up at Jason. "This may sting a bit."

The goon pressed a tiny button on the left armband, and Jason yelped. *The thing fucking bit me. It bit me! Sting a bit?* It felt like he'd been stabbed by a dozen little needles. A couple of little drops of blood trickled down his arm. *Christ. It did stab me.* His arm was on fire. He gripped the chair and sucked air in through his teeth.

The goon stepped over to Jason's right arm, and he had time to realize what was happening and cry out once in protest before the same thing happened on that side. He arched his back, scrabbled his heels forward, and yanked at the restraints, but he couldn't move the chair or dislodge himself. He groaned, gritting his teeth, fear and pain and anger mixed together.

Wilders appeared unmoved.

"All right, let's get started. We have our initial coordinates in place." He picked up the device next to the computer, the thing with the wand, examined its touchscreen, and then handed it to the older goon who moved to stand behind Jason.

Jason's fingernails dug into the armrests. He was panting, both arms burning, tiny pockets of blood gathering in the crooks of his elbows. He couldn't see the goon behind him. He tried to look around, but a pair of gloved hands seized his head, pushed it forward so he was looking down, scared, shaking, his arms throbbing, and something pressed against the base of his skull and everything exploded.

Black. Black punctuated by flashes of light.

Roaring, a constant rushing in his ears.

Off in the distance, Jason could hear a sort of gasping, hiccupping. The roaring gradually faded, the gasping got louder, and Jason recognized his own gulping breaths. He was still in the chair, bent forward and gripping the armrests, eyes squeezed shut, teeth bared in a grimace. Echoes of pain washed through his head, reverberating but dying away, until finally he was able to open his eyes and stare unfocused at his feet. Green felt slippers. He hadn't even registered the slippers before.

Slowly, his breathing steadied, quieted, but he remained slumped over, staring at his slippers.

He heard, as if through cotton, "...going to alter one of our calculations. Let's see, I think it may be the medication, but we'll try this...here. Get him up. Is he awake? Get him up."

Jason remained frozen. He closed his eyes again, held his breath, hoped maybe they'd leave him alone.

They didn't. Someone tilted his chin up, pried open his eyelids. He was momentarily blinded, as a penlight flicked back and forth between his eyes. He could hear rapid beeping from the EKG monitor. He blinked a few times. Wilders was still sitting across the table, tapping at his laptop, ignoring him. The wand device was back on the table.

The thinner goon—Ramon—murmured, "I think he may need a few minutes, sir."

Wilders stared at his laptop screen for a beat longer, pursed his slack lips. Swiveled his chair to glower at the offending goon but said nothing, only held out the wand device.

Ramon muttered, "Sorry, sir," took it and stepped behind Jason.

Jason shook his head. Panic rushed over him. "No. No. No—" and someone pushed his head down and the world exploded again.

And again. And again. Every blackout a vivid nightmare, a level of agony that was almost a violation. He couldn't keep track of time, couldn't even keep track of how many times it happened, couldn't understand why. *What do they want anyway? What is he expecting? What's the point? Is he just a sadist?* Jason didn't know what to do, what to say to make Wilders stop.

He wanted to resist. He wanted to fight, but he couldn't, he didn't even have the energy to pull himself up...no, he didn't even want to fight.

He just wanted to curl up in a ball and pass out or cry or die. Or maybe all three.

Off in the distance, he heard Wilders again. "Is he awake? We have one more, I think."

Light in his eyes again, then the lights were gone, replaced by darkness and indistinct figures, and the distant image of green felt slippers. His head was spinning, and he braced for the rhythmic tides of pain that would come splashing around his skull.

A hand on his shoulder, pushing him forward.

A whispered plea, "Stop, stop it," but even he couldn't really hear it, and something pressed against the back of his neck again and he tensed for the inevitable explosion—

And he fell, crumpled into a heap on the floor, wrapping his arms around his head.

He lay curled on the floor for a few beats, waiting for the spasms to subside. It dawned on him that his arms were free, that he was no longer in the chair. He opened his eyes to see an unfamiliar room.

Holy shit. I jumped.

He struggled to sit upright, looked around, squinting in the bright light. His clothes were gone, his nakedness almost reassuring in its familiarity. He tried to get his bearings. He seemed to be in…what…a room, like the white room, but orange instead. His chair was gone, the desk gone, but there was a door in the same place, a mirror in the same place. There were bug-eyed cartoon elephants and zebras on the walls, a sunset with silhouetted giraffes. Somewhat worn carpet on the floor, felt toys in a bin, a playpen, a half-full clothes hamper, and cameras in each corner of the ceiling.

A playpen.

A playpen?

He pushed himself backwards till he hit the wall, leaned on the wicker hamper as he struggled to his feet. His arms hurt—stung—when they contacted the wall. He glanced down, annoyed, at the armbands biting into him.

The armbands. They're still on. How is that possible?

He pulled on one of them, but it just started oozing blood again. He stopped, staring at the playpen. *A baby's room. This is a baby's room.* A baby's room, in the exact location as the white room in the lab.

His head spun.

He stumbled over to the playpen, peered inside.

The infant was sleeping, or had been sleeping, but awoke as Jason peered in. Lying on its back, without a blanket, just a few toys scattered around. Smooth perfect cheeks, bright brown eyes, a tiny little nose, dark curls over its forehead. A spray of microscopic pimples over its temples.

Dimples when it saw him and giggled, a couple of teeth peeking out.

In the distance, Jason thought he heard alarms, shouting, scuffling. He ignored it.

He paused, blinking, transfixed, the pain in his head momentarily forgotten. Leaned over the edge of the playpen, reached down toward a tiny waving hand that caught his finger and tugged it—

And suddenly, violently, he was yanked back, jerked away from the child, jerked out of the fabric of space, thrown down on the hard, uncarpeted floor of the white room, the two guards seizing his arms and pulling him back up and into the chair. He screamed, from the pain and from confusion and inexplicable but palpable loss, struggling, fighting, twisting, slipping, and finally blacking out entirely.

⌗

Through the window of a downtown cafe, Brigid watched the tourists meandering down Michigan Avenue and through a park across the street. Some shining chrome monstrosity gleamed in the distance, barely visible beyond a grove of trees. A waiter appeared over her shoulder, setting sandwiches down before Ana and David. Brigid had a bowl of soup. Chewing was still something of an ordeal.

"Any luck on your end?" David asked politely.

Brigid shrugged. "I got an email from the Boston cop that I worked with, you know, after the break-in. He seems a little pissed. I'm not sure, someone may show up here. I mean, I can't be 100 percent sure that they're not in on it? You know, if this is a government thing. But I got a good vibe from him. He didn't trust that FBI guy. I mean, that speaks volumes in my book. Right?

"I was thinking also, if the police do show up…in terms of having any sort of evidence to support our story. What do we have? There's the guy who broke into my condo. He's in custody. I assume he was working with FBI guy…non-FBI guy…but I don't know what his status is, like whether they dug up any background on him that might connect him to the lab. Maybe they did. That would be helpful. And there's FBI guy. I mean, I don't think he's actually FBI. I think he's fake. But, truthfully, I don't actually know. There is the chance this is some sort of government conspiracy. Which would be…a problem."

Ana tilted her head thoughtfully. "You think the government took over the lab?"

"Well, I don't know. What happened, exactly? Jason wasn't clear. I don't think he understood."

Ana leaned back and crossed her legs. "Hmm. That's an interesting thought. I had wondered, briefly, as well, now that you bring it up." She sipped her iced tea and set the glass down on the table. "The short version is, I worked in that lab for…oh…nearly two decades, I think. That may be a bit misleading. Much of the original work was theoretical, not with actual subjects. Jason and the rest, they were my first group of human subjects. Prior to that, we ran some animal trials, and of course there was the whole development phase…but no, my point is that we had been there for a long time, working. Originally, I had a grant from the NSF, which funded me up through the initial research."

"What is that, NSF?"

"National Science Foundation. Once we started developing the distractor technology itself, though, we had to look for funding elsewhere, as you may recall that federal funding for scientific research was cut back fairly significantly a few years ago. We ended up getting a private grant from an institute called the John M. Hereford Foundation. We called the project 'Alternate Wavefunction.' That was independent of any federal or government funding. It did come with certain stipulations. For one, any papers had to be cleared by the executive board before being submitted for publication. I resented that. Research, in my opinion, should be divorced from any meddling by individuals outside of the scientific community." She frowned. "You understand? Individuals who may have ulterior motives, individuals who maybe do not understand the significance of the work. There was a clear reluctance to allow publication of new discoveries, even…especially when we made major breakthroughs. This, this…concealment, this hiding of advancements, it handicaps the scientific community as a whole. You understand? We were not designing, I don't know, a computer operating system, or app, or similar. We were trying to unlock the secrets of space, time, quantum physics. It is a collaborative process, not a secretive one." She shook her head. "It was absolutely the wrong approach. But we needed funding. We could not move forward without it and, when we lost the federal grant, we failed to find any adequate alternatives, so we saw no way around it."

"So...the private grant, what, ran out?"

"No. We were very careful with our budgeting. Very careful. No, one of the other stipulations of accepting the Hereford grant was that we had to allow certain individuals to come, er...observe our work. Initially, that was not a problem. No one was interested. Quantum physics is... sometimes difficult to explain to a layperson. The JMH representatives would show up, we would try to explain our process, and the next day they would be absent. But once we really started to make progress, they were around more and more. Eventually, we were notified that a team of men would need to be present for all trials, that we were obligated to turn over copies of all raw data to them even before we had finalized our work. It was all...very irregular."

Brigid nodded. "Oh. Yeah, Wilders, right? Jason mentioned him."

"Slimy little bastard. He didn't just observe, you understand. He... interfered. He would try to direct the course of the experiments, the trials. And he had a—to say nicely—a limited vision. He was excited about our success. Jason especially, he had a knack for it, he learned how to phase shift much more quickly than I had expected. But Wilders seemed to be...well, he wanted to take advantage of potential technological advancements that my subjects might encounter in alternate worlds. And I certainly understand that temptation." One of her eyebrows wandered upwards, facetiously. "But we had barely begun to understand phase shifting as a whole. We had barely scratched the surface. We didn't even understand how it was affecting the subjects, and that, frankly, was a matter of no little concern."

"What do you mean?"

"Well, consider. When we first sent people into outer space, they came back with certain health ailments, because the human body is not designed to stay in space for prolonged periods of time. You understand? For example, radiation damage, muscle atrophy, loss of bone density. And we did not understand the details, the specifics of these issues until we had actual physical data from astronauts, after they came home. Now, Jason and my other subjects, they were traveling not to outer space but to entirely separate and parallel realities. What would this do, physically? We had no idea. Well, that is not completely true, of course. We had had animal trials already, akin to Laika—"

Brigid held up her hand. "What's a laika?"

"You remember, the dog the Russians sent into space? Laika. We also sent animal subjects to alternate realities. We did learn much, it allowed us to make alterations to our final prototype for human use, but still there were some limitations. And we were very concerned, very concerned indeed, about some of the physical damage that we were seeing in our subjects. Ultimately, I recommended that we suspend further trials with our human subjects, to allow us to modify the devices, study the effects we had been seeing. Protect our subjects from…unnecessary endangerments. But our sponsors, no, they did not like this idea. And, shortly after that, I was informed that my research team—that was my postdoc Erin and my research assistant Vijay—that their positions had been terminated. And then I was informed that the funding had been withdrawn, and since, as part of the original contract all the research and data belonged to JMH Foundation, well, they took all my data, all my work, they banned me from the lab."

"None of that sounds legal."

"No. I agree, I do not think it is. We have been focusing, over the past year, on taking them to court over this. I meet with my lawyer maybe once a week. But, thus far, we have not had much luck." She shook her head again. "It is a frustrating thing. But maybe, now that we have your testimony, your new information, maybe we will find something we can use."

卐

Jason came around slowly, a pain-siren from the back of his brain, everything smeared together like a hand wiped through wet paint. He could hear murmuring in the distance, voices, but the words escaped him. He lolled his head over, watched one of the goons—fat goon, not Ramon—unlock and remove the armbands. Tiny needles on the interior surfaces of the armband rings tugged at his skin as they came away. His arms started bleeding again. The goons wrapped him in a hospital gown, pulled him back into the chair, bandaged his arms with gauze.

"Very good. Very good. Did you save those settings? Good. Jason… Jason. Come on, now. It's time for your debriefing."

Jason moaned. *Debriefing. A weird word. Interrogation might be a better one.*

An interrogation. Describe the surroundings. What color was the room? What size? Where was the mirror? What sort of furniture was in the room? What sort of lighting? Were there other individuals present? Did you notice any specific odors? Sounds? Music?

Jason mumbled vague, monosyllabic responses, too exhausted to do much else.

Wilders typed laboriously, two fingered, mounting frustration clouding his features. "Did you see, or see evidence of, an infant or child? Children?"

Jason balked, froze for a second. "No." *Shit. Wilders knows. Something. He knows something.*

Wilders looked up, saw Jason staring at him, narrowed his eyes.

Jason shifted his gaze to the laptop, unfocused. He was breathing faster than he should be, his eyes darting around of their own accord. *He can tell I'm lying. He has to know.* "No. No baby. Just a room. Nothing in it."

"It would behoove us all if you participated with honesty, Jason."

Jason blinked, shook his head slowly, tried to slow down his breathing. "Just a room." He rubbed his at his arms, gently, cautiously. "I feel sick. I'm gonna be sick." He leaned over, rested his elbows on his knees, hanging his head.

"You can go as soon as—"

Jason retched. Someone placed a wastepaper basket by his feet and a hand appeared on his shoulder.

"Sir, maybe…maybe this would be better once he's a little stronger." Ramon's voice, Jason thought. He glanced gratefully in Ramon's direction, but a wave of dizziness forced him to close his eyes again.

Wilders was silent for a few moments, presumably considering, then Jason heard the laptop click shut and Wilders snapped, "Fine. Reschedule. Go on, take him back."

Ramon and fat-goon half-dragged, half-carried him back down the hallway to the dorm suite. He watched them type in the code to the door. 4668. *I should remember that. Right? Probably.*

They dropped him on his bed. He curled up, pulled a sheet over himself, his eyes unable to focus. *What was that? Who was that?* He felt like something invisible had stabbed him in the chest. All he could see was an infant face smiling at him, familiar dimples, shining eyes. A tiny hand grasping his finger, tiny fingernails, tiny knuckles.

Chris came over, offered him a cup of water. "You do okay? Feeling all right?"

He pushed the cup away, even though this made the pounding in his head worse, moaned, hugged the sheet around him.

Chris left him alone.

⊞

Brigid woke the next day under the same frilly bedspread, but a bit less disoriented. Again, she heard the rattle of dishes and distant voices. Ana was up before her. *Lord save us from early risers.* Lithium jumped off the bed and whined impatiently at the door.

"Right. I'm up, I'm up." She rolled out of the bed, yawned, stretched. Pulled on a pair of jeans, a bra, a t-shirt, and a sweater so she could take Lithium out for his walk. "Morning," she said, as she walked past the kitchen and pulled on her shoes.

"Ah, Brigid! We were thinking…today perhaps we go to find Jason's family? See what they know, what they have been told. Perhaps it will help."

"Okay. Yeah. I'll be right back." She walked down the street, slowly because Lithium was sniffing every exotic blade of Midwestern grass and every heretofore unexamined gatepost.

There was a shiny black car parked half a block from Ana and David's house. Brigid eyed it suspiciously. *A government car, maybe. Looks like the government cars in TV shows about government conspiracies.* She noticed it had an Illinois license plate…and there was a stick figure family on the back window. *Nice touch. So, fifty-fifty, maybe government spies, maybe soccer mom.*

Back in the house, in the teenager's bedroom, Brigid examined her face again. It looked better, she thought. Not as puffy, and a lot of the reddish bruising was fading to a lovely yellowy-green. Probably a little more presentable for meeting Jason's parents.

She checked her tablet. Another flurry of emails, mostly junk. *What the hell, why am I still getting Myspace updates? Is that still a thing?* One from work, somewhat frostier than the previous one, informing her that if she remained incommunicado her position would be considered terminated. *Great. I haven't really been gone that long. Not really, right? Doesn't seem fair.* She was, after all, doing something more important than telemarketing. *Few things are* less *important, as far as I can tell.* She sighed, stared at the email, wondered if she should reply. *I'm going to lose my job.* She supposed she should feel regret about that, but, well, she didn't, even though it would probably be a good idea to have a job to go to when this was all done. *But, honestly, this might never be done. I'll probably end up in jail anyway.*

She remained incommunicado.

There was also another from O'Leary.

> Ms. Sullivan: Again it is very important that you contact me with regard to these pending cases. Please make yourself available or notify me of where we may locate you. This is a very serious matter please treat it as such.

Oh, he's getting mad, now. That actually affected her more than the threat of losing her job. She liked O'Leary, wanted his support, but he wasn't going to trust her if she kept avoiding him. She considered going down to the local police station. Maybe they'd arrest her, but maybe they wouldn't, and she would just build up some good credit. She bit her lip, conflicted. Ultimately didn't do anything, just closed her email. *Should definitely deal with it later, though. Definitely not just going to ignore it.*

"Brigid! Are you ready? We are going to head out soon, okay?"

Brigid looked up, stretched her back, fought the urge to yell back, "God, Mom! I'm *com*ing!" She unfolded her legs from her cross-legged position on the bed and tucked her wallet into her pocket.

The doorbell rang downstairs. Lithium woofed, tail wagging.

Brigid took one last look in the mirror and headed toward the stairwell. Downstairs, she heard the door open and Ana greeting the person. "Yes? How can I help you?"

"Hello, ma'am, I'm sorry to bother you. I'm Officer Jones, Chicago PD. I'm here on behalf of the Boston PD. We have reason to believe a person of interest in an incident in Boston may have attempted to contact you."

Brigid froze on the stairs, crouched down. Lithium bounded toward the door. She hissed at him but didn't follow. She couldn't see the door from her position, which meant the person standing there couldn't see her either, which struck her as fortuitous.

"Have you by any chance seen this person?"

Pause.

"No…who is this? What is this about? Shh, puppy, get back."

"This is with regard to a breaking and entering incident, and subsequent assault, in the Boston area. This person's name is Brigid Sullivan. Have you had any contact with her?"

Pause again.

"I did get a phone call from a Brigid. She had some questions for me regarding my research—I am a physicist. I believe Brigid had a friend who used to work with me? But I have not seen her. I spoke to her…hmm…yesterday or the day before, I believe. Nothing since. I am so sorry. Should I be worried?"

"No, ma'am. We're just here as a courtesy. But if you happen to hear from her again, please contact us immediately. Thank you. You have a good day now." There was a creak and the click of the door shutting.

Brigid straightened up slowly, then slipped downstairs with some trepidation. She found Ana in the kitchen, washing breakfast dishes. Lithium was sitting by her feet, staring up brightly, evidently hoping she would put a dish down for him to lick. "Hey. Uh, who was that?"

Ana turned around, beaming at her. "Ah, good morning. That was a police officer. He had a picture of you, he was asking me if I had seen you. Will you have coffee? Yes?" She took a mug from the cabinet, filled it from a half-full pot. "It's fine, I told him I had not. Well, I told him that you had called me. I don't know, maybe he will believe me. He went away. I do not think he cared very much. So! Today, perhaps we will visit Jason's family. You have their address? I think they will most likely be home, as it is Sunday. But perhaps we should call first? They may be at church. What do you think?" She handed Brigid the steaming mug. "Milk? Sugar is on the table there."

Brigid took the mug, wrapped her hand around it. "You told him you hadn't seen me?"

"Yes. Of course!"

"But…" Brigid gazed into the steam coming from the coffee, her brow furrowed. "You lied to the police? Why?"

"Well, I think we still have some work to do, yes? We can talk to the police when we are done. But, today, we will talk to Jason's parents."

⌗

Jason lay curled up in his bed in the dim morning, half asleep, aware of people moving around but not in any particular mood to join them. He'd been dreaming about something, couldn't remember what. It felt important, or at least appealing, and he felt like he could maybe slip back into the dream if he could just fall back asleep, so he allowed himself to drift along, drowsy, sedated. Unbidden images swirled around in his head—a kaleidoscope of shapes, colors, patterns without order. He watched them passively, let them invert and reform and evolve. Blue, yellow, red, blue again. Voices, it seemed, muffled, sounds that should be words. Sounds that were words.

"…will be grumpy later…" As if from a distance, amplified.

Blue, yellow, pale blue again. Vines reaching skyward against pale blue clouds.

"…If she doesn't…" Clearer.

Yellow coalescing into a form, a figure, walking through the vines, bouncing gently, turning toward him. A person, a woman, a familiar woman, cradling a wiggly bundle in her arms.

"...go down for a nap now."

Jason jerked awake, heart racing. Molly? Molly, clear as day, wearing a yellow t-shirt, holding a squirming infant, walking through a room with pale blue striped wallpaper. The baby was crying. He could remember the crying now, the thin wails. He could see Molly's face, see exasperation and fatigue. The crib against the wall, the toys on the floor, a changing table with a small stack of disposable diapers and a box of baby wipes, a bureau with one drawer ajar. Peach carpet on the floor, discolored where it had been walked over. A defect in one of the vertical stripes on the wall, interrupted by an electric outlet. Faint odor of baby powder. All of it, real, physically there, right in front of him. It vanished the instant he woke, replaced by nondescript off-white walls, a rumpled blanket. *Dammit, why am I awake? Fuck!*

He pushed himself up and sat leaning against the wall. From the other room he could hear quiet talking. There was a faint odor of coffee. He supposed he should probably shower, change clothes, but he didn't really have the motivation and he could sense a headache lurking but not quite manifest, waiting in the shadows. He felt muddled, confused, elated. *Molly.* The thought alone flushed him with excitement. *But why? Or how? Was that a jump? A hallucination? A dream? Didn't feel like a dream. It felt real. I could see them. They didn't see me.* A half-jump, or something...a window, a one-way mirror.

He got up, went to the bathroom, splashed some water on his face. Looked at his reflection. Bags under his eyes, lines forming around his mouth. A bit of stubble already. He braced himself on the sink, leaned close, peered at his eyes. Were his pupils larger than they should be? There was a tiny burst blood vessel in the white of his left eye, a little red pool reaching toward the brown iris. His mouth was dry, sticky. He wondered if that was from the pills, too, or just neglect of dental hygiene. The ghostly headache tapped at his skull. He closed his eyes, rinsed his mouth out with water, dried his face.

He found Chris and Moe in the common room, drinking coffee, reading the paper. Shuffled past them to the kitchen to get himself a cup.

Kechia was there, poking through the cabinet. "Hey, good morning. You sleep okay?"

"Yeah. Okay if I get some coffee?"

"Knock yourself out. You haven't seen a tub of raisins, have you? I can't find them."

"No. Thanks." Jason poured himself half a cup of coffee, watched Kechia for another moment, returned to the common room and sat down. "Where's Diana?"

"Sleeping, I guess. It's early." Moe put the paper down. "You okay? You sort of passed out last night."

"Yeah. It's the pills, I guess. Or…and I was tired."

"You missed dinner. It's okay, though. Chris ate it for you."

Chris's face appeared over his paper. "Hey! Shut up."

Jason grinned a little. "I wasn't hungry anyway." He flipped through the sections of newspaper on the table. The date seemed wrong, but he wasn't quite sure what the date should be. The only sections remaining were sports and the weekend magazine. He looked through the weekend section. Lots of activities that he would not be able to attend. He dropped it again. Leaned back in his chair with his coffee, thinking of the blue room, the orange room, Molly and the baby. God, he wanted to talk about this. He wished Brigid were around, wished he could ask her advice, her opinion. Well, just wished he could tell her, tell someone, without Wilders catching on. He gazed into his coffee, at the oily sheen on the surface, wrapped his hands around the mug looking for warmth.

The door beeped and opened, and Ramon pushed in a cart stacked with malodorous trays covered in foil. He left it by the door and handed Jason a little paper cup. Jason obediently took the cup, tipped the pills into his mouth and chased them with a swallow of coffee. The coffee was too hot. It burned, going down, and Jason coughed a few times.

Ramon nodded and knocked on Diana's bedroom door, opened it and slipped inside. Jason watched. Curious. He looked at Chris questioningly.

"Yeah, they have a thing. It's supposed to be all secretive and stuff, but…" He snorted. "Truthfully though, he's not a bad guy. He's the one who'll get us things on request, for the most part. There's like five others, but they don't like to talk to us."

"Yeah, well, if he were really concerned about our well-being, or cared about her, you'd think he would've…I don't know, blown the whistle…or at least, like, smuggled in a cell phone or something," Moe said, his eyes fixed on the closed bedroom door. Quiet voices were audible from within. "End of the day, he's still just a coward."

Chris went back to the paper.

Jason coughed again. The coffee was bitter and coated the back of his throat, and the smell from the cart was making him nauseous.

Moe picked up a tray, peeled back the foil, poked at some watery scrambled eggs with a plastic fork. "Well, great. Bacon and eggs. I swear they just do this to fuck with me." He looked over at Kechia. "You want one? Don't you get tired of cottage cheese and raisins?"

Kechia smiled wryly over her bowl. "No thanks."

Moe shrugged, offered a tray to Jason. "Jason, you should eat something."

This struck Jason as morbidly funny for some reason, and he laughed, or coughed, or both. His nose started to run, and it smelled like coffee. *Eat something. Who could eat at a time like this?* He couldn't stop thinking about Molly, about the vision of her and the baby, the vision that wasn't a vision, that was certainly real.

The room fell silent, other than the scraping of plastic on plastic. Jason stared unseeing at the newspaper on the table, wiped his nose. *Molly. Baby. Molly.*

After about half an hour, Ramon emerged from Diana's room, a bit flushed, his hair mussed. He looked over at Kechia. "You ready? You're up." Kechia put her mostly untouched bowl onto the coffee table, brushed off her shirt and pants. She glanced back at Jason as she walked to the door, left with Ramon.

Ana called Jason's parents and arranged to meet them at a café in Champaign, near where their daughter went to graduate school. A shorter drive than to Springfield. Brigid hadn't realized how far apart everything was in the Midwest.

She thought it would be prudent to meet in a public area, just in case. She wasn't completely sure she wasn't still being followed, or surveilled, or something. They—Wilders et al—they had tried to kill her. Surely, they weren't going to just forget about her now. *I wouldn't be surprised if someone was watching Ana's place, which of course means they're probably just a few cars behind us, but still. At least in a café it would be hard to sneakily kill us all. Hmm. Unless they just pull out a machine gun and mow everyone down.*

These trains of thought were disturbing.

Ana spent the first part of the drive explaining the minutia of her early research, how she'd first determined the possibility of shifting waveforms or wave functions or phases or something.

Brigid couldn't follow this for any length of time. After a little while, she was just automatically murmuring, "Yeah," and nodding, without registering anything Ana was saying.

Eventually, Ana stopped talking. After a brief silence, she suggested, chuckling, "This is maybe a bit much to comprehend at once, eh?"

Brigid, mirroring a polite smile, muttered, "Yeah, kind of." She elected not to try to explain to this woman—with her eight hundred academic degrees and decades of study and sheaves of publications—that she had an associate's degree and fifteen years' experience in trying to sell strangers shit they didn't need over the telephone and that these things had not prepared her for unlocking the secrets of space, time, and the cosmos.

She was quiet for the rest of the drive, ruminating on the debt she was accumulating to Ana. She really was going out on a limb to help her, Ana was. Lying to police, talking to lawyers, driving them out to interview Jason's parents. True, some of it was in her own self-interest. It was her lab, after all, and her research that had been stolen from her. It made sense that she should dedicate herself to getting it back. But this felt like more than that. Ana seemed genuinely concerned about Jason, the other lab subjects, and what was happening to them.

Well, maybe that shouldn't be a shock. She's a human being, of course she cares. What sort of person would turn their back on people in danger, people in need? Obviously, she'll do what she can to help, even if it means putting her own self and family in the crosshairs. Human nature, right?

Sure. Maybe.

They finally reached Champaign and found the café Jason's parents had suggested. The place was largely nondescript, yellow walls and white tables, pastries displayed in a glass case. Ana went to the counter and ordered a couple of fancy coffees while Brigid found them a table and sat, looking around. There was a corkboard mounted on the wall with the standard flyers—guitar lessons, art shows, that sort of thing. Funny that people still left flyers on corkboards, now that the Internet existed. She liked it. It felt nostalgic and sweet. She checked her watch, looked at the clock on the wall, checked her watch again. *How long should we wait before we decide that no one's coming? Well, they aren't supposed to arrive for another fifteen minutes. So probably at least fifteen minutes.*

The Reyeses arrived ten minutes later. Brigid was halfway through her coffee, the arty design on the foam long eradicated. She'd been debating getting up and buying a slice of coffee cake when a couple entered the cafe, scanning the faces of the diners. The woman was maybe ten years her senior. No gray in her black hair but lines around her eyes and mouth, an anxious expression. The man was shorter, heavyset with close-cropped salt and pepper hair, and a downturned mouth bordered by fleshy jowls. He was wearing a button-down short-sleeve shirt. The woman saw them first and approached with some trepidation. "Dr. Hernandez?"

"Yes! Yes, Ms. Reyes? My name is Ana, this is Brigid, it is so good to meet you. Sit! Sit, please. Can I get you something to drink, or eat? Please, sit."

The woman sat down, nodded politely at Brigid. "Hello, nice to meet you. I'm Jasmine. This is my husband, Danilo." She had an accent, foreign, difficult to place. "You knew my son?"

"Yes. Jason was a subject in my research. Perhaps he told you? He volunteered to participate in a research study, I was in charge of it. I knew him well, until I was forced to relinquish control of the project.

Since then I have not seen him, but Brigid here met him recently. She came all the way from Boston, to find me, so that we could help him."

Jasmine turned to stare at Brigid, a look of bewilderment on her face. "You...recently? What do you mean?"

Danilo scowled at the two of them. "Is this a joke? Some sort of scam? What is going on? Perhaps we should leave." He took his wife's hand, but she didn't acknowledge him.

Brigid started. "Wait. What? Why...why would this be a scam?" She looked at Ana for clarification but found none. Ana looked confused as well. For a few moments, the room seemed eerily silent.

"Jason is dead." Danilo spoke with the sort of aggressive neutrality that cloaked pain. "He died over a year ago, in an accident."

卐

Chris eventually gathered the half-empty trays and took them to the kitchen. Moe flipped over the newspaper, dropped the section back onto the coffee table, pawing around for something else of interest.

Jason leaned forward, dropped his voice. "Hey, Moe."

Moe glanced up, still shuffling through the paper. "Yeah."

"Did, uh...when you have your...sessions or whatever, with Wilders, where do you go?"

Moe abandoned the paper, sat back in his chair. "Where do I go? Another lab. Not super different from here, I guess, but the walls are painted green. And the people are different. They're working on something related but not quite the same. They weren't too mind-blown when I showed up, believe it or not."

"Green?"

"Yeah. Light green. Kind of reminded me of a prison."

"Was there...was there a baby?"

Moe stared at him mutely for a few seconds.

Behind him, Chris responded. "The baby again. Always with the baby." He returned to his seat. "Wilders is obsessed with the baby. No one knows what it's about, but he's always asking about a baby. He asked you, too, I assume."

"Yeah."

"Well? Was there a baby?"

Jason paused. "No. Just…wondering. Who is the baby? Whose baby is it? Why is he—"

"No one knows," Moe interrupted. "No one has any more information than you."

"Well…" Chris hedged a bit. "There are rumors. Diana's asked Ramon about it a few times."

"I'm not sure Ramon is a reliable source," Moe growled.

Chris sighed. "Look, yeah, you're never gonna be pals with Ramon, but that doesn't mean he was lying or something." He looked to Jason, leaned forward, dropped his voice. "This was before he started working here, so nothing that he witnessed firsthand. But he says that, word is, sometime last year, someone had a baby, and the baby was…special, somehow. Or he thought it was."

"Someone here had a baby? Did someone?"

"No, we sort of assumed it was either bullshit or maybe like in an alternaverse or even…we don't know…but even another lab like this one, here. Like maybe there are others. Or…" Chris's eyes shifted. "You know, it would've been a little after Molly…uh…disappeared, and you and her were pretty hot and heavy."

Jason nodded slowly, but his heart was racing. His face felt flushed, he hoped no one could tell. Her baby had died…hadn't it? Died with Molly? But this all made sense, now. He'd known it, sensed it from the start. Of course it was his baby. His child. His child with Molly. He was thrilled, ecstatic, terrified at once. What to do now? He had to protect it, he had to find it, he wanted to hug someone, jump up and dance—

"Dude. Dude? You all right?"

Jason jumped, looked over at Moe. "Yeah. Sorry. What?"

"Sort of zoned out there for a minute. Something happen? Did you see a baby, for real?"

Jason shook his head, too fast, twitchy, giddy, trying to settle his thoughts. "No. I didn't." He chewed absently on his thumbnail, trying to process this new information, but all he could see was Molly, his child, his family, his world.

Ana turned to Brigid, wide eyed. "What? What are—"

Brigid shook her head vehemently. "No. No. I saw him—Jason—a couple of days ago. He's not dead. He's in trouble, yeah, but he's not dead. Someone's been lying to you."

Jasmine's hands started to tremor. Tears filled her eyes.

Danilo broke eye contact and snarled, "This is some sort of prank. You should be ashamed, playing these games. Ashamed." He squeezed his eyes shut, pinched the bridge of his nose.

"Look! Look. I have a picture." Brigid pulled out the dossier, found the ID photo of Jason. "This guy. Jason. I found him in Vermont, hitchhiking. He stayed with me for two or three nights, and then he was kidnapped by some people in an ambulance...uh...a few days ago." She glanced at Ana. "How long have I been here? A few days. This is your son, right? This is Jason?"

Jasmine looked at the photo, covered her mouth, nodded. A tear splashed onto the table in front of her. She was shaking violently.

Brigid stabbed the photo with her finger insistently. "I know this man. I do. Uh...he has a sister...right? He didn't graduate from college, because he ran out of money. That's why he signed on for the project, so he could pay for college. He had a girlfriend named Molly, she was in the study, too. Uh..." How did she know so little about him? "He doesn't look like the picture anymore, much, because he's lost a lot of weight, but...oh! Wait! I know! He had his appendix out, when he was a teenager. Right? He's got a little scar, right here." She pointed to her belly. "Looks like someone knifed him...right? That's him, right?"

Ana peered at Brigid but said nothing.

"Uh...I saw him with his shirt off once. I asked him about it. You believe me? I mean, what made you think he was dead?"

Jasmine's hands were clamped over her mouth. She stared at the photo, not breathing.

Danilo smacked the table with his palm and snapped, "We have a death certificate. We had a funeral. We saw his *body*."

Brigid blinked, pushed back from the table. "You saw his body? How...that's not—"

"That wasn't him. That wasn't him. I told you. I told you, I would know my own son, that was not my son." Jasmine took a napkin, wiped her eyes. "The body...they showed us a body, but I knew it wasn't him. I knew they were lying."

Ana looked from Jasmine to Danilo, clearly baffled. "I do not understand. How—"

Jasmine crumpled the napkin in her hand, wiped her eyes again. "He'd been in an accident. They told us. He was...damaged...he was unrecognizable. They said they'd checked—with dental records, with fingerprints. But the body, the body...we couldn't tell. We believed them. We thought, why would they lie?"

"Who?"

"The police. They said he was in an accident. We buried him. Danilo, we buried someone who was not our son. Where is he? Where is Jason now?"

Danilo was shaking his head. "Wait. No, Jasmine, we don't know these people. Why should we believe them?" He turned to Brigid. "Why are you telling us these things? How can we trust you?"

Brigid was silent for a moment. Something Jasmine said was niggling at her. Something about identifying the body. Something...

She lit up. "Oh! No, I have it! I can prove it! I can prove Jason was with me a few days ago." She stared, wide eyed, at Ana. "O'Leary has proof. They lifted his fingerprints from my apartment...after the break in. They ran his prints, they identified him. They showed *me* his picture." She turned to Danilo and Jasmine. "The Boston cops, they have a record of him. I can call them, we can go to the cops, tell them everything. Tell them that Jason's not dead, that there was a coverup. You know this is from the lab, it has to be. They must've given you a fake body." *Shit, that means someone else must be dead. Who was that body?* "But we think that Jason's probably been taken back to the lab now, so all we need to do is get the cops involved. God, we have all the evidence now! Ana, I think this is it! This is what we need."

"Wait—" Jasmine held up a hand. Her eyes burned into Brigid. "Where is Jason? You say he's alive, you think you know where he is. Where is he? Where is my son?"

"Uh..." Brigid glanced over to Ana, looking for support. "This is gonna take some time."

🔲

The door lock beeped, then he heard the faint squeaking of the wheels on the cart. Lunch had arrived.

Jason peeled back the foil from the tray. A moist, grayish mass sitting on what appeared to be reconstituted mashed potatoes. He replaced the foil. He wasn't hungry, had no interest in eating. Bigger things to think about. He'd been mulling over the situation for hours, sitting motionless in his chair and staring off into the distance while the others floated unseen around him.

The orange room. The orange room and the blue room. They were definitely in the same universe, the same alternaverse. They had to be. Wilders must have...he didn't know...triggered a bridge, or something. He couldn't understand the link, but it had to be there. It had to be the reason he'd been able to reach out and see them, see her. They were right here, just out of reach, just on a slightly different frequency, but right here. He'd been there once already...so then there had to be a way to get back.

He plucked a bread roll off his tray, looked around. "These jumps... that Wilders, like, directs..." He pulled a corner of the bread off, regarded it thoughtfully. "They're controlled? They're not dangerous or anything?"

Moe smirked. "They're plenty dangerous. Haven't you been paying attention?"

Jason dropped the morsel of bread, tugged off another. "They don't worry about that?"

Diana responded, "I'm sure they worry about it. I'm sure they're working on something—"

Moe interjected. "Oh, come off it, Diana. They're not working on anything. They're going to use us up and, when we're gone, they probably have a whole new set of people lined up to take our place. They don't care about us."

"Moe, that doesn't make sense. Of course they care. They're not monsters."

"Diana, they are literally killing us. How do you not get that? They are. Literally. Killing us."

Jason looked over at Diana. She was focused on her salad, didn't meet his eyes. She shrugged. "No one thought it was going to be easy. But, you know, people have endured worse. It's not like it's a Filipino death march or something."

Jason recoiled. "What the fuck is that supposed to mean?"

"Nothing. Sorry. Nothing."

Jason glowered at her for a moment, deciding whether to push the issue, decided it wasn't worth it. Addressed Moe instead. "But he directs you. Always to the same place. And you can stay there...how long? Have you tried running? While you're over there, I mean?"

"Yeah, of course we have. Right?" Moe looked around for support. Chris nodded, but no one said anything. "The shifts, they don't last very long. I'm not sure if it's their doing. I mean, I don't...I don't have any control over it. I think I last like five, ten minutes or so, then, zzzzp, back here again." He sighed, leaning back in his chair. "So yeah, I tried running. The first time, I got about halfway down the hallway, the second time I got a little further, and then...then they put me in solitary confinement for I don't even know how long, and I haven't tried since then." Moe shuddered and blinked rapidly for a few seconds before looking back at Jason. "It sort of breaks your spirit, sitting alone in the dark for days on end. Think I would've preferred it, honestly, if he'd just kicked the shit out of me...then it would have been over faster."

Jason nodded dully at Moe, rolled a piece of bread between two fingers, dropped it. Objectively, he realized that he ought to be horrified. Well, he was horrified, sort of. He was just distracted, thinking about other things. He didn't care anymore, didn't care about getting out, about escape, about getting anyone else out. The only thing that mattered was Molly and the baby. They were so close—he could see them, smell them, taste them even—well, not quite, but so close. Everything else faded into a nondescript buzz in the background.

The door beeped and opened. Chris got up and slipped his arm under Kechia's shoulder, helped her to her room.

Brigid finished talking and the table went quiet.

Danilo broke the silence, finally. "Jason is in Chicago." His voice was unsteady. He had his hands clasped tightly on the table before him.

"I think so, yes. I don't know where else they would have taken him."

"And, all this time, the last year and more, he was alive."

"Yes."

Ana had her elbows on the table, her hands steepled and her fingers resting on her lips. "A year? A year ago, that was when you were shown this body, told he was gone?"

"Over a year. January 22nd, they said it happened." Danilo responded. "They told us on the 25th, said they had trouble identifying him. The worst day of my life."

"I lost control of the lab a year and a half ago. October. When did Jason escape?"

"I'm pretty sure it was less than a year ago," Brigid volunteered. "I'm not 100 percent sure on the details, but I got that impression."

"But why? Why would they...if he was with them, alive, why lie? Why go through this charade? What advantage could it possibly confer?" Ana ran her fingers through her hair. "It makes no sense. The entire project was to last eight months. Maybe twelve. What was to happen after?"

Brigid's throat tightened. She hesitated, spoke slowly. "There wasn't going to be an after. That's why. They didn't want anyone looking for him." She wondered if they had done the same for the others at the lab. If there were other dead doubles, other grieving families. The thought made her nauseous.

Danilo closed his eyes, shook his head. "No. Why would he not have contacted us? Why would he let us think he was dead? This makes no sense. Why would he have let us...let us grieve, let us mourn? He was not a thoughtless boy. I cannot understand why...what would have... why he would have done this."

Brigid shifted uncomfortably. "I don't think he knew. He never told me that you thought he was dead. He said he was afraid to contact you, because he thought he would be caught. He assumed you were under surveillance. And, like, he was afraid to log into his email or make phone calls. But, I mean, if he'd known, I'm sure he would've done something. You know, found some way to let you know he was alive." She rubbed her arms. She disliked speaking on Jason's behalf. "I don't think he had a real plan, in terms of...um, fixing the situation, I guess. He was scared, he was running, I don't think he thought too far ahead."

Jasmine clasped Danilo's hands. "He was never one to think ahead. He was an impetuous boy." She looked up, eyes shining. "*Is* an impetuous boy. You know where he is? We need to go. We need to go and get him, now. I don't want to sit here any longer. We must go."

Ana shook her head. "Wait, please. I need to advise a bit of caution. I want to go rescue Jason as well, and the other subjects that are still there. These are great friends of mine, you understand, good people with whom I worked extensively. The notion that they are being mistreated is abhorrent to me. But we need to play our hand right. You understand? If we go barging into the lab now, with accusations but no concrete proof, all it will do is give them time to adjust, time to hide or conceal what they are doing." She turned to Brigid. "You have a contact with the police, yes? A contact who can confirm that Jason was alive as of a few days ago?"

Brigid nodded.

"This is our advantage. We will involve the police, inform them of the...this discrepancy. They will have an obligation to investigate. A dead boy is not dead! Why were you given false information? Where did that information come from? Who is dead? The body was misidentified, someone else has lost their child. All these things...they will be obligated, as I say, to open up an investigation."

Jasmine tapped the table impatiently. "But Jason. We need to find him, now. I won't wait any longer."

Brigid agreed. "Yeah…I get the feeling that if we go strictly through official channels, it'll just give them time to cover their tracks. I think we need to catch them off guard. In the act, so to speak."

"Yes…" Ana mused for a moment. "Maybe you are correct. Let me think…"

"We need to go to the lab," Brigid announced. "Go there, bring the police, if we can physically show them what's happening…but we need to get inside, right? If we just show up, pounding on the door or whatever, that won't do anything. How do we do that? How long does it take to get a warrant? Or isn't there some contingency that, like, you don't need a warrant if there's a suspicion that people are in danger? I feel like that's something I've seen on TV, at least."

"Well." Ana still looked doubtful. "First, at least, call your policeman. You trust him, correct? The man in Boston."

"Yeah, I trust him. I don't know what he thinks of me at this point, but I think he's reliable." She pulled out her tablet and opened up her emails. "I think he sent me his phone number. Yeah…should I call him now?"

"Yes!" Jasmine was pressing the knuckle of her index finger against her teeth, her eyes darting between Brigid and Ana. "Call him. Call whoever. Just do something."

Ana passed her phone to Brigid, who found herself suddenly gripped by anxiety, reluctant to dial the numbers. *What do I say? What if he doesn't believe me?* She stared at the screen, looked up. Three sets of eyes were fixed on her. *Fuck.*

She dialed the phone, touched the speaker option.

"O'Leary."

"Hi, uh, Detective O'Leary, it's Brigid Sullivan."

Pause.

"Ms. Sullivan. I'm glad you called. What can I do for you?"

"Yeah. So, I, uh…do you remember, after the break-in at my apartment? You remember that you lifted some prints, you showed me a picture? I told you he was a guy who crashed with me for a night and then I took him to the train station?"

Pause. "I recall. Where are you now, Ms. Sullivan?"

"So, okay, here's the thing. I wasn't quite honest with you about that guy. His name wasn't...uh...whatever I said it was, right? His name's Jason. He didn't...I didn't take him to the train station. He was staying with me in a motel for a couple of days after the break-in. And then some men, some men with an ambulance, they broke into the motel, and they kidnapped him, and then that guy with the FBI badge, Smith, he kidnapped me, and took me to, uh...where was it...Revere, in the trunk of his car, right? That was when I called you, that night. But so, Jason...here's the thing, I think he's in this lab in Chicago now. I emailed you about this. Did you get it?"

Silence.

"Well, okay, and here's the other thing. Right now, I'm sitting with Jason's parents. And they were told—by the police in Chicago—they were told that Jason was killed in an accident a year ago."

Silence. Brigid felt her face flushing.

"What?"

"I mean, I know this is going to sound kind of crazy, it's a long story, but he was a research subject in this lab here, in Chicago, him and a bunch of other people, and he was being kind of abused so he broke out and was sort of on the run, right, when I met him, but I think it was the lab that told his parents that he was dead, I think there's some...vast... conspiracy going on. And Jason's in danger, and I think so are a bunch of other people who were subjects there, so I think, like...you need to ... um, raid the lab?"

Silence.

"What?"

Brigid's face was very hot at this point. "Okay, look, this all sounds pretty crazy. But the point is, Jason Reyes—the person whose fingerprints you lifted from my guest room—is definitely alive, or was definitely alive like a few days ago, right? You can confirm that?"

"Ms. Sullivan—"

"You can confirm that, right? But call the Chicago PD. Or look him up. Or whatever. He's supposed to be dead. Long dead. Why is that? You know? Ask yourself. Ask anyone. It doesn't add up, right?"

"Ms. Sullivan. I need to ask you to turn yourself in to the nearest authorities. We're not looking to arrest you, you aren't in trouble, but you are a person of interest in multiple investigations here, and we need to be able to talk to you. Do you understand?"

Dammit. This is not going well. People at other tables were starting to stare.

"Will you look him up? Call Chicago PD. Ask them. Will you do that? And, if I'm right, if I'm not bullshitting, will you have someone go to the lab and raid it?"

"I can't make any promises about raiding a lab in Chicago."

"Call Chicago. Ask about Jason."

There was a sigh from the other end. "Ms. Sullivan, look, like I said, I can't make any promises about Chicago. That's not my jurisdiction. I tell you what, though, I'll look into it, ask around. But, in return, you need to check in with the police. Come answer some questions."

"You promise? Call Chicago PD and ask. Then I'll come in. Okay?"

"All right."

"Okay then." She had a flash of inspiration and announced, "I'm going to be at the lab tomorrow morning. This is the location." She looked at Ana, waving her fingers. Ana muttered "Oh!" and dictated the address. "Whoever wants to can come meet me there. Police or whatever. But call and ask. It's important. Lives are at risk. Please." She disconnected, looked uneasily around the table.

⌸

When he eventually got tired of staring at his bedroom walls, Jason returned to the common room. Through the open door, he could see Diana in her bedroom, earbuds in, doing sit-ups. Chris was curled up on one of the lounge chairs, also wearing earbuds, reading an e-book and nodding rhythmically to himself. *Guess they find ways to pass the time.* He glanced back at his own bedroom, thought about the blue wallpaper he couldn't see anymore.

Gotta pass the time somehow.

He leaned back into a chair, curled his legs under him, closed his eyes. Cleared his head. Focused on emptiness, focused on nothing, paradoxically. Breathed in, relaxed, breathed out, relaxed further. Crept slowly away from the waking world, slowly, slowly.

Off in the distance he thought he heard voices. His heart leapt, his eyes snapped open—

Still in his chair. Same chair. Same common room. *Shit. Start over. Try again.*

It was hard, this business of focusing on nothing. The drugs made him lose his train of thought, or non-thought, or maybe it wasn't the drugs and maybe he just needed to be more disciplined, but whatever it was, it was hard. Maybe he was too excited, too hopeful, too eager. He wanted desperately to see the blue room again, to see Molly and the baby. If he could see the room, maybe he could figure out how to jump there, maybe he could slip out of this nightmare. But the want itself, the insistent and impatient desire, that was a barricade. It clouded his mind, closed him off. The only way to get what he wanted would be to *not* want it.

"Hey, man. You okay?"

Jason started.

Chris had pulled one earbud out, was staring at him.

Jason nodded, rubbed the back of his neck. "Where's Moe?"

"He's in our room, watching a movie or something. I think Kechia's sleeping. Hope so anyway. We had to ring for some painkillers for her a few hours ago. She's pretty banged up this time." Chris glanced over at the closed door to Kechia's bedroom, evidently anxious.

"You have painkillers here?"

"Well, we have to ask for them. They don't let us just have a bottle."

"Oh."

Chris set his e-reader down. "You look pretty down, man. Did you eat anything?"

"No. It got…it looked kind of gross. I just couldn't. I will, though."

"Yeah, it is gross. Still, you need to eat." Chris glanced toward the kitchen. "It's a shame they won't just give us the basic staples. We could cook our own food, but they don't want us handling sharp objects."

"They think we might attack them?"

"Them? No, not them. Let's be honest, we've all considered that there might be an easy way out here."

Jason grunted an acknowledgment.

Chris slipped his earbud back in place, went back to his e-book. Silence again.

Jason closed his eyes, slowed his breathing. Let go of his intentions, his desires, his machinations. Relaxed into the chair again and concentrated on nothing.

Nothing, for an eternity. Until, from a distance, a muffled familiar voice.

With a massive effort, Jason maintained his relaxation. Slowly, carefully, he opened his eyes.

Chris was still curled up in his chair, but his outlines were vague, fuzzy, out of focus. When he shifted positions, he left an echo behind. The walls behind him were altered, no longer white, but decorated with stenciled designs and framed photographs. A figure moved through the room, ghostlike, red and black, a trail wisping away behind.

Jason blinked, delicately, focusing on keeping his mind empty.

A second figure entered the room, coming from the blue room. Jason could see the blue now. Things were clearer. Thick, dark hair in a puffy ponytail. A yellow t-shirt, jeans. Rubbing her hands on her hips as if to dry them. Dropping to her haunches to retrieve some object from the floor—a bottle, an empty baby bottle.

Then a voice, hollow, as if from an empty auditorium, "Someone's going to slip and break their necks, seriously. This isn't hard, just pick up after yourself once in a while—"

The door lock beeped, jerking Jason awake. The vision evaporated like a puff of smoke in the wind. Two of the jumpsuited men wheeled in a cart with more foil-wrapped trays.

"Oh," Chris murmured, "dinner already. I lost track of time." He looked over at Jason. "You're going to eat tonight, right?"

Jason was frozen, staring at the space where Molly had been standing, not breathing, trying to cling to the insubstantial images, failing, a tiny burning rage igniting deep within him.

Ramon wasn't here tonight. One of the goons approached him. "Your pills."

Jason shook himself out of his reverie, glared at the two tablets. The tablets that were keeping him from Molly. They were keeping him here. They were his jailers, as much as Wilders or his guards were. He choked them down, hating himself, hating everyone.

Chris set a tray in front of Jason. "I'm serious, now. You have to eat."

Jason glowered sullenly at the tray. "Yeah. I just want to go…I have to pee."

In the bathroom, Jason stared at his reflection, hardly recognizing himself. His stomach was knotted. He could almost feel the pills in there, dissolving, poisoning him.

Wonder if there are cameras in here. Or microphones. Wouldn't be hard to imagine.

He turned the shower on, shut off the lights. Knelt before the toilet in the darkness. Braced himself and shoved two fingers into the back of his throat.

Gagged. Retched. Nothing else.

Did it again. Gagged. Retched…painfully this time. Nothing. He hit the wall with his fist, knocking something plastic off the sink. It skittered around on the floor in the dark. There was a knock at the door. Jason switched on the lights, opened the door.

Chris was standing there, a plastic-wrapped bread roll in his hand. He handed it to Jason, leaned in, murmured urgently, "You need to have something in your stomach," and left.

Jason closed the door again. The room was starting to fill with steam. He leaned against the sink, studied the bread roll, thought about what Chris had said.

He ate the bread roll in about four bites, choked a bit on the dryness of it and washed it down with water he scooped into his palm from the faucet. Shut the lights off again, knelt, poked the back of his throat with his finger, retched violently and vomited the bread roll.

He turned the light back on with cold unsteady fingers to confirm two small white pills floating among the pieces of bread and streaks of bile in the toilet.

⊕

Ana drove in silence for much of the return to Chicago. Brigid watched the landscape pass by the window, musing. *Did I do the right thing, telling O'Leary that I'd be at the lab tomorrow? Should we just go tonight?*

She didn't know, couldn't figure it out, so she just continued to watch the cornfields.

"What are we gaining by waiting, do you think?" Ana asked. "By waiting till tomorrow? What do you think?"

Brigid tore her eyes away from the scenery and looked at Ana, who appeared tense, the corners of her mouth drawn back slightly. "I don't know. I was wondering that, too." Brigid rubbed her mouth thoughtfully. "We could go tonight. I guess the main thing I'd be worried about is that we told the Reyeses we'd be there tomorrow. But, also—worst-case scenario—if we go like start banging on the door tonight, what if we just get arrested, no one looks into the lab?"

"True. Though *they* would still be around. Jasmine and Danilo."

"Yeah, that's true. I still think we're better served by not getting arrested tonight, though." She tried to sound more convincing than she felt. Part of the issue was, to be completely honest, that she was scared. Scared to take what felt like a final step, an all-or-nothing gamble to fix everything. *And, once it's done…if I fail, what then? Jason would be forever lost, Ana will never get her lab back, and I'll be…what? In prison? What if that happened? What would happen to Lithium? Who would look after him?*

There was a part of her that wanted to just say, "Fuck it," and run back to Boston, beg for her job back, return to her apartment, go back to her nice comfortable, boring, unfulfilled life.

Still, though, that wasn't a realistic option. There was still the matter of Agent Smith, or Not-Agent Smith, or whoever he was, and the fact that she'd left him battered and handcuffed to a tree. *So…whatever. Old life pretty much gone, may as well move forward with new life.*

There were times she wished she was still a smoker. She wanted a cigarette right now, more than just about anything. But she'd given it up for Lithium, after she'd read that dogs could get sick from secondhand smoke. She sighed. There was no nicotine in the sigh. *Ugh.*

Lithium.

Ana glanced over. "Brigid, are you all right? You look upset."

"Yeah...it's just, I feel like there's a decent chance things might not go well tomorrow, like it's possible I'd be detained or arrested." Brigid rubbed her arms. Saying it out loud made it so much more real. "I just...I'm worried about Lithium, what's going to happen to him. I don't have any...uh, any contingency plan for him, if something happens to me."

"Brigid, my dear! Of course we will look after Lithium until you can come back. Don't worry! Whatever happens, we will be sure you are taken care of. Both of you. It will be all right."

"Are you sure?"

"Yes! Yes, of course."

Brigid felt an unexpected surge of relief. "Thank you so much. I can't even tell you...thank you."

"It is no problem. So, tonight we will enjoy one more evening at home together and say a prayer for tomorrow." Hernandez beamed at her, encouragingly.

Brigid returned the smile, pushed down her lingering anxiety and returned her gaze to the passing cornfields.

⌗

Jason had trouble sleeping. He woke up every couple of hours, spent an eternity trying to get back to sleep, then would wake up again before he realized he'd dozed off at all. There was a residual vomit taste lingering in the back of his throat that wouldn't dislodge, no matter how hard he coughed or blew his nose. *Probably need a good sneeze. Wish I could sneeze.*

He'd eaten dinner, finally, once the nausea had subsided a bit, basking in the glow of successful emesis. He felt as happy as he had in a long time, it felt like, and so he'd eaten the soggy, rubbery piece of unidentifiable fish and noodles. Then he felt nauseous again for a while.

The drugs, the drugs. How long do they last? How long till they're out of my system? His head felt clearer already. *Maybe they're gone already, maybe that's why I can't sleep. Maybe it's as simple as that.*

He sat up in bed, stared into the darkness.

Maybe if I jump now I'll find Molly.

But then what? What will I do, if I can find her? What if I can't even jump?

What if I can?

The clock changed from 05:42 to 05:43. Other than the red illumination of the clock display, the room was dark.

Fuck it. Jason rolled onto his back, closed his eyes, took a deep breath and cleared his mind.

Deep breath. Clear head. Deep breath. Clear head.

Eyes still closed, he pushed himself, pushed...

Familiar tremor, familiar chill, familiar sense of wrongness. He knew he'd done it before he even opened his eyes. Though this was partly because of the fall to the ground.

His heart pounded. His eyes opened, his lungs filled to call for her...

But no, no, this is all wrong. No carpeting, no blue striped wallpaper, no changing table. *Fuck. This is...what...a mall?* He was surrounded by racks of sunglasses and mirrors, a glass door leading to a hallway, a countertop with a cash register and displays of impulse buys. Lens cleaners, dust cloths. All the signs were written in a language he didn't recognize. German maybe? Something European. He was a little curious. In a different situation, he might have done some exploring.

But not now. Now the only thing that mattered was that it was the wrong other-universe. The wrong alternaverse. Not Molly's, not the baby's.

He synced back, found himself in his own darkness, sat against the wall and pulled his sheets around him. Took a few steadying breaths, waited for his head to stop spinning, for the chills to subside.

The clock by the bed read 05:49, or something close. The numbers were fuzzy, refused to focus. *Still. Enough time to try again. A few hours to keep searching.*

⌘

Brigid woke up at four o'clock, tried to go back to sleep, woke up again at five o'clock, closed her eyes, opened them again at 5:20, gave up trying around 5:30 and sat up, leaning against the headboard, staring into the darkness. Through the window, the sky was starting to lighten. Lithium was curled up next to her. He picked up his head and pricked his ears as she moved. She leaned in and hugged him.

She was scared. More and more, she was convinced that she'd be arrested as soon as the police arrived. She had legitimately assaulted someone, and she wasn't sure exactly what his story would be, whether she'd be able to support her story of self-defense. *What if I can't? And what if things don't go well today? What if O'Leary didn't look into Jason's death report? What if he did, but doesn't consider it significant or reliable? Or what if he just doesn't care? Suppose the police do show up, take me into custody and just leave, without investigating the lab at all?*

Maybe I shouldn't worry. I'm not in this alone anymore. There's no way that Jason's parents will let this drop. Jason's their son. They'd chase down the possibility that he's alive to their last breath. I'm sure of that. Ana's pretty invested, too. She has the chance to reclaim her life's work, basically. And she has connections, legal connections. And she's clever…and, also, she hasn't recently committed any crimes. Bonus for her.

Lithium rested his head on her thigh and sighed. She grinned at him, stroked his ears. The room was filling with the pale light that precedes sunrise, the clean and hopeful glow of dawn. She admired the dawn's optimism. *Not completely sure it's warranted, but whatever.*

She heard footsteps in a distant part of the house, hushed voices, water running. Ana must be up too, then. The day was officially starting. Brigid gazed at the bedroom door, bit her lip. Hugged her dog one more time.

This is happening. This is happening.

⌗

Jason pulled the sheets around him again, whispering obscenities under his breath. He wiped his nose on the increasingly soiled fabric. It had been bleeding for an age, or an hour, give or take, and the sheets were getting pretty gross. He pinched his nose shut, breathed through his mouth, closed his eyes against the pounding in his head.

Eight jumps. Eight jumps and not one of them even close. Hell, not one of them even resembled Chicago. He'd found himself in a hospital anteroom filled with patients, of whom only about a third seemed to register his presence. The rest were coughing into tissues while medical people wearing surgical masks and gloves whisked through the room. He'd tried again—a crumbling building with netting over the windows and whining insects around his head. Again—the stairwell of an apartment tower, a flickering fluorescent bulb illuminating layers of graffiti on the walls. Again and again and again. No peach carpeting, no blue striped wallpaper, no baby, no Molly. And every time his head hurt a little more.

Fuck. This isn't working. Why isn't it working? I don't get it, it should be working! It's not fair! He winced, kneaded his temples, waited for a wave of pain to abate. *I can't control it, can't control where I'm going. I never could before. I don't know why I thought I could now.*

Stupid.

I need a better plan. A direction. A guide.

I need Wilders.

⊞

Ana peered sadly out the car window. "This is much changed. Since it was my lab…it is much changed."

"That was your lab?" Brigid faltered. She didn't want to sound dismissive, but this was not what she was expecting. They'd parked across from a facility that most closely resembled a prison compound. A nondescript square white building was surrounded by a perimeter fence with razor wire tilted inward, a locked gate with a keypad and camera, and an interior second perimeter fence with more razor wire. She could see security cameras placed strategically around the compound. What looked like an attached garage protruded from the front of the building, engulfing the paved road in. A set of retractable auto doors sealed the entrance, with a small side door on the right. The lawn between the building and the fences was overgrown, weedy. Neglected. No signs, not even a visible address. Brigid had imagined Ana working in pristine sterile facilities, all stainless steel and white coats, skylights over whiteboards with elaborate mathematical formulas scribbled in black marker. This looked like the bunker for some anti-government radical splinter group.

"It is much changed." Ana leaned back in the driver's seat and thoughtfully ran her hand over her mouth.

Brigid scanned the surrounding area, which didn't seem quite as industrial. Farther down the street she could see a car wash, an auto body shop, a couple of fast food places. Moderate traffic, a few cars parked along the curb. A normal commercial strip, all things considered...other than the daily rifts in space and time taking place nearby.

"Do you see Jasmine and Danilo?"

Brigid shook her head. "No, it's early, though. We should wait for them, I think. I mean, we should have all the support we can get here." She wasn't sure if she was just procrastinating or speaking in earnest. *Probably earnest. Right?* She looked over at the lab again and tried to suppress a shudder. It was foreboding. Scary. Terrifying, really.

Ana nodded. "Yes. We should wait. I will call them if they do not arrive soon. Do you think your police have come? I do not see anyone."

"I'm not sure. Probably would be unmarked, though, right? *If* they show up. But who knows. This is all new for me." She smiled, uncertainly. "I'm pretty nervous. You think this'll go well?"

Ana didn't answer but tapped Brigid's arm excitedly. "Look! Look!"

Brigid followed her gaze. A black sedan had pulled up to the first of the two perimeter gates around the lab. Someone leaned out of the window, tapped on the keypad, then drove through the gate as it opened. The second gate opened without a keypad. Maybe it was controlled by whoever was on the other end of the cameras. The car pulled up to the garage door, which slid up. Slid down again as soon as the car was inside.

"Who was that? Do you think it was Wilders? Did you see the license plate?"

"Maybe. I couldn't tell. It was really too far to see."

Nothing more happened for a while. They waited, watching for police cars, watching for Jasmine and Danilo. The sun climbed higher into the sky, which was bright blue with a smattering of clouds. It looked like it was gearing up to be a gorgeous day. *Thank fuck.* She was sick of the constant gray, the cold drizzle that dragged down the spring. Now the weeds and grass between the buildings were dazzling green. The air smelled clean, the sun shone clear and warm. *A lovely day to save the world. Or fail spectacularly. One or the other.*

⌗

By the time breakfast arrived, Jason had managed to staunch his nosebleed, taken a long hot shower and made himself sort of presentable. He shuffled into the common room, where Ramon took one look at him and promptly dropped the little cup with his pills. The pills rolled to a stop on the floor.

"Shit, you look terrible. Are you all right? Do you need anything?" Diana looked over. "Oh, my god. What happened? Are you sick?" Jason blinked. *I don't look that bad, do I?* "Migraine. It's okay. It's fine."

Ramon nodded, picked the two pills up off the floor, proffered them to Jason. "Sorry about that. Here, I can come back with some Tylenol, if you want."

Jason meekly took the little paper cup and swallowed the two pills with a cup of water sitting on the table. He could smell something that was close to eggs and sausage but was just a shade off. It didn't help his head.

He investigated the contents of the breakfast. Something definitely trying to be eggs and sausage, though the sausage looked suspiciously plastic. Another bread roll. *This place is gangbusters for carbs, evidently.*

He unwrapped the bread roll and ate it without margarine. The margarine didn't seem to make much of a difference anyway. He glanced around at the others, who were picking at their breakfasts. Kechia had abandoned hers and was in the kitchen, presumably looking for her cottage cheese. None of them seemed to be paying any attention to him so he headed back to the bathroom.

"Hey," he heard behind him, "you feeling okay?" He shook his head, didn't look back.

In the bathroom, he flipped up the toilet seat, turned the shower back on, and shut off the light. The room was still damp with condensation and the toilet clammy to the touch, which made kneeling before it even more unpleasant than normal. He wiped his hands on his shirt, took a few bracing breaths, and stuck his fingers down his throat.

He retched, but nothing came up.

Dammit.

Tried again, but no luck. *Fuck. The pills are gonna melt, they're gonna start kicking in soon...I have to get rid of them.* Tried again. Retched for what felt like an age, but nothing. His stomach had evidently clamped shut that particular exit.

He leaned back on his heels, panting, starting to panic. *I can't fail now...I'm almost there.*

He gazed up at the medicine cabinet over the sink. Switched on the light, opened it, saw a toothbrush, a mini sewing kit, a pair of tweezers, a small first aid kit...and a bottle of peroxide.

He stared at the peroxide. Turned and looked at the frustratingly clean toilet. Rubbed his hand over his head.

This is a bad idea...

He switched off the light again, opened the peroxide, took a deep breath, took a deep swallow.

Weirdly, it didn't taste that bad. A little bit foamy, kind of...almost yeasty.

Nothing was happening. *What was I expecting? Maybe I should take another—*

He doubled up as a sudden spasm of pain seized his abdomen. He dropped to a knee, banged his elbow on the toilet bowl, curled over in agony. He couldn't breathe. His stomach was convulsing, burning, ripping apart.

Shit...shit...this was a mistake...I'm dying...I'm dying...

He vomited, copiously and agonizingly and repeatedly. When it was finally over, he was curled over the toilet bowl, his head resting on his arm, breathing shallowly. His hands were cold and shaky, his nose had started to bleed again, and he was covered in a fine sheen of chilled sweat.

After a few minutes, he took a deep breath, stood up, and switched on the light to see what was in the bowl. Bread and foam and streaks of blood and two little pills.

卐

Brigid's butt had gone numb some time ago. Some long time ago. She shifted uncomfortably, which only served to amplify the ache in her hips. *How long are we going to sit here waiting? Nothing's happening. No one's here.* She chewed on her lip. *What the fuck. Why did we even come?*

Ana tapped her arm again. "Look. There. That may be them, yes?" A car—a slightly battered, slightly outdated mid-sized sedan—was pulling up in front of the lab, moving tentatively, slowly, before parking on the far side of the entrance gate. Brigid leaned forward, tried to see the occupants. *Nah. Too far. Stupid elderly eyes.*

The doors opened and Jason's parents got out of the front. A young woman emerged from the back—long shiny black hair that she brushed behind her ears as she stood up, jeans and a tunic shirt, tall and lean. Their daughter, Brigid realized. Jason's sister.

Brigid got out of the car with relief, arching and rubbing her back. The Reyeses came over, apologizing for the delay. They'd come as fast as they could but got caught in rush hour traffic. "Have the police come? Can we go in?" Jasmine eyes were laser focused on the lab. "He is in there? Jason?"

"Yeah. Um...yeah, I think so. It's the only place I can think of where they'd take him. The cops aren't here. I'm not sure...they may not be coming, I'm not..." Brigid faltered. "I'm not sure."

"So, what are we doing then?" The daughter crossed her arms, glowered at Brigid and Ana and the lab in turn. She was lovely, Brigid noted, sharing Jason's almond eyes and dark lashes, with regal cheekbones and full lips. Late twenties, maybe thirty. There was a certain confidence, almost arrogance, to her bearing.

Brigid extended a hand to her. "Hi, I'm Brigid. I met your brother."

"Yeah, I heard." She had a firm, dry handshake. "Laura. What do you think, then? What should we do? Knock?"

Jasmine looked conflicted. "I don't think—"

"Mom. Joking. We're not going to knock." Laura peered at Brigid. "Still, though. We have a plan, right? So...should we call the cops, or what?"

Brigid froze. "Uh. I guess. Maybe?" She looked to Ana for support. "What do you—"

"I am not certain. We maybe should wait a bit more," Ana replied.

Laura rolled her eyes impatiently. "Mom, give me the keys. I need something from the car."

Brigid watched, uneasy, as Laura jogged back to their car. "I don't know, honestly. I don't know. I hadn't really accounted for the police being no-shows—" She stopped talking. A new car was pulling up to the entrance gate, parking across the drive. A big, black, hulking SUV with tinted windows.

Ana squinted. "Who is that, now?"

Brigid didn't answer. *Something's off here. Something's very wrong.*

The SUV door opened and, out of the driver's side, wearing a new suit and mirrored sunglasses that did little to distract from his chewed up and mangled face, stepped Not-Smith.

⌸

The stomachache and headache faded after a while. Jason lay curled up but relaxed on his bed, hands no longer balled into fists, eyes shut though he was awake. There was an echo of pain sort of lurking in the background, threatening, but almost pleasant in its absence. His head was much clearer now. Over twenty-four hours since he'd last taken any drugs. *Will I go into withdrawal? What were those drugs again?* Moe had told him, but he couldn't remember the name. *Doesn't matter, though. So long as they're gone.*

There were hushed voices from the common room. He wasn't sure if anyone had been taken for a Wilders session today. *Maybe they'll come for me. Maybe. Hopefully.*

He rolled over onto his back and stared at the cracks in the ceiling. His stomach protested weakly, but he ignored it.

The door beeped and opened. He turned toward the common room. Ramon and his fat friend. *Well, not that fat, if I'm honest. But fuck that guy anyway. Fat friend.*

They approached his bedroom and Ramon knocked on the door frame. "Hey. Come on. We need to finish your debriefing."

Jason blinked at them slowly. *Debriefing. Oh, right. That. I forgot about that.* What a stroke of blind luck... He grimaced dramatically and pulled himself upright, found his green felt slippers and shuffled down the hall with his two companions. He stumbled once, for effect, shoulders hunched, head down. *Am I going overboard? Can they sense a difference?*

Do they care?

Wilders was waiting in the room, arms folded over his chest, pacing. Impatient.

For what? Does he have a deadline or something?

Ramon and his fat friend led Jason over to the chair. He sat down obediently, hands in his lap, eyes downcast. They didn't bother restraining his wrists this time. Wilders sat down at the table, fidgeted with his toys on his desktop, tapped hesitantly on his laptop. Hissed to himself in frustration, or exasperation.

He was a lousy typist. *Should get himself a nice secretary. Fucking awful job to condemn a nice secretary to, though.* Jason stole a glance at Wilders, snarled involuntarily, looked back down and fixed his face into a mask of submission before anyone noticed.

"All right. To resume our previous conversation...we'd been discussing the...er...the surroundings you found yourself in, after our last...our last experi—"

Jason interrupted, keeping his eyes down, his hands folded. "Yeah. A room. Orange...an orange room...like this."

"Can you give us some more...some more details about what you saw? Decorations on the walls, any odors you may have noted, any papers or books, or..."

Jason shook his head slowly. "An orange room. I don't remember it well. I was confused, I was...I was hurt. Things are fuzzy. You know, it was two days ago, I can't remember everything, not clearly."

Wilders narrowed his eyes, refocused on his laptop, typed with two fingers. "Just an orange room. No details? Furniture, decorations?"

"Just...no, just orange. Maybe..."

"Maybe what? Work with me, Jason. Tell me what you saw."

Jason rubbed his eyes and mouth. Dropped his hands again. *I'm being too coy. How much do I ham this up before he catches on?* "Maybe some cartoons. You know…on the walls. Like for a kid's room."

Wilders lasered in. "Did you see a child?"

Jason kept his eyes down, scrunched up his face. Shook his head. "I don't know. I don't remember." He raised his head, met Wilders's eyes, tried to appear plaintive. "Look, it's not my fault. It was two days ago."

"You don't remember?" Clearly Wilders was getting frustrated. "Think. Did you, or didn't you?"

Jason shrugged.

"It's not hard. Focus." Wilders was growling, glaring at him. Jason could feel it even without looking up. "Anything else in the room? Noises. Odors. Anything."

Jason shrugged again. "It was two days ago…and I had a headache and I didn't notice. I was there for like two seconds. I don't remember anything."

There were a few moments of loaded silence.

"In that case, maybe we should refresh your memory."

Jason looked up, widened his eyes. His heart kicked up a gear. His face felt flushed, he hoped it wasn't visible, or that Wilders attributed it to panic. *Yes,* he thought, *yes, yes,* and said, "No. No."

"Sir, I'm not sure that's a good idea, so close to the last one…I mean, I'm not sure it's safe."

Shut up, Ramon. Shut up shut up shut up.

"Well, unless his memory comes flooding back, I don't see an alternative." Wilders tapped an index finger on his desk impatiently. He looked really pissed.

Jason tried to look sufficiently intimidated and shook his head mutely.

Wilders paused, waiting a beat, but Jason stayed silent. Wilders's features darkened visibly. He yanked open a drawer and slammed a familiar black device down onto the table. The cattle prod thing with a wand. "Get him strapped in. Get him ready."

Jason's heart was racing now, his breathing shallow and rapid. His eyes were fixed on the black device. He felt his arms get secured to the chair, distantly heard someone asking about armbands and monitoring.

Wilders dismissed the questions. Jason registered this vaguely. Wilders wasn't interested in gathering data, then. He just wanted to force a jump, just wanted to punish Jason.

Fine. Fine…so long as it's to the right place. With an effort he looked to Wilders. "Please. Just one, okay? Just for a minute? I'll do better. I'll remember this time, okay? Please?"

"You *will* do better. You'd better do better."

Ramon picked up the device, stepped behind Jason. Jason dropped his eyes again for a moment, focused himself, took a slow deep breath. Felt hands on each side of his head, positioning him.

Jason raised his eyes one final time and met Wilders's gaze.

He allowed a triumphant grin to split his features as the device hit the back of his neck and he felt himself gloriously hurled away, out of this crappy universe, to Molly, to his family.

FIVE

That familiar explosion of pain and light, pressure. Everything washed out and slowly came back into focus.

Jason was lying naked in the orange room. His heart skipped a beat. The lights were off, it was dark, but he could still make out the cartoon animals on the walls and toys scattered on the floor, could smell the baby powder, see the shapes of familiar furniture. A nightlight was plugged into the wall, next to a pile of laundry discarded on the floor. He pawed through it, put on a pair of sweatpants and an oversized t-shirt, which was stretched out and had a crusted stain on one shoulder. He scraped absently at the stain, looking around, giddy and triumphant, dizzy with glee.

The door opened and the light came on. Jason turned toward the door and his heart exploded in his chest.

Molly was standing in the doorway. Molly, robust and healthy and glowing, thick curly black hair held back by a headband, wearing jeans and a fitted cotton shirt that hugged her belly and proudly displayed the curves of her chest and abdomen and arms, those familiar curves, that ideal shape. She'd opened the door and flicked on the light without looking, was talking to someone outside the room, smiling, and for one eternal moment she was perfect.

For every eternal moment she was perfect.

Jason's legs gave out beneath him. He collapsed to his knees, clutched the bureau drawer for support, gaping, gasping for breath.

Molly laughed at whoever she was talking to, turned and walked into the room, yelped and jumped forward, her hands up in a defensive pose. "What the…what…who the…oh my god…Jason? Jason? Jason, my god, Jason, Jason—"

She bounded across the room, dropped to her knees, to his level, wrapped her arms around him. Clutched the back of his shirt in her fists, pulled him into her as if she wanted to absorb him. She was shaking, she was sobbing.

He didn't think, couldn't think, just pulled her into him as well, buried his head in her shoulder and held her tightly, maybe too tightly, maybe too much, but he couldn't relax, couldn't let up. Molly. Molly. Molly was here, was real, was in his arms again. Finally. Everything he'd wished for, everything he'd dreamed of. He was crying, too, the two of them shuddering in synchronicity.

卐

Brigid's chest seized up so fast and hard she thought she was literally choking. She dove behind Ana's car, all instinct, and crouched by the trunk, shaking. *Shit. Not-Smith…he's found me…he wasn't arrested, isn't in prison, he's here, and he's found me and now he's going to kill me, kill us all.*

"Ana…get down…everyone get down. Hide, hide!"

Ana did not get down. Neither did either of the Reyeses. Danilo peered around the end of the car at her, perplexed. "What—"

"That man—that man, he's here to kill us—you have to get down. Get down!" *No one's listening to me, goddammit, what's wrong with these people?* "Run! Run, call the police, or…fuck…" She peeked past the tires. Not-Smith was walking toward them in a leisurely manner. A second man in a suit and mirrored sunglasses emerged from the passenger side of the black SUV and followed a few steps behind him. Beyond them, she could see Laura standing by the open door of the Reyes's car, staring at them.

Ana appeared at her side. "Brigid, what is happening? What are you doing?" She looked toward the two men. "It is the police, do you think? Or—"

"No! No!" Brigid hissed, frustrated. "It's that guy who tried to kidnap me, right? When they took Jason? That guy! Not the police!"

Where the fuck are the police? "We have to get out of here. They're here to kill us. I know it. I know it."

Ana took a step back, took out her phone and dialed. She watched the two men warily but made no move to run or hide. And they kept walking, kept coming. Brigid was sure she could see guns in holsters under their suit coats.

Maybe. Fuck. No one's doing anything. I have to do it. Again.

Brigid took a deep, shaking breath and stepped out to face the two not-agents.

卐

Jason didn't know how long he and Molly knelt there, tangled in each other. A millisecond. An eternity. Not long enough, no matter how long it was. But eventually she pulled back, took his face in her hands, studied him with eyes bloodshot and wet.

"Jesus…Jesus. Jason. What happened? You're so…thin. God, I barely recognized you. What happened to you? What's happening?"

Jason shook his head, unable to articulate everything he wanted to say, and so unable to utter anything at all. "I…Molly, god, Molly…" He kept stroking her hair, the hairband becoming dislodged. He didn't care. "I've missed you so much. So much."

"I missed you too, Jason…but what's going on? Explain to me what's happening. Okay?"

A figure appeared in the doorway. "Hey, what…Molly? Who's that? Do you want me to—"

Jason looked over. The face was familiar.

"Vijay?"

Molly nodded. "Yeah, Vijay, he's living here now, he's still working on the project, he's graduated since you…since you've been gone. Me, too." She cocked her head, sniffed and wiped her nose. "Maybe you know that already?"

Vijay was staring, aghast. "Is…is that Jason? Holy cow."

Jason rubbed his eyes with the heels of his hands. "Hi, Vijay. Long time."

Molly hugged his shoulders, beaming. "God, it's so good to see you. What is this? Where are you from? Is this a trial? Is Dr. Hernandez still running tests? I was wondering if we would ever encounter—"

Jason pulled back. "Dr. Hernandez? No, she's gone. This isn't a test. It's Wilders, I'm trying to…it's all…it's all gone to shit, Molly. It's a nightmare. Wilders, he's…like…he's torturing them, he's got them prisoner, me too… He had me drugged, I couldn't jump, I had to vomit, like, pills… This is the first time I could make it out, I need to get…I need to, I don't know, get the police, get the authorities, I don't know…" *None of this is coherent. I can't coherence. Is that even a word?* He couldn't organize his thoughts, his words, it all just tumbled out, jumbled out. "And Molly, you're gone. You're gone. I found an autopsy report, you died, the pregnancy, I don't know if that was why, I don't know what happened to the baby, but you're gone and it…it…I just….couldn't…" He buried his face in her chest, breathed in her scent, closed his eyes and wished he could stay in that moment forever.

Molly shook her head. "Hey, Jason, calm down." She rubbed his head briefly, stood up, tugged on Jason's arm but he sank back down onto the carpet. "We just need to figure out the timelines. Right? You're not from here, this universe, we know that, but we know we share a history. We just need to figure out where our paths diverged."

Jason nodded. His head was starting to hurt again. *Shit.*

"Wilders, then. He's still around? Not in prison?"

Jason shook his head. *If only.* "Should he be in prison? I mean, yeah, but—"

"Well, yeah. We did that. Me and Dr. Hernandez, mostly. We, like, revolted. Got the lab back. After you died."

Jason stared at her, confused. *This makes no sense. Those words make no sense.* An ache was coalescing at the back of his skull.

"I what?"

Molly knelt down next to him, ankles crossed underneath her. "You died, Jason. You fucking died. I came in one morning and you were lying on the floor, just—" Her eyes slid away from his, blinking rapidly. "You were…you had been, I don't know, crushed or something. We assumed you'd shifted somewhere and been hurt. You came back, but you were…god, Jason. You were…just…" She stopped talking, covered her mouth with her hand and screwed her eyes closed. Tears leaked out all the same. "You were dead. You were hurt, so hurt, so…crushed, I don't know, and you were dead. There wasn't anything we could do." She wiped her nose on her wrist, smeared the tears away from her eyes. "It pretty much destroyed me, to be honest."

Jason couldn't quite wrap his mind around this. He sat slumped on the ground, staring at the floor in front of him but not seeing anything. His head was starting to spin. "When?"

"January 22nd. A little over a year ago. Worst day of my life, Jason." She leaned against him. "I loved you. More than anything. I loved you."

January 22nd. He didn't remember anything significant about that day. *I died? But I'm here now. I could stay here, maybe? Replace dead Jason. Just be here with Molly, in this much better universe, where Wilders isn't around and it's just Molly and Vijay—*

Wait. What's Vijay doing here, exactly?

His mind dodged that question. The ache in the back of his head was growing. Less an ache, more a needling.

"You got Wilders thrown in prison? How?"

Molly looked down. "I managed to contact Dr. Hernandez. I was so angry, I mean, after losing you. I broke out of the lab one night, I tracked her down, we exposed the whole deal—that research subjects were being held hostage, that some of them had disappeared, some had died. The trial was this past winter. Trial of the century, you know? We made all the headlines."

He shook his head, tried to clear it. "The baby, Molly. There's a baby, right? I've seen it. During an experiment…and in, like, a kind of vision…there is a baby, right?"

Molly smiled, hugged him again. "Yes, of course. Our baby." She released him, pulled him to his feet. "Come meet your daughter."

Molly led him down familiar yet unfamiliar hallways, to the dorm, to the baby's room, the blue room. Vijay followed at a distance, looking a bit uncertain. Jason peered over the edge of the crib. The baby was sleeping on her back, her head turned to the side, tiny lips slightly ajar, a tiny filament of dribble on her lower lip. In the dim light, he could still make out the dark eyelashes against her cheek, the tiny fingernails on her hands. He had to put his hand over his mouth, trying to suppress his delight, trying not to wake her.

Molly reached in, stroked the baby's cheek with the back of her finger, smiling. The little eyelids fluttered, opened. The baby stared at the faces over her and squared her mouth in a thin wail. Molly picked her up and cradled her over one shoulder, fingers spread over the back of the little head, bouncing up and down, cooing. After a minute or so, the crying stopped, and Molly turned to Jason, eyes bright. "You want to hold her?"

Jason didn't know how to hold a baby. He was afraid he'd drop her and had to sit down, remember to support the head, tuck his arm under her back. She was heavier than he expected, wiggly, squirmy. He couldn't find a comfortable position. Shouldn't this feel natural? It didn't feel natural, it felt awkward. The baby tolerated him for about six seconds before she started crying again, and he froze, confused, until Molly took her back and cuddled her back to quiet. Jason tried to suppress a pang of jealousy.

"How old is she?"

"Eight months yesterday."

"What's her name?"

"Yasmin. After your mom."

Jason smoothed the dark curls back from the baby's forehead. The needling in his head needled deeper. He grimaced. "Yasmin? My mom? She's around?"

"Yeah, she's been amazing. I don't know what I would have done without her. Your parents have an apartment rented nearby, just down by the lake, they stay here most weekends. She babysits, pretty regularly, gives me a chance to rest and get some work done. You know."

"What work?"

"Well, you know, the experiments were stopped after we got the lab back. Too dangerous. But we're still researching. Actually, Hernandez took me on as a research assistant. Vijay and me." She kissed the baby on her forehead, placed her back in her crib and led Jason back to the common room where Vijay was still standing awkwardly by the door.

"How are you here, though? What happened?"

Jason shook his head. "It doesn't matter. None of it matters. I'm here now." His left eye twitched. He kneaded it with his knuckled finger. It twitched again. He rubbed again.

Molly glanced at Vijay. "Yeah, um, I mean you're here. For now, yeah."

Jason removed his knuckle from his eye. The eye spasmed. He swore softly and resumed rubbing, looked at Molly with his good eye. "Not for now. I'm here. I'm staying here. I can't go back." He grimaced. A flash of pain burst in his head, receding after a moment. When Molly's face came back into focus, she wore a conflicted expression. "What? What is it?"

"Jason, sit down. Tell me why you…why you don't want to go back. Okay? Tell me what's going on."

⛶

"Hey!" Brigid winced internally. She'd wanted to sound intimidating, aggressive, but it came out tinny and squeaky. *Shout from the diaphragm,* she thought. *Puff your chest out, throw your shoulders back, project, project.*

"Hey, you! You two! You can just stop right there!"

Still squeaky. Fucking hell. But the two not-agents hesitated, broke stride for a moment.

"I know who you are! I know what you're doing! Yeah, I know you, you fucker. How's the fucking face? Huh?" In her periphery, she could see the Reyeses staring at her, aghast. Ana was still on the phone, out of earshot, talking quietly and urgently to someone.

With some effort, her knees shaking so violently she thought she might tear a ligament, Brigid took a few steps toward the two men. "Yeah, we know all about it, all the shit going down here. We know about it, we talked to the cops, they're on their way." *I hope that's true.* "This whole place is going down today. You hear me? We've told everyone. Everyone. You guys, you're fucking *done.*"

The two men had drawn even and exchanged a brief glance. One of them, the stranger, pulled out a phone and held it to his ear. His expression behind the mirrored lenses was unreadable. Not-Smith made a ghastly attempt at a smile, hampered by the bandages on his cheek. "Ms. Sullivan. I'm going to need to ask you to cooperate. We're here on official business. No one needs to get hurt, we just want to—"

"Yeah, you can just shut the fuck up, right there, fella. Like hell you're on official business." Brigid looked around, up and down the street, then jumped up and down, waving her arms over her head. "Hey! These people are trying to kill us! Hey!" There weren't many people around, but it caught the attention of a couple of pedestrians. *Good.*

Not-Smith started walking toward her again. "Ma'am, please. We're just here to talk. There's no need for a scene."

"Ha, ha, there's no need for a 'scene,'" she snorted. "Hey! Help! Fire! Rape! Help!"

"Brigid, Brigid." Ana tapped her on the shoulder, and Brigid heard a blessed sound—the cry of angels, the truncated "whoop" of a police siren as a cop car pulled up behind her with lights flashing.

卐

"So you're in trouble. All of you. The rest of you."

Jason rubbed his head, which was throbbing now. "Molly, you want to know my serious thought? I think the whole world's in trouble. I don't think Wilders knows what he's doing, I think he's going to screw something up. For all I know, the whole universe is going to get sucked into a black hole or something."

Molly hugged him. *God, that feels so good.* Like something cold and dead deep in his core had awakened, had warmed.

"Well, I hope that's not going to be the case," she said. "They're in this building, still, though? Have they changed the rooms around or is everything still basically the same?"

Vijay looked up. "Molly. Are you thinking—"

"Yes, I am. We need to know what's happening. *I* need to know. And I need to help. Vijay, it's Jason. You know I have to do this."

Jason squinted at her, confused. "Do what? We don't need to do anything. I'm here now. Everything's all right now."

"Jason." Molly turned to him, locked eyes. "Everything is not all right. You're not staying here. You know that. And you can't leave everyone else abandoned back there. If things are as bad as you say, what do you think's going to happen to them?" She got up and tugged at his hand. "Come on. Let's find the data storage room, see what's happening, see what we can do about it." She turned to Vijay. "Stay here and watch the baby."

Part of Jason wanted to argue but he didn't have the energy. The needling in his head had upgraded to ice picking. He got up obediently and followed Molly down the hallway, around a few corners, to the data storage room which was conveniently labeled *Data Storage*.

"Molly, what are we doing?"

Molly tapped a code into the keypad by the door and entered the room with Jason following behind her. "We're going back to your world, you and me. We're going to look through the records—hopefully they'll be there, or here, in their version of this room—figure out what's happening, figure out how to fix things."

"We? You and me? Wait, how—"

"We're gonna co-shift. Shift together. It's fine, I've done it before. A few times."

Jason scanned the room. Four computers, all the screens dark. Papers piled up between them, some in plastic baskets, some just scattered around. A recycling bin under the desk filled with paper. Three ergonomic chairs. Jason wondered if the fourth person had to stand to use the last computer. A bunch of file cabinets, with labels on the drawers he couldn't understand. Or, more precisely, couldn't see, because his eyes were tearing and he couldn't focus. The pain in his head had evolved. He had visions of tiny goblins inside his skull, rending his brain with carving knives, stabbing through gray matter and blood, withdrawing and stabbing again. He reached toward one of the ergonomic chairs to steady himself, forgot that ergonomic chairs tend to spin, stumbled and fell into a file cabinet.

"Shit!" Molly caught him by the arms, supported him. "Shit. We better go. Jason, hold on, you ready?"

Jason nodded with eyes closed, felt Molly's arms encircle his chest, her body press up against him, and in a moment of euphoria that almost eradicated his brain-agony, felt her lips on his.

The kiss was sudden and perfect, unexpected and familiar, overwhelming him with her taste, her fragrance, her warmth and pressure. It lasted forever but was over too quickly. He opened his eyes to find the two of them embracing naked in a strange room.

Home again.

⊡

"Oh, thank god, thank god..." Brigid had to fight the urge to run over to the cop car, yank open the door, and hug whoever was inside. The relief washing over her was almost physical, palpable. The cops were here, everything was going to be okay, everything was all right now. She threw both middle fingers up in the air and grinned triumphantly at the two fake agents, both of whom had frozen and raised their hands deferentially.

"Brigid Sullivan? I'm gonna need to you kneel down and put your hands behind your head."

Wait, what?

She whirled back to the cop car. Two officers had gotten out. One was standing behind the car, the other had one hand on his holster, one arm extended toward her. She couldn't possibly seem like a threat, could she? *What the hell?*

"What? No! No, you don't get it, those two—those two came here—they're here, they're trying to kill us—Go! Go get them!" She was tripping over her own tongue. Her brain was fritzing out. Didn't matter much, though, since Ana and the Reyeses were also now shouting over the cops and each other, with the effect being that of a small but very angry mob. She looked back at the two fake agents and saw with dismay that they'd each pulled out a fake badge.

Hopefully fake.

One of the cops approached the angry, and still shouting, tiny mob while the other walked over to the two fake agents, who put their fake badges away. They conferred quietly.

Brigid watched with a sense of dread. *They're gonna leave*, she thought, *they're gonna leave and take me with them and I'll be arrested and Jason'll still be in the lab and nothing will change, this will all have been for nothing.* "Hey!" She focused on the closer cop—a young guy, thirty something, bullish and stocky. "Hey, look. I'm Brigid Sullivan, yeah, and I'll go with you, I'll go with you quietly, but you have to look in the building there…there are people inside and they're in danger. You have to look in there. Please."

"What sort of danger?" The cop squinted at the lab, doubtfully. "Calm down, everyone, calm down—"

"I will not calm down! My son is in that building and he's in danger, so you go! You go and get my son! You…you told me he was dead and he's not, he is in that building! You go and get him!" Jasmine was on fire. She actually shoved the cop in the chest before Ana and Danilo managed to pull her back.

The cop, already clearly a little freaked, now also looked pissed. "Hey! Settle the fuck down. Settle the fuck down!"

Brigid took a step back. The two fake agents and the other cop were walking back toward them now. *Fuck, none of this is going according to plan.* The cops were pissed, the fake agents were faking them out. She felt someone seize her, unexpectedly roughly, by the upper arm. She jerked away automatically, but the cop jerked back, and she stumbled, and everyone started yelling again, the noise almost drowning out the roar of an engine and the squealing of tires but not even remotely drowning out the crashing sounds as a slightly battered, slightly outdated, mid-sized sedan barreled through the two gates, through the garage door, deflected off the car parked inside and plowed into the building wall within.

⌗

Molly twisted out of Jason's arms, taking in the contents of the data storage room. There were two desktop computers in this version of the room, two ergonomic chairs, and a wall with nine video screens showing what looked like security camera footage. Jason barely noticed the room. He was having trouble tearing his eyes off of Molly. Even through the dizzying throbbing in his head, even though he realized they were on a mission, he just wanted her. Wanted to pull her back into his arms, collapse onto the floor together, run his fingers and lips over every inch of her exposed skin—

"Jason. *Jason.* Hey, pay attention. What is that? Can you tell?"

She was pointing to one of the video screens. He squinted at them. Most of them seemed to be empty hallways, but one showed an outdoor area, a field surrounded by two fences with a paved road through the center. Two were different views of his dorm suite—the common room, where he could see figures sitting on the couch and chairs, and a bedroom that wasn't his. The images changed every few seconds, rotating through the cameras, he supposed.

He found the image of the white room. Wilders was pacing back and forth, seemed to be yelling, obviously enraged. Someone Jason didn't recognize was typing on the laptop and periodically inspecting the wand device. A couple of guards jogged past other screens, their origins and destinations unclear. An exterior view showed a couple of cars parked by a gate, a group of figures standing nearby, too far away to see clearly. Jason smirked to himself. *Wilders must be freaking out.*

Molly turned her attention to the computers, sat down in one of the ergonomic chairs. Jason collapsed into the other, closed his eyes, massaged his temples, opened his eyes again to stare at Molly. Her belly rested on her thighs and her heavy breasts rested on her belly, large dark nipples capping them. Pale stretch marks tiger striped her abdomen. They were new, *his* Molly hadn't had them. Despite everything, Jason realized that his dick was also reacting to her proximity, her scent, her nakedness. He tried casually sitting, crossed his legs and draped a hand over his lap, but honestly doubted anyone would be fooled. He looked around for something he could use to cover himself. Nothing.

Molly, meanwhile, appeared unfazed by her nudity. She'd always been comfortable in her own skin. She tapped on the keyboard, powering up the monitor. When it requested a password, she hesitated, fingers poised in front of the keyboard. "So…what are the odds they use the same password?"

"Huh?"

Molly typed something in. The password screen vanished, a desktop backdrop appeared in its place. "Ah ha. We're in luck."

"Molly, how do you know the passwords?"

Molly turned, regarded him wistfully. "Well, I mean, after you died—over there, you know—it sort of screwed up the whole project. I mean, obviously. They weren't going to just keep going like nothing happened. Dr. Hernandez released all the subjects, paid us all the stipend. But she hired me as a research assistant, and they gave me access to the files. You'd think they would've changed all the passwords, but...guess not." She returned her focus to the computer, clicked on an icon, clicked on another. "I've been working with Vijay. Erin graduated last year, she's in, um...Portland, I think." The screen was filling with PDF files, Word documents. Molly scrolled down one, mumbling to herself, "What the what...I mean...what..."

"What is it?" Jason leaned forward, trying to read over her shoulder, but it was hard to focus on the words with his head still pounding, and hard to resist slipping his arms around her and nibbling her neck and spinning her ergonomic chair around and— *Dammit. Stop.*

"Well..." Molly clicked on another icon, scrolled through another document. "A lot of this is just, like, random data. Stuff I guess they've been gathering, but they haven't done anything with it. And it's messy, nothing's controlled. Look, here, there are...hmm...looks like physical measurements for someone...someones...after some sort of experiment, but stuff is missing. Like, the subjects, were they male or female? What's the timeline? When were these data points taken? It's...amateur, I guess, for want of a better word. And there's no indication that any of these experiments were repeatable, or if it was like a one-off thing. It's just..." She frowned and shook her head. "Messy."

"Is that important?"

"Well, yeah. If you want any of your findings to have any relevance, then yeah. You can't have this sort of just...whatever he's doing, screwing around. That's not research. That's a kid playing with a toy he doesn't understand."

"Is there anything about a baby? Is there a baby here?"

She clicked around, her forehead crinkled with concentration. "I don't see anything. Why? Did your Molly have a baby? Oh, here's something interesting. A fail-safe protocol." She was silent for a while, reading whatever file she'd opened on the screen. "Jesus, Jason, listen to this. They've got the whole building wired, whoever's in charge."

Jason nodded. "Yeah, cameras everywhere. I know."

Molly shook her head urgently. "No, I mean, like with explosives wired. There's a protocol here. If security's breached, the whole place is designed to burn down. To cover their tracks, get rid of evidence. Most of the data should be backed up on some remote server so it's supposed to act like a wipe of any proof of wrongdoing."

Jason blinked. His throat tightened. "What? There's explosives in the walls?"

"Yeah. Holy cow, this just seems like…massive overkill. There's a lot of paranoia in these documents. They must know they're doing illegal shit, too. But it's cold, man. Look right here, in the event of compromise, there's a fifteen-minute grace period to get out of the building, but it specifically dictates that all subjects be returned to the dorm area." She looked at Jason, her eyes horrified. "Do you get that? The subjects—you guys—you're not getting out. They've designed the place to burn down with you in it."

"Can you disable it? Stop it? What do we do?" Jason's heart was racing, which didn't particularly help his headache. He felt trapped, backed into a corner. *How can we even get out now? If I do manage to get out, notify police or whatever, won't they just activate the fail-safe at that point? Then Chris, Moe, Kechia, Diana, they'll all get killed anyway. It's a miracle Wilders didn't do it when I first got out. Maybe it wasn't in place then, the protocol. Maybe it was because I stayed hidden, didn't bring any attention to the place. Shit, what if I do now? What if I'm going to be responsible for their deaths?* His head spun.

"Well, we just need to figure out a way to get you all out of the building. Don't panic. I mean, it hasn't been set off or anything, there's no rush—"

Her voice was drowned out by the blaring of an alarm.

There was a solid thirty-second period of silence as everyone stopped and stared at the dust puffing out of the half-demolished garage. Well, ten- or five-second. Anyway, a moment of shocked, stunned awe in the aftermath of the crash.

Jasmine was the first to break it, shrieking at levels previously unreached. At first, Brigid couldn't understand what she was saying, screaming really. Just inarticulate sounds that slowly resolved into a recognizable word.

"Laura!"

Oh, fuck. Laura. That was Laura, driving the car.

Jasmine and Danilo charged toward the wreck. Ana stood frozen with her hands over her mouth. The cop still had his hand on Brigid's arm, but now he leaned toward the radio on his shoulder, asking for backup—fire department, ambulance, something along those lines. Acronyms she didn't recognize or care about. She yanked against the cop's grip, to no avail. He snarled at her to stay where she was, but she barely registered him.

Danilo was the first to reach the garage, now gaping open with dust and smoke drifting out. The battered, now totaled, sedan appeared in the entrance, rolling slowly backwards. It stopped moving as it bumped into the battered garage door, which was now lying on the ground. The front end of the vehicle was crumpled, the windshield cracked though not shattered, smoke billowing from under the hood. Danilo pulled the driver's door open and Laura stepped out gingerly. A half-deflated airbag sagged out of the steering wheel.

"Shit," Brigid muttered, jerking against the cop again, but he just squeezed harder. She was going to end up bruised. "Look," she pleaded, "look, we need to get over there. We need to make sure she's okay. Come on." *Honestly, he's just being obstinate now.* "She could be hurt, come on, I'll go with you, okay?"

The cop glowered at her but, having finished his conversation with whomever was on the other end of his radio, he grudgingly acquiesced. Laura was buried in her mother's embrace, cradling her left arm. Blood dripped from her nose, and she had a few cuts on her forehead.

Danilo was rubbing his hand over his head, leaning on the half-crumpled car, clearly shaken. "What were you thinking, Laura? What? What did you think this would accomplish?"

"Well, we had to get in, right? We had to get in?" Laura's words were a little slurred.

Brigid worried she might have a concussion. *Probably does, actually.*

"We had to get in. So, now we can get in. Just go in and get Jason, go in and get him. You can just walk right in."

"What?" Jasmine's voice was unsteady.

Laura gestured at the garage. "Well, there's a big fucking hole in the wall now."

Brigid peered into the garage, through the smoke and dust. There was, in fact, a big fucking hole in the wall. She spun to face the cop, who was still holding her arm. He seemed bewildered, clinging to her because he didn't know what else to do, because it gave him a sort of control in a chaotic scene. "You're gonna have to go in there now. Right? Right? Go in there, get everyone out?"

The cop looked conflicted. He looked back to his partner, maybe hoping for some support, but his partner was still standing with the two non-FBI agents with their convincing badges, staring at the wrecked car from a safe distance. Laura wriggled out of her mother's embrace, crawled over the rubble toward the big fucking hole in the wall, muttering inaudibly, tossing back her black hair as it tumbled over her shoulders.

"Hey!" The cop finally lost interest in Brigid's arm, released it so he could pursue Laura. "You need to get out of there, it's not safe. Get back, please, miss. Get back, please, the fire department needs to come and assess the situation, miss, please."

Like she's ever going to listen to him. Brigid rubbed her sore arm, tried to see through the settling dust in the garage, see into the building.

The side door burst open and a man wearing a business suit under a white lab coat came storming out.

卐

Molly and Jason froze, staring at each other for a few seconds as the alarm blared, echoed, blared again. "Shit. Shit. Did they find us? They found us." Molly spun back to the computer, but her hand hovered uncertainly over the mouse. "What do we do? Shit. Should we go back? Shift again? Shit…" She turned back to Jason, her eyes wide. "Jason, we have to run. We have to get the others and run. Now. Now!" She tugged at his arm. "Come on! Run! Let's go!"

Jason stared back, bewildered, stationary. *What's happening? What did I miss?*

Molly pointed to the computer screen, where a pop-up window had appeared with a timer on it, counting down. 14:45. 14:44. 14:43. "Jason, this is a security breach! The fail-safe! The fail-safe! We have to get the others and get out! Move, goddammit!"

Oh shit.

He finally broke free of his paralysis, yanked the door open, and the two of them bolted down the hallway. They made it approximately twenty feet before they were stopped by a locked door. A set of double doors, steel, closing off the hallway.

"Shit. Fuck. Fuck!" Jason rattled the push bar, slammed the heel of his hand into the door, which continued to not open. He took a step or two back, pressed his hands on his temples, squeezed his eyes shut. It couldn't end like this, the two of them trapped in a hallway, so close to freedom.

Well, but it won't end like this. All I have to do is jump, cross to the far side of the door, jump back. With Molly. No problem. He reached out for her hand but missed. His balance was off. He stumbled, fell. Molly caught him by the arm, steadied him. "Molly, the—" *This fucking alarm…the fucking alarm is killing me.* "We have to jump, get to the other side of the door, right? We can do that." He closed his eyes, tried to concentrate, tried to initiate a jump, but he couldn't collect his thoughts, couldn't shut out the blaring noise or the escalating panic in his chest. A realization rose through the chaos in his head, which he tried desperately to avoid facing, that he had no chance of making a jump successfully in his current state.

It's going to end like this after all.

Molly dropped him. He fell to his knees, blindly, clutching at his head. Between the alarm blasts he heard a squeaking, a scuffling, Molly's voice. "Dude! Come on!" He opened his eyes. Molly was holding the door open.

She got the door open! Goddamn that woman is magical. He staggered through the door, leaned against it to keep it open, realized what had happened. One of the jumpsuit goons—Ramon—was running down the hallway. He stopped at the next set of doors, swiped a keycard at a sensor on the wall. The sensor flashed red. He had to swipe it twice more before it switched to green, and by then Molly had caught up with him and full-on body slammed him into the doors. Ramon was caught off guard, not prepared for one hundred and fifty pounds of naked desperation barreling into him, and the two of them collapsed together in the now-ajar doorway. He shoved her off, scrambled to his feet. Molly lay curled up in the doorway, keeping the door from shutting. Ramon looked back and forth, panicked, turned and dashed back the way he'd come. Jason flinched away from him as he passed, but he didn't seem to have any interest in Jason, just kept running. Molly pulled herself upright, beckoned Jason through the door, slammed it behind them.

Fuck, though, now we're in exactly the same predicament. Stuck in a hallway behind locked doors. He looked to Molly, despairing.

Molly was grinning.

Molly was holding a keycard.

⌗

Brigid found it hard to tear her eyes away from the lab coat/business suit man. She waved in Ana's direction. "Is that him? The guy? Is that him?" She took a step backwards, hesitated for a second before running after the cop. "That guy! Arrest that guy! He's a kidnapper…he's got prisoners in there…my friend's in there!"

Ana was already striding toward Wilders, furious and indignant and righteous, stabbing the air with her index finger and shouting something Brigid couldn't quite make out over the din, but which was probably a polite request to allow access to the building or something.

The cop barely glanced in Wilders's direction, chasing after the Reyeses instead, who were chasing after Laura who had vanished through the hole in the wall.

Brigid halted as she reached the shattered garage door. Her heart was pounding, her arm sore. The smashed car was making knocking noises and steam hissed out from under the hood. Strobe lights blinked out of the hole in the wall, and an alarm rang from the bowels of the building. She looked back to the other cop, who was running in her direction and talking into his shoulder radio. Surprisingly, the two fake FBI agents were not coming toward her. Their expressions were obscured behind their matching mirrored sunglasses, but Brigid suspected "worried" as they took a few uncertain steps backward, muttered something between them, started trotting together toward the street, away from the fire engine which pulled up to the curb and disgorged a bunch of burly men from its flashing cab.

"Hey! Hey!" She waved both arms over her head. "Hey, they're going, stop them!" Neither of the cops seemed particularly interested. One was pulling Laura, protesting, out of the garage. The Reyeses were shouting at him, or at Laura, but Brigid couldn't understand a word of what they were saying. Ana continued yelling at Wilders, who was backing up slowly and trying to shout over her. An ambulance joined the fire engine at the curb, followed by two more police cars. Uniformed figures began swarming the area, shooing away rubberneckers who had phones out to video the events as they unfolded. The two fake FBI men slipped into the growing crowd. *Fuck,* Brigid thought, looking from them to Laura and the settling cloud of dust in the garage. *They're gonna get away, they're definitely gonna get away. Should I chase after them? No, who am I kidding...*

A couple of the firemen arrived and crawled over the wreckage, into the garage. Brigid heard a series of angry curses and Wilders charged past, Ana in pursuit.

Wilders threw himself in front of the firemen and physically shoved one of them. "No! No! No one has authorization to enter this facility! This is a classified facility! No one enters! No one!" No one listened. The firemen stepped past Wilders as if he didn't even exist and crawled through the hole into the building. Wilders paused for a moment, looking at the hole, the strobe light and alarm pulsing out. He looked around, met Brigid's eyes briefly, and bolted toward the wrecked perimeter fence.

центр

With the keycard, Jason and Molly were able to get back to the dorm rooms relatively quickly. Still, Jason wasn't sure how much time they had left. Things were getting kind of jumbled up. As they sprinted to the door, Jason couldn't help but register the inconvenience of running nude. The swinging, slapping inconvenience.

They got to the door, panting. No keycard swiper here.

Instead, they were faced with a keypad.

Molly looked at him, wide eyed. "Shit. What do we do?"

Jason stared at the keypad. He closed his eyes, tried to block out the sound of the alarm. He'd seen the code. He knew this. He knew this, he could do this—

"Jason!"

"Shh. Shh. Let me think. Wait." The alarm was messing with his brain, scrambling things. *There was a six. Definitely a six...* He tried 3664... no...6448...no.

He closed his eyes again, tried to visualize fingers typing in the code. 4688. No.

Fuck.

Fuck.

4866.

Fuck.

4886.

Fuck.

4668.

The keypad flashed green, the door clicked and opened.

Jason gasped, victorious delirium splashing through him, as four confused faces turned toward the open door.

Molly shoved the door fully open, shouting, "We have to go! Come on, we have to go, it's an emergency, everybody come on! Now now now!"

They stood up uncertainly, hesitantly. Jason checked down the hall—clear still—and beckoned frantically. "We have to go, come on, come on!" That seemed to do it.

Moe and Chris leapt up and dashed to the door. Kechia bolted to Molly, wrapping her arms tight around her. Diana disappeared into her bedroom.

Goddammit. Jason followed her. *What the fuck? Is she seriously refusing to leave? The fucking building's about to go up in flames and she's gonna decide to take a stand here? Now?*

He ran into her as she came charging out of her bedroom. She slapped a pair of light green scrubs against his abdomen as she passed, passed another set to Molly, and followed the others out the door. Molly dropped the shirt, picked it up, dashed to the front of the pack, swiping the keycard at the next set of hallway doors. Jason hopped after her, trying to pull on the pants. He managed to get them up over his hips, but they were about two sizes too small and consequently changed his gait from a run to more of a waddle. He didn't bother tying the drawstring, just chased the others down hallways, through a set of doors, into a new hallway.

Noises and dust emanated from beyond the set of doors in front of them. Voices, a bunch of them, all shouting...and sirens between the shrieks of the alarm.

Molly hesitated for a moment, glanced back at Jason, unlocked the door.

Past the door, Jason could see a hole in the wall and a couple of firemen peeking through, kneeling on the rubble on the ground. One looked up, noticed them, held up a hand and barked "Stay there!"

Jason forgot about the discomfort of the tight pants, forgot about the pain in his head and the blaring of the alarm, forgot about everything for a moment, stumbled and caught himself against the door, delirious and lightheaded. The end. They were at the end, there was an exit, there was a hole in the wall—

Molly yanked on his arm. "Out! Out out out! We're out of time! Go!"

Right, right, the explosives.

Brigid, frozen, watched Wilders's white lab coat flutter to the ground behind him as he fled. *Isn't someone going to stop him? Isn't anyone paying attention?* A female police officer had appeared by her side and was attempting to escort her away from the building, though Brigid barely noticed her. There were now two or three cops wrestling with Laura, who was still trying to claw her way into the building. Others were arguing with the Reyeses and with Ana, everyone shouting, no one coherent, a chaotic scene that felt on the edge of becoming an outright riot. Suddenly, Brigid heard a guttural roar and turned to see Jasmine bull her way through two policemen and a fireman, charge past the wrecked cars and throw her arms around a slight figure who'd emerged from the hole in the wall.

It was Jason. *Jason! Fuck, Jason!*

Jason and his mother dropped to their knees together, wrapped in an iron embrace, oblivious to the scene around them—the scene which consisted of another five individuals, all wearing light green scrubs with the exception of one woman who was totally naked, scrambling past them and out of the garage. The naked woman paused by Jason and his mother, pulling on their arms, saying something Brigid couldn't hear over the din. After a heartbeat, they got up and followed her outside. Laura twisted her arms free and ran to her brother to pull him into a hug with Danilo, all of them tangled together, even while they stumbled out of the garage and into the disheveled yard.

The naked woman took a few steps outside, paused just long enough to pull on a set of light green scrubs that were clearly too small. She tugged the shirt down over her chest while backing up, shouting, "Everybody get back, get back, get back!" and staring at the building with trepidation.

A muffled *whoomp* came from deep within the building, then a series of additional whoomps, a halo of dust puffed out, and the whole place folded inwards and burst into flames.

The shockwave from the collapse knocked Jason, as well as all of his family, over. They still had their individual arms wrapped around him as if they were worried he would disintegrate at any moment. He actually felt a little suffocated, but he didn't care. When his mother had appeared in front of him, her face was so unexpected that he almost didn't recognize her, didn't realize the reality of her presence until he felt himself buried in her embrace. He didn't quite understand, but it didn't matter—his family was here, of course they were, this was his daring escape! His family was here, Molly was here, his friends were escaping, everything was finally coming together. He had never felt so triumphant.

Some uniformed people appeared around them, pulled them up and ushered them all away from the building, from the heat of the fire. Jason managed to peer around, tried to process the scene. He thought he could see Dr. Hernandez's face popping into view here and there between police and firemen and paramedics. It was weird to see her in street clothes, not in a lab coat. *And Brigid! No? Yes! Definitely Brigid!* She looked like she'd been in a car accident. *Was she in a car accident?* He tried to wiggle free, but his mother was having none of it. Sirens approached as a second, then a third fire engine pulled up, and men in heavy yellow coats rushed past them, dragging large canvas hoses. His mother cupped his face in her hands, weeping, tears tracking through dust and soot on her face. Somehow, they'd moved to the street. Paramedics handed out blankets, shone lights in eyes, and checked pulses. Molly appeared wearing scrubs that were too small, and he beamed at her, took her hand and pulled her to him, rested his chin on her shoulder and held her.

Molly was silent.

⌘

The shockwave from the collapse knocked Brigid onto her rear, and a wave of heat hit her face as if she'd just opened an oven door. Two women in light green scrubs had fallen in the weeds near her. One of them, blonde and lean, stared at the rubble in shock for a moment, then screamed "Ramon...Ramon! No! Ramon!" before heading back toward the fire. The other woman, dark-skinned and ponytailed, seized her around the waist and pulled her struggling to the ground.

"God. Oh, god." A blond guy, also in scrubs, sat up and twisted around to watch the flames flickering out of the depths of the wreckage. "What happened? Who are you? Did you do that?"

"I'm a friend of Jason's. Yeah, I mean no, we…I don't know. We knocked a hole in the wall there, but Jesus…I wasn't expecting the whole place to…" She stared at the blaze. *Had it taken out a load-bearing wall or something? Did a car explode while I wasn't looking? What sort of shoddy fucking construction…*

The other guy, the darker one, tore his eyes from the fire. "You're a friend of Jason's?"

"Yeah. Hi. I'm Brigid. His family's here, too…and Ana… Dr. Hernandez."

The guy looked astonished, mouth gaping slightly. "You're Brigid? No way! He said you might come, I thought he was full of shit. No fucking way." He was grinning now, delighted. "That's fucking amazing. You fucking broke us out. Chris! Did you hear that?"

"Yeah…" Chris, the blond, propped himself up on his elbows, his eyes wide. "Wow. That is incredible."

"Oh, yeah, Chris. He mentioned you." She turned back to the other one. "So then you would be…uh…" Brigid flushed. *Great googly moogly, this guy is hot.* She couldn't remember the other names. *One was Tyrone, but he was gone, right? Fuck, it would've been so cool if I could've just named him, off the cuff.* This dude was so sexy, even in scrubs. He had messy black curls over thick eyebrows and intense green eyes that scanned the area with controlled interest. Stubble over his cheeks. She mentally shook her head. *Settle down. Now is not the time or place. Not the time or the place…but wow, though.*

His gaze returned to rest on her. Searching. Piercing. "I'm… Mohammed. I'm sorry, I just can't get over…I can't believe you came. This is amazing. You did this? You're amazing."

She could feel her cheeks burning, had to drop her eyes, looked over at the two women. The blonde one was still screaming but had stopped thrashing, and the darker one was holding her, rubbing her back, trying to comfort her. "Diana…oh no…"

A knot formed in Brigid's throat. She wondered if there were people from the lab who hadn't made it out. She struggled to her feet and backed away from the fire. Uniformed people appeared behind them, guiding them to the street, which was filled with emergency vehicles—ambulances, fire trucks, more and more police cruisers. Someone handed her a blanket. Someone else told her not to go anywhere, something about questions later, blah blah. She looked around for Jason, saw him leaning against an open ambulance with a blanket around his shoulders, hugging someone, his sister and parents around him.

Jason saw her, jogged over with a sort of weird waddling gait, leading a woman by the hand. He embraced her briefly. His face was suffused with elation, unadulterated joy. "Brigid, thank you, thank you—" He pulled back a bit. "What happened to your face?"

She shook her head. "Nothing. Are you okay? Is everyone out?"

"Yeah. Yeah, we're all okay." He gestured to the woman next to him. "Brigid, this is Molly."

Brigid gasped. "No way. Really? That's incredible." She reached out, grasped Molly's hand. Molly was shorter than she'd envisioned, with mocha skin, puffy hair. Her eyes were wide set, dark and intelligent, her handshake firm. Her scrub top was stretched tight over her chest, same with the pants over her hips. "I thought you…uh, I thought you hadn't made it."

"I didn't. Not here." Molly cast a look back at the burning lab, grimaced briefly. "It's good to meet you, and I don't mean to be rude, but…Jason, we need to talk."

⌘

Brigid stepped back, wearing a bewildered smile.

Jason felt a wave of dread wash over him, tried to tell himself he wasn't sure why, but he was lying to himself. Nothing good could come after that phrase. Nothing good. He shook his head, his joyous expression becoming fixed, false. "No. No, we don't." He looked toward the police car. He could see Dr. Hernandez in the distance, wanted to take Molly's hand and run over, wanted to keep having happy reunions, keep hugging and laughing and crying. He wanted to feel the sun on his skin, taste the crystalline and smoky air, fill his heart with his newly won freedom. He did not want to talk. Not that talk. That talk never needed to happen.

Molly rubbed her eyes. "Yes, Jason, now." She sniffed, ran her hand under her nose and left a smear of blood on her lip.

Jason's chest tightened. His headache, briefly forgotten, resurrected at the base of his skull.

Molly looked down at the blood on her hand ruefully. She wiped her nose again, then met Jason's eyes. "You know I have to go. You know that. And you know you can't come with me."

Jason's vision blurred. He shook his head vehemently. "No. No." He wasn't even sure what he was denying. He just didn't want to hear what she was saying.

"We belong in our own universes. Jason, that's the truth. We can't... switch them out." A trickle of blood reappeared under her left nostril. She winced briefly, and when she opened her eyes again he realized how bloodshot they were.

Have they been like that the whole time? How did I not notice?

"No one has ever managed to stay in an alternative universe for long. Never for more than an hour, not without serious damage. I'm on another resonance. I need to go back. If I stay here much longer, it'll hurt me. It might kill me."

"No. This isn't fair. It's not fair!"

Jason's mother appeared from somewhere, cooing sympathetically about something she couldn't possibly understand, put her arms around his shoulders. He shrugged her off and stalked away. He didn't want comfort. He didn't want sympathy. He suddenly just wanted all of them to go away, to leave him and Molly alone. *Fuck, why does everyone have to witness this?* He turned back to the collapsed, burning building. *Did the goons make it out? Probably dead. Good. Someone should pay for this, someone should be hurting, someone besides me.*

Molly came up behind him, pulled him around by his arm. Her eyes locked onto his, steady, resolute, but wet. "No, it's *not* fair. It's not. It's not fair that *my* Jason died, it's not fair that *your* Molly died, but here we are. We have to live with it." She smiled, a bit wryly. "As it were. And I can't leave Yasmin. I have to go back."

"Fine. I'll go back with you. She's my—"

"You know you can't do that either. You won't survive."

Dammit, why does she have to be like this? She isn't listening, isn't even trying. Why does she always have to be so stubborn…so fucking frustrating? "I don't care. I just got you back, I can't lose you again."

She shook her head. "You don't care…*I* care, Jason. I can't watch you die again. I will not. This is a no-alternative situation." She had to stop to wipe blood off her lip again, put a hand on his shoulder. At first, he thought it was out of affection, but she was swaying slightly, leaning on him. Her legs gave out and he had to catch her under the arms. She was in bad shape, much worse than he'd realized. She'd been here, in this universe, for too long.

Jason's heart dropped. A vise closed in his chest and it was suddenly hard to breathe.

She has to go. She's dying, again, right here, because of me, and she has to go.

He pulled her close again, wrapped his arms around her familiar warm body, his hands balled into fists, buried his face in her shoulder. "I'm sorry. Okay. I'm sorry. Just…maybe I can find you again, maybe I can see you…"

Molly sighed, her head pressed against his chest, her arms tight around his waist. "Maybe."

She pulled back slightly, looked up into his face, leaned in and kissed him. One last kiss tasting of blood and pain, filled with all the hope, horror, joy, dread, and rage he was holding in his heart. One kiss for one moment, for every moment, before she broke off and fixed him in place with her dark shining eyes.

And then she was gone, and he was left holding a light green scrub shirt, alone.

⌘

The rest of that day was one of the longest Brigid could remember.

The five lab subjects were taken to the local hospital for checkups. Mohammed went reluctantly, as he'd been lingering around Brigid, staring, reminding her periodically about how incredible she was, how brave, how smart. By the end she found it almost funny. He agreed to go with the paramedics only after she gave him her email address and promised to stay in contact.

The paramedics wanted to take Laura, too, but she insisted she was fine and refused to go. There was some debate as to whether she'd be arrested for destruction of property but, in the end, she was released. Jason's family, Ana, and Brigid were all taken downtown for interviews, which lasted all day.

Brigid got in touch with O'Leary, demanding to know why Not-Smith wasn't in custody and whether she was going to be arrested. He wouldn't tell her anything, just insisted she return to Boston to be interviewed ASAP. She wasn't sure what was going on with the two fake agents or Wilders. They all seemed to have vanished.

Jason and his family returned to Springfield that night. Brigid went home with Ana. They were silent on the drive home, both of them exhausted. David met them when they arrived, embraced Ana, asking, "Are you all right? What can I get you?" Brigid dropped to her knees as Lithium came bounding out, happy and wiggly like always. He let her hug his neck for a few moments before squirming out so he could sniff her clothes and hair. She did smell pretty strongly of smoke and dust.

"Come on, come in. Come have a drink. Sit down. Relax," David said.

Brigid stood up, smiled gratefully at him, and entered the house with Lithium still sniffing at her pants. *A drink, yeah...a shower, even more yeah.*

An hour later, she was sitting at her hosts' dinner table, sipping a glass of wine, her hair still damp from the shower, her skin scrubbed raw and clean. The enormity of everything that had happened that day was finally starting to become clear. There were so many conflicting emotions bubbling through her, it was hard to pick one to focus on— the victorious thrill that they had freed the lab prisoners, dismay that the building and whatever research data was in it had burned down, delirious joy at having returned Jason to his family, grief for his loss of Molly. Again.

She nibbled on some peanuts Ana had set on the table while dinner was being prepared, sipped the wine. Tried to piece together the sequence of events of the day. Most of it had come out in hushed discussions with the lab subjects, and particularly with Jason, though he'd been emotionally devastated to the point that only snippets of information were forthcoming.

Ana came out from the kitchen, placed a bowl of salad on the table and sat across from Brigid.

"What a day, eh?"

Brigid nodded, set her wineglass down. "Yeah. For sure." She reached to scratch Lithium between his ears. "Crazy. You know, I've been thinking, like...what are the odds?"

Ana cocked her head slightly. "What do you mean?"

"Well, you know how once I asked Jason why..." Brigid had to stop and gather her thoughts. "Why those guys didn't run into alternate versions of themselves all the time, and he said it was because the odds of going to a similar alternate universe were astronomical, because of infinite universes? Something like that?"

"Yes?"

"So, it's just really crazy that Jason managed to find the one alternate universe where there was a Molly who knew him, and knew about the experiment, and knew how to get him out, all of that stuff. Just...really long-shot odds. You know?"

Ana nodded. "Yes. You are right. You are of course completely correct." She leaned back, her eyes focused on something distant. "Look at it this way. For every possible outcome today, a new alternate reality was born. Yes? Take for example, Jason shifted to an alternate universe this morning. To simplify things, say there are 500 possible alternate universes he might have gone to, and only one had Molly. Now there are 499 alternate realities in existence in which Jason failed to escape the lab. Taking that one universe where he did find Molly, suppose they did not manage to get a keycard to unlock the doors. So, now there are some...at least one...alternate realities in which he found Molly, but they could not get out of the building. Some alternate realities where they couldn't get the others out of their locked room. Somewhere Laura did not drive into the building and set off the alarm."

Brigid was getting confused. "Yeah..."

"Those are all valid realities. They exist, so to speak. They just don't happen to be the one we're in. This is one of an infinite number of possible outcomes, yes. But as long as it is a possible outcome, it exists as a reality."

"Yeah…"

"What is amazing, truly, is not that all of these…er…strokes of luck happened. What is amazing is that we exist in *this* one specific universe. Because out there in the multiverse there are millions, billions of versions of you and myself that are not sitting here at this table, safe and warm. We are fortunate, not that all of those lucky strokes happened today, but that we happen to be the ones inhabiting the one universe in which they did happen. They would have happened for someone."

Brigid thought this was starting to make a bit more sense, though she suspected in half an hour she'd be confused again. "Okay, yeah, I get it…I think."

"What is mind boggling," Ana continued, her eyes bright and animated, "is that you and I, we share a history with all of these infinite alternate versions of ourselves. There is a version of you, right now, in the multiverse, who was indeed the same as the you who is sitting here now, right up until we got to the lab this morning, but branched off and is now, I don't know, sitting in a jail cell or driving back to Boston or even dead maybe. They all exist, they are all you, but now this is the only you that you realize. Think of it! And tomorrow there will be another set of versions of you, another maybe infinite set, and every one will consider herself the one true self, but in truth they will all be the same as the self who is here now."

Right. Confused again. That didn't take long.

"What we should be thankful for, humbled by, is that we are in this one unique reality. Think of the odds that we would not have been! Infinity to one, eh! It brings me great joy, whenever I think of what could have been. How fortunate I am that I exist in the universe in which I have a husband whom I love, that I have my daughter. How fortunate that you appeared on my doorstep, how fortunate that we were able to help rescue Jason today. I thank God that we are here. I am filled with gratitude." Ana beamed and sipped her wine.

"But…" Brigid faltered. She hated to rain on the parade, but she felt like this logic was flawed somehow. "But not everything went right. You know? Molly, she's still gone. Jason's pretty messed up about that. There are still, like, some of the lab people who didn't make it out. The Reyeses, they spent an entire year thinking Jason was dead. That's all really f—…um, bad stuff."

Ana nodded. "Again, you are completely correct. Wouldn't it be wonderful if everything went right all the time? Perhaps that world is out there, somewhere." She smiled again. "Yes, some things went wrong. Where I find comfort, in those situations, is in the knowledge that there is…there exists…a reality where those things went right after all. There is a real, physical…no, metaphysical," she corrected, "place in which Jason and Molly left the lab, married, had children, are living happily. Where Tyrone and Pedro and Angela and Ji are alive and fulfilling their potentials. It is not here, and this brings me sadness. But it is out there, in the multiverse."

Brigid nibbled on the peanuts, mulling this over. *Seems like…like she's cherry-picking the best aspects of the whole situation, only looking at the happy things, ignoring the bad. I don't know that I'm capable of that degree of optimism. Yeah, there's a universe where Molly's still alive, a better universe, and we're not in it.*

She looked down at Lithium, who noticed and raised his head off the floor, pricking his ears. *But then there's also worse universes, where the worst things possible happened. Jason still locked up. Or me, dead in a swamp in Revere. Or Lithium hit by a car and killed while on a walk.* She shuddered at the thought, seeing herself kneeling over his broken body, helpless and torn apart inside. A universe filled with pain and death and anguish.

She stroked his ear.

But that isn't this universe. This is my universe.

So be happy. Be happy that we're here.

EPILOGUE

U nder the dull gleam of a midnight streetlight, Brigid threw her suitcase into the back of her car, returned to fetch Lithium, locked the house, twisted her back a few times and jumped into the driver's seat.

She was excited. Really excited. *All I have to do is drive for the next, what, twelve hours? Fourteen? Sixteen? Who knows, exactly. I don't care. GPS can direct me, I don't even really have to pay attention.* She was going back to Chicago for a full week's vacation. She hadn't seen Ana in way too long—months, after they'd been together almost 24/7 for the first few weeks. Same with the Reyeses. And, honestly, she missed Jason…or, more specifically, she worried about Jason. He'd been silent for the past few weeks, after an initial flurry of intense emails and texting and Skype conversations.

But, also, I'm going to see Mohammed again.

Squee.

Which means I'm going to get laid again.

Squee-heeee.

It was nearly a year since she'd begun a relationship with Mohammed. *Agh! Relationship! What a scary word.* It was undeniably a bit of a struggle, given the distance between them—he still lived in Chicago, as he was still tangled up in all of the residual investigations and lawsuits that had sprouted from the ruins of Wilders's lab. Brigid had returned to Boston, though. She'd been un-fired from her job—after the details of the lab, the kidnappings, the heroic and explosive rescue had hit the media—and she still had another year's lease on her apartment. Also, she was reluctant to uproot her life for a man. No matter how great the sex might be.

Oh, but it is great.

So great.

Driving through the darkness on the interstate, half-singing along to the radio, she remembered the day they first got together. A favorite memory, though a bit morbid, since it had been the day of Molly's memorial service.

A confusing time, emotionally. It turned out that all of the lab subjects had been declared dead, all on the same day in January. The same day that Jason's parents were told he'd died. The official police theory was that, after Angela died, Wilders decided that if all the subjects were thought to be dead then he wouldn't have to worry about curious family members showing up and poking around. That would be why he'd been so hell-bent on finding Jason, after he escaped. Jason could have brought the whole thing crashing down...if things had played out a little differently.

All of their families had been mourning for over a year by the time the lab was destroyed. There was so much joy when Mohammed and Chris and Kechia and Diana were reunited with their families. Brigid couldn't control the fountain of happy tears, witnessing it.

But the other families...five sets of parents who'd arrived filled with hope for the same, thinking their children were being miraculously restored to them, and whose grief returned compounded when that hope was crushed. Five memorials for the five lab subjects who were still dead. Molly's family happened to arrive at the police station while Brigid was there, giving a statement. She'd seen them from across the room, watched Molly's parents crumble as they were given the news. Even over the background clamor of the station, Brigid could hear the sobs.

She'd attended Molly's memorial with some trepidation. She hadn't technically known Molly, though she felt like she had. She had conflicting feelings that she was butting in somewhere she didn't belong, but she wanted to be there to support Jason, and to pay her respects. So, in the end, she showed up and sat in the back, lurking, hands folded on her lap and back ramrod straight. Mohammed appeared, sat next to her, silently handed her a tissue when Jason stood up to make a statement and tears started running down her cheeks. Slipped an arm around her shoulders, giving her a tiny but supportive squeeze.

After the memorial, the two of them walked out of the chapel and wandered through the cemetery, through the worn headstones and moss and silent echoes of ancient grief. She couldn't remember the details of their conversation. Something about his parents, how his closer relationship with them was an ironic happy outcome of his incarceration in the lab, how he was looking for silver linings and trying to focus on the positive. At some point, he put his arm around her shoulders again and stopped walking, and she turned to find him gazing at her. He said—without inflection, as if he was pointing out that the sky was blue or the sun was warm—"You're very pretty."

"Ha," she responded, sneering, because she was not pretty, knew she was not pretty, had never been pretty and now was pudgy and middle aged, with puffy eyes and smudged mascara. "Well, you're nice."

He didn't reply, just kept looking at her, cocking his head slightly as if curious. Her initial impulse had been to recoil and hide her face, her lined, saggy, worn out face. But, after the memorial service, her defenses were down, her emotions raw and vulnerable. On a whim, she instead met his eyes, slipped a hand onto the back of his neck, kissed him long and hard...and completely inappropriately, given that they were standing in a cemetery.

In hindsight, she thought after much reflection, *he didn't look at me and see someone pretty. He looked at a woman he liked and perceived her as pretty. A subtle difference, maybe. Perception is funny. Perception is reality.*

She grinned, now, thinking of it, bit her lip, glanced at the headlights in her rearview mirror, and took a sip of the coffee she'd prepared. For all the hell that the last year had produced, she had to think that she herself had come out on top. She had friends again, she had a social life again. She had become outgoing. Stronger, more confident. Happier. Thinner, too...well, or at least healthier. She was on a first-name basis now with the gruff, tattooed old men who staffed the L Street Bathhouse down by the beach, where she would jog with Lithium a couple of times a week. She suspected they were retired gangsters or ex-cons, but they were happy to keep Lithium company for her while she worked out at their gym. They spent most of the time feeding him cookies, so Lithium was actually getting a little chubby, but Brigid was looking good.

And, if Mohammed doesn't notice, I'm going to smack him and then we're going to have lots and lots of sex.

Everything was better.

Everything except for Jason.

⌸

Jason was sitting on his bed scrolling idly through his phone when he heard gravel crunching. He hopped over to the window. Brigid's car was pulling up behind his parents' cars in the driveway. He perked up, muttered to himself, "Hell yeah," and trotted downstairs. His parents were already halfway down the walk to meet her when he got outside, and he had to wait impatiently for both of them to hug her before he got his chance.

"Hey, Jason," she whispered. "It's so good to see you." She leaned back, held him at arm's length. "Sorry, I must smell awful. I've been sweating pretty much since the sun came up. You're looking good! Doing okay?"

"Yeah, yeah, good. So good to see you!" He broke off and dropped to his knees to greet Lithium, who bounded over and twirled and wriggled around him, doing that whole-body tail wag thing. He paused to sniff at the cuffs of Jason's pants, and Jason took the opportunity to scratch him behind the ears. "Hey buddy, I missed you!" He straightened up and beamed at Brigid. "Let's head on in, we've got some stuff set up out back. Dr. Hernandez is on her way, I think, and the others. Chris and Dan are here already. Laura couldn't make it, she says hi though."

They headed to the back deck where chips and peanuts were set out on a glass table, next to a cooler of beers. Chris hopped up to wrap his arms around Brigid. His boyfriend, Dan, a stout Canadian with a thick black beard and charming Quebecois accent, gave her a perfunctory squeeze. Kechia rose to hug her as well. Jason handed Brigid a beer and opener, and they both settled into plastic deck chairs, as Lithium enthusiastically explored the grassy yard and occasionally squirted a bit of pee on the vegetation. Brigid glanced at her phone surreptitiously while sucking on her beer.

Jason poked her shoulder playfully. "He's on his way. Relax."

Brigid giggled. "What? I'm not..."

Jason leaned back, sighed contentedly. They hadn't all gotten together like this for months, after being together almost daily after the demise of the lab. Every day there'd been interviews, meetings, depositions, more meetings, therapy sessions, more meetings. There was an ongoing manhunt for, and criminal investigation into, Wilders, who'd vanished after the lab burned. The investigators had dug up a spiderweb of shadowy corporate backers with possible ties to the government. Nothing confirmed, lots of denials, lots of digging around in deleted emails and documents and stuff that Jason didn't really understand. There were a series of lawsuits, the biggest one obviously raised by the families of the five surviving lab subjects, which was still pending. In addition, wrongful death suits had been brought by the families of those who didn't make it out, though none of their remains were ever recovered. And there'd been no mention of an infant, living, dead, or otherwise.

A lot of stuff still unresolved.

But, after Brigid moved back to Boston, after the media spotlight wandered off to find another scandal, they all sort of drifted apart. Not that they weren't close anymore, it was just hard to find time for all of them to get together at once. And, sometimes, it was just too much effort. Jason had periods of time when he couldn't face the world, sometimes suffering through weeks of insomnia, paranoia, anxiety. It was PTSD, he was told, and he'd been prescribed medications, but he refused to take them. Figured he'd had enough of drugs.

So it was particularly good to see them together again. All except for Diana, who responded to his invitation with a polite but terse, "My therapist is discouraging me from exposing myself to any situations that might trigger me." To be honest, that wasn't surprising. Diana had never really forgiven Jason for Ramon's death. She placed the blame squarely on him, though he thought that was unfair. A little unfair. If he allowed himself to think about it, he would have to admit that yeah, it was his fault. He hadn't meant it, but it was his fault. But he didn't want to face the guilt that came with that, so he mostly didn't think about it.

Jason was on his second beer when Moe finally arrived. Brigid lit up like a Christmas tree, glowing, almost literally. *So weird to see her like that. Also, so weird, her and Moe together. Sure, they've spent a lot of time together, and yeah, they clearly have chemistry or whatever. For sure she's super into him, but...* He mentally shook his head. He still couldn't wrap his head around their age difference. The whole reason they'd gathered today was for Moe's thirtieth birthday. *And, what is she, like forty-five or something? She told me once, I think. I can't remember.* He had to admit that she seemed younger when she was around Moe. Brighter. More alive. *Moe's looking good, too. Guess he's been going to the gym again.*

Moe went around the table, giving Kechia the obligatory greeting-hug, shaking the men's hands, but Brigid got up beaming and stood on her toes to kiss him. Kechia laughed, shaking her head. Dan raised a furry eyebrow, smirking. Moe draped his arms loosely around Brigid's waist, leaned in, and whispered, "You look good."

Brigid blushed furiously. Jason realized with some chagrin that she did look different. She was thinner, maybe? Fitter? He'd failed to notice earlier. He wondered if there was some appropriate thing to say in these situations. "You are dramatically changed since I last saw you! Please do not take my obliviousness as a personal slight." *Hmm, probably best to say nothing.*

Dr. Hernandez and her husband arrived about twenty minutes later, by which time Jason's dad had the grill turning out an absurd abundance of charred burgers and hot dogs only made edible by copious volumes of ketchup and relish. Dr. Hernandez made the rounds, greetings and small talk, before getting around to Jason. She held a chilled glass of white wine in one hand and wrapped her free arm around his shoulder. "Jason, I am so happy to see you. It has been too long. How are you? Are you doing all right?" Her eyes were searching; she wasn't asking politely. Jason shifted uncomfortably.

Dr. Hernandez had taken a special interest in him, he felt, since the whole lab incident went down. Maybe because of their shared relationship with Molly. Maybe he was just imagining it. But it seemed like she was overly invested in how he was doing and, for this reason, he'd been kind of avoiding her for the past few months. Well, and because she kept pushing him to remove the implant, the distractor.

He still had it. He still wanted it. Everyone else's had been removed, without complications, nearly a year earlier. He'd refused. And, apparently, this bothered her so it felt like every time she saw him it became a cloud hanging over them. *Why should I get rid of it? Why give it up? What does anyone else want with it?*

So he only smiled tersely and nodded. "Yeah, yeah. Um, you?"

⌗

"Brigid," Jasmine was gushing, "you look too thin! Are you eating enough? What is wrong?" She leaned over to her husband. "We need to feed her. Get her another hot dog. Do you want a hot dog?"

Brigid giggled. "I've already had like a million hot dogs. I'm about to burst. Thanks." She'd slipped far too many bites to Lithium, who was inevitably going to have terrible gas later. That might be a mood killer, she realized, but that wasn't going to stop her.

"We missed you at Christmas! Certainly we understood, but we would have loved to host you. Someday you will need to come! Next year perhaps."

Brigid shrugged. She'd wanted to join the Reyeses for Christmas but, ultimately, she couldn't imagine Christmas without her mother, so she spent the day sitting at her mother's rest home silently watching old movies and nursing that old familiar ache. *Sad, yeah, but if I'd skipped it I'd never be able to forgive myself.*

She looked over at Jason. She'd barely had a chance to talk to him since she'd arrived, barely had a chance to ask how things were going. He was talking to Ana, his face uncomfortable, his posture stiff. She was pushing him on something. That was typical. She wasn't one to back away from difficult conversations, though Jason looked very much like he wanted to back away.

⌗

Dr. Hernandez rubbed Jason's arm, stepped back to survey the party and sipped her wine. "I am so happy to see everyone together again.

Almost everyone. I have missed you all! You know, I worry." She turned back to him. "I know I say this every time, but—"

"I'm not taking it out."

She sighed. "All right, Jason. It is your choice. But how are you handling things, really? You are still in therapy?"

Nod.

"Anything to report? Any news? Are you seeing anyone?"

Jason shook his head.

"Have you given any thought to returning to your education? Finishing your degree?"

Jason stared off into the neighbor's yard. "Um, maybe. Not right now. Sometime later." *Shit, she's making me feel so inadequate.* Truthfully, mostly these days he just hung out in his room, in his parents' house, browsing the Internet or binge-watching TV shows he'd missed out on or playing video games. It kept his mind off of other things.

Dr. Hernandez crossed her arms. "You know, of course, anything you need from me, all you need to do is ask—"

Jason nodded again. "Yeah. Thanks. I know. Um, I have to…uh…I gotta go to the bathroom, um, sorry."

He dashed off, hid in the bathroom. *Shitballs. This party's going to hell.* He stared at his reflection, gripped the bathroom sink. His knuckles went white. He closed his eyes, took a few deep breaths. The meditation training still came in handy these days, therapy or no. He opened his eyes again, focused on his face in the mirror.

It'll be all right. Just keep it together. Everything's gonna be fine.

Slow blink. He relaxed his hands. *It's gonna be fine.*

⌘

Brigid set her beer down on the deck table. It was mostly empty anyway. She brushed her hands off, excused herself from the Reyeses, who'd turned their attention back to the grill, and approached Ana. "Hey, uh… what's going on with Jason? I haven't seen him for a bit."

Ana sighed. "Well, have you had much of a chance to talk to him recently?"

Brigid shook her head. "A few texting chats here and there, nothing very deep, not for a few weeks." She followed Ana's gaze toward the house. "You're worried? He seemed okay to me."

Ana murmured, under her breath, "He still won't let me remove the implant."

Brigid grunted quietly. *I wouldn't call that a surprise. It's his one last link to Molly, at least as far as he's concerned. I can kind of understand why he's reluctant to let go of it. So long as it's just a memento.*

But it isn't, is it? That's why she's worried. Of course he's still using it. Wouldn't I, if I were him?

They'd already performed a series of interventions, way back last year, when Brigid was still staying in the area. Ana explained, in lurid and painful detail, why he had to abandon any notion of finding Molly again. The odds against it were astronomical. The damage done to himself, every time he phase shifted...well, it was going to end up seriously hurting him. Triggering a stroke or an aneurism or something. And, even if he did find her again, even if he managed to locate one version of Molly who knew him and had a history with him and hadn't moved on, which was infinitely unlikely, what would that accomplish? He wouldn't be able to stay there. Molly wouldn't be able to join him here. How would it help, seeing her for ten, twenty minutes?

Back then, he'd nodded, agreed, claimed to understand. But, since then, he'd been caught three separate times in suspect circumstances. Once, he'd been picked up by the police, wandering naked through the overgrown vegetation by the lab ruins. Another time, Chris found him in an alley near his old studio apartment, panting and sweaty, with blood smeared under his nose and down his chin. Then, he was found one night down by the lakeshore, skinny dipping. Or claiming to skinny dip. Not a popular activity in Lake Michigan in the fall.

"What should we do? I mean, what *can* we do?"

Ana sighed. "I do not know. I wish I did. The truth is, we cannot force him to give it up. We cannot force him to take care of himself. Not when he is obsessed with this...this quest of his. But I hate to watch him destroy himself. I hate to watch what he is putting his parents, his family, through...they lost him, and he returned. What a gift. And now he is…" She stopped talking, her arms folded across her chest, two fingers resting on her lips.

"I know," Brigid said. "Yeah, but you know, you're right. I don't know what we can do about it. We're sort of…stuck."

"Yes." Ana looked at her sadly. "As is Jason. Stuck."

⊡

Ten minutes standing gripping the bathroom sink did little for Jason's state of mind, and he finally decided to go cool off in his bedroom for a little while. He snagged a beer from the kitchen first, managed to slip upstairs unnoticed and flopped down on the bed. *A couple of minutes of privacy. Then I should be okay to face everyone again. Just a couple of minutes.*

He'd lost track of time, scrolling aimlessly through his phone, when there was a knock at the door. His mom, presumably. Wanting to know why he was being antisocial.

"Jason?"

Fuck, that's not my mom.

He tossed the phone aside, opened the door. "Hey, Brigid. I just…I just had to get away for a little bit. You know?"

She nodded, looked behind him into his bedroom. "Yeah, I know. That's okay." She looked back at him, smirked. "You're gonna have to deal with me for a little bit, though. We haven't really had a chance to catch up."

"Yeah." Jason suddenly felt awkward, standing in his doorway, blocking her. He took a step back and gestured an invitation. Brigid walked to his desk and sat down in the chair, spinning it around slowly, taking in his room. He hoped there wasn't anything too embarrassing visible. He sat down on his bed, cross-legged, facing her.

"So…" Brigid's eyes wandered around in a leisurely manner before alighting on Jason. "You're doing all right?"

"Yeah, yeah. Fine."

"Because, you know, Ana is kinda—"

"Yeah. I know," Jason said, rolling his eyes. "She's worried, blah blah. She wants me to take the implant out." He glowered at the window, avoiding Brigid's gaze. "Look, it's not up to her. It's my body."

"Well, yeah, but like technically, it's her device…"

"Well, she put it in *me*, didn't she? I'm sorry, but she sort of gave up, like, ownership rights or whatever when she did that."

Brigid pulled her legs up, crossed her ankles, leaned forward to wrap her arms around her knees. "I don't actually think that's the way it works. But that's not the point. That's not why she's worried, and you know it."

"I'm not using it. I'm not…I haven't made any jumps in, like, forever."

Silence.

"I'm not."

Silence.

Goddammit. "And even if I was, that's my choice. That's my right. No one else has any right to…to…"

"Jason, no one's arguing about whether it's your right…or your choice, or whatever. What all of us—and I'm including your parents—" Her eyes widened pointedly. "—are worried about is that you're hurting yourself. And you know you *are* hurting yourself if you're doing these phase shifts, and for no reason." She reached over, opened his beer and took a sip, handed it back to him. "I know we've had these talks. Nothing's changed."

Jason took his beer back, dangled it by the neck, stared at it dejectedly. He'd drunk about four already and would probably have four more before the end of the night, because he always thought it would help, even when it didn't. *Yeah, we've already had these talks. Yeah, nothing's changed. But, yeah, I'm still making jumps.*

He was still looking for Molly. Looking for her and their baby. Talking was for nothing. There was a gnawing, aching emptiness inside him, a blackness that threatened to slither its tendrils around his entire being and swallow him whole. He felt as if at every moment there was a weight on his throat, threatening to crush him from the inside out. An almost sentient misery that had amplified since the lab burned, since he'd last seen her, held her, kissed her. Losing her again had ripped something vital out of him. He had a family out there—a partner, a daughter—and without them he was nothing. He had to do something. He had to try to find them, or he would fall apart.

"Jason."

"Yeah, I know." His face felt hot. His eyes were watering. *Dammit, I did not want to spend this fucking party crying.* He sniffed angrily, drank about half the remaining beer. "You don't understand, though. You don't know how it feels."

"No, I don't. You're right. But that doesn't mean I can't see what it's doing to you."

"No, fuck that. Fuck that…and fuck me." He wiped his eyes, but tears managed to spill down his cheeks anyway. "I can't just…it…it feels like there wasn't any resolution. There wasn't any…" *Fuck.* "I don't have any closure."

"Yeah, I get it." Brigid leaned back, dropped her legs again. Found a box of tissues on his desk and tossed it onto the bed. "You want a happy ending. Everyone wants a happy ending."

"You got one. You and Moe. Me, what happened to me? I'm just left…alone. She's still dead, she's still gone." He sniffed. His voice was shaking, unsteady. "But she's also still out there, she's still alive out there, but just not here, not in this, whatever, reality, but she *is* in another. You know, of course I have to look for her. I have to."

"Okay…okay." Brigid had been staring at the window, her face dark and tense, frowning. She turned back to him again. "But, the thing is—and this is a hard thing to face—there's not going to be any resolution. Not everything gets resolved, you know? Things just change. Sometimes stories end in the middle. You're chasing this dream that if you find her, you'll… what, find closure? But you won't. I mean, first, odds are you won't find her, and second, if you do, it won't make you happy, not for more than a moment. And then you'll be back here again. There's no closure there."

"No. No. I don't accept that. I found her once. I can get back, I can find her again. Maybe they've figured out…figured out how to stay…how I can stay. You don't know. There are infinite possibilities, right? That's the whole thing, the whole point. There's still hope. There's always hope. Why don't I get to keep on hoping?"

Brigid didn't answer, just gazed at him sadly.

Jason wiped his eyes, blew his nose. Stared out the window again. He could see Lithium in the garden, sniffing at something and digging a hole through the baby lettuce. His mom would be pissed about that when she found it. He shook his head. He didn't have the energy for this argument right now. "Okay. I get it. I'm sorry."

"You're still seeing your therapist?"

"Yeah."

"Did they suggest any—"

"I'm not taking the pills."

"Okay."

Jason's tears abated and he tossed the tissue onto the floor. "She suggested these exercises, like mental games, and said I should try to find like a hobby or a job or something to take up time. She thought maybe writing a memoir would help."

"Yeah, that's a good idea. I'd read it."

Jason shrugged. "Yeah. I'm…I'll think about it." He smiled a bit more convincingly, he thought. "We should head back downstairs. I'm just gonna clean up a little first."

Brigid nodded and hopped off the chair. Leaned over to give him a little hug. "It'll be okay, Jason. You know you can always call me, count on me. You have people who love you here, you know. Don't forget that."

"Yeah. Thanks, I know."

As soon as Brigid left, Jason pulled the door shut behind her.

He sat down on the bed again, lay on his back and stared at the familiar whorls and cracks in the ceiling.

Took a couple of deep breaths.

Cleared his thoughts.

Emptied his mind.

Closed his eyes.

ACKNOWLEDGMENTS

I would like to acknowledge all those who, wittingly or unwittingly, suggested that I could do this thing—my family; my friends in Boston, DC, and PC Senegal; and *sama waa ker* Dabo. I would particularly like to thank Ed Melaugh, of New England Small Circle Jujitsu, for teaching me how to fight; and my editor and publisher, Emily Victorson, for giving me this opportunity and guiding me through the process.

ALSO PUBLISHED BY
ALLIUM PRESS OF CHICAGO

Visit our website for more information:
www.alliumpress.com

THE EMILY CABOT MYSTERIES
Frances McNamara

Death at the Fair

The 1893 World's Columbian Exposition provides a vibrant backdrop for the first book in the series. Emily Cabot, one of the first women graduate students at the University of Chicago, is eager to prove herself in the emerging field of sociology. While she is busy exploring the Exposition with her family and friends, her colleague, Dr. Stephen Chapman, is accused of murder. Emily sets out to search for the truth behind the crime, but is thwarted by the gamblers, thieves, and corrupt politicians who are ever-present in Chicago. A lynching that occurred in the dead man's past leads Emily to seek the assistance of the black activist Ida B. Wells.

◆

Death at Hull House

After Emily Cabot is expelled from the University of Chicago, she finds work at Hull House, the famous settlement established by Jane Addams. There she quickly becomes involved in the political and social problems of the immigrant community. But when a man who works for a sweatshop owner is murdered in the Hull House parlor, Emily must determine whether one of her colleagues is responsible, or whether the real reason for the murder is revenge for a past tragedy in her own family. As a smallpox epidemic spreads through the impoverished west side of Chicago, the very existence of the settlement is threatened and Emily finds herself in jeopardy from both the deadly disease and a killer.

Death at Pullman

A model town at war with itself...George Pullman created an ideal community for his railroad car workers, complete with every amenity they could want or need. But when hard economic times hit in 1894, lay-offs follow and the workers can no longer pay their rent or buy food at the company store. Starving and desperate, they turn against their once benevolent employer. Emily Cabot and her friend Dr. Stephen Chapman bring much needed food and medical supplies to the town, hoping they can meet the immediate needs of the workers and keep them from resorting to violence. But when one young worker—suspected of being a spy—is murdered, and a bomb plot comes to light, Emily must race to discover the truth behind a tangled web of family and company alliances.

◆

Death at Woods Hole

Exhausted after the tumult of the Pullman Strike of 1894, Emily Cabot is looking forward to a restful summer visit to Cape Cod. She has plans to collect "beasties" for the Marine Biological Laboratory, alongside other visiting scientists from the University of Chicago. She also hopes to enjoy romantic clambakes with Dr. Stephen Chapman, although they must keep an important secret from their friends. But her summer takes a dramatic turn when she finds a dead man floating in a fish tank. In order to solve his murder she must first deal with dueling scientists, a testy local sheriff, the theft of a fortune, and uncooperative weather.

◆

Death at Chinatown

In the summer of 1896, amateur sleuth Emily Cabot meets two young Chinese women who have recently received medical degrees. She is inspired to make an important decision about her own life when she learns about the difficult choices they have made in order to pursue their careers. When one of the women is accused of poisoning a Chinese herbalist, Emily once again finds herself in the midst of a murder investigation. But, before the case can be solved, she must first settle a serious quarrel with her husband, help quell a political uprising, and overcome threats against her family. Timeless issues, such as restrictions on immigration, the conflict between Western and Eastern medicine, and women's struggle to balance family and work, are woven seamlessly throughout this mystery set in Chicago's original Chinatown.

Death at the Paris Exposition

In the sixth Emily Cabot Mystery, the intrepid amateur sleuth's journey once again takes her to a world's fair—the Paris Exposition of 1900. Chicago socialite Bertha Palmer has been named the only female U. S. commissioner to the Exposition and she enlists Emily's services as her social secretary. Their visit to the House of Worth for the fitting of a couture gown is interrupted by the theft of Mrs. Palmer's famous pearl necklace. Before that crime can be solved, several young women meet untimely deaths and a member of the Palmers' inner circle is accused of the crimes. As Emily races to clear the family name she encounters jealous society ladies, American heiresses seeking titled European husbands, and more luscious gowns and priceless jewels. Along the way, she takes refuge from the tumult at the country estate of Impressionist painter Mary Cassatt. In between her work and sleuthing, she is able to share the Art Nouveau delights of the Exposition, and the enduring pleasures of the City of Light, with her husband and their young children.

◆

Death at the Selig Studios

The early summer of 1909 finds Emily Cabot eagerly anticipating a relaxing vacation with her family. Before they can depart, however, she receives news that her brother, Alden, has been involved in a shooting death at the Selig Polyscope silent movie studios on Chicago's northwest side. She races to investigate, along with her friend Detective Henry Whitbread. There they discover a sprawling backlot, complete with ferocious jungle animals and the celluloid cowboys Tom Mix and Broncho Billy. As they dig deeper into the situation, they uncover furtive romantic liaisons between budding movie stars and an attempt by Thomas Edison to maintain his stranglehold over the emerging film industry. Before the intrepid amateur sleuth can clear her brother's name she faces a serious break with the detective; a struggle with her adolescent daughter, who is obsessed with the filming of the original Wizard of Oz movie; and threats upon her own life.

THE HANLEY & RIVKA MYSTERIES
D. M. Pirrone

Shall We Not Revenge

In the harsh early winter months of 1872, while Chicago is still smoldering from the Great Fire, Irish Catholic detective Frank Hanley is assigned the case of a murdered Orthodox Jewish rabbi. His investigation proves difficult when the neighborhood's Yiddish-speaking residents, wary of outsiders, are reluctant to talk. But when the rabbi's headstrong daughter, Rivka, unexpectedly offers to help Hanley find her father's killer, the detective receives much more than the break he was looking for. Their pursuit of the truth draws Rivka and Hanley closer together and leads them to a relief organization run by the city's wealthy movers and shakers. Along the way, they uncover a web of political corruption, crooked cops, and well-buried ties to two notorious Irish thugs from Hanley's checkered past. Even after he is kicked off the case, stripped of his badge, and thrown in jail, Hanley refuses to quit. With a personal vendetta to settle for an innocent life lost, he is determined to expose a complicated criminal scheme, not only for his own sake, but for Rivka's as well.

◆

For You Were Strangers

On a spring morning in 1872, former Civil War officer Ben Champion is discovered dead in his Chicago bedroom—a bayonet protruding from his back. What starts as a routine case for Detective Frank Hanley soon becomes anything but, as his investigation into Champion's life turns up hidden truths best left buried. Meanwhile, Rivka Kelmansky's long-lost brother, Aaron, arrives on her doorstep, along with his mulatto wife and son. Fugitives from an attack by night riders, Aaron and his family know too much about past actions that still threaten powerful men—defective guns provided to Union soldiers, and an 1864 conspiracy to establish Chicago as the capital of a Northwest Confederacy. Champion had his own connection to that conspiracy, along with ties to a former slave now passing as white and an escaped Confederate guerrilla bent on vengeance, any of which might have led to his death. Hanley and Rivka must untangle this web of circumstances, amid simmering hostilities still present seven years after the end of the Civil War, as they race against time to solve the murder, before the secrets of bygone days claim more victims.

Honor Above All
J. Bard-Collins

Pinkerton agent Garrett Lyons arrives in Chicago in 1882, close on the trail of the person who murdered his partner. He encounters a vibrant city that is striving ever upwards, full of plans to construct new buildings that will "scrape the sky." In his quest for the truth Garrett stumbles across a complex plot involving counterfeit government bonds, fierce architectural competition, and painful reminders of his military past. Along the way he seeks the support and companionship of his friends—elegant Charlotte, who runs an upscale poker game for the city's elite, and up-and-coming architect Louis Sullivan. Rich with historical details that bring early 1880s Chicago to life, this novel will appeal equally to mystery fans, history buffs, and architecture enthusiasts.

◆

The Reason for Time
Mary Burns

On a hot, humid Monday afternoon in July 1919, Maeve Curragh watches as a blimp plunges from the sky and smashes into a downtown Chicago bank building. It is the first of ten extraordinary days in Chicago history that will forever change the course of her life. Racial tensions mount as soldiers return from the battlefields of Europe and the Great Migration brings new faces to the city, culminating in violent race riots. Each day the young Irish immigrant, a catalogue order clerk for the Chicago Magic Company, devours the news of a metropolis where cultural pressures are every bit as febrile as the weather. But her interest in the headlines wanes when she catches the eye of a charming streetcar conductor. Maeve's singular voice captures the spirit of a young woman living through one of Chicago's most turbulent periods. Seamlessly blending fact with fiction, Mary Burns weaves an evocative tale of how an ordinary life can become inextricably linked with history.

Set the Night on Fire
Libby Fischer Hellmann

Someone is trying to kill Lila Hilliard. During the Christmas holidays she returns from running errands to find her family home in flames, her father and brother trapped inside. Later, she is attacked by a mysterious man on a motorcycle...and the threats don't end there. As Lila desperately tries to piece together who is after her and why, she uncovers information about her father's past in Chicago during the volatile days of the late 1960s...information he never shared with her, but now threatens to destroy her. Part thriller, part historical novel, and part love story, *Set the Night on Fire* paints an unforgettable portrait of Chicago during a turbulent time: the riots at the Democratic Convention... the struggle for power between the Black Panthers and SDS...and a group of young idealists who tried to change the world.

◆

A Bitter Veil
Libby Fischer Hellmann

It all began with a line of Persian poetry . . . Anna and Nouri, both studying in Chicago, fall in love despite their very different backgrounds. Anna, who has never been close to her parents, is more than happy to return with Nouri to his native Iran, to be embraced by his wealthy family. Beginning their married life together in 1978, their world is abruptly turned upside down by the overthrow of the Shah and the rise of the Islamic Republic. Under the Ayatollah Khomeini and the Republican Guard, life becomes increasingly restricted and Anna must learn to exist in a transformed world, where none of the familiar Western rules apply. Random arrests and torture become the norm, women are required to wear hijab, and Anna discovers that she is no longer free to leave the country. As events reach a fevered pitch, Anna realizes that nothing is as she thought, and no one can be trusted...not even her husband.

Where My Body Ends and the World Begins
Tony Romano

On December 1, 1958, a devastating blaze at Our Lady of the Angels School in Chicago took the lives of ninety-two children, shattering a close-knit Italian neighborhood. In this eloquent novel, set nearly a decade later, twenty-year-old Anthony Lazzeri struggles with survivor's guilt, which is manifested through conflicted feelings about his own body. Complicating his life is a retired detective's dogged belief that Anthony was involved in the setting of the fire. Tony Romano's delicate handling of Anthony's journey is deeply moving, exploring the complex psychological toll such an event has on those involved, including families...and an entire community. This multi-faceted tale follows Anthony's struggles to come to terms with how the events of that day continue to affect him and those around him. Aided by a sometime girlfriend, a former teacher, and later his parents—after long buried family secrets are brought into the open—he attempts to piece together a life for himself as an adult.

FOR YOUNGER READERS

Her Mother's Secret
Barbara Garland Polikoff

Fifteen-year-old Sarah, the daughter of Jewish immigrants, wants nothing more than to become an artist. But as she spreads her wings she must come to terms with the secrets that her family is only beginning to share with her. Replete with historical details that vividly evoke the Chicago of the 1890s, this moving coming-of-age story is set against the backdrop of a vibrant, turbulent city. Sarah moves between two very different worlds—the colorful immigrant neighborhood surrounding Hull House and the sophisticated, elegant World's Columbian Exposition. This novel eloquently captures the struggles of a young girl as she experiences the timeless emotions of friendship, family turmoil, loss…and first love.

A companion guide to *Her Mother's Secret*
is available at www.alliumpress.com. In the guide you will find resources
for further exploration of Sarah's time and place.

◆

City of Grit and Gold
Maud Macrory Powell

The streets of Chicago in 1886 are full of turmoil. Striking workers clash with police…illness and injury lurk around every corner…and twelve-year-old Addie must find her way through it all. Torn between her gruff Papa—who owns a hat shop and thinks the workers should be content with their American lives—and her beloved Uncle Chaim—who is active in the protests for the eight-hour day—Addie struggles to understand her topsy-turvy world, while keeping her family intact. Set in a Jewish neighborhood of Chicago during the days surrounding the Haymarket Affair, this novel vividly portrays one immigrant family's experience, while also eloquently depicting the timeless conflict between the haves and the have-nots.

A companion guide to *City of Grit and Gold*
is available at www.alliumpress.com. In the guide you will find resources
for further exploration of Addie's time and place.

CPSIA information can be obtained
at www.ICGtesting.com
Printed in the USA
FFHW021546130519
52414799-57851FF